GEARS AND LEVERS 1
A STEAMPUNK ANTHOLOGY

EDITED BY PHYLLIS IRENE RADFORD

SKY WARRIOR BOOK PUBLISHING LLC.

Published by Sky Warrior Book Publishing, LLC.
PO Box 99
Clinton, MT 59825
www.skywarriorbooks.com

This is a work of fiction. All characters and events portrayed in this book are fictitious, and any resemblance to real people is purely coincidental.

Editor: Phyllis Irene Radford.
Cover art by Peter Bradley.
Cover layout by Mitchell Davidson Bentley.
Publisher: M. H. Bonham.

Printed in the United States of America
9 8 7 6 5 4 3 2 1

TABLE OF CONTENTS

COPYRIGHTS

EDITOR'S INTRODUCTION
PHYLLIS IRENE RADFORD

In *Gears and Levers* we at Sky Warrior Books have tried to stretch beyond classic Steampunk in Victorian England or Western Europe. We have tales from the weird west to China and Japan, to central Europe, and Africa. We've pushed the envelope of colonial attitudes and hopefully present some sideways alternatives to make you think, make you laugh, and maybe inspire you to go out and make a costume. But don't forget the goggles.

Steampunk is a combination of adventure, Romance (in the classic literary sense), with marvelous toys and gadgets, and an attitude. Steampunk starts with real history we can tweak in ways that made sense and yet thumbs a nose at prejudices and haughty scholars.

Steampunk is more than just the things you can do with steam. It is a sensibility, an approach to life, and a new way of looking at issues—through goggles if you will.

I have found Steampunk all around me. Not just in books, movies, and TV shows that shout steam at every turn, but in subtle ways. In interior of the Tardis on *Dr. Who* looks and sounds as if it belongs in a Jules Verne tale. In watching the DVDs of the TV series *Farscape*, I find some of the same flowing elegance in the living ship *Moya* as I do in many a luxurious upscale steam train.

The huge "What if" factor in both of those shows is similar

to the Steampunk movement.

At **PDX** Gearcon 2011, my first Steampunk convention, one of the topics tossed around frequently was that Steampunk allows us to explore the human relationship with technology. In our current reality we seem addicted to technology, almost the slave to the next upgrade rather than the master. We no longer have the knowledge or ability to understand the microscopic layers of silicon and circuitry. With steam, the inner workings are large enough that we can follow the hoses and coils, the pipes and the fuel, visually discover the logic of the design and fix it if need be with "found" tools and material.

Steampunk may have grown huge through the costume movement. It lingers for other reasons than just lace, velvet, goggles, and grease.

Steam engines are not just practical; they are elegant, as elegant as an artfully draped skirt or beaver top hat. They come from an era when craftsmen designed beauty into their creations and took the time to make every seam align and flow into decoration. The gilding and flounces were as much a part of the function as the hoses and coils, the heat and the hiss.

As we romp through the stories and adventures, marveling at the possibilities of science and magic entwining, the mysterious flux and flow of the ephemeral steam, we also get a chance to tweak with the laws and morality of the Victorian Age that have come to dominate modern life. In Steampunk, (this is *Alternate History* after all) women can stand beside the men as equals; they can tromp through jungles, climb mountains, and fix the bloody engine. All the while they will do it with grace and aplomb with an eye toward sensible fashion. After all, a corset is not just a symbol of sexual bondage; it contains useful raw materials and tools within the stays. It can become a woman's barrier against unwanted advances. And when she chooses to take it off? Oh, the slow and wonderful possibilities that can follow.

I invite you to explore the age of steam, the sensibilities, the marvelous "what if" factor, and the optimistic, or cautionary, energy of Steampunk.

LOVE IN THE BALANCE
DAVID D LEVINE

Theophile Nundaemon closed the book, shaking his head over the images he'd found therein. So sad, so mad...he closed his eyes and set the book aside, a few maroon particles of the decaying cover dusting the ormolu surface of the table.

Unobserved, a cleaner descended silently and snuffled the debris away. It sniffed at the book as well, but Theo's scent on the cover indicated this was no discard. The little creature puffed itself up to grapefruit size and drifted off to its nest in the corner of the room. Immature cleaners peeped supersonically and opened wide their jaws.

Theo opened his eyes and stared out the window. Beyond the glass loomed the fog of endless night, and bulbous shapes drifting. Here and there a spotlight picked out the sigil of one or another House on a pennant or tail fin. The red bat of the Unknown Regalia...the silver spoon-and-circle of Theo's own Guided Musings...and there, the gilded fish of the Pulp Revenants. Angrily Theo twisted the brass and crystal handle beneath the worn sill, and wooden slats snapped shut over the view.

How *dare* Kyrie summon the zombies again—on this day of all days, and upon the Musings of all Houses? How *dare* she?

Theo picked up the book and shoved it back on the shelf.

That compendium of ancient lore and legends was nearly as useless as the endless mutterings of the House Fathers. He paced before the shuttered window, heedless of the books' shuffling and muttering as they rearranged themselves alphabetically, and lit his pipe. Then a low familiar foghorn sounded outside the window, and Theo sighed and opened the shutters.

Looming from the dark and fog came the nose of the *Grand Edison III*—the personal airship of Kyrie Strommond, the flagship of the Revenants, and the long-estranged lover of Theophile Nundaemon.

Theo still felt fondly toward the *Edison*, and he knew that, despite everything, she still held some warmth in her engines for him. But those cooling ashes of love would be no protection at all from the zombie warriors the *Edison* now bore within her gravid silver hull. For fluttering from the foremast was Kyrie's own sigil—Capricorn on a field of stars.

That damnable goat.

A tear gathered in the corner of Theo's eye. "Zenobia," he called to his personal servant. "Prepare my zeppelin gun."

Not waiting for a response, Theo strode from the library and descended the brass-railed oak spiral stair to his quarters. There he shrugged on his black wool overcoat, with the high, stiff collar and gold-braided epaulets of a Commander of the Musings. He descended two more flights, then took a long corridor—his thudding boots raising dust from the worn carpet below portraits of long-dead zeppelin captains—to the reception bay, where the house slaves had already opened the doors and extended the boarding ramp to meet the descending *Edison*. A cold, damp breeze blew in from the endless night. Theo fastened his top coat button.

He stood silent, marinating in memory and regret, as shouting slaves tossed lines to the *Edison* and made her fast. Then her hatch opened, the boarding stair unrolling itself like a great slatted tongue, and Kyrie Strommond descended to the ramp, majestic in the green uniform of a Commander of the Revenants.

Though the threads of gray in her hair now outnumbered the

black, Kyrie was still a handsome woman, with keen, intelligent green eyes and clear, pale skin. But the mouth tightened in a hard line as she saw who had come to meet her. "Honor to you, Theophile," she said, "and honor to your House."

"Honor to you, Kyrie," he replied, "and honor to your airship."

It was a calculated insult, barely within the bounds of protocol, but his only reward was a single blink. Despite himself, Theo had to admire her steel. It was a shame they could never be friends.

"I require quarters for my troops," she said, "as stipulated by the Compact."

"That may be...difficult. At this time of year. How many?"

"Three hundred." At that, Theo blinked. So large a contingent had not been seen in centuries. What could the Revenants be planning? "But they require no food or water, and only the minimum of space."

"Of course." He escorted her to an alcove in the wall, where a wooden model of the House of the Guided Musings floated in the air. He touched one of the brass knobs that studded its surface, and the model obediently split open, revealing the warren of rooms and corridors within. Thousands of tiny wooden pegs populated the spaces—mahogany for men, maple for women, fir for slaves—their fitful motion reminding Theo of a disturbed anthill. "As you see," he said, "the Reunion Day crowds have already arrived."

Naturally, since this model was in a public space, much of the information was lies. But Theo's lip quirked in amusement at the two pegs, maple and mahogany, that stood by the alcove in the model's reception bay.

Theo turned the model this way and that, opening and closing its various sections. "Ah, I believe the children's squander-ball games can be moved from the lesser gymnasium. Would that do?"

Kyrie pondered the model gymnasium, as though trying to discern its size. The model did not show the steel doors and mantraps that surrounded it, of course, but Kyrie would be looking for tell-tale voids and discontinuities. Theo sweated under his heavy coat. He had supervised the reconstruction of the Red Diamond section himself, and the model's complex of feints and deceptions was superb, but Kyrie was a formidable strategist.

"Yes," she said at last, "that will suffice."

Theo pointed out the route from the reception bay to the gymnasium. "Your troops will be escorted, to prevent them losing their way."

"Thank you." She gave a smile that appeared nearly genuine.

As Kyrie returned to the *Edison*, Theo climbed an aluminum ladder to the glass-enclosed mezzanine. There he stepped to a brass trumpet set in the wall and pulled the chain for privacy. Immediately the reception bay's clatter and banging were stifled to a dull mutter, accompanied by a feeling of pressure in Theo's ears.

The grating voices of the House Fathers emerged from the trumpet. "What does Kyrie plan?" they demanded without preamble.

"There can be little doubt she will attempt to take the House, most likely tonight," he replied. "I have quartered her troops in the lesser gymnasium."

"Excellent. We will transfer Cherub and Centaur divisions to that section immediately."

"You must also prepare to cut the section loose, if necessary. Even with all our preparations, three hundred zombies are a formidable force."

The Fathers muttered in consternation, but finally replied "We will begin the calculations. We hope it will not come to that."

"As do I." Theo hesitated. The final element of his defense plan would be highly controversial, and he considered keeping it to himself until the thing was done. But the long habit of duty compelled him to speak. "There is one other thing."

"What?"

"Kyrie's airship. The *Grand Edison*."

"What about it?"

Theo swallowed. "I intend to kill her."

At that the Fathers' chorus fragmented into a confused babble. "…impossible…unprecedented…against the Compact…"

"Hear me out!" Theo shouted into the trumpet, his throat tight with rage and anguish. "Even if we prevail in this battle, the Revenants have made it clear that they will not hesitate to summon the zombies again and again until they achieve complete domination. They have bent the Compact nearly to the breaking point already. Killing the *Edison* will only complete a process that the Revenants began. And without her, their strength will be reduced to the point that the other Houses can once again balance them. We can restore the spirit of the Compact only by breaking its letter."

Theo's outburst silenced the Fathers for a long moment. "We cannot officially sanction such an action," they replied at last.

"I understand." The privacy field pressed in on Theo's head like a vise. "Any action I take will be my responsibility alone."

Theo took a moment to compose himself before returning to the floor of the bay, where the zombies were already lining up. The smallest of them was over six feet tall and heavily muscled, and their dead gray skin and lifeless eyes hinted at their incapacity for pain and fatigue while belying the speed of which they were capable. Each wore a poison-green uniform, with Kyrie's Capricorn sigil at the shoulder, and carried a heavy spider-rifle. Theo noted that the rifles' bores and magazines were exactly at the limit prescribed by the Compact.

A company of Musings troops, uniformed in black with Theo's own trident-and-anvil on their shoulders, confronted the zombies with razor-whips at the ready. Theo nodded in approval; standard-issue confusers would be of no use whatsoever against zombies.

The last zombie marched off of the *Edison* and lined up with its fellows. "This is Sergeant Shrive," Theo said to Kyrie. "He and his men will conduct your troops to the gymnasium. Once they are settled, would you do me the honor of joining me for dinner?"

"The honor would be mine," she replied.

"It will be a formal occasion, of course."

They leveled stares at each other like lances at a joust. Under the Compact, a formal dinner was a web of obligations and prescribed courtesies, offering many opportunities for insult. The Revenants' last three battles had all begun over protocol violations at formal dinners—one of them might even have been justified.

As the invited party, Kyrie had the choice of wine. "I have an Upwelling Iris '623 in my cellars. Would that be appropriate?"

"Delightful," Theo replied. The Revenants always used poisons from the cadenine family with that vintage; he made a mental note to issue the appropriate antidote to his steward. "One of my men will bring you to my quarters at seven bells."

They bowed stiffly to each other, sealing the invitation. But with the formalities concluded, Theo had one more request. "As you may know, I once served aboard the *Edison*. While you are seeing to your troops' comfort, may I come aboard for a visit? An *informal* visit."

Kyrie hesitated. Theo knew she was torn between denying him the intelligence he would gain and granting him the pain and distraction the visit would cause. "Certainly," she said at last. "My captain will escort you."

Theo smiled a grim little smile. As he had expected, Kyrie's sadism had won out over her strategic judgment. His stratagem had succeeded, but now he would have to live with the consequences.

The captain was a lean, cadaverous man who seemed half zombie himself. He conducted Theo across the creaking boarding ramp, stretched across infinite blackness from the House of the Guided Musings, and up the *Edison*'s warm and faintly pulsing steps. Once inside, Theo was assaulted by an appalled nostalgia—his old lover's familiar halls, railings, and wainscotings were now covered with a gray coat of fireproof military paint, and oak sideboards had been replaced by racks of laser-guided scramblers.

Theo was led on a circuitous route to the airship's audience chamber. The route itself told him much—clearly something major had been installed on deck three between the fore and mizzen engines, and the captain didn't want him to see it. He thought it might be a bay for boarding-craft, but then the scent of hydrazine in section twenty-five told him it was even worse: guided missiles. Inwardly he trembled, even as he continued counting men at duty stations and analyzing the upgraded firefighting systems.

"This is the audience chamber," the captain said unnecessarily. "You may have ten minutes."

"Thank you," Theo said, and slipped down through the opened hatch.

Unlike the rest of the ship, here nothing had changed. It was still close and moist and warm, echoing with the thrum and gurgle of the great zeppelin's life fluids.

"Hello, Theo." The airship's voice was warm and maternal, but still gave Theo an erotic tingle.

"Hello, Edie."

"I'm surprised you came. I thought you wouldn't want to see me."

Tears pinched at the back of Theo's throat, but he refused them. "I...it was a hard choice, Edie. But, the way things have been going lately, I thought it might be my last chance for a while." Maybe forever, he thought.

"I'm sorry, Theo." Warm pseudopods extended from the wall and rubbed his shoulders, and Theo relaxed for a moment into the familiar touch. "Kyrie is keeping me so busy these days."

Theo sat up and brushed the pseudopods away. "Yes, I know. That's what I'm here to talk with you about."

The seat of Theo's chair stiffened and grew cool. "The answer is still no."

"Damn it, Edie!" Now the tears did come, though he sniffed them back. "How could you abandon the Musings—how could you abandon *me*? I loved you!"

"And I loved you too. But the Revenants are the future,

Theo. Why can't you see that? The Musings, the Regalia, the Apocrypha...they're trying to hold on to the sky by their fingernails. How many Houses have gone down in the past year?"

"Eight," he replied automatically.

"Eight," she repeated, "and madly flapping the Compact isn't going to keep the rest in the air forever. As long as each House holds its thaumaturgies and technologies close to its vest, each will float or fall on its own...and each one that falls takes all its secrets with it. Only by pooling our best ideas do we have a chance to keep what remains of humanity aloft."

"The Compact has provisions for information sharing."

"The system isn't working, Theo. The lesser Houses—the ones that float lowest and are closest to losing buoyancy—are naturally the most driven to create new techniques. But because of their reduced status, none will trade with them, and so they fail, and so their learnings are lost to us."

"And the Revenants' forced labor and torture are better?"

"We've already learned so much, by combining the work of the Whistlers and the Philosophers and the Radiant Ones. Once all the Houses are united under Revenant guidance, we will surely find the final solution. And then these unfortunate practices can be brought to an end."

"'Unfortunate practices'? 'Final solution'? Edie, what's become of you?"

"Nothing's changed, Theo. I'm still trying to do what I was built to do—keep you all alive, in the best way I know how." The sounds behind the walls changed, as though the great airship's heart were beating more slowly. "Whether you understand it or not."

The hatch opened, sending the harsh military light of the cabin above into Theo's stinging eyes. "Time's up," said the captain, and without a word Theo climbed out of the audience chamber.

He thought he heard "I love you, Theo," as the hatch closed. Perhaps it was only his imagination. But as the captain walked him back to the boarding ramp, he pushed the question out of his mind and focused on the enemy airship's defenses.

Seven bells. Theo paced his dining room, sweating in his dress uniform. Five battalions of the Musings' best troops were hidden in the walls around the lesser gymnasium. Tanks of acid were pressurized and ready to spew, frenzied eagle-cats snarled and battered great wings against the walls of their cages, and trans-dimensional fields strained the vertices of their dark crystals. All was in readiness, but the forms of the Compact must be observed.

As the sound of the seventh bell echoed away down the oak-walled corridor, the door opened and two men in radiation armor escorted Kyrie in. A tiny constellation of five pea-sized diamonds orbited above each of the epaulets of her dress uniform.

"So pleased you could join me, Kyrie." He proffered his arm. "May I show you to your seat?"

"Why, thank you." Her uniform sleeve was lined with ceramic plates, which struck rigidly against the defensive field grid sewn into his own.

He pulled out her chair—the one facing the door, as required—and brushed off the seat with his handkerchief. She sat, and he helped her to push in her chair.

Kyrie peered at the table. All the cutlery was in the proper positions. The napkins were folded appropriately for the time of day and the season. The number and size of servants were within prescribed limits. Theo was certain there was nothing Kyrie could use to provoke an incident. "What a charming table."

Theo bowed, and called for the first course. A serving cart rolled out on silent rubber wheels, parked obediently by the table, and raised its silver dome, revealing fairy shrimp steaming in a glistening brown sauce. The steward carefully ladled out a precise portion on each plate.

Kyrie took a bite...and immediately spat it out. "This tastes like shit!" she said.

"Yes," Theo said, and smiled. "My own, to be precise."

Kyrie sat, mouth open, too stunned to say anything.

"I decided to cut short the agony of waiting and give you

your opportunity to attack in the first course."

"You..." Then she snapped her mouth shut and gave him a brief bow of acknowledgement, not taking her eyes off him. "Very well. I, Kyrie Destinia Strommond of the Pulp Revenants, do take the gravest offense at this violation of protocol, and under Article XVII, Section 7 of the Grand Compact of Humanity, I invoke my right to restitution." And then she clapped her hands together and vanished with a blue flash, leaving behind the tingle of thaumaturgical energies and the smell of ozone.

Theo bent down and spoke to the brass trumpet fastened to the arm of his chair. "We are at war."

"Acknowledged," came the voices of the Fathers, and alarms sounded throughout the House.

Throwing his napkin on the floor, Theo hurried up the spiral stair to the library. The bookshelves had already been cleared away, replaced by screens and crystals showing views from throughout the House and the air nearby. On one screen, zombies in pale shimmering armor waded through hip-deep acid, their spider-rifles spitting poisonous metal spiders at the defenders. On another, an enormous zombie, stripped to the waist, mowed through Theo's black-uniformed troops with a broadsword in each hand.

But Theo's attention was riveted to the three-dimensional display in the center of the room, a rotating web of crystal threads that depicted the House and the airships nearby. With the exception of the *Edison*, they were all Musings ships; on Reunion Day, all members of each House would be with their loved ones. And the Musings' best zeppelins were no match even for the *Edison* in which Theo had served, never mind her new configuration.

Nonetheless, Theo ordered his zeppelins into combat. *Tarantella* and *Eagle Scout* immediately slipped their moorings and drove ponderously toward the *Edison*, followed shortly by *Razor* and *Wedgwood*. *Edison* responded smartly, whipping out of her berth with the full power of her seven enormous engines. She began hammering the Musings' airships with missiles, lasers, and black coruscating webs of arcane energy; soon *Razor* and *Eagle Scout* had been reduced to embers, fluttering down into the endless dark, and *Tarantella* was listing badly.

Theo cursed the loss of life, but the attack had achieved the desired effect: it had brought *Edison* out into the range of his zeppelin gun. He ordered his first subcommander to take charge of the aerial defense and clambered up the ladder to the highest point in the House.

Zenobia had done well. The zeppelin gun gleamed, its long brass barrel polished to perfection, its sights precisely aligned, its every nickel-plated wheel and lever gleaming bright. The harpoon was loaded and charged, humming with electricity and shimmering with thaumaturgical energies.

This one harpoon had cost nearly half of Theo's defense budget five years ago. The arguments had gone on for months. Now he was vindicated, and nothing could have made him more miserable.

Theo stepped into the zeppelin gun's shoulder braces and placed his hands on the grips. The dome overhead divided smoothly, letting in a wedge of night and fog. He peered through the gunsight at the *Edison*, heeling hard to the right as it unleashed a flight of missiles at *Wedgwood*. With only the one harpoon, he had to be certain of his aim.

"Commander!" cried his second subcommander from the room below. "The zombies are breaking through into the Blue Star section!"

Theo spat out a curse, then spoke into the trumpet to the House Fathers. "Cut loose the Red Diamond section immediately."

"Acknowledged." A new set of alarms sounded, ear-shattering and urgent. On the displays, those Musings troops not directly engaged with the enemy dropped their weapons and ran. In the library, subcommanders and lieutenants began securing equipment.

The voices of the House Fathers sounded over the public address system. "The Red Diamond sector will be separated in sixty seconds." It was the first time Theo could recall the Fathers speaking to the entire House at once.

"Fifty seconds." In the sight, the *Edison* had finished

off the *Wedgwood* and was turning to strafe the House. She would be closer than the gun's minimum range in less than a minute. He engaged the harpoon's tracking, evasion, and anti-thaumaturgical systems.

"Forty seconds." Theo breathed a prayer and pressed the firing stud. The floor shuddered and, with a scream of superheated steam, the harpoon flung itself out of the gun, trailing its cable behind.

"Thirty seconds." Steam obscured Theo's view. The floor thrummed as the cable paid out. Theo cursed, over and over.

"Twenty seconds." The view in the gunsight cleared just as the harpoon pierced *Edison*'s silvery envelope. The great zeppelin twitched all over at the impact, then convulsed as a mighty charge flowed into the harpoon from the alchemical batteries beneath Theo's feet. He could almost hear her scream through the gunsight.

"Ten seconds." *Edison* continued to quiver and shake as though with fever, jerking and twisting, but the harpoon held firm in her envelope. Reluctantly Theo stepped back from the gun and slid down the ladder.

"Five. Four. Three. Two. One." Theo held onto the ladder as though it were his long-lost sister.

A rumble as though the whole House had indigestion vibrated through the floor, the wall, and the ladder, as chemical and magical explosions severed the structural connections between the Red Diamond section and the rest of the House. Half the displays went black; most of the rest showed pandemonium.

In the center of the room, displayed in a tracery of crystalline filaments, a large lobe fell slowly away from the House, while three huge gasbags detached from the top of the structure to compensate for the lost weight.

Meanwhile, *Edison* thrashed at the end of her line. Then, suddenly, she reversed herself and dove toward the House. "No!" someone shouted—Theo realized it was himself.

The ghostly, crystalline *Edison* smashed into the top of the ghostly, crystalline House. The impact drove the House sideways, knocking everyone in the library except Theo, who still clung to the ladder, off their feet. The lights flickered, along with the technological displays; when they cleared, it was plain that two of the House's gasbags had been destroyed by the collision. Above them the *Edison* floated free, still connected by the slack cable but no longer twitching. It was unclear whether she was dead or alive.

Theo dragged himself to the nearest trumpet, as the floor shivered and tilted and a queasy feeling of uncontrolled descent flowed through his stomach. "Deploy emergency lift!" he shouted to the House Fathers.

"We have already done so," came the reply. "It is not sufficient. Too much reserve gas was lost in the detachment of the three gasbags that supported the Red Diamond section."

Theo sagged against the wall. The House of the Guided Musings was doomed. Helpless, he watched the altimeter drop. The room tilted slowly to one side as the crystalline model of the House fell away from the model of the *Edison*.

And then the *Edison* came to the end of the cable. Or perhaps the House did. In either case, there was a sickening jerk and the floor suddenly tilted fifteen further degrees. Theo's head slammed against the wall and he lost consciousness.

When he recovered, probably only a few seconds later, the three-dimensional display showed the *Edison* floating at the top of the cable, docile as a child's balloon. The altimeter was nearly stable; the great zeppelin had just enough lift to compensate for the two destroyed gasbags.

Theo stumbled across the tilted, debris-littered floor to the ladder, then clambered up to the gun room. The cable stretched through a gash in the dome, thrumming like a guitar string, and the whole room groaned with structural stress; there was no telling how long the cable, or the drum to which it was attached, or the structure to which the drum was in turn secured, would hold out.

He climbed up on the zeppelin gun, now bent nearly in half, and put his head next to the cable. Peering along its length, through the broken dome, he saw the *Edison* rotating slowly high above. Gas leaked from the rent where the harpoon pierced her skin.

And he heard his own name.

He looked around, but he was alone in the gun room, and the voice was so soft it could not have come from very far away.

Then he heard his name again, and this time he felt it as well—felt it thrumming under his fingers in the cable that held the House to the *Edison*.

He pressed his ear to the cable.

Theo, came Edie's voice, vibrating down the cable to his ear. Or perhaps it was just his imagination. *Theo, Theo, Theo... I still love you, Theo, though you have killed me.*

"I still love you, too, Edie," he whispered to the cable.

All around him the shadows deepened, as the House's lighting failed and the endless night crept in.

SECUNDUS
BRENDA W CLOUGH

Part 1

From the journals of James Laurence, lately of Concord, MA
Catania in Sicily, August 1868

Oh, my boy! My boy!

A suicide. He killed himself. That accursed girl! Jo March's last letter to him, rejecting his proposal of marriage, was in his traveling desk. May they burn in Hades: Meg, Amy—the whole pack of March girls. Oh! But not Beth. No, no, that dear child—she will be with the angels soon enough. I must not let bitterness overwhelm me. No hand but his own was responsible for Theodore's death. I should have intervened years ago, when he first began pursuing Jo.

Would that I had died for thee, Teddy—my boy!

<>

The provincial carabinieri traced Teddy's journey up Mount Etna to the top. But to retrieve the body was beyond their simplicity. The resourceful American consul here in Catania, one Samuel Whiddimore, came to my aid. "Be of good cheer, sir," he said. "In the consulate gardens my staff uses a steam plow—have you ever seen one? I modified the German design extensively."

His kindness brought tears to my eyes. "God bless you, Whiddimore," I choked, wringing his hand. "If you can help me—I will recompense you. Anything!"

"Never in life!" Mrs. Whiddimore's tears of sympathy did not slow her tongue at all. "My Samuel will not accept a cent. That darling, curly lad! I cannot think how you bear it, Mr. Laurence. Your only grandson! It is no more than a Christian should do, to lend a hand in this calamity."

It took them all day to load the massive steam plow onto an ox-drawn sledge, and haul it up to the top. The following morning, Mrs. Whiddimore helped me into her own pony trap, and we set off up the mountain road. Above us the terrible peak loomed dark against the brightening morning. Only one skein of pale smoke twisted from the summit.

As we ascended, the baleful influence of the volcano became plain to see. Gradually all vegetation ceased, and we plodded uphill through a gritty and barren desert. Gray as mummy powder, the ashy dust was kicked up by our wheels and the pony's hooves. The road ended where the foul belchings of the mountain had last halted. Jet black stone, still hot from its forging in the belly of the earth, rippled uphill to the ultimate verge, which was haloed with a fiery glow.

The steam plow was still up on its sledge. The gardeners had just finished stoking its great brass boiler. Whiddimore shed his coat and turned up his shirt sleeves, entrusting the garment and his bowler hat to his wife. He clambered onto the sledge and then up into the saddle to fuss with the dials and levers. Gradually the engine took up the load and the treads began to creep around. The helpers scurried to steady the ramp that allowed the vehicle to trundle down to the ground.

Even through my grief I could appreciate the cunning of the artifact. A wide flat steel shovel was clamped to the front of the vehicle. In happier times this doubtless facilitated the transport of heavy potted plants or small trees. Now the metal treads could creep safely across the hot unstable rock. A couple of the boldest Sicilians stood on the shovel blade, pointing ahead and crying directions up to Whiddimore. Theodore's footprints were still visible in the gray ash that dusted the cooled lava. At all costs, my boy, I will claw you back from the abyss!

Beside me Mrs. Whiddmore called, "Don't stall out, Samuel, whatever you do!" He waved his handkerchief at her and then mopped his brow with it. Even here at the edge the heat of the scarce-cooled rock struck right up through a leather boot sole. Out where the upwelling lava was newer it must be unbearable. Oh my boy! Was this any way to die?

A distant yell and babble brought my heart up into my throat. Could they have found him? The sulphur stench of the volcano made me sick and dizzy. As the steam plow thumped and clattered back, Whiddimore waving triumphantly on top, I saw a log on the shovel blade in front, at the Sicilians' feet. It was scorched black. Only one shirt cuff and the curly pate was recognizable. When I fell to my knees, wailing, the hot rock scorching through clothing against my flesh was not so painful as my heart's agony.

Oh, my boy!

<>

Every block of ice in Sicily was brought to the consulate cellar; my grandson lies on a bier that an emperor would envy. But with the last wagon-load Whiddimore brought me more bad news from the local church. "We are Protestants, sir!" I cried. "This is an outrage!"

Whiddimore shook his head. "This is a profoundly Catholic island, Laurence. Even the Anglican expatriate cemetery cannot accommodate a suicide."

At this last word I could not help flinching. "Now, Samuel." Mrs. Whiddimore frowned at her husband's plain speaking. "Mr. Laurence, we know of another solution, if you will consider it. The recent cruel War Between the States has brought only one benison to the grieving parent."

"Yes, yes," Whiddimore broke in. "That new alchemical art. They call it embalm-ment."

When Whiddimore explained this downright Egyptian procedure I was appalled. "Chemicals? Into his very veins? How is this less a violation than reanimation? Or even soul-transfer?"

"Here? In Europe?" Whiddimore's jaw dropped, and Mrs. Whiddimore's eyes went so wide that I apologized immediately, pleading the disorder of grief. But when they left me to recover, I took time to reflect on my own words.

The good citizens of Concord do not know how our family made its fortune. Because I have kept my counsel, the assumption is that its foundation is tainted: slavery. Little do they know! A fortune founded on the vile Triangle trade would be sweet as the perfumes of Araby, compared to the facts. But now? Now that Theodore lies dead and cold, I will dare to call on my father's old knowledge: the lore of the Poet King.

◇

Old Sir Willoughby would have been the man for the job. He was last heard of in 1863 in Siam. But fortune was with me. Charles Fanshawe, his chief artificer, parted brass rags with Willoughby over some political issue, and returned to Europe to work at a laboratory at the University in Heidelberg. And I must say, stimulated by my massive payments, he made a superb job of it! Purloining parts from Sir Willoughby's secret workshops is merely a venal sin—I can easily settle accounts with W. upon his return—but the transfer of Theodore's soul into the mechanical man is indeed a crime in Europe. I fear I have given Fanshawe a hold upon me.

But oh! When the metal eyelids fluttered for the first time, and Teddy himself looked out of the Murano-glass eyes! It was worth every cent, to have my boy back again!

Part 2
Christmas Day, 1868
Hotel d'Angleterre, Nice

Amy March was late in paying her duty to old Mr. Laurence because her dance card was so full, but at length she had to sit down to rest her feet. She was too well-mannered to remark upon how her old neighbor had changed. Perhaps travel really did bear harder upon the aged? His countenance, always reserved, now seemed ravaged and gray—a locked and shuttered house shattered by gunpowder and shot. He now used a gold-headed ebony cane to support his ageing step. But it was always safe to ask about his grandson. "So Teddy is still studying eidolonic mechanismics in Rome. Fancy! He has quite turned over a new leaf then, to be in his laboratory over Christmastide."

"He has progressed amazingly," Mr. Laurence said.

Mrs. Carrol, chaperoning her daughter Flo and Amy, chipped in. "His delightful Christmas present has created quite a stir."

"It is rather a present to us girls," Amy declared. "So sweet of Teddy! As soon as Flo's waltz is done I mean to have another turn."

The American hosts had taken the largest *salle à manger* at the hotel, the one hung all down one wall with mirrors. Candelabra set against each one doubled the light and made the room merry and bright. Amy admired the automaton's impeccable black swallowtail evening coat—quite gentlemanly.

Its steel face and hands glinted in the multiplied candlelight as it twirled and stepped. For her part Florence Carrol, in his arms, looked pleased but surprised. A robot dancer of this dexterity was an incredible mechanismic leap.

"It is the best dance partner you could conceive of," Amy declared. "It never misses a step and never gets tired."

"No conversation, though," Mr. Laurence said.

Amy smiled. "Silence is less a flaw than you might imagine, when you consider the insipid chatter of the usual ballroom partner."

"I am told that the vox mechanica is still beyond Theodore's skill. Perhaps next semester."

The waltz ended with a patter of polite applause. Florence approached with the mechanical dancer on her arm.

Amy said, "It even has a look of Teddy."

"It does, does it not?" Mr. Laurence agreed. "Something in the way it holds its head."

"Did Teddy give it a name?"

The automaton's dark eyes were crafted of glass, unusually expressive. Mr. Laurence's left hand was in the pocket of his evening coat as he spoke easily. "He left that to me. I named it Secundus."

"Then shall we, Mr. Secundus?" She rose and held out a slender hand. With silent gallantry the mechanical man bowed over it. As it led her out onto the dance floor, Mr. Laurence glimpsed beyond the forming set to a hotel bellboy ushering in a short stout figure. Mrs. Carrol and Florence were occupied with re-pinning an errant corsage. They did not look up as Mr. Laurence rose to his feet with the aid of his cane. He moved discreetly toward the terrace. Any conversation with Charles Fanshawe would go better out of doors.

Even at the end of December, the Riviera was clement. White and full, the moon swanned across the Mediterranean sky through a modest drapery of high cloud. Fanshawe stared soulfully up at it and took off his bowler hat. "Beautiful night, isn't it, Mr. L?"

"What are you here for, Fanshawe? Could your business

not wait until after Christmas?"

"Bless you, Mr. L. Creditors don't take no holidays. The bills got to be paid." He held out a sheet of paper closely written with numbers and sums.

Mr. Laurence made no move to take it. "Our accounts are settled, Fanshawe. Be off with you."

"Sir Willoughby's suppliers can't be stiffed like that, Mr. L.," Fanshawe returned. "They'll go complaining to him, see, and then he'll have to take it out of you. Better to get it over now, and then the boss don't have to get stuck in."

"And you think he will enter the lists for you? Besides, Willoughby died in Siam." This last was a bow drawn at a venture. After all, Siam was so far away, anybody there might die without being heard of.

But Fanshawe hooted at the suggestion. "Guess you haven't met him in awhile, eh? We're partners in crime, Mr. L. You can't turn down a pal, not when he could peach on you to the French police. I know you've liquidated all your European holdings, but there's word of a big house of yours, in Yankee country."

Mr. Laurence did not care to mention that he had already set John Brooke, the family factotum, to mortgaging the mansion. Instead he strolled deeper into the shrubbery, out of view from the hotel windows. "Be off," he repeated, "or it will be the worse for you." He slid his left hand into his coat pocket.

"Come now, Mr. L," Fanshawe said with reproach. "You can't threaten the maker with his own creation. That's a game for blood-and-thunder novels. So you ring for the automaton— the aetheric controller works a treat, don't it? But I put him together."

The tubby little man watched, smiling, as Secundus came down the steps toward them. The moonlight silvered the machine's metal so that it almost could have been the fairest of human skin. In the pale light the worked bronze could simply have been ruffled dark curls tumbling over the broad smooth forehead.

"You made him well," Mr. Laurence said. "Stronger than you know. Secundus, if you would?"

With smooth speed, the mechanical man seized Fanshawe by the checkered tweed sleeve. Fanshawe sighed. "Downright shame, really." He used one booted toe to kick the side of Secundus's knee. There was a small popping sound and suddenly the automaton toppled sideways. It fell heavily onto the thick turf, the metal hands not moving to break its fall. "Nothing to it, if you know how the joints are riveted."

"I've always been old-fashioned," Mr. Laurence replied. He gave the gold head of the ebony cane one twist, freeing six inches of steel blade, and in almost the same motion stabbed it to the hilt into Fanshawe's back. Fanshawe fell to the grass in his turn, thrashing and choking out a horrible gurgling cry. Mr. Laurence felt certain that no one in the ballroom could hear it over the sound of the orchestra. He wiped the blade clean on Fanshawe's tweed coat and clicked it back into the cane again before addressing the machine. "Come, boy. Sit up and let me see."

Commanded, the automaton moved, rolling to sit up. Mr. Laurence clicked his tongue at the split knee of the dress trousers. "No more dancing for you tonight." From his right pocket he produced a pocket knife with half a dozen tool attachments. Stiffly he lowered himself to kneel on the grass. It would be a simple job, to align the broken joint and then tighten the connections properly. As he began the automaton put a pleading hand over his. "No conversation for you," Mr. Laurence responded. "It's too dangerous in public. Allow me to guess your questions, and offer a reply."

"Do you recall when we first discussed this trip, that my original plan involved some business in London? Good. It would be pointless now, to hide from you that our family's financial affairs are closely wound up with the estate of the allegedly late George Gordon, Lord Byron. I shall not confide the details of the connection to you now, but suffice it to say that when I needed a soul to be transferred into an automaton, the resources of both money and knowledge were to hand."

Mr. Laurence's attention was fixed on the tiny hex screw he was tightening in the steel kneecap, but he was aware of the fine fingers, sensitive and quick though made of metal, tensing under the pressure of unspoken questions. "No, my boy. This time I shall not fail. Never again will you be at risk, for I love you too well. Your father ran off into disaster, and you did the same. But now you will be safe forever—your soul securely housed in an everlasting metal body. A body that I control. I swore I would drag you back from the abyss, and I did."

"But—but that's *slavery*!"

Startled, Mr. Laurence looked up. "Miss Amy—how do you come here?"

"I was looking for my dance partner," she said. Veiled in tulle and illusion, her white satin ball gown magnified her petite form the way the mist magnified the moon. She stared with horror into the metal face and the great glass eyes. "Teddy! Can it really be you in there? And who is this man? Has there been an accident?"

The automaton made not the slightest gesture. It sat on the grass, one knee drawn up, still as a statue. In heavy tones Mr. Laurence said, "My child, forgive an old man's last folly. You have not heard—it is a dreadful secret—that poor Theodore killed himself last summer in Sicily."

Amy gasped. "Oh, dear God! No, I did not know!"

Mr. Laurence rose stiffly, leaning on the cane. "He had received a final letter from Jo, and it overwhelmed his reason. In the pit of my despair, I had this automaton crafted, a metal substitute. That is why it is named Secundus. It is not truly ensouled. That is just a fiction I tell myself, a pretense to poultice this terrible grief. I beg you: do not tell of this to the folks at home. Let me break the tragic news to your mother, your sister, in person."

"Teddy, poor Teddy! How horrible! But—but this automaton. His eyes—" Tears welled up in Amy's own blue eyes and rolled down her pale cheeks. "They are so like!"

"I had them especially made that way." Mr. Laurence's voice quavered pathetically. "Brown glass from Murano, in Italy."

With a wheezing groan Fanshawe rolled to one side. In his

hand was a single-shot pocket derringer. "You lying bugger," he gasped.

Amy screamed. The automaton moved almost too swift for sight, seizing her by the waist and throwing her backward in a flurry of blonde curls and petticoat. Mr. Laurence swung the cane to knock the derringer aside. In the same instant Fanshawe fired over the heads of both girl and mechanical. Mr. Laurence swayed for a moment, a look of immense disdain creeping over his aristocratic features. Then he crumpled.

"Cunning git," Fanshawe groaned, and said no more.

Fighting to take a decent breath against her tight corsetry, Amy sat up gaping like a fish. She was alone with an automaton and two fallen men! If there had been any other person present she would have been relieved to faint gracefully away. But without anyone else to bear a hand, she had no option but to cling to consciousness. With a grim effort she wallowed upright, irretrievably staining her white gloves on the grass and dragging the heavy skirts and crushed horsehair bustle. Years of charity visiting with Marmee now stood her in good stead. Her first responsibility must be the wounded.

Mr. Laurence's white shirt-front was so blood-boltered that it was impossible to believe he yet lived. In the moonlight the wide pool of gore stained the grass black around him, squelching disgustingly under her white satin slippers as she stepped closer. Shuddering, she clutched her lace shawl tight around her shoulders and turned away to approach the other man. He lay on his side, also unmoving. She could not see his chest rise with breath. In the sickroom with little Beth she had learned how to take a pulse. Very gingerly, with one finger, she pressed the thick hairy wrist protruding below the checkered tweed sleeve. There was nothing.

Finally she turned to the automaton. It sat like a stock, one knee still drawn up for repair. How did you tell if a mechanical man was alive? Amy licked her lips, nerving herself to address it. "You saved my life," she declared, tremblingly.

Then it did move. It looked away. Amy stepped around and bent to look into the metal face. "Teddy?"

Something in the glass eyes did not look mechanismic. She pressed on. "Teddy, is it you? Please! You can confide in me— your old playfellow, Amy."

A long pause. Then, very slowly, the bronze pate glittered in the moonlight as the machine nodded. It held up a hand, and Amy helped it stagger to its feet. The knee joint wobbled but did not give way. Quickly she scooped up the ebony cane and put it into its hand so that it could support itself. With this aid it limped over to Mr. Laurence's fallen form. From the left coat pocket it extracted a mechanical controller the size of a large cigar case, a miracle of burnished bronze and smooth steel bristling with brass levers and vernier wheels. The slim metal fingers slid over the controls. Slowly the steel lips parted, and a thin voice haltingly creaked, "Aetheric. Controller. Grandfather—he... turned. Off. The. Vox."

"Teddy! It *is* you!" Amy wanted to shout with joy, but there was no time. The implications of his plight surged through her mind. "Teddy, we cannot stay. You know that it is still illegal in Europe, for souls to be transferred into machines. If you stay in France the gendarmes will, will—" Her imagination failed her. A smelting furnace? Forcible disassembly? Surely an ensouled mechanical's fate here could not be but dire.

She could hear the gears click around in the automaton's chest as the vox mechanica selected word cards. "My. Own. Grandfather. Made. Me. A Slave."

Amy thought more rapidly than she had ever done in her life. "We must tell the authorities that Mr. Laurence perished being— yes, being robbed by this person lying here. Then we will go straight back to America. At home, Papa read Mr. Lincoln's Emancipation Proclamation out loud to us. Our martyred President freed not only the Negroes, but mechano-Americans as well. If you will trust yourself to me, Teddy, I will declare you to be my property: a Christmas gift from your grandfather to—to Jo, back home. Doesn't that sound convincing? And then, once we are back in Massachusetts, you will be safe—and free."

"No."

"No? Teddy, can you wish to stay here? What will they do to you? Are you—" A fresh terror seemed to grip Amy's heart. Everyone knew that a dying man's last words were truth, and so it must be that old Mr. Laurence had been lying to her—but what had been the lies? Could Laurie still be bent on self-destruction? Was he embracing disassembly and oblivion?

He shook his head. "Dangerous. For you."

"Oh, for Heaven's sake." In her relief Amy could have smacked him, as Jo had done when they were children. "Teddy, we are behind enemy lines. This is no time for gallantry! My own Papa, your tutor Brooke, our boys in blue—they fought to free all the slaves. We must not—I will not!—let them down by deserting you."

She watched the metal countenance carefully. Perhaps with practice she could learn to read its thought, but now it was inscrutable. But then he moved. Gently he took up her hand and put the aetheric controller into it. "I am. Yours," he said.

She clutched it, careful not to disturb the setting of the levers and silence him again. "Only until we are safe out of Europe, Teddy. I shall be your Harriet Tubman, guiding you underground to freedom."

The face and mouth were forever immobile, but the brown glass eyes spoke volumes: admiration, acquiescence, and more. "Yours," he repeated softly, and her heart knew the words had nothing to do with emancipation.

NIGHT WITHOUT DARKNESS
SHANNON PAGE AND
MARK J FERRARI

In which the lamentable Mr. Wendell Shrewsbury, Esq., proffers his astonishing recollections regarding the spectacular events which transpired on the evening of December 7, 1886, in the Cambridge manor laboratory of Sir Rupert Collin Frost.

<>

... The laboratory in flames, generating ever-larger flashes of blinding light and searing heat. The terrible din of exploding bottles and jars assaulting his ears. Tinctures and potions combining as they were never meant to do, filling his lungs with noxious fumes. The high, choking screams of Lord Frost... suddenly silenced.

Shrewsbury stands, frozen as always, held within this horrifying scene by guilt and remorse—real or imagined, he no longer knows—unable to avert his eyes as Lord Frost bursts from the conflagration, a man aflame. The doctor's nearly vanished lab coat is a shriveling, blackened wick, billowing up on gusts of heat as it is consumed. His sizzling skin sends a cloying stench into the air... "Shrewsbury!" With that anguished, accusing croak, Frost pitches forward, perishing for the thousandth time at the feet of his horrified protégé.

A dark, flitting presence begins to mock Shrewsbury from within the flames and smoke, from behind Frost's ruined face—from inside Shrewsbury's very mind. As it whispers sins—of commission, and omission—he is appalled to realize that it has been there all along, hiding in his thoughts, his dreams, slyly driving him... to this.

"Officious fools!" it hisses triumphantly, as if borrowing voice from the flames themselves. "What would England be without its dreams—and us to shepherd them?"

<>

An insistent knocking brought Shrewsbury to what remained of his senses. He bolted up in bed, gasping for breath, pulling the covers up against the chill of the deep February night. Had he been shouting? Very likely... his throat felt dry and sore.

He looked around, blinking in the dimly lit room. It was not his own; he was abed in a well-appointed guestroom at the home of barrister Ian Rutherford, Esq.

An old friend and Cambridge classmate, Rutherford had made significantly better progress in the world than had Wendell Shrewsbury since their graduation together some twenty years before. Ian's warm if unexpected letter inquiring into Wendell's strange elusiveness these past few years, and inviting him to come rekindle their old friendship, had drawn Shrewsbury hesitantly out of hiding, hopeful that a change of scenery and some social interaction might relieve his difficult condition.

Apparently not.

"Wendell? Wendell! Are you quite all right in there?" The knocking grew a little gentler, if no less insistent.

It was the first night of Wendell's visit—and, he feared, after this display, his last.

<>

A quarter-hour later, the two men sat downstairs in Ian's book-lined study. A coal fire had been laid and lit by Ian's aged, live-in housekeeper, Mrs. Sapphira Lamblittle, and was now bestowing some begrudging warmth upon the room. This elusive comfort had been augmented by the half-drained snifter of brandy at Wendell's elbow. He took another sip and adjusted the belt and lapels of his dressing-gown self-consciously. He could not meet his old friend's eyes, choosing instead to watch the low flames, despite their dreadful evocation of his fiery dream.

"I am terribly sorry for waking you—and Mrs. Lamblittle," Shrewsbury ventured at last.

"Not at all!" Rutherford cried, too cheerfully. "I am only glad that you happened to be here and not alone while suffering so terrible an episode."

"Ah..." Wendell gazed into the fire. "Well... Yes. It can be quite troubling..."

"You've had such fits before?" his friend asked gently.

"I have." Wendell took another sip, nearly finishing the snifter, and set it down on the mahogany table beside him, only to have Ian reach for the decanter and pour him another generous glass. "Almost... every night."

"Every night?" Ian blanched and took a healthy draught of his own brandy, then shook his handsome head. "What devilish torment! Is there no one of sufficient expertise in such matters to offer you hope of relief?"

"There was," Wendell lamented. "There was..." The liquor was beginning to affect him... that, and the terrible paucity of sleep. Despair crept ever closer. "But he is lost forever now— and...I fear this torment I endure is all too richly deserved."

"The devil, you say!"

"The devil, indeed." Wendell teetered on the brink of indecision. He could make his excuses and leave tonight—or on the morrow, more politely—to continue bearing this burden alone. Or...

A sudden resolve prodded him to speak before he quite knew he'd decided to. "Oh, Ian, dear friend, I cannot contain it any longer. I must tell someone, though it leave me in as much need of your legal assistance as of any medical counsel. Yet, confess I must, if only in the desperate hope that guilt acknowledged and justice satisfied may rid me at last of this endless nocturnal scourge. May I burden you, old friend, with a dreadful tale—from which I dare hope our long friendship might emerge intact?"

His friend stared back, blue eyes glinting in the firelight. "After such an introduction, how am I to sleep now without hearing it?"

"I fear you'd best not count on sleeping either way," said Wendell. "Does the name Sir Rupert Collin Frost mean anything to you?"

"I've heard of him, of course. Who hasn't? Such a titillating catastrophe!" Ian leaned forward, keen interest on his ruddy face. "Did you know him?"

"More than that," said Wendell. "I was his research assistant for some years."

"You jest! How can I have failed to hear of this before?"

"I have taken pains to see the fact unadvertised." Wendell did not entirely succeed in keeping his voice steady.

"Surely..." Ian said, "you weren't there when..."

"Oh yes," Wendell whispered, lost in painful memory. "I was there. I am not sure I have ever truly left that night behind. It has not left me. That much is certain."

Wendell accepted another refill of his brandy, cleared his throat, and set out to confide at last the lurid truth of Lord Frost Collin Frost's spectacularly fatal attempt to rid England forever of nightmares.

<>

"You know, of course, that Lord Frost was a brilliant man of science."

"Of course," Ian murmured. "Sleep research, was it?"

Wendell nodded. "And not merely sleep—he was also enquiring into the anatomy, and possible uses of dreams."

"Yes," said Ian. "I read his *Systems and Practices of the Nocturnal Mind* with great interest. A seminal tract. Quite revolutionary."

"You cannot begin to know... the half of it," said Wendell.

"Do tell." Ian settled more comfortably into his chair. "I am awash with curiosity."

Wendell knew that he was stalling for time, considering his approach, as though just the right combination of words might somehow sanitize the awful truth.

He took another swallow of brandy, then stared again into the fire as he spoke. "Though it's been scarcely more than whispered beyond certain inner circles since his... horrific demise, Lord Frost believed that nightmares might not be merely dreams at all, but invasive psychonomic parasites—an entirely new and utterly uncatalogued form of life which preys upon, or engenders some malevolent symbiosis with, the dreaming human mind." He kept his eyes firmly upon the low flames, anxiously awaiting his friend's response to this outlandish assertion.

"Please, go on." Ian's voice was low and calm.

Wendell risked a glance at the barrister, finding him apparently at ease. "During my employment with him, Lord Frost did, in fact, invent, and was perfecting, a series of ingenious devices capable of extracting these parasites from the minds of numerous tormented subjects. In fact," he ventured timidly, "we had managed to imprison a fair collection of these... creatures... in hermetically sealed glass vacuum bells for study and extermination."

"Fascinating."

Wendell sighed. "It's likely treason to be telling you all this. But I don't care... Not anymore. What can they do to me that could be worse than what I suffer now?"

"Treason! Good God, man! Why?"

Wendell considered his impeccably educated, worldly friend, wondering how he of all people could fail to grasp the implications. "Imagine our advantage over other nations, were the sleep of all English citizens—and theirs alone—never troubled by such anxieties and terrors; if every head in England woke well rested each morning; if England's children grew up free of the subconscious fears that so distort and disable young minds elsewhere in the world. How many fewer criminals might we have to cope with? How much more fearless confidence might this country's future generations take for granted in the course of their endeavors?"

"You don't mean that he intended to keep such a boon secret from the wider world?"

"Indeed. He was commanded to do so by none less than the prime minister."

"What of Scotland?" Ian asked, a slight resentment creeping into his heretofore encouraging tone. "And Ireland? Would all of Her Majesty's subjects have so benefitted, or only those closest to the throne, if you take my meaning?"

"I do not know, old friend," Wendell said, shaking his head. A lump of sorrow—or anger—settled in his chest. "Nor shall we ever know. Not now..."

<>

Ian soon proved so engrossed, that, against all expectation, Wendell found himself warming to the task of describing Frost's ingenious devices. Chief among them, he explained, was a massive piece of sealed headgear rather like the helmets worn for deep sea diving. This 'extraction bell,' as Frost had called it, was encrusted with smaller mechanisms cleverly contrived to produce, through the highly pressurized release of steam from tiny pinholes, ultra-sonic frequencies inaudible to human subjects but extremely unpleasant to the fiendish parasites. Upon penetrating the subject's brain, these frequencies had compelled the ethereal creatures to flee through various orifices in the victim's head. From there, sonic devices had moved along tracks attached to the vacuum hoses, generating a moving pulse which forced the fleeing beasties through a network of complexly-valved and insulated vacuum hoses sealed to the headgear. In this way, the parasites had been conveyed into large glass bell jars, instantly vacuum-sealed by pumping out their atmospheric contents through a sonic barrier which the creatures themselves would or could not pass. The gaseous parasites alone were left inside to be observed through various filters and lenses, and experimented upon by numerous other means and mechanisms of Frost's invention.

Describing these marvels gradually transported Wendell back to the happier days of his mentorship under Lord Frost. As a man of science himself, Wendell could not help but admire the genius behind such a truly elegant system. He even began to recall some of the pride he'd once taken in his own contributions to their work. "We were going to change the world!" he declared, waving his empty brandy glass expansively. "Top government ministers—I mean *top* ministers—" he fixed Rutherford with a knowing gaze "—visited our laboratory every week, eager for our latest reports and demonstrations. And rather ready with support, if you take my meaning... Lord Frost's fortune, though vast, was not inexhaustible, and groundbreaking scientific research is not for the financially faint of heart."

"I can well imagine," his host said, replenishing Wendell's beverage once again.

Shrewsbury took another fortifying swallow. Confessing himself had clearly been the right decision. He already felt his awful burden dissipating. How much torment might have been avoided had he found the courage to try facing all this sooner? In fact, he wondered what had kept him hiding all this time. Could even that be laid to the pernicious influence of...but no. Those were the musings of a madman, alone in the dark with his thoughts. He was not that madman, and not alone tonight.

The thought returned him to his surroundings. The coal fire was burning low; Mrs. Lamblittle must have retired once more.

"A truly fascinating tale, Wendell," Ian said, pouring a bit more brandy into each of their glasses. "But... I find no evidence within it to explain your earlier assertion."

"What assertion do you mean?"

"That this nightly torment you endure is well deserved?"

"Ah yes, of course," Shrewsbury muttered, gazing downward. His prideful reminiscences collapsed and fell away.

"I shall hasten to the point, then, so that we may both have hope of at least a few hours slumber before dawn."

"Do not rush on my account!" Ian leaned back in his overstuffed chair. "But tell me: did you not undergo the experiment yourself? Or was Lord Frost unable to perform this extraction of your own nightmares?"

"Ahhh... " All unknowing, and from entirely the wrong way 'round, his host had hit upon the dark heart of it. "No, more's the pity; I never did. Had I experienced anything resembling an overt nightmare during those last fateful months, I'd doubtless have been bolted into Lord Frost's collection device as fast as you could say Wee Willy Winkie, and that would have been the end of it."

"The end of what?" his old friend asked with visibly rekindled interest.

"If only I had seen the truth in time," Wendell lamented, "I'd likely enjoy a station far loftier than yours by now." Ian's smile dimmed somewhat, but Shrewsbury gave it no thought as he fell deeper into reverie. "Alas. No such happy fortune is accorded me." He took a larger draught of brandy than good manners might have countenanced, and heaved a sigh of resignation. "Here's the awful truth of it, then."

Ian set his brandy down, and leaned forward in his chair to listen.

"I must assume," Wendell said, "that one of these fiendish creatures somehow glimpsed the nature of our activities while sorting through the contents of my own mind at nights. Not only that, but it apparently then had the cunning to conduct itself in ways not recognizable to me as nightmare... Not *then*. No..."

"I am... not sure I take your meaning," Ian said, in a stiff voice. Wendell glanced up at him. The shadows of the dying fire played upon his old friend's face unpleasantly, though Ian smiled as if anticipating some reassuring explanation.

In for a penny, in for a pound, Wendell thought, gripped now by the determination to unburden himself completely of this dreadful secret. "I believe it infects me still."

"What? ... One of these parasites you speak of?"

"The very creature whose tender ministrations you so mercifully interrupted earlier this evening," Shrewsbury acknowledged.

Ian withdrew into the shadows of his plush chair, and raised the snifter to his lips, obscuring his expression.

"Once they are housed in the skull," Shrewsbury explained, "such creatures can live and grow, apparently, watching and waiting, biding their time..."

"You speak of these... parasites... as if they had intelligence and agency," Ian observed.

Wendell leaned forward, gazing at his friend. "But they do—it does! These are no mere automatons, mindlessly feeding and breeding and dying like so many other members of the animal kingdom. They think. They plan, and scheme," he whispered, half forgetful of his friend, "but subtly, oh so subtly."

"So... this nightmare you've been suffering... is not just a living organism lodged within your mind, but actively contriving some enduring plan to harm you?" Ian asked.

Shrewsbury nodded miserably, aware that he had finally outpaced his host's credulity.

"But why?" Ian pressed. "I too have nightmares from time to time. Who does not? They do not remain after waking to keep waging some campaign against me. Even if you are correct, and these dreams really are the work of some elusive organism, what purpose could a parasite have in persecuting the host from whom it presumably benefits?"

"Revenge, I assume," Shrewsbury replied with a desolate shrug. "We persecuted others of its kind, and would certainly have done as much to it if we had guessed in time that it was there. Having used me to defeat my mentor, it now seems to derive more pleasure from my extended torment than from just dispatching me as it contrived to do to poor Lord Frost."

Ian set his snifter down abruptly and lurched forward in his chair. "Surely you're not claiming that this insubstantial... *insect* is somehow responsible for Lord Frost's death!"

"It... *and I*," Shrewsbury murmured, once again unable to look anywhere but into Ian's dying fire.

"I do not believe it," Ian said. "I would sooner think you mad, old friend, than a murderer of any kind. I will help in any way I can, financially if necessary, and, of course, you may count on my absolute discretion, but I think you must seek help immediately in regard to this delusion that you suffer."

"That is very generous," Shrewsbury said in disappointment, "but I am quite certain that this is no delusion. Would that it were! I am well aware of how incredible these claims must sound, but the entity of which I speak is, sadly, all too real. You have not seen its cousins in the laboratory as I have. You... were not there... that night..."

Elsewhere in the house, Wendell heard footsteps and the muffled thump of a closing door. Mrs. Lamblittle, no doubt, up again for something. He hoped she might consider coming in to tend the waning fire.

"What did happen... *that night?*" Ian pressed, if less enthusiastically than before.

That night... Wendell thought despondently.

"It started well before then," he said at last. "Having discerned the threat we posed to it before we discerned its threat to us, the pernicious demon refrained from inflicting any overt nocturnal terror. Rather, it simply hid within my mind, subtly manipulating both my thoughts and dreams to induce within me a growing urge, first to prove, and later to aggrandize myself before Lord Frost. It exploited my propensity for pride, my vanity and weakness for conceit. No gentler description is merited, I fear. I found myself increasingly compelled to pretentious displays of zeal for meticulous detail and obsessive perfection in my work, not that I found anything strange in such behavior. What young man does not seek the attention and approval of his employer in hope of advancement? Unfortunately, this new proclivity soon proved so insatiable that I began inventing opportunities to demonstrate my usefulness by fixing things that were not broken—first between myself and the lesser members of Lord Frost's staff and household, then between myself and Lord Frost, himself, and eventually presuming to *improve* upon the lab's equipment and devices themselves..."

"What sorts of improvement?" Ian asked.

"Small things. Trivial, in fact... at first." Shrewsbury sighed. "Needless attention to parts I thought wanted lubrication or polishing to remedy some rough edge or improper motion. Things meant to have no real impact beyond that of impressing upon Lord Frost what a careful, knowledgeable, *important* resource I was. Indeed, Lord Frost was initially delighted by my industrious attention to detail—which just encouraged my evolving mania." Wendell gazed bleakly at his host, who stared back in silence. "How is one to know he builds a weapon, Ian, if he never sees more than the one small piece he's given to contribute at a time?"

"I... could not say," his friend answered carefully.

"They are diabolic creatures, these nightmares," Wendell said. "This one, anyway. By this excessive maintenance, it learned at least as much as I did about our equipment's every part and function. I saw nothing then save my own *good* works, and cannot say, even now, exactly when I shifted from inconsequential meddlings to more significant attempts to usurp both the direction and implementation of Lord Frost's research. No longer content merely to magnify myself as his assistant, I now hoped to engineer recognition and reward as a peer and co-author of the breakthroughs we pursued."

"Had you even any medical degree yet?" Ian asked.

"I... still have nothing but the degree in general sciences I took at Cambridge," Shrewsbury admitted with chagrin. It was as if the tale were telling him now, rather than the other way 'round, but Wendell felt compelled to make Ian see this was no mere madness to be coddled and contained at some gentle sanatorium. If even his old friend could not be made to see the truth, then what purpose had there been to this whole exercise?

"Under the devious influence of my invasive parasite, I had become convinced that practical experience trumped any mere certificate bestowed by tired, old, wine-soaked dons. I imagined myself Lord Frost's *right hand man*, and merely sought to help others, including himself, recognize the fact." He shook his head in self-disgust.

"On the fateful night in question, I arrived at the laboratory hours earlier than necessary—as had been my overeager practice for so many months by then—and, predictably, found myself alone there. I lit the lamps, reviewed Lord Frost's most recent notes, and set about preparing the materials and devices for that evening's procedure. It was to be a challenging extraction. The subject was a deeply troubled young woman." Wendell shook his head sadly. "She had sought us out on the advice of Lord Frost's cousin in Dorset where they both resided. Her dreadful and relentless nightmares had brought her to fear sleep itself. Much like..." He trailed off with a small shudder. "We were, of course, earnestly determined to free her of this affliction.

"As I ignited the device's engines, and adjusted output levels, it suddenly seemed to me that stronger frequencies than normally applied were surely called for in a case of this severity." As the dreadful reminiscence grew more vivid, Shrewsbury became all but unaware of his rapt audience. "I can still recall how the machine hummed to life under my fingers, as if eager for my commands... I turned the knobs higher, strangely convinced that the apparent strength of that night's quarry demanded strength in return, and that my employer's usual practices were overly cautious, perhaps to the point of endangering our subject." The recollection filled Wendell with an urge to sob, which he manfully suppressed. "I assured myself that Lord Frost would examine the machine himself, once he arrived, and override my decisions if he chose to.

"My preparations were barely concluded, however, when I heard a tentative knock at the laboratory's inner door. I went to see who it could be and found Miss Ingleside, our unfortunate client, arrived at least an hour early. The housekeeper, it seemed, had simply escorted her up and left her at the laboratory door. I remember thinking she should be reprimanded for such conduct. In retrospect, Miss Ingleside's premature arrival seems uncannily well timed to facilitate what was about to happen. I have sometimes wondered since if these creatures may be capable of some communication over distance with others of their kind. Could her parasite have conspired with mine?"

Wendell bowed his head. "This is yet another question we will likely never answer, now." He sighed deeply.

"I recall that Miss Ingleside was dreadfully pale. There were dark, greenish patches below her sallow eyes. Her dress hung off her thin, brittle frame as if off a broomstick. She asked timidly if I were Lord Frost, and I told her, no, that I was his associate. Flooded with compassion for the poor creature, I invited her to sit down in the room's only chair, to which she would be later strapped for the procedure." Wendell reached once more for his brandy glass, which Ian had quietly topped up. "She sat there shivering, though the laboratory was quite comfortable. Only when she declined the offer of a blanket did I realize that she was trembling with fright, if not exhaustion too, rather than from cold.

"My heart filled with the tender, urgent desire to assist her at once. I felt bizarrely certain that Lord Frost would heartily approve of my decision not to make her wait a moment longer for relief. I had performed this sort of procedure countless times by then, or, at any rate, assisted Frost in doing so, which seemed much the same thing to me at that ill-fated moment."

Ian made a small, apprehensive noise, and rose to set a few more coals onto the fire himself, nudging them into place with a long, wrought-iron poker.

"Have I been wrong to tell you this?" Shrewsbury asked.

"Of course not," his host replied, settling back into his chair. "It is just... not the kind of tale to be listened to in darkness."

"Of course. Quite right," said Shrewsbury, so thoroughly engrossed in his own account by then that he'd not even noticed the fire had finally died. "It was foolishness," he went on. "Utter madness. Lord Frost was a meticulous researcher, always careful to maintain precise records and complete control of each experiment. Though I'd been permitted to maintain and calibrate the engines and delivery systems, and pump out the collection jars upon capture of an organism, there was never to be any hand but his on that final switch... He had made that very clear." Shrewsbury gripped his glass, fairly quivering with outrage at his own disastrous arrogance. "Yet, after months, I now surmise, of my nightmarish handler's grooming, I somehow felt myself perfectly qualified to help this poor girl without waiting for Lord Frost, whom I did not expect for some time yet."

Ian sat in silence, his face blank of any readable reaction to such hubris.

"I bade Miss Ingleside make herself as comfortable as possible, and adjusted the chair's restraining belts to her small frame, then fastened her delicate arms into the leather straps upon its own. Lord Frost and I had quickly discovered how forcefully the distressed parasites could cause our subjects to thrash about in pursuit of escape once the procedure began.

"She quavered a bit, as I finished my work, but I had explained the treatment to her very carefully before strapping her in, so she did not complain. I placed the extraction bell over her head, and sealed it around her neck, made sure her breathing-tube was functioning properly, and, after giving her a final, reassuring pat, stepped to the controls."

Shrewsbury put his head into his hands in abject misery. "I wish I could claim to have hesitated before placing my hand upon that lever... but I did not. All was ready and checked two or three times over. I was fully confident of all my calculations.

"I threw the master switch.

"Steam billowed from exhaust portals just outside the laboratory windows, as usual. Miss Ingleside gave a small shriek, muffled by the diving bell and breathing tube, which, as I've mentioned, was not unusual either. I cautioned her to be still, but she responded by writhing even more aggressively against her constraints. Seeing how mercilessly the beast within drove her, I surmised it must be very powerful indeed. Motivated by this speculation, I increased the frequencies yet another notch— hoping to drive her tormentor out the faster."

"I do not think I like where this tale seems to lead," Ian murmured.

"Nor should you," Wendell answered sadly. "As you've clearly guessed, guided by my own still undiscovered passenger, I kept finding reasons to turn the dials further up, just the merest nudge. Miss Ingleside began to thrash about so wildly, that she actually managed to free one of her wrists from its strap, and, a second later, her upper arm. *So much strength in such a tiny frame!* I thought, rushing to stop her as she began to rip the other straps away with her freed hand. I grappled with her, but her strength proved truly superhuman, and I found no way of gaining ground against her efforts without risking harm to her myself. I had no idea what to do.

"Even more unfortunately, the panel of controls was close enough to the chair that as we struggled with each other, she was able to reach out and slap frantically at its knobs and dials, apparently attempting to stop the procedure. All she succeeded at was boosting half the frequencies to levels I would never have employed in any state of mind. Worse yet, as they were knocked completely out of calibration, the sonic instruments began to generate dissonant vibrations that rattled half the objects in the room, including my own teeth.

"I still see that moment, with such dreadful clarity, as the bell jars began to shatter from the sound."

"The nightmares!" Ian gasped. "Did they escape?"

"Oh yes. But not just to flee, I soon discovered. Abandoning the struggling woman, I leapt for the collection of vibrating jars, attempting to contain the damage, but had hardly started before the air seemed filled with terrifying sounds." Wendell brought his hands up to the sides of his head. "I barely heard Miss Ingleside begin to scream anew as the room filled suddenly with monstrous forms. I felt pressed about with filthy, sweating, stinking bodies. I cried out, trying to push them back, but they simply pressed in harder.

"Panic turned to terror in my head and chest. The air became rank, entering my lungs like viscous, septic syrup. I no longer saw the laboratory at all—but the interior of a crowded passenger-coach, loaded with convulsing corpses. It careened down a narrow, winding street, rocking wildly as all of us inside it cried in panic, gouging, scratching, kicking to get out. I tasted blood, felt it coat and clog my throat!

"Gasping, I groped desperately around me for a pull-cord to alert the driver—but everywhere I reached, I just felt more putrescent flesh, more rotting, blood-drenched clothing, matted hair, ragged fingernails... When my hand at last found what I was sure must be the cord, I yanked upon it with all my strength, and was rewarded with a flash of light and heat, as if the very coach around me had exploded.

"Amidst this maelstrom, I heard the shouts of my employer. As if punctured by his voice, the illusory coach vanished, and I found myself lying on the floor as Lord Frost struggled nearby to free the now unconscious Miss Ingleside from her remaining restraints. The laboratory was engulfed in flames! Hoses had been torn away, spewing the highly combustible experimental fuels we used to heat our boilers all about. These had somehow ignited. Gazing about in horror, I saw that all of the laboratory's accoutrements had been scattered and demolished! Had I caused all this damage flailing at imagined corpses?

"Lord Frost bellowed something at me, seeming angry and confused. I drew breath to explain myself, but my lungs were stung by smoke and searing heat, and I was merely wracked with coughing.

"'Get up, man! Help me get her out of here!' he cried, trying to drag me to my feet.

"Still influenced by my internal foe, I heard only blame and outrage in my mentor's voice. After all my efforts to win his admiration, he clearly now felt nothing but contempt for me. I found his censure quite unfair. He had no idea of the trials that had befallen me. With his help, I pulled myself upright at last, still intent upon explaining. But before I could, his face became that of the Devil itself—twisted, red and leering. I shrieked and scrambled back, shoving him away... quite forcefully..." Shrewsbury's restraint failed at last, and the anguished sob that had been building in his chest—for years—erupted. "I pushed him... straight into the conflagration!"

"Wendell!" Ian exclaimed. "Calm yourself!"

"*Oh, dear God!*" Shrewsbury wailed, rising from his chair. "*Dear God, I killed him, Ian!*"

"It is but a memory!" Ian shouted, rising now as well to grab Wendell's arms as if to keep him from destroying the study as

Wendell knew he'd ruined Frost's laboratory in his panic. "No one seeks to hurt you here! Be calm, old friend!... be calm."

"I could have saved him, Ian," Wendell sobbed, collapsing into his friend's bewildered embrace. "I could have saved them both, but I just stood there, frozen, immobilized by the sudden understanding of what I had done—not just then, but all along." He wrenched himself from Ian's arms, and staggered back to fall into his chair. "That is when the demon within me finally made its presence known. It started whispering accusations, audibly gloating at how easily I had allowed myself to be manipulated—as it still does... to this very night."

"How could you have known?" his friend insisted, trying feebly to comfort him.

"How should I have not?" moaned Wendell. "In all the world, I was one of just a handful who *could* have known.... Who *should* have known..."

"Ian, dear friend," his host insisted, "what is gained by such self-torment?"

"I saw him die," Shrewsbury whimpered. "It was too terrible... I ran, Ian." He buried his face in his hands again. "I left them both, and ran to save myself.... It is only right that each night now I am required to return... Unable to run... Forced to watch..."

"There are doctors who can help you," Ian pled. "There is no demon in your brain, my friend. Only guilt and horror, for which no one, least of all myself, could blame you after such an ordeal."

"They are free!" Shrewsbury rasped. "Do you not understand? With cause to fear us now—to hate us even—and the only man who might have stopped them dead! By my hand!"

Ian seemed about to speak again, but they were interrupted by a loud banging at the front door of his residence. Startled, Ian looked at Wendell, as if wondering whether it were safe to leave him there, then headed for the study door. Before he reached it, however, Mrs. Lamblittle burst in, followed by two burly constables.

"There he is!" the housekeeper cried, pointing at Shrewsbury.

Wendell made no effort to resist as the men hurried past her to seize him. Well-drunk on brandy, and quite depleted from so many months of such badly interrupted sleep, he just collapsed into their grasp.

"What is the meaning of this?" Ian demanded. "Unhand him! He is my guest here."

"He's no proper guest, Mr. Rutherford, no he ain't!" Mrs. Lamblittle broke in shrilly. "It was treason he were talking! Said so himself. Treason and murder. I heard him, I did! I were listening in the hall the whole time, and glad of it." At the scowl this brought to her employer's face, she added, "I'm saving us all, and you'll thank me for it later, I've no doubt."

Wendell watched his host struggle to frame some response, and lose that struggle. *Quite wise, old friend,* he thought. *An up and coming barrister might not want to be heard defending a murderer caught in the act of treason. And just as well. If I am lucky, they will hang me now. Then again, to sleep, perchance to dream... Aye, there's the rub...*

As the constables carted Wendell toward the door, he felt the thing within him seize his body, and a shrill, unnatural laughter burst involuntarily from his mouth. Wendell screwed his eyes shut, trying to suppress this violation of his sovereign self, but to no avail. The thing inside him pried his lips apart once more, and a voice that he had never heard before outside of dreams screeched, "Self-destructive fools! You think yourselves so wise, your science so indomitable, but without *us* there can *be* no dreams! And what will England be without its dreams?" it cackled. "What will England be?"

THE SHUNNED BUTTERFLY
LIVIA FINUCCI

When she blew out the candles of her birthday cake, Kathy decided to run to the entrance-hall window. Standing on a chair, she pressed her pudgy nose against the glass. She jumped from the chair with joy when she spotted her father's coated silhouette in the chilly spring evening. He was about to ring the bell, when she rushed to the door and opened it. Picking her up with one arm, he carried her into the dining room where her mother waited.

Along the way, he said, "Do you think I wouldn't be able to celebrate your seventh birthday, my little Kathy? I made sure to take the early train so I could be here on time."

After hugging his wife, Kathy's father caressed Kathy's curled hair and gave her a small box made of blue velvet, wrapped with a pretty red ribbon. Kathy noticed the nearly empty, almost hollow lightness of the box. When she opened it, holding her breath against disappointment, she uttered a delighted cry. Placed on the velvet was a two-inch mechanical butterfly. Bright wings of colorful crystal and a body of pure gold with delicate golden antennae tapered into two small, sparkling diamonds shimmered in the dim light as if the creature waited breathlessly for the command to fly.

Seeing Kathy's happy face, her father took the butterfly in his hands and said, "I am glad you like your gift, Kathy. I bought it from a clockmaker in Switzerland. Be very careful with this pretty thing, because it is fragile and it was expensive. This butterfly is unique. I will show you how it works."

He placed the mechanical insect belly-up on his palm and revealed to Kathy a tiny engine skillfully embedded in its body. He wound the springs and the butterfly shook its wings. Suddenly it took off and, after circling the dining room, landed gracefully on Kathy's shoulder. She bounced with glee and kissed her father, promising him she would be very careful with her precious birthday gift.

The next day Kathy woke up early and, as soon as she had finished her breakfast, she hastened to the garden in front of the house, eager to play with her new toy. She sat on a bench, wound the engine and watched the butterfly while it flew in the direction of the flowers, its crystal wings shimmering under the spring sun.

The butterfly landed on a striped white-and-pink tulip. However, when it stretched its legs the tulip closed its petals in a defiant attitude. It was as if the flower said, "Get away; you are not welcome."

Taking off, the insect flew to a red rose nearby. On the rose there was another butterfly that spread its wings, preventing the mechanical newcomer from landing. It seemed as if the live butterfly had done this on purpose to deny it access to the rose.

The mechanical butterfly still insisted on landing somewhere. Maybe it would have more luck with a humbler flower. This time it decided to alight on a daisy. It didn't work, though. When it landed on the flower, the dew stored on the petals made the butterfly slip and fall onto one of the leaves further down. Then the flower shook its leaves slightly, and there went the poor butterfly to the ground, belly up, unable to fly again.

Kathy, who was watching everything from her bench, rushed to help her butterfly, and placed it on her shoulder. The poor thing's antennae seemed to droop with sadness. Anger made Katyh's cheek hot and clench her fists when she saw this. She went back to the house, shouting at the garden,

"Bad flowers! Very, very bad!"

When Kathy closed the door behind her, she had an idea. Whistling a happy tune, she skirted past the staircase and darted into the dining room. On top of the dining table sat a vase with some orchids made of fine colorful silk. Kathy's father had bought them on one of his trips to China, and since then they had never left the dinner table.

Kathy wound her toy and it flew right away to one of the orchids' leaves. The orchids seemed to like their little visitor, because they stood motionless while the butterfly slowly opened and closed its crystal wings. Kathy clapped her hands with excitement and trotted to the sitting room to tell her mother about the perfect spot she had found for her mechanical butterfly. The butterfly had finally found suitable lodgings.

Moral: Birds of a feather must always flock together.

A RUMOR, A BLADE, AND A DISCOURTEOUS INTRUSION
RHIANNON LOUVE

I arrived late to my own birthday ball. I liked to make an entrance, and I wasn't disappointed. The band stopped playing, and everyone looked up to admire my expensively-tailored yellow silk dress, covered in ribbons and lace, flaunting fashion with its elaborate design. I'd piled my chestnut curls high, arranged in perfect ringlets, and my wide, dark lips and rosy cheeks required no paints.

I paused on the stairs, to give everyone a good look, then gracefully accepted my brother's arm as he led me to the dance floor. It was 1896, and I was seventeen. The ensemble resumed their tune, and I waltzed among the guests with dear Frederic, future Duke of Grafton, ignoring the buzz of gossip around us.

"A lovely stir, Lady Evelina," Freddie said, so that only I could hear. "You do look fetching. How many weapons are you wearing?"

Mother hated my unfeminine practice of going armed. I hadn't worn my rapier tonight, of course; even the army men had left their sabers outside. Swords might be back in fashion— what with the increasing availability of aetheric personal defense fields—but one didn't bring them to the duke's country palace for a celebration.

I did, however, have a derringer tucked into my garter belt, and a stiletto hidden as an ornament in my hair. A person never knew anymore when one might encounter packs of Baron von Gottschalk's clockwork dinosaurs, Comte d'Ombreville's ninja spies, or the ever more various Creatures of Science that plagued the countryside. I wasn't the typical lady to helplessly await rescue in such circumstances.

I can't imagine why Mother wished I were.

Nevertheless, I smirked quietly and left my brother to wonder. Best that he needn't need lie if Mother asked him.

"So," I began instead. "What delicious gossip did I miss while Delia finished lacing my corset?"

Frederic grinned. "I'll tell you the biggest first, shall I?"

I nodded, excited by the twinkle in his eye. He had something good.

"See that man with the dark hair and the blue cravat? Next to Colonel Taylor?"

Again, I nodded.

Freddie went on. "He arrived with the Spanish Ambassador's party, though he's as English as I. Was introduced as Reginald Hammond, a scholar of Spanish literature. Well, rumor would have that it's a false identity, and you'll never guess who they're saying he really is." He waggled his eyebrows absurdly, and I resisted an urge to stomp on his toes.

"The king of Bavaria," I hazarded, without seriousness. "Thomas Edison in disguise. Madame de Pompadour."

Frederic chuckled gamely. "You know, your second guess is remarkably close, since Holmes is in America just now, helping Tesla over some bother with a murderous automaton."

I puzzled at the hint. Edison was Tesla's scientific nemesis, and Tesla was with Holmes, so...

"No!" I hissed, stifling a giggle. "Professor Moriarty? He can't possibly!"

Freddie shrugged. "That's what they're saying."

Our waltz drew to a close, and Freddie made an old-fashioned bow over my hand. When he met my eyes again, he said, "You should dance with him, and find out."

He escorted me to the edge of the floor, and I did my level best not to stare at Reginald Hammond all the way.

Of course, as soon as I stood among the idle guests at the buffet table, I was far too surrounded by friends and well-wishers to catch a glimpse of anyone. Then Father insisted Frederic and I join our parents on the reception dais, where I could greet each guest in turn and receive my birthday gifts. I acquiesced graciously, but by the time I took my place and turned to scan the assembled gentry, Hammond had vanished.

Ah well. I dismissed the man as unlikely to prove interesting. He certainly wasn't the famed nemesis of England's most prized detective and criminologist. I turned to the task at hand—receiving my birthday presents.

The experience was tedious, a pointless array of bracelets and baubles, perfume bottles and other tawdry finery. I'm girlish enough in my way, but I've little patience for excess beyond a certain threshold, and I already owned more scents and jewels than I would ever wear. Besides, most people, no matter how well-intentioned, have truly appalling taste.

I thanked them as effusively as if I liked what they'd brought. Our chamberlain, Ralph, mercifully noted who'd given what, as I could never have kept track myself. Only two gifts stood out in my mind that night.

My aunt Diana, father's much younger sister, presented me daringly with an illustrated book on combat for ladies, with chapters on fencing, gunpowder firearms, and the new aetheric energy weapons as well. It advised on dressing to compliment one's fighting style, and discussed the ethical philosophy of a well-armed femininity. I could have kissed her.

Mother glared, but Father indulged his youngest sibling even more than he did me. Diana was the one person who could gift me that book without fear of it being confiscated.

"I'll visit next month, and we can discuss it," she promised.

I couldn't have been more thrilled.

Then—two hours later!—as my feet ached from standing and I nearly wept with gratitude to see we approached the end of the queue, a bear of a man loomed into my vision, one Sir Gerald Davis. He murmured something inaudible, and handed me a box with a forgettable brooch inside.

When Davis moved aside, only one guest remained behind him, a man who'd been hidden by the other's impressive bulk.

"Mr. Reginald Hammond, I believe?" I asked as he bowed.

Up close, Hammond was tallish, with a figure cut for dueling. His suit was a somber grey and fit him most attractively, but I'm afraid I noticed little more beyond his eyes. They were black. Like forest pools on a moonless night, I thought I might fall into them and drown. They seemed older than the stars, too old for his face, full of regret and a strange, sad hunger.

"My lady," he said. "Best wishes on the anniversary of your birth. Please accept this token of my gratitude for your welcome."

He held forth a box of carved cherrywood, sized like a case for a fine dagger. The carvings themselves were so lovely—an intricate parade of wild animals—that I prepared myself to find the box empty. Coming from a stranger, here only to attend the Spanish ambassador, so fine a box was a fitting gift in itself.

I opened it. It wasn't empty.

A murmur arose from those gathered nearby. The gift within lay on midnight-blue velvet. I heard shock and disapproval from many hovering guests, but others gasped in sheer admiration.

Hammond's box contained a dagger indeed, but like none I'd ever seen. Its hilt was simple and plain, with a ladies-sized, leather-wrapped grip and a narrow cross-bar of some unfamiliar pale alloy, rather than ordinary steel.

As for the blade...

I stared at it in wonder. It looked like hollow glass, with a complex arrangement of gears and copper wiring inside it—a strange weapon to be sure—but I'd heard of such a design.

Someone behind me—the Viscount of Arbuthnott I thought—whispered reverently, "A lightning dagger!"

The "glass" was scientifically-grown crystal, stronger than steel, and, when activated, it held an edge of crackling, aetherically-enhanced electricity. It was said to burn through nigh anything, as fast as a sword could slice. I hadn't known they were real.

Why would Reginald Hammond—or Professor Moriarty for that matter, though I believed him no-one of the kind—gift me with such an item? We'd never even met.

I loved it, so I felt as if I stabbed myself to utter my next words. "Mr. Hammond, I can't accept this. So fine a gift on so little acquaintance..."

To my chagrin, I heard a whimper of relief from my mother.

"My humblest apologies," Hammond intoned, sweeping another graceful bow. Now that I watched him, there was something sly about the man, a touch too charming, but his eyes haunted me. Whatever explained him, rumor didn't know the half of it.

In any event, he made no move to reclaim his lightning dagger.

"My lady," he said instead, "please forgive my impropriety, but I must beg you to reconsider. Pray set the blade aside for now. I will discuss the matter with you and your good father the Duke, and if I cannot convince you both of my gift's seemliness, I will reclaim it ere I depart. Will you do me this favor?"

Taken aback—and frankly, hoping to be convinced—I looked to my father for guidance. The duke's habitually mild expression had turned as bemused as I felt. When I caught his eye, he gave only a slight shrug. I was on my own.

"As you will, Mr. Hammond," I said at last. "But few tales, I think, could convince my father."

Especially so, since half the still-civilized country had turned up to witness tonight's festivities. If Hammond had revealed the weapon in private, allowances might have been made, but Father had our reputation to consider.

"Your indulgence is most gracious, lady," was all Hammond said. "I ask no more."

With that, the presentation of gifts had ended, and the band struck up another tune. Gossip buzzed like wildfire, but Hammond managed once again to fade into the background. Before I could seek out his vaunted explanation, a young African prince asked me to dance.

I couldn't refuse. His name was Jean-Richard, and I'd met him twice before. His country, Senegal, was fabulously rich in aetheric emanations, and had recently thrown off the yoke of French oppression. Mother quite hoped I would marry him, and I did like him well enough thus far. He'd been schooled in England for nigh on ten years now, and was a hundred times more dashing than any of the local gentry. He got on well with Frederic too.

Tonight, as he whisked me skillfully around the floor, his tawny brown eyes were alight with curiosity. Truly, he was a handsome man, with his chocolate skin, and fine white teeth between sensual lips.

"I've been asking about your Hammond," he confided once we'd run out of small talk. "I hope I've not overstepped my bounds."

He hadn't a trace of accent, and I was struck once more by the melodic richness of his voice. I shook my head.

"What did you learn?" I asked. "Not that he's Professor Moriarty, I hope?"

"So you heard that?" He chuckled and nodded sagely. "A maid assigned to the ambassador's party saw him receive a secret missive. She glimpsed only part of the envelope, but clearly read the letters M-O-R to start his name. Since then, she and other servants have reported all manner of strange, covert activity, and you have to admit, he has a certain... scheming aura."

He watched for my response.

"Lots of names start with Mor," I said neutrally, "and covert activities can accompany habits as pedestrian as seducing other men's wives."

Jean-Richard grinned. I liked that he seemed pleased by my intellect. A girl wants a suitor who appreciates her mind as well as her face.

"Oh, but that's just the beginning," the prince revealed with a wink. "Clairmont of Portland swears that he heard of a Reginald Hammond who disappeared in Spain last fall, and that now no record can be found of the report he heard, nor any living relative to vouch for Hammond. No one knows him, and you know Moriarty can't show his face since that debacle with the Contessa di Casoria and her winged monkeys. What better place to hide than behind the identity of a missing person?" Jean-Richard was terribly excited about the whole thing, reminding me in all the best ways of my dear older brother.

Nevertheless, I frowned and shook my head. "I think if he were really Moriarty, he'd have done a better job of covering his tracks." I gave a light shrug as we swept along together, our steps perfectly matched. "I'll dance with him next, shall I? We'll see what I can learn."

The song drew to a close, and Jean-Richard reluctantly released me. "Be careful," he advised, sobering.

I promised I would.

It took several more dances, with peers of varying rank and grace, to even find Hammond again. By then the other guests whispered and glanced at him most discourteously, shaming me to see anyone so treated at a fete in my honor. I maneuvered myself toward where he stood, isolated, beside the grand southern windows. He'd a glass of cordial in one hand, and a rueful smirk beneath those ancient, black eyes.

Retaining his dignity despite the stares, I could still note his calculation, and the odd falseness I'd seen as sly, and Jean-Richard had called scheming. Nevertheless, I was hostess here, and I could not suffer a guest to be ill-treated. Besides, I'd wanted to dance with him all night.

"Have you a partner for the next song Mr. Hammond?" I asked on approach.

A lady shouldn't invite a man to dance, but the breach retained little scandal in my regard. I'd never been one to sit out a single song, not when I had breath to request a partner. Those who knew me were used to it by now.

Hammond, to his credit, didn't bat an eye.

"'Twould be my honor, lady," he said, gallantly offering his arm.

I took it, and let him lead me onto the floor.

"So," I began. "It seems you're a man of mystery, Reginald

Hammond."

He chuckled. If he found my directness uncomfortable, he gave no sign. "Yes, another week of this and I'll be burned at the stake for witchcraft."

I couldn't help but smile. He really was charming, if in a slight confidence-man sort of way. He didn't look old enough to have been in school with Detective Holmes, but it was a near thing, and age can be difficult to gauge. Still, he didn't exude the towering intellect one might expect from so great a criminal mastermind. Nor, despite his slyness, did I sense true malice.

He seemed to me more a man adrift, lost on the tides of destiny.

I couldn't say what made me think so.

"Well," I told him, "I'm convinced you're *not* Professor Moriarty. I'm not convinced, however, that your name is Reginald Hammond."

He gave a nod of commendation. "Surprisingly," he said, "you, my lady, are thus far living up to your legend."

"My legend!" What on earth could he mean? I was among the more scandalous English noblewomen of my generation, I'd give him that, and all for reasons I considered admirable, but I would hardly call myself a legend. Still, his tone indicated neither flattery nor mocking. I awaited more explanation, watching his handsome, dishonest face, and those strange, black eyes.

"Lady Evelina, I have precious little time. Acquiring that dagger was more complicated than I'd hoped, and I nearly arrived too late." He swallowed and met my gaze with an open sincerity I suspected foreign to him. "I'm afraid I must tell you everything, and hope you'll believe."

Mysteries upon mysteries! "Go on," I allowed.

"You're right on both counts," he admitted, and chuckled. "I've never even met Moriarty, and I assumed Hammond's identity not three months gone." At whatever he saw in my face he hastened to add. "The real Hammond is fine, hiding in Portugal. I paid him well for the exchange."

I wasn't sure whether to believe him, but I kept listening,

at least.

He went on. "That's not the strange part. Please open your mind, my lady. This may stretch your credulity quite far."

Charming as he was, he began to stretch my patience. I raised my eyebrows and said nothing.

The man calling himself Hammond cleared his throat. "I'm a traveler in time," he said. "A woman from your future, an American, invented—or will invent—a time machine. As for my own identity, well..."

Those ancient eyes of his closed in a moment of pain, but before they did, I glimpsed a man quite far out of place in the world. His tale seemed mad, but... those eyes...

"It's a sad story, and you'd never credit it. Let's just say I'm from the past. In my own time... well, your Moriarty and I might have more in common than I'd like to remember. As to why I'm here..."

This time he met my eyes with a shocking intensity. "I was sent to save your life, Evelina of Grafton. Three timelines fork tonight, at this party, and in the best of them you live to be one day crowned Queen of Great Britain."

I blinked at him.

To be fair, me as queen was a more plausible notion than himself as a time-traveler from the past. I was tenth in line for the throne, and during Gottschalk's manufactured plague last winter, the whole nation nearly thought me placed to become Crown Princess, what with everyone but Father and me delirious and fevered for well on a month.

Before the plague, I'd been significantly further than tenth in line.

I'll also say that I didn't much question my own fitness to rule. Nevertheless, the notion clenched my gut painfully. The price was too high, and not merely because I liked Cousin Victoria.

"My father?" I whispered past a throat gone dry, "a—and Frederic?"

Hammond nodded. "I can't reveal much more, but... your father's fate won't be what you fear. As for Frederic... hope is your friend and his. Your brother's timeline remains complex."

I tried to absorb this information, mad though it seemed. I had a horrible suspicion that the man whirling me across my father's ballroom was neither insane nor lying to me.

"Prove it," I murmured, feeling dizzy.

"You'll have all the proof I can offer by midnight," he said. "When the time comes, dive for the blade I brought you, and defend yourself. I'll do what I can, but nothing short of a lightning dagger can keep you safe tonight."

He stopped dancing and released me. I realized only then that the music was silent. Shaken and incredulous, I watched him melt back into a chastened crowd, themselves endeavoring now to honor my example of courtesy.

Still, I must have looked terribly pale, gazing after him. Frederic appeared at my side, his eyes worried.

"Evvie?" he asked. "What is it?"

"Dance with me, Freddie," I said. "You'll never believe this."

<>

I never did learn whether he would have believed. Before I could get out another word, my gaze chanced to fall on our ballroom clock. Five minutes to twelve.

You'll have all the proof I can offer by midnight.

Struck speechless in a kind of anticipatory excitement, I glanced around for Hammond. I didn't see him. Instead, I saw the blade he'd brought me, lying in its box, not twenty feet from where I danced with my brother.

I looked back up at Freddie, his clever, handsome face a picture of baffled curiosity.

Your brother's timeline remains complex.

Fear for his safety shot through me.

"Go get your sword, Freddie," I said then. The tremor in my voice surprised me, and my brother's eyebrows shot up in response. At what point had I gained such faith in Hammond's story? "And any firearms you can lay hands on. There's no time to..."

Before I could finish, the ballroom exploded in an unholy din of breaking glass and women's screams. I forced myself to look, toward the very window which Hammond had stared out earlier.

It was destroyed, of course, lying in fragments on the ballroom floor, or embedded in the flesh of wailing guests as the less-injured scrambled to drag them to safety.

In the wreckage, where the panes of glass had been, stood an armored beast I can only call an ogre. Malformed and hideous, but with gnarled arms thicker than tree trunks and a height measuring upwards of thirteen feet, it stomped onto the ballroom floor, brandishing some sort of enhanced club. It nearly stepped on Lady Eunice Taylor, who'd fainted, but her husband, the Colonel, swept gallantly to her rescue.

Somehow, that snapped me from my shock. I glanced at Frederic, but he was already moving. No more explanation was needed. He'd be back with weapons as soon as he could.

I darted for the lightning dagger. How Mr. Hammond had known no longer mattered a whit to me. I'd decided to accept his extravagant gift.

I was still yards away from it when the ground lurched beneath me. A roar shook the ballroom, rattling the walls and sending one crystal chandelier to crash down onto the buffet table. Several guests screamed again and stumbled to the ground. I felt myself falling too and dove into a roll toward the dagger.

When I looked back, a long, jagged crack split the ballroom floor, from where I'd stood right back to the ogre. The beast glared at me. His science-enhanced club, still resting where it had struck the floor, thrummed and smoked with the aftermath of whatever shockwave it had unleashed in my direction.

The ogre grunted annoyance and raised the club again, perhaps to attempt a second strike. Before it could, men engaged it from several sides at once.

I'd no clue how this creature had gotten past our guards without raising an alarm, but the dukes of Grafton are not notoriously easy to defeat in their own halls. Father and others ranged around the thing, brandishing weaponry from the antique collection in Father's smoking room. I saw Colonel Taylor dart to flank the thing with a Japanese saber. Arbuthnott leveled a revolving Colt rifle, took aim, and fired, but the ball bounced harmlessly off the ogre's thick, and apparently mechanized, plate armor.

Who had equipped this monster? Someone had sent it, but I didn't credit even Gottshalk with technology so advanced.

Time machine. I shuddered and pushed myself toward the lightning dagger's case. Wrenching it open, I gripped the hilt inside. It fit my slender hand to perfection, my thumb slipping neatly over the elegant electrical switch on the cross-bar. I took a moment to assess that I knew how it worked, then dashed toward the fray.

Aunt Diana had joined the battle. She wielded only a tiny stiletto, much like the one hidden in my hair, but she darted to and fro with acrobatic grace, drawing the slow giant's attention and neatly dodging the swings of its terrible club.

Even as I admired her skill, I feared for her. She looked so small, and the club so vast and powerful.

One hit. A human might survive that much, if lucky, but the weapon was simply too big. A single blow would crush bone at least. There would be no parrying it either. Anything short of a Highlands greatsword would shatter under the strain, along with the arm that held it, most likely.

I took a few more steps with the dagger, watching in horror as the ogre destroyed our ballroom with its unstoppable club. It didn't use its shockwave along the floor again. Perhaps power for such a feat had limits.

Yet the beast had been ready to use it twice in as many breaths, when aimed at me.

Hammond was right. I was the target. I swallowed hard, feeling very young.

Jean-Richard looked even younger, yet almost painfully handsome. He'd taken up Father's old German morningstar flail. Through a side door, I saw Freddie return at a run, the door guard at his heels and both their arms full of guests' surrendered swords and other weapons. I doubted my brother's own blade numbered among them, but that hardly mattered. He'd run for a nearer arsenal, much as Father must have. I was proud of them both.

Then the ogre caught sight of my approach and made to aim another strike at the floor, in my direction.

"No!" my father shouted. He dove into the club's path.

I screamed, running forward at full tilt. I heard Freddie do the same.

The ogre grunted annoyance and changed the direction of his swing, slamming his club into the duke's side, though blessedly not engaging another shockwave. My father flew through the air to slump unmoving against one wall. My mother shrieked and ran to him.

I ached to join her, but I had no time. Diana, enraged by such treatment of her brother, leapt carelessly to cling to its massive arm. She struck with her stiletto for a gap in its armor, but missed as it flailed to dislodge her.

When the ogre grabbed her and tossed, Arbuthnott caught her, but both of them tumbled out the broken window, outside my field of vision. The beast made to follow them, but Jean-Richard and Colonel Taylor put themselves in its way.

The Colonel got in an excellent strike across the ogre's breastplate, but whatever the armor was made of, instead of crumpling fatally inward—as plate armor should beneath so well-wielded a blade—it rang like a bell and took not the slightest dent. Taylor's katana-saber shattered in his hands like so much glass. The Colonel blinked at his hilt one second too long, and the ogre tossed him outside as well, after my aunt and the viscount, neither of whom had reappeared.

That left only Jean-Richard, with Frederic and I on the way.

I entered the circle of the ogre's reach, and its baleful gaze fell upon me once more.

"Ev-e-li-na!" it bellowed bestially. Once more, I became its target, and the world slowed down as its massive weapon hovered above my head. This was it. My first real battle.

Up close, I had one heartbeat to notice that this brutish

being looked to have once been human, made vast, grotesque, and stupid by scientific meddling. Who had done this? Who would want me dead?

I dodged the descending blow by rushing forward, inside his guard. Somehow, that was exactly what he wanted. Machinery clicked and whirred, and I glanced up to see a wicked, sparking blade extend downward from inside the strange club's handle. The ogre drove it toward me, and there, between its vast, powerful arms, I found myself trapped, unable to dodge away.

"Don't you dare!" Jean-Richard cried, voice naked with terror for me. He struck out at the descending club, and his flail wrapped around it, entangling itself.

Annoyed again, the ogre did grant me a reprieve, long enough to rip the medieval weapon from my young suitor's grip and shake it away. In its left hand, the beast lifted Jean-Richard by the throat. The prince's dark skin darkened further as he struggled for air, legs kicking helplessly beneath him.

At just that moment Freddie arrived, slamming into the monster's side, with little effect. My brother's borrowed sword rang off the armor, bending back until Frederic nearly stabbed himself before it snapped at the hilt.

I flicked the switch on my lightning dagger and drove it forward, aiming for a joint in the ogre's huge armored thigh, as tall by itself as I was. Clockwork hummed to life inside the dagger's transparent blade. The edges began to glow.

I don't personally claim to grasp the workings of a lightning dagger. I'm more fighter than engineer, myself. I do know the weapon is powered aetherically, like much of Modern Science, and thus governed by New Physics, not subject to such outmoded concepts as Conservation of Energy.

I struck the ogre's armor with a blaze and crackle, sparks flashing along the suit. The monster went still a moment, and fear flashed in its small, stupid eyes. Then, as if the mechanized suit had somehow righted itself, my would-be assassin surged back into motion.

Using Jean-Richard's body as a bludgeon, the beast managed to sweep both the African prince and my brother out the window, where all but my father had already been thrown. From my closer vantage, I could now see battle raging in the darkness outside, a glimpse of Father's militia taking Colonel Taylor's orders, and Aunt Diana neatly dispatching some black-clad figure.

The ogre hadn't come alone. Bright lights and shouting inside the ballroom had simply concealed the rest of the combat. I still didn't know how they'd arrived so suddenly, but as the ogre swung back to face me—now its only assailant—I hardly had time to puzzle it out.

The beast struck at me, and I dodged neatly. I was faster than it, at least. I essayed another strike, but the ogre deflected it from his elbow joint to the smooth plate on his upper arm. My dagger didn't break, nor did it cease its humming glow, but neither did it affect the ogre in the slightest. I might as well have used a feather.

So the battle continued for some time, me darting and dodging like a hummingbird, while the ogre blocked my strikes and patiently, inexorably, kept fighting. I wracked my brain for some hope of advantage, but nothing surfaced. It was too tall for a thrust at its unprotected face, and slow or not, it was still too deft to risk climbing its armored body.

I could stay out of harm's way a long time, but eventually I would tire, and it wouldn't have to chase me if I ran, not with that shockwave club it wielded.

I clenched my jaw against tears of frustration as I dodged another swing. At least my skirt hadn't tripped me yet, nor caught on anything, but that too was all but inevitable, given time. These delicate shoes were not ideal for combat either.

And I didn't even know if my father lived!

The fear had long since left the ogre's gaze. It watched me now with an unsubtle amusement, clearly eager to see me squashed. I waited to attempt another strike. I needed a plan.

Hammond had brought the lightning dagger for a reason. If he was a traveler in time, here to keep me alive, then he'd known what was coming. He thought the lightning dagger was the answer.

Where was Hammond anyway? Some protector, leaving me to fight alone. What if he hadn't come to help at all? What if it was all some sort of ruse?

No sooner had the thought filled my mind, clouding me with doubt, than the ogre gave a mighty roar. Something landed on it from above. A black blur of motion lashed out at the beast's weapon, ensnaring it in some sort of net.

The ogre howled in rage and twisted, batting at this new irritation. I recognized Hammond, clinging to its shoulder, holding the reins of some blacker-than-night filament—so dark it was hard to look at. It held the monster's club at bay, but not for long. The ogre would fling Hammond aside soon enough.

"Now, Evelina!" my rescuer shouted.

I had no time to think.

I took a running leap away from the ogre, toward a stable-looking beam of the burst window frame. Careful of my skirts as I jumped, I hit the beam with both feet at nearly head-height, kicking off it to fly back toward the ogre. It still wrestled with Hammond on its shoulder, swinging so wildly that I nearly missed my grip and fell to the floor. At the last instant my free hand found purchase on the lip of the beast's armored collar.

Dangling by one hand across the monster's chest, I drove the lightning dagger deep into its armpit, between two plates.

I felt my blade bite deeper this time, sliding in past the armor. The dagger lodged, stuck between the strange metal plates, and I had to let it go. I remembered well what had happened with my first strike.

Hammond must have had the same thought. Together, we leapt away, rolling on the glass-strewn ballroom floor and covering our eyes.

The same lights as before arced across the ogre's suit, but magnified a hundred fold, crackling and sparking like fine Chinese fireworks. The ogre howled in pain, an awful, animal sound, until I nearly pitied the thing.

As it fell, though, I remembered my father.

I whirled toward where he'd fallen. Mother still crouched at his side, fussing and weeping.

I sought his face. His eyes blinked back at mine. He was alive! Relief flooded me, and I started to run toward him. He shook his head, fatigued but firm, and raised a tired hand to wave me off.

"I'm fine," the duke mouthed in my direction. Though he clearly lied, I did gain the impression that his wounds weren't immediately mortal. My father, at least, believed he would live. He held my gaze and pointed behind me, toward the fallen monster. "Who?" he mouthed.

Yes, of course. If the ogre or its allies lived, I needed to interrogate them.

Chastened, I nodded and returned to my duty. My erstwhile attacker lay in our ballroom window's wreckage, its suit blackened in places, and still lightly arcing in others. The creature itself, however, still breathed shallowly, grimacing. I pulled the stiletto comb from my hair and knelt near the monster's face.

Outside, I could hear the other battle subsiding. I allowed myself one glance to take stock, but that was all I could afford. I saw Diana and Arbuthnott flanking a solitary enemy. Nearby, Jean-Richard helped a grinning Freddie to his feet. Whatever disaster loomed over my brother's future, it hadn't come tonight. Relief, once more, surged through me.

One last detail I caught, before forcing my eyes back down to the prisoner. At one corner of my gaze, I saw Hammond mounting an odd black horse, preparing to ride away. Damn him. I had so many questions!

But first, the ogre. I gave the dying creature my best glare, and brandished my stiletto at its eyeball.

"Who sent you?" I demanded. "Who wants me dead?"

The pain in the monster's face eased, as it met my gaze with a chuckle. Apparently this information wasn't secret.

"Sta-lin," the ogre muttered. Then it died.

Who?

I leapt to my feet and propelled myself out the window, toward the departing Hammond.

"Stalin, Hammond?" I shouted after him. "Who is that? I've never heard of him."

Hammond reined his horse at my call, but he never looked around.

"You will," he called back mysteriously. Then he rode away.

The ballroom clock struck midnight. Had it been a mere five minutes since the attack?

Frederic came up behind me and laid his hands on my shoulders. "So, he's not Moriarty then?" my brother asked.

"Apparently not," I answered, bemused, "But beyond that, I haven't the slightest notion."

"Well," Freddie said, philosophically. "Then I suppose for now we'd better start cleaning up."

A helpless grin overtook my lips. Freddie could always make me smile.

"We do have a mess on our hands," I agreed, though in truth, I didn't care. I was too happy we were all alive. I could worry about the mess—and this Stalin—later.

THIS OTHER PLACE
BRUCE TAYLOR

Oliver Stanton was a big man; not overweight just—big. Jowly, with loud blue eyes and pale sand colored hair, he looked like anything but a curious man—rather he could look like a foreman, even more so dressed in jeans and a red shirt that gave him an air as if somehow used to giving commands. Even he thought of himself that way; no nonsense him, not at all, which, made what he did surprise himself even more when, walking down the street near Occidental Park on that beautiful May day, in the city of S. by the mountains, by the sea, he (after, having coffee and a morning scone at the bakery at the park) began to feel the urge to move on, getting his daily walk in and so doing, came to a street that he'd have to cross when the light turned green—he stopped, turned. "A bookstore—" he said to himself. "How many times have I been down here and—never seen it until now?"

Not particularly a man of books, he none the less felt compelled to go in and so doing, met the owner, Miss Jessica Wingate, age fifty or so, delicate of features with eyes hazel green peering out through glasses in pale blue frames.

Oliver stepped in and found Jessica looking at him, with a hand resting on open pages of a thick book. He looked to her and in a tone that even surprised him, in terms of its softness, said, "I've been by here so many times, I don't know why I've not seen this bookshop before."

Jessica smiled. "So many say that," she said, "it's rather odd. I've been here so long. What kind of a book are you searching for?"

Oliver felt puzzled and said, "Why, it's strange, I don't really know—I don't usually read books—manuals yes, I've been an engineer much of my life and now looking for a new job. Always been fascinated by steam power you know? What would have happened had steam energy truly been our primary energy source?" Abruptly he stopped. "But I don't suppose such topic would be of much interest to you."

"On the contrary," said Jessica, "my great grandfather Cornelius owned a Stanley Steamer or two and raved about what wonderful machines they really were and how they were just on the edge of solving all the technical problems. Had the Stanley twins been better at promoting their work—" She shrugged. "Are you looking for something of said subject matter?"

"Well," he laughed, "it's funny, I hadn't thought so—" And he stopped and looked about the store, to the crowded shelves and books stacked on the floor and the row of books that lined the sill of the window from which he looked out over the park. "It's just funny you know? How you can walk by a place so often and not really see it? But even so—" He stopped, noticing the blank book on the counter in which Jessica's hand delicately rested on the pages there as if a five fingered bookmark. He laughed. "And so you sell even blank books?"

She flipped back the pages to reveal beautifully handwritten script. "Oh, my, no," she said. "Someone brought this in just a while ago—it looks like a diary but clearly it has some sort of engineering ideas of which I cannot decipher—perhaps you?"

He took the curious black leather bound book from Jessica's hands, just a simple affair, on the front lettering, "Diary, 1895-1898" in gold lettering, and rather elegant in its simple way.

"Of what interest would such a diary be to me? Especially one of engineering whose ideas are most likely antique?"

"Don't be so hasty, so quick to disagree. Maybe open it and look at a few pages or so—"

Oliver looked at Jessica, not quite sure what to think, but opened the book to the front. "Why, this is so odd—" he began, "here is a diagram of a machine I've never seen—something that looks like it runs on steam—" He looked more and the pages became a blur as in his mind, things began to stir, his curiosity now fully engaged, and finally he looked up from the page and reached around back for his wallet—but Jessica shook her head and said, "Why don't you take it and see if it works? You can pay me later and that would be fine."

Startled, Oliver replied, "Not even a dime?"

"Not this time; after all it is a story that is not finished yet; a book with no final chapter or a poem without final rhyme."

Oliver stood rather transfixed. The generosity was clear and was not a trick. "Well," he said, "thank you—this is a most interesting find. I plan to study it well; and I shall return and tell you what it is this book speaks of."

Jessica nodded. "Payment enough."

Oliver left then, and went on his way, finally getting home and the rest of the day studied the book and when his friend Jackson called later that afternoon, Oliver answered and said, "Jackson, my friend, I have found the most incredible thing—a diary with plans for a machine that has never been built—a steam machine, but the purpose of which I can't fathom what it might be—"

Jackson was quiet a moment, and then finally said, "I'll be right over. *This* I just *have* to see."

In just a half hour, Jackson was there. A short man he was, with salt and pepper hair, square jawed and lean, almost as if himself an efficient machine. He came into Oliver's small but ample home (with a view of mountains east where often hiking, they'd roam for days and for nights, experiencing the forests, the alpine delights of heather, bear grass and rushing creek, often in view of a glaciered peak) and he sat at the table with Oliver and they both looked over the book and Jackson said, "I confess. It's a machine, a machine of which I can't imagine the purpose,

I swear I cannot but—" he smiled, "if it has not been built, then it should be," he laughed, "should it not?"

Oliver nodded. "Of course. Indeed—why not?" Looking at the schematics a bit longer, he said, "What do you suppose—"

Jackson said, "The idea was probably ahead of its time, technology not yet advanced—but, now it's our find."

The next evening, in Jackson's huge home with a basement outfitted for such adventures, with work bench and shelves and in the corner, a hydra shaped furnace, with a low growl of utilitarian flames, they began working and discovered, yes, that was the problem: a machine ahead of its time though what it did and was—that was still rather opaque but they worked on it and found, by visiting machine shops, just what they needed, be it condenser or pulleys or dials galore, all easy to find and soon a machine of brass now stood in Jackson's back yard. And on noon the twenty-second of June, they stood there, admiring the finished machine and Oliver said, "I've gone through the book yet again, and I still can find no idea what it's supposed to do and unfortunately the writing just ends—as if the inventor suddenly stopped in mid-thought."

"Well," said Jackson, quite taken with this all, "I brought some champagne."

Oliver grinned. And, that said it all as they looked at what it was they had built: some four feet across, five feet high, maybe nine feet in length with a boiler, two lateral pistons on each side, and above it all, a bench to sit on with handholds on each side. And at knee level, a short and narrow instrument panel with several switches and gauges which somehow, seemed quite ample.

Jackson and Oliver grinned at each other and Oliver took the champagne and said, "I christen the machine the—" he looked to Jackson who looked back at him and both shrugged, "The Great Steam Unknown."

Crash with the bottle, the champagne foamed about; both Oliver and Jackson then climbed up on the machine. Sitting on the bench seat, Oliver said, "Hold on—I guess." And he tripped a toggle switch with a bright *snap*.

Neither knew of course, what to expect but in seconds, the boiler was operating well, it would seem, the pressure was fine, and—

Jackson turned to Oliver, "Well, guess we now find out what it will do."

"Be nice to know."

But Oliver's attention was drawn to an intriguing round gauge, the markings on which went from zero to ten. Suddenly a needle on said gauge advanced upward to four then five, finally stopping at nine. He touched Jackson, then pointing to the odd dial, "What do you make of this?"

Jackson shook his head, gave a short laugh. "I just followed the instructions; got me on that."

Abruptly, they were cloaked in a thick but bright mist followed a very sharp jolt. They both grabbed the handrails—and suddenly, the machine stopped.

"Well, guess that's that," Jackson said, after trying in vain to start the machine once again.

Oliver looked around. "Have we traveled into a cloud?"

They slowly climbed off The Great Steam Unknown, both feeling a bit of amusement and some dismay that apparently the machine operated in some mysterious way that they had not fathomed or done right or—?

"Oh, well," said Oliver, "we just followed a madman's dream to its logical end and—"

Abruptly the mist cleared he turned and stared.

Jackson also turned and his mouth dropped open. "My house," he whispered, "where oh where is my house?"

Indeed, indeed, for it was not only his house, but also all the houses that had been there—were gone.

"Oh, my Lord," said Oliver, as it began to dawn on him as well that something *had* happened. "Did that machine alter our dimensionality? Did we travel in time?"

"Oh, God," said Jackson, "if that's true, how will we ever get back?"

Oliver stopped and pointed. "Look—a road over there. It looks like it's in the same place as the one that was out in front of your house."

They walked over to it; it was wide and made of the familiar concrete except, "Odd," said Oliver, "wasn't that road in front of your home made of asphalt?"

"I don't understand," said Jackson, most fitful and quite upset.

Oliver just looked and then said, "A rise over there, that's where the road goes, let's see what's what from the top."

And so they walked for a short distance and cresting the ridge. "Oh, my Lord," whispered Oliver, as they both looked over a scene quite altered from what they had known. Still the broad valley as before with the narrow river below, but instead of the old bridge that they knew, it was now spanned by one quite new and of the *most* elegant design. In the distance the road rolled on to a city of spires and skyscrapers of pale blues and greens and subtle reds. Skyscrapers and spires graceful indeed and soaring so high; a city *so* beautiful, Oliver wanted to cry.

Suddenly they heard the blare of a horn and up behind them came a quiet car.

The driver stopped. And the window rolled down, and the head of a dark mustached and bespectacled fellow poked out the window and yelled, "What's eating ye? You're in a road, can'cha see?"

Oliver and Jackson stared at the car, something so sleek and deep blue with the engine just a low purr.

The driver's features softened a touch. "You fellows lost? Do you need a ride? I can certainly fit you inside."

"Where—what year—?" said Oliver.

"You're serious? Dear lad. Whatever's happened to you it's happened real bad. It's AD and GSE—Great Steam Era 2012—and that city out there, it's the City of Sandburg— as it's always been."

Jackson said, "I don't recognize—what—"

Oliver said, "I'm sorry, we come from some other place…"

The man looked at them. "Strange language you speak. Almost sounds like ancient Greek. You've never learned the government mandated poetic speech?"

Oliver and Jackson just looked at each other.

The driver studied them a few moments more. "Let me give you a ride; to walk to Sandburg, will make you footsore since it's a dozen kilometers or more. And it will be dark before long. You can stay at our place; we've room for more."

Oliver felt startled. *Kilometers*. But then they both got into the car. The gentleman extended his hand. "Rory McElroy. Executive Poet, the Ministry of Poetic Expression for the Province of Frost, the County of Chaucer, now that's who I be. And you, my fine friends and new company?"

"Oliver Stanton," said Oliver, first.

"Jackson, Jackson McHenry."

"Well," said Rory, "those are decent poetic names you both have." He stepped on a pedal and instantly the car moved into top speed. "Care for the paper? It is yesterday's *Times*, of New York but still relevant, might not you agree?"

Oliver, in the front, just nodded dumbly as he read the headlines: "President in a bit of a fix; upset with Congress and remains ticked." And another headline: "Women's fashions using more red; use of bright colors is hardly dead." And, "Mars Lander to land in ancient lakebed in Crater Gail; the search for life soon shall set sail."

Putting the paper aside, he looked straight ahead, then down to the dashboard, to the chrome letters there. "Stanly Steamer Deluxe/ T. S. Elliot GT"

And for a moment, all rode in silence, but secretly Oliver smiled. Wherever it was that he and Jackson might be, The Great Steam Unknown had now put them on a grand journey indeed.

THE GESTALT PRINCESS
JAMES BROGDEN

1 Once upon a time there was a girl who was born without a body, so she made one of her own.

Her name was Angela Harcourt, daughter of Professor Denton Harcourt, the renowned scientist and engineer, whose wife had been cruelly taken from the world before she was able to provide him with children. It is hard to say which left him more bereft: her death, or the echoing sorrow of an empty house with a playroom which would be forever silent and cold.

And so, he reasoned, since Nature in her arbitrary cruelty had cheated him thus, it was only fair that he cheat her in turn. He would create the most perfect daughter a father could ever wish for—beautiful and talented, wise and pure—through technology alone rather than the mischances of gross biological matter.

He travelled the world over, searching for the most accomplished women in their fields—the arts, sciences, philosophy, and literature—immortalizing their words and actions with an oculoscopic camera designed by himself to such exacting tolerances that their images could not be told apart from reality. At length he returned with his recordings and set about preparing his home for a new child.

He commissioned the construction of a Babbage Engine so

massively complex that it filled the whole of his cellar and all of his workshops, and required the construction of a small railway line to continuously supply enough coal for its boilers. He installed an intricate array of magic lanterns, reflecting prisms, and lenses throughout the house, and had the very air itself enriched with a cocktail of noble gases to permit clearer propagation of light waves. Finally, every window was bricked up so that no chaotic light from the outside world would interfere with the projection equipment upon which her existence depended.

When the time finally came to bring her to life, his hands were trembling so much that he could barely operate the contact relays. Deep beneath his feet, the calculating engines thrummed into life. Lamps burned, prisms flashed and spun, and his daughter shimmered into being like the coalescence of a thousand rainbows.

She flickered at the edges, uncertain, unfocussed. A thousand different faces blurred together and finally settled into a tentative smile. Gradually she became more confident and began to move, looking around at the room curiously, and then at him.

"Do you know who you are?" he whispered, frozen with terrified hope.

She frowned, puzzled. Many floors beneath his feet, the huge Babbage engine whirled, brass armatures and cogwheels sifting through infinite combinations of oculoscope footage to provide her with a dazzling smile—the totality of a thousand recorded smiles—and it took his breath away.

"Yes of course!" she replied, in a voice which was the totality of a thousand recorded voices. "I am your daughter, Angela. Hello father."

Forgetting himself in the transport of his joy, he threw out his arms to embrace her, but they closed only on empty light.

"Silly father!" she laughed, and began to explore her new surroundings.

In the years that followed, the Professor did his best to teach her as much about the world as he was able, augmenting these lessons by recording more of the Outside with his oculoscope and adding to her library of raw images.

As he had intended, she was an eager pupil, quick to learn and of a curious disposition. But eagerness soon grew into impatience, and she began questioning the limitations placed on her.

"Dear father," she would say, "grateful as I am for all the news of the Outside that you bring me, why might I not see it with my own eyes?"

"My sweet daughter," he would answer, "you know as well as I that your projections simply cannot survive in the light of day."

To this she had no reply, but simply pressed him further to bring back as much news of the Outside as he could.

And so, for a while, both were content.

2 Now there came a time when Professor Harcourt was obliged, by virtue of his membership of various scientific and professional institutions, to entertain a gathering of his colleagues. Whilst he considered the whole affair awkward and unnecessary, Angela was giddy with excitement at the prospect of meeting other flesh-and-blood people for the very first time. She didn't know what to wear or how to appear, and spent a dizzying few hours flashing through an array of outfits and hairstyles like the pictures in a child's flip-book.

He, on the other hand, was seized with apprehension over what his colleagues would do if they discovered her. At the very least they would demand to know the secrets of her creation. At worst they might try to disassemble her altogether. Reluctantly, he told her that she would be unable to attend the feast—moreover, that for her own safety she would have to remain in her room.

"Oh but father!" she cried in dismay. "That is monstrously unfair! How can you possibly ask this of me?"

"It is for your own protection," was his only reply, and when the evening of the feast came he disconnected the prisms and mirrors throughout the house so that she could project herself nowhere but her own chambers. Angela could do nothing but listen to the distant sounds of revelry and weep tears of bitter loneliness which sparkled and disappeared before they reached the floor.

And yet, she would have been more terrified to learn how entirely his suspicions were justified.

The process of developing the technology which had brought her to life had been waymarked by a succession of minor breakthroughs in optics and thermodynamics which he had published to the scientific community—partially out of a spirit of intellectual philanthropy, but also in the hope that by throwing out such small tidbits he could distract speculation from the Great Work which was their culmination. In this, he fooled precisely no-one.

It was obvious to his colleagues from an early stage that

he was working on a groundbreaking invention. Curiosity bred rumour and gossip like maggots on a corpse, and so it was that evening, behind the faces of amicable neutrality around him at the table, Professor Harcourt fancied he saw darting glances of avid curiosity and ears alert for unguarded hints of the Great Work. To make it more difficult, each of his dinner guests was accompanied by a retinue of assistants, secretaries, and general flunkies—all of whom needed to be watched like a hawk.

<>

One such hanger-on was a young laboratory assistant by the name of Justin Soames. He was intelligent, honourable, passionately devoted to the advancement of the physical sciences, and currently having the worst evening of his life.

It wasn't just that he was awkward in social situations—it felt like his tongue had two left feet most of the time anyway, and he'd attended his patron at several of these symposia in the past, so he was quite used to them. It was more that this was the first time he'd ever been compelled to burgle his host.

His patron had equipped him with an aether drill—a highly restricted piece of equipment designed by the dentistry profession for extracting tricky teeth but which was also surprisingly effective at loosening all manner of mechanical devices including locks. It was approximately the same size and shape as a ratchet screwdriver and it hid in a coat-pocket just below his heart, like a guilty secret.

Justin was as honest as the day was long, so the saying went, but he was 'prenticed to an unforgiving master whose own researches ran to sticking electrodes in rabbits' brains and then recording the shapes of their contortions, and who kept Justin short of pay and long of day, as the other saying went. He would not scruple to fling the young man back into the Stepney Slums, and given that Justin's wages were all that stood between his ailing mother and the Poorhouse, Justin found himself with little choice.

Accordingly, he waited for an opportune moment of

distraction and slipped away from the feast to see if he could find and steal the secret of Harcourt's Great Work.

The mansion's upper hallways were cold and dark. Occasionally a small clockwork servitor would scuttle past on an automated errand, making him jump. Everywhere he came across what he assumed were pictures with their frames shrouded by dust-sheets, until he discovered that they were mirrors—they were *all* mirrors. Other than that he found room after room to be empty and clean to the point of sterility. No furniture, carpet, or curtains.

He was beginning to despair of finding anything interesting when, at the end of a long corridor, he saw a light under a door.

Breathlessly, he approached, and became aware of a sound which he had at first taken to come from the merriment downstairs: a woman singing. It was of such mellifluous beauty that he quite forgot any sense of decorum—for what could it be other than a lady's chamber and hence inconceivable to enter, thief or not—in a sudden and irresistible desire to see the owner of such a voice.

His aether drill made short work of the lock.

In contrast to what he had seen of the house so far, this room was opulently furnished. It was also inhabited by, quite simply, the most beautiful woman he had ever seen in his entire life. She stood before a tailor's dummy, working on an elaborate bodice of gold filigree and diamonds with the help of several small servitors which scurried up and down it and about her ankles like mechanical squirrels. She was singing with such an air of melancholy that he didn't know whether his heart was about to burst with love or longing.

All this he saw in the few seconds before she noticed his intrusion. She cried out in alarm, backing quickly to the far side of the room.

"No, wait! I'm sorry…" he began, taking a pace inwards, but found his way blocked by the servitors which menaced him with their various mismatched limbs. They were a motley collection, seemingly built out of spare parts.

"Who are you?" she demanded.

"I'm—*ow!*" He'd tried stepping forward again, and something like a sharpened egg-whisk had jabbed him in the ankle.

"That is more than close enough," she warned. "Tell me who you are and what you are doing here, if you value your lower appendages."

"My name is Justin," said Justin. "Please be assured Miss, that my intentions, though they are not what one might exactly call honourable, nevertheless include no harm or dishonour to your person."

"No indeed?" Her scepticism was plain.

"I am here merely to burgle your father."

"Imagine how reassured I feel."

"Please understand," he continued in tones of such desperate urgency that she could not help feeling sympathy for him a little, "I take no joy in this act. I am constrained by the orders of a cruel master without whose reward my sick mother will surely die in the Poorhouse."

"And what have you come to steal, that is so valuable?"

"Nothing less than the secret of your father's Great Work itself."

"Really? What might that be?"

His face fell. "I confess, I do not know." Then, just as quickly, it brightened again. "But I'm sure I'll know it when I see it," he added optimistically.

She couldn't help smiling. "I'm sure you will," she replied. A queer, fluttering sort of feeling had started in her stomach. It was like nothing she had ever felt before, and she wondered if something were not wrong with her. She interrogated the computing engines which carried the totality of her knowledge and gave shape to her thoughts, but nothing in their miles of gearage could explain such a feeling. Was it possible that her father had deliberately kept something from her? Some small but vital facet of human experience? If it were the case, was she now spontaneously discovering it for herself? Was she no longer just the sum total of his collected information but becoming something...more?

The automated boilers in the cellar struggled to meet the demands of her racing thoughts, dumping their excess heat into the house's central heating system. It was noticeable to the feasting guests as a marked rise in temperature. Brows were mopped, collars loosened, and Professor Harcourt excused himself from their company to locate the source of the malfunction.

"Then we have that much in common, at least," she replied. "I am trapped in this house by a cruel father who has never let me see the blue sky or another human face."

Justin was horrified. "Then let me help you escape this place immediately!"

"Alas, it is not that simple. I am beset by technical contrivances of his which prevent my escape. It is within my power to free myself but there are certain tools and materials which I lack—bring them to me and in return I will show you the secret of my father's Great Work."

"Miss, believe me when I tell you that I would help you even if you had nothing more to offer me than a smile of gratitude."

She looked at him wonderingly, and felt that strange fluttering again. "I do believe you," she said.

Then the sound of footsteps echoed in the hallway outside, along with her father's voice calling "Angela? Are you there, my daughter?"

Justin froze in panic.

"You must not be seen here!" she hissed.

He dithered, which was at least an improvement. "How am I to escape?" he pleaded. "There are no windows!"

"Stand there!" she demanded, indicating the corner. "Stand absolutely still. Do not move!"

Her tone permitted no refusal, and so he obeyed. From the corner he watched in surprise as several of the mirrors in her room angled themselves on hidden mechanisms, bathing him a strangely quivering light which made his head swim. It was so disorientating that when the Professor entered he really could do nothing more than blink.

"Angela," said her father reprovingly. "You did not answer me."

"My apologies, father," she replied. "I was concentrating on my outfit." She had thrown a sheet over the tailor's dummy and was smiling her sunniest and most innocent of smiles at him. He did not seem to have noticed Justin at all.

"And when are you going to let me see this mysterious outfit which you have been working on for so long?"

"It is a surprise, father," she tutted. "I have told you."

"Hm. Well, so. What can you tell me about a sudden surge of energy in the cellars?"

"I? Why, nothing. Perhaps there is a faulty thermostat somewhere?"

"Hm. Perhaps." He took a few more steps into the room, looking around, right at and through Justin as if he wasn't there at all. Then without another word he turned on his heel and left.

The mirrors swivelled, the shivering light faded, and Justin shook his head clear. "How did you do that?" he asked. "What did you do?"

"I simply projected an image of that corner of the room over the top of where you were," she said as if it were the most obvious thing in the world. "We have no more time for discussion. Tell me where to contact you, and I will send you a list of the items I require. Succeed in this and I will be able to answer all of your questions. But you will have to be patient. It may take some time."

3 It took three years.

In the first year he brought her pistons, actuators and gear assemblies, and he saw that she was adding limbs to the tailor's dummy.

"You are building a mechanical man!" he said excitedly.

"No," she laughed, "by no means am I building any sort of man."

In the second year he brought her precision milling equipment and tools so delicate that their working ends were thinner than a human hair.

"With these," she said, "I will build my nangines."

"Nangines?"

"Babbage engines built from the very smallest particles of matter—so small that a single nangine is no larger than a speck of dust. The entire computational power of my father's cellars will soon be reproduced in the size of a sugar cube."

He saw then that what he had taken to be gold filigree and diamonds was in fact an elaborate system of miniaturized lenses, mirrors, and lanterns interconnected by thread-thin hydraulics.

"Why, they look exactly like veins and arteries," he observed.

"Why they do, don't they?" she replied with a secret smile, and refused to be drawn further.

In the third year she asked him to bring nothing more than a large plumber's wrench. When he asked why, she took him down into the sulphurous humidity of the cellar, where her father's calculating engines performed their eternal ballet of brass and machine oil. To Justin's ears, the whirring of their multitudinous rods and cogs sounded like the workings of a giant insect hive. Indeed, the scurrying of many clockwork servitors—cleaning, carrying, adjusting—added to the impression.

"I once told you," she said, "that I would show you the secret of my father's Great Work."

"Yes, and this is it?"

"A little more than this, perhaps. This is *me*. I am *this*."

"I don't understand."

She indicated herself, explaining, "What you see before you is nothing more than a projection," and to prove it she projected herself across to the other side of the engine room. Justin gasped in astonishment. "Everything I am—everything I know, or think, or remember—comes from these machines."

"I don't believe that."

"But you must!" Her voice was filled with sudden urgency. "Over these years I have come to love you; you must believe the truth of what I am or my heart will break!"

"What I mean to say is that I don't believe this is all you are. I have loved you from the moment I first saw you, and while I feel that love in my heart I know that my heart is not where the love comes from. Whatever I am, it is more than just corpuscles of flesh and bone; whatever you are, it is more than just wheels of iron and brass."

"Will you help me to finally free myself of this prison?" she asked.

"I will do anything you ask of me."

"Then take your wrench and remove the primary pressure control assembly, just there." She pointed to a cluster of pipes and dials.

"But that will…"

"I know. You must trust me."

"Daughter! What is the meaning of this!" Justin had been about to obey when Harcourt's outrage echoed across the chamber. He stood bristling with fury, and armed with a revolver pointed directly at Justin's heart.

"Father," she warned. "Do not do this."

"You presume to order *me*?" he thundered. "Faithless girl! After all that I have given you!"

"And for that I am thankful. I love you father, but I am no longer yours to control. Nor am I his," she added, indicating Justin, "though I love him just as dearly. I am mine."

A figure appeared behind the Professor, grasped his arms with prodigious strength, and forced the gun down. It was in every respect identical to Angela.

"Dearest father," said this new version of his child. "You

will note that I now have a physical body. I beg you, do not force me to test the limits of its strength." For a fleeting second the outer projection flickered and Justin caught a glimpse of the augmented tailor's doll underneath: the shining lenses of her eyes, the diamond sparkle of her projection nodes, and the clean grace of her piston limbs.

The first Angela nodded to him again from the other side of the engine room. "Everything I am is there too," she reassured him, "but with the freedom to leave and see the Outside for myself. Please now, do as you have promised."

Justin did as he had promised.

With the primary pressure control assembly in pieces, the steam powering the huge computation engine escalated rapidly out of control. Great blasts of superheated vapour scalded the air and tremors shuddered through the foundations. Brick arches started to crumble. The new Angela watched as her incorporeal self flickered out like a candle flame. Then she grabbed the two men dearest to her in all the world, and carried them up and into the safety of the Outside.

4 Once upon a time there was a girl who was born without a body, so she made one for herself.

She stood at the rail of the steamer plying its night journey past the coast of Cyprus, watching the phosphorescence tremble in its wake while the stars shone hard and clear above, and she lay her metal head contentedly on her lover's shoulder.

"I have a memory of this," she said wistfully. "But this is the first time I have seen it with my own eyes. Isn't that funny?"

Justin took her hand, weaving her cold fingers with his warm ones, and listened to the tick and whirr of her thoughts. "We will make new memories together," he said.

"I think my parents journeyed here when mother was alive." She looked up at him, and let the projection of her face fall. He was the only one for whom she would ever do so; and her lenses of brass and crystal shone with love. "My father will see that your mother is cared for," she said. "Have no fear of that."

"I fear nothing when I am with you," he replied. "I have only one question."

"What is it?"

"Back in the cellar. Why did you need me to destroy the engines? Why couldn't you do it for yourself—you had a body then, after all."

Her face reappeared, and she shuddered as if with cold. "I was afraid," she said. "Simply afraid. I didn't know what would happen when the first me disappeared. Maybe I would die. Maybe I did. Am I the same person, or just a copy who thinks she is?"

"What do you think?"

She shrugged. "I think I love you."

"Then that will do for me."

Together they left the ship's glittering wake to slip away astern, and went forward to see what the world ahead would bring them.

THE TYPHOON OF 1901
CHRISTOPHER L EGER

Captain John Davidson sat at the polished mahogany desk in his cabin aboard the battleship *USS Kersarge*, slowly stirring his coffee in its elegant china cup. The comforting and familiar taste belayed the fact that the entire world had changed around him in the past fortnight in the most unbelievable of ways. He had first felt the sea on his face more than thirty years before on the old sail frigate *Constellation* as a midshipman and was supposed to retire in August. He was from a different age and a different era as was that old sail frigate. However, he would not trade the *Kersarge* for a dozen *Constellations* in the coming fight.

The new steam powered navy was something his son had trained to command. As he thought of John, Davidson absentmindedly spun with his thumb the Naval Academy ring that his son had recently had sized for him. Over the years, his hands had grown continually smaller and the ring had to be taken in. It still did not fit properly but Davidson would have never mentioned it, preferring to remind himself of his son whenever he had to push it back up.

He thumbed through the dispatches and telegrams assembled out on his desk as he stirred. His wife's picture, with those soft warm eyes of 28-years of marriage looked fondly at him from a heavy silver frame, now bordered in black.

◇

16 June 1901
News Dispatch from New York Herald to all syndicates.
Commercial Telegram transmitted over open wireless and intercepted.

Strange Clamshell Vessel Surfaces Inside New York Harbor;
Navy keeping sightseers away. Collector of Customs unable to make contact with vessel. Early morning pandemonium in the metropolis as a strange vessel, shaped like a clamshell, surfaced directly inside New York harbor today near the Statue of Liberty with no notice. Marine surveyors state that vessel is 575-feet in length and 75-feet in beam, making it larger than every known ship afloat. Its purpose and flag are unknown. The whole population has turned out to witness the event and there is much activity in the streets near the dock. The crowd became so great that at noon reserves from the police stations in the outlying boroughs called in to assist with preserving order. Never before in recollection have so many persons congregated along the river and docks. Every small boat in the city has taken to the water, filled with spectators. After the Collector of Customs could not hail the strange craft and no activity emitted from within it, the US Navy gunboat *Wasp* along with the battleship *Kentucky* took up station near the clamshell vessel to discourage ramshackle launches from coming too near the mysterious craft until its intentions known.

◇

16 June 1901
Western Union Telegram
To Captain John Davidson, SR, USS Kersarge, commanding
From Ensign John Davidson, JR,
Sent from New York Naval Station

Dear father, please know that I have, through the good offices of certain members of the Naval Board no doubt known to you, received appointment as gunnery officer of the monitor *USS Tonapah* in Boston. I leave this afternoon by rail. Mother is in a fit that she will now be home alone with the strange new clamshell craft in the harbor, but Aunt Helen is arriving today. Uncle Thomas on the *Kentucky* is probably beside himself. What wonderful times we live in.

<>

17 June 1901
News Dispatch from Boston Daily News to all syndicates
Commercial Telegram Transmitted over open wireless and intercepted

NEW YORK DESTROYED BY ROCKET FROM CLAMSHELL VESSEL. From the center of New York harbor north to Canal Street in Manhattan, to Jersey City in the West, south to Bayonne and East to Ocean Parkway in Brooklyn, not a single building remains standing. Water boiled away from the giant city's aqueducts and none was available to quench the 200-mph firestorm of flame that shot out as far away as Perth Amboy and Levittown. Only shadows of human beings etched into concrete remain. Ship's anchor thought to be from the *USS Kentucky*, directly under the explosion, found in the center of a farmer's field in Connecticut. A stark cloud of debris hangs over what used to be the great city and gray ash continues to rain. Untold thousands dead. Many more ill with disease referred to by local doctors as Ash Sickness. All Army and Navy men in Boston on high alert as Clamshell sighted surfacing near this city's harbor.

<>

18 June 1901
Official Naval Department Dispatch
To: Commanders of All ships and stations, US Navy
From: Commander of the Atlantic Fleet, Hampton Roads

Subject: Battle of Boston

Confidential, decode with cipher 21. Restricted distribution.

Let it be known and remembered that on 17 June, 1901 the steam monitors *USS Tonapah, USS Puritan*, and *USS Terror*, were lost with all hands in gallant action with the invader known as the Clamshell. Their sacrifice allowed the city of Boston precious extended time to evacuate, saving many civilian lives. Their commitment to duty is in the highest tradition of the service.

All Atlantic area ships to assemble at Hampton Roads, soonest.

<>

21 June 1901

News Dispatch from the Dover Democrat to all syndicates.

Commercial Telegram transmitted over open wireless and intercepted

Cities in Ruin; Navy in Retreat. Following on the heels of the unpredicted destruction of the great cities of New York, Boston, and Philadelphia under the rockets of the Clamshell invader, the last US Navy ships in the waters of Delaware hurriedly weighed anchor and sailed over the horizon for points unknown today. After three of the sea service's ironclad monitors were rapidly sunk within minutes by revolutionary underwater rockets in Boston harbor, there have been no further engagements between the Navy and the unflagged Clamshell vessel, which travels from city to city underwater. All along the east coast, an epidemic of Ash Sickness is following the destruction by the Clamshell. The sickness causes victims to lose hair, fingernails, and teeth before dying in agony for which no treatment is known. Seacoast towns are emptying as panic has inflamed the country and citizens ask where is the Navy?

<>

23 June 1901

Official Naval Department Dispatch

To: All ships and stations, US Navy
From: General Naval Board, Washington DC
Subject: Battle of Hampton Roads
Confidential. Decode with cipher 27

With the destruction of the 1st and 2nd Naval Divisions of the Atlantic Fleet at the Battle of Hampton Roads and the loss of the Atlantic Fleet commander, all remaining Atlantic area units are to assemble on the northern end of Chesapeake Bay and will come under the direct command of the General Naval Board.

◇

24 June 1901
From, General Naval Board, Washington DC
To: Captain Davidson, Commander, *USS Kersarge*
Secret. Decode with cipher Z8. For addressee only.

It is of pressing importance that you proceed at once to Baltimore harbor, take on passenger, and as much coal as possible. Said passenger is of the utmost importance and all cooperation is to be extended to him in his urgent mission. Expect the converted yacht *USS Vixen* to meet you at Baltimore. Your tactical command will extend over both vessels. I am sending identical telegram to Secretary of Navy.

◇

Captain Davidson dabbed his lips with a linen napkin, pushed his cup away, and stood, straightening his spotless heavy woolen uniform and adjusting his brass buttons before he donned his white gloves once again and moved out of the cabin. As he walked the passageway of his command, he was in awe once more of its presence and power. His ship was no decades-old ironclad as the three boats lost at Boston.

His charge, *USS Kersarge* was the largest battleship in the western hemisphere and weighed some 11,540 tons. Longer than a football field, she needed 24 feet of deep water just to float. Most of her bulk came from hundreds of tons of Harvey steel armor plate. Wrapped around her in a belt up to 17-inches thick, it was strong enough to withstand direct hits from any naval gun at sea.

The ship was alive with activity through every compartment he passed, returning salutes as he moved. More than a hundred men stoked row after row of heavy, coal-fired boilers that provided her engines up to 10,000 horsepower, pushing the leviathan to an amazing 17.3 knots of full speed, faster than any previous first-class warship in American waters. Hundreds of ratings operated her weapons, conned her small boats, pulled in her anchor lines, peeled potatoes, and maintained the ship's hull and plates. A total crew of 553 officers, sailors, and marines inhabited her maze of decks and spaces.

He made his way toward the bridge of his battleship, and as he did so, stopped in on the ship's newest addition.

Mr. Nikola Tesla sat in what was formerly the navigation room of the *USS Kersarge,* now taken over by the strange inventor. Fresh from experiments in Colorado Springs that Captain Davidson could scarcely understand, Tesla had arrived at the docks in Baltimore at the head of a team of twenty scratch engineers assembled at the insistence of President Teddy Roosevelt himself. The bewhiskered former Assistant Secretary of the Navy had grabbed Davidson firmly by the shoulder and advised him to show Tesla all the courtesy due a full commodore in the Navy, and nothing less. The truth was, the strangely accented engineer held that rank, pending Congressional approval of course.

"Good morning, Mr. Tesla," Davidson managed as he entered the space. The former chart table was covered with scale models, electrical parts, and items that he could pretend no knowledge of. Tesla had been developing a device that he professed would disclose the Clamshell's arrival no matter whether it had surfaced or not. He even boasted that he could pinpoint its location to within a few hundred yards.

Tesla scarcely noticed him and continued somewhat

arrogantly with his work.

"How is the progress coming with your apparatus, sir?" Davidson asked, perusing a half-unrolled set of drawings.

Tesla reached a smooth hand out and rolled the prints up neatly. "Indeed, I should be ready for testing today, Captain," Tesla said softly, with a hint of eastern European accent caressing his words. "Please have the *Vixen* standby for this afternoon."

The *USS Vixen* was a 182-foot steam yacht converted hastily into an airship tender for the eccentric engineer's device. From the rear deck of the *Vixen,* a helium-filled kytoon airship that was half balloon and half kite had been assembled. The experimental craft would hold aloft a mile of energized copper wire connected to the receiver that Tesla fiddled with.

"Indeed," Davidson replied with meaning, drawing the word out over a good three seconds. The gesture did not faze Tesla, who simply continued his work.

The day previously, the engineer had described it in detail. "The Clamshell is, of course, constructed of some sort of ferrous metals. Judging by its dimensions, such a large craft would displace more than 24,000 tons in seawater. Such a large deposit of moving metal would create a magnetic anomaly along the earth's own electric current. By means of electrodynamic induction, I believe that it should be relatively easy to discover the vessel through use of a detector attuned to just such a magnetic anomaly."

In short, the *Vixen*, as a hunter would find the Clamshell and point it out to the *Kersarge* to kill just as it surfaced. Davidson could hardly wait.

<>

They had positioned themselves at the top of Chesapeake Bay, just three miles offshore. During the nighttime hours, the gaslights and chimney sparks of both Washington DC and Baltimore could be seen. The two cities were the largest left on the Eastern Coast of the United States. Teddy Roosevelt, true to his Bull Moose tendencies, had refused to leave the White House even as he ordered the Library of Congress quietly evacuated and the papers of the Founding Fathers taken to an undisclosed Army post in Ohio. When the *Kersarge* had taken on coal at Baltimore the day previously they had found the town nearly deserted, with stray dogs outnumbering residents near the docks.

It was there they had taken on a provisional company of more than 150 US Marines. Led by Captain John Archer Lejeune, a 33-year old Louisianan who was a stern disciplinarian and a born fighter, the Marines pressed into every free space on the *Kersarge* to grab whatever sleep they could. With each of the sea-going soldiers burdened down by a Winchester-Lee 6mm straight-pull rifle, a 9-inch steel bayonet, and 180 rounds of ammunition, they were ready for war. To bolster the force, Davidson had armed fifty of his seamen with cutlasses, pistols, and rifles, ready to board the alien vessel if given the chance.

With Tesla's operation moved to the *Vixen*, Davidson once more had his battleship to himself. He was enjoying his morning coffee in his cabin when Lejeune burst through his door, gasping for air and full of excitement.

"They found it," the marine officer announced with his southern drawl.

Davidson drained his cup in three careful swallows, replaced it on the desk, and stood. Confidently, with all of the air due the commander of the greatest battleship afloat, he walked to the bridge, Lejeune leading the way by several paces. The open-air bridge of the warship was buzzing with conversation as Schaffer; the gunnery officer, busily spoke into voice tubes.

"Prepare all batteries for action. Load armor piercing rounds. All gun crews standby for rapid reloading drills," the officer called first into one tube and then the other. When he saw Davidson, he stood at full attention and directed his conversation to him. "The *Vixen* signaled by flag that they have the Clamshell below water two miles away sir, moving toward Washington, sir."

Davidson nodded. "Very well, Mr. Schaffer, you may carry on." With the order and a nod, the bridge crew resumed activity with increased vigor. He turned to Lejeune. "Mr. Lejeune, you may see to your marines. Keep them out of the way but be prepared for a boarding should the opportunity arise."

As Lejeune saluted and disappeared he began barking orders in the distance to his lieutenants and sergeants, and the decks of the battleship thundered with hundreds of running men getting below decks as the ship began to sail.

From what Davidson had been told by the member of the Naval Board, it had been a very one-sided battle in Boston. As soon as the three monitors could work up steam in their boilers and clear their decks for war, the relics sailed forth to pick a fight. With their battle ensigns flying proudly, they were sunk within minutes by rapid hits from small, unbelievably fast underwater rockets from the Clamshell before they were able to get a shot out of their guns.

His son had deserved better than that.

All of the leviathan's boilers had been lit and kept warm in preparation for fast movement and it allowed her to begin sailing within minutes toward the bearing provided by the *Vixen*. They soon hit 16-knots and the *Vixen* fell fast away in the distance, struggling to keep up. With great clouds of black smoke belching from her twin stacks, the *Kersarge* split the calm waters of the bay, leaving a churned froth in her wake. Davidson felt the sea spray from the bow on his face that soon turned to salt with the cool breeze. "A whale, a whale!" called a lookout in the crow's-nest directly overhead of the bridge, "1500 yards to port!"

The young sailor was sadly incorrect as Davidson peered through his telescope at the object just under the sea, racing toward them. Moving incredibly fast the 'whale' disappeared under the battleship's hull only to reappear on the other side. It continued on its single-minded race toward the horizon, leaving a trail of bubbles and wake behind it.

"One of the reported underwater rockets, Captain!" Schaffer called out, craning his head over the side to look at its path.

"Indeed, Mr. Schaffer. It seems both that we have lost the element of surprise, and that they have missed their first shot at us," Davidson answered as calmly as he could. He had to set the example and remain levelheaded. It was what was expected of a naval officer in battle. "Signal to fire the Armistead Mines."

The order was repeated and soon a small signal rocket was fired from the quarterdeck. A US Army signalman standing on a platform onshore near Cape Saint Clair saw the red streak of light and smoke trail from the battleship and then picked up his sound-powered telephone, furiously cranking the signal box to get someone at the telephone exchange to answer. A sergeant took the call, asked that he repeat the fact that he had seen a signal, scribbled a sheet of paper and then hung up the phone.

Another phone call placed to a fire control center deep inside the concrete of Fort Carroll was answered by an Army engineer major and confirmed. Scarcely a minute later, the chain of 60 Armistead Mines exploded in the waters just south of Baltimore in Chesapeake Bay. The mines, named after the experimental project at Fort Armistead that had rushed the devices from drawing board to production in a week, each contained more than 500-pounds of high explosives wrapped in a heavy cast iron casing. Laid by the Chesapeake fishing schooners and set off by an electrical fuse attached to floating buoys overhead, the daisy chain of explosions were designed to do one thing; force the Clamshell to surface before it got into Baltimore harbor.

As Davidson looked on, the Bay just past the *Kersarge* erupted in dozens of immense geysers shooting high up into the sky. The water had scarcely becalmed when their prey showed itself once again. Broaching the surface like a prehistoric shark jumping for the sky in a fit of rage, the gray-black shape unlike anything Davidson had ever thought possible materialized. Sitting dead in the water some 4,000 yards away was the destroyer of cities, the bringer of the apocalypse—the Clamshell. It was twice the size of his own ship and although was flushed from its hiding place, seemed visibly undamaged.

Davidson, never one for theatrics, quietly spoke his orders to Schaffer. "Open fire, Mr. Schaffer."

Thirty feet forward of the bridge a pair of 13-inch/35 caliber rifled naval cannons spat fire and flame in a spectacle that would have made any medieval dragon envious. Davidson watched from his telescope as a pair of 1,130-pound shells packed with high explosives traced an arc towards the Clamshell. Traveling at 2,000 feet per second, the shells fell alternatively one long and one short, bracketing the alien invader in tidal waves of water as they missed, but only nearly so.

Sixty long seconds passed with the *Kersarge* steaming for the Clamshell, her gunners stripped to the waist and furiously working with chain and sling to reload her two forward cannons.

"Rockets in the water!" the lookout yelled for all he was worth above them in the crow's-nest as the man saw a pair of the deadly underwater rockets streak from the strange craft toward the battleship.

"Sir, should we come about to evade the rockets?" asked the helmsman on the wheel of the *Kersarge*.

The young man reminded Davidson of his son. He imagined what his son's Captain would have said to him as they steamed toward the Clamshell in Boston. He calmly extended a hand out and physically placed it on the wheel next to the helmsman's. "Our gun crews are almost ready to fire again, son."

With an exchange of a look the young sailor hardened his gaze and resolved to continue onward relentlessly towards the Clamshell. Closer and closer the 11,000-ton battleship raced like a locomotive of the sea on a direct course for the 24,000-ton Clamshell, wallowing before her. The two underwater rockets from the enemy ship reached out for the *Kersarge* like spectral arms open in an embrace of death.

"Captain, number one mount is showing ready to fire and we have corrected aim point," Schaffer announced, his forehead bathed in sweat.

"Fire," Davidson said at the same instant the crow's-nest lookout reported the rockets only feet away from the battleship's hull.

The helmsman shuddered and closed his eyes, bracing for the impact. With a rumble and flash, his young world turned upside down in a storm of concussion and smoke, flame and shrapnel. The last thing the helmsman saw as he somersaulted over the wheel and through the crushed front of the bridge windows was the recoil of the ship's twin 13-inch cannon below.

Davidson himself was thrown against the bulkhead and

only narrowly saved himself from the same fate by clawing his way to a halt against the ship's wheel. The huge battleship lifted under his feet, bulged, and contorted below him. A flash of pain raced from the balls of his feet through his knees and into his pelvis as his legs were crushed, twisted, and corkscrewed from the force of the dual rocket explosions directly under the bow of his ship. He blinked through the pain and struggled to remain conscious long enough to see his mission through.

He took grim satisfaction as he saw the impact of the *Kersarge's* last rounds upon the exposed hull of the Clamshell a thousand yards in front of the shattered battleship. The first round tore a groove across the craft and exploded harmlessly in the open water. The second round, however, was a direct impact dead center of the small structure that sat on top of the strange vessel. The explosion of a half-ton of black powder and Explosive-D vaporized the structure and left a gaping hole in the top of the Clamshell's deck from which fire and smoke poured.

Davidson was aware of someone shaking him from behind. Lejeune, the marine officer had returned to the deck and was yelling at him yet he could hear no words. Davidson felt at his right ear with his free hand and it came away sticky and bright crimson with blood. He refused to be carried away from the bridge and instead slumped on the exposed deck, watching his ship continue to plow forward even though the first forty feet of it had been sheared off as if by a giant's scissors. Even mortally wounded the *Kersarge* was still on a collision course with its murderer.

The momentum ended with the impact of the battleship directly into the smoking Clamshell. Now locked together they formed an immense T-shaped sinking island of steel and steam. Davidson watched as blue-uniformed marines and white-uniformed armed sailors swarmed over the wreckage of the *Kersarge's* bow and onto the alien ship. Trapped in his cloud of silence he could still pick out the muzzle flashes of their rifles and revolvers as they engaged the crew of the Clamshell. Emerging from the smoking hole in the center of their craft were what appeared to be men in masks, carrying rapid-fire handheld weapons whose rate of fire rivaled the best Gatling gun Davidson had ever witnessed. He watched the pitched battle unfold as Lejeune, who had departed his side, directed his men into the attack.

Captain John Davidson lost consciousness just as the marine's larger numbers carried the day and the masked, bug-eyed creatures made a last stand, perishing in a final bayonet charge. As he died, his Naval Academy ring slipped from his thin elderly finger and clinked metallically on the deck.

<>

Recently promoted Major John Archer Lejeune stood in front of the General Board of the Navy Department at the Washington Naval Yard, only blocks from the White House. Presiding over the board was Admiral of the Fleet George Dewey, hero of the Battle of Manila Bay two years before. The mustachioed and perfumed admiral had just heard from Mr. Tesla his analysis of the wreck of the Clamshell. The new words uranium, fusion, reactor, and nuclear had been added to the board's vocabulary through repeated use by the engineer and inventor.

"Major, let me get this correct, your marines attacked and killed sailors and naval infantry men who now claim to be Russian? And their ship was a ballistic missile submarine named the *Typhoon*?" Dewey asked rhetorically.

"Er…Soviet is what they claim," answered Lejeune. "The Soviet Union appears on no map; however under interrogation the handful of survivors speak Russian. It is my belief they are mad sir, that the extreme stress of handing their underwater craft has created some sort of mass hysteria. They all claim, to a man to be from the year 1989. They claim they submerged while conducting what they refer to as missile drills off the coast of the United States.

"When they surfaced again after passing through an electrical storm and could not communicate with their naval high command, they carried out their orders for such a scenario, which was the systematic attack on our cities. They further state that the lack of what they referred to as satellite communication forced them to manually calculate their rocket attacks from virtually point blank range."

The government of the Tsar from their Washington embassy had disavowed any knowledge of the *Typhoon*, a fact quickly confirmed by the US ambassador in St Petersburg. After several days, the Russian Naval attaché was allowed to question the survivors of the submarine at the naval brig. A linguist from the US office of naval intelligence took notes of the conversation, which seemed centered on the year 1917 and a man code-named Lenin whom the Tsar's attaché showed much interest.

Dewey stroked his mustache. "Your men captured one of their rocket's warheads intact, isn't that correct. As well as some of their automatic rifles?"

Lejeune confirmed this. The *Kersarge* had filled with water from her sheared bow and eventually dropped below the surface, taking more than three hundred sailors and marines with her, including her Captain. When the *Vixen* arrived followed by several steam tugboats alongside the battered Clamshell, Lejeune and the survivors of the battle went to work quickly saving what they could. He felt that is why he won his fast promotion above all else. Tesla had told the board the technology was generations ahead of what they had currently.

Dewey was pleased. When the board dismissed Lejeune, the Fleet Admiral stopped him to ask one more thing.

"Major," asked Dewey. "Would you be so kind as to stop by the White House and collect Commodore Davidson's Congressional Medal of Honor and present it to his family on our behalf? Since you were there for him in the end."

Lejeune turned and addressed Dewey once again, "I will, Admiral. He never mentioned his family but I will inquire about them."

Dewey nodded gravely, "I see. Perhaps you should return to the barracks instead. We are going to need you to put together a force to escort the warhead to Mr. Tesla's laboratory."

TOMMY TALES
BOB BROWN

The leather straps, tight around my wrist and ankles, bound me to the table. Above me, inside the white domed ceiling, the sharp angles of the skylight's cut glass chopped the light into narrow beams of color.

Bright copper wires fitted into cleverly threaded clamps on a flat bar that curved across my shaved chest. If the ferry's boiler hadn't been constructed with such magnificent precision, I might not be laying here, naked except where the white gauze clung to the oozing crust that covered much of my body.

The taste of the opium juice was still bitter on my tongue. I looked again through the skylight into the blue above. The sky swam in my mind, even when I closed my eyes. I had ignored such blue for years as I had worked the open river until the boilers imprisoned the watermen into foul holds where the shoveling of coal replaced the pulling of oars. Had I stayed in my boat, I might not be here. But I was.

The doctor with the blue glasses leaned over me. He had told me his name but it was now washed away on an opium breeze. I inhaled deeply and grimaced from the resulting feel of cracking skin. "It's all right," he whispered and the last strap went over the bridge of my nose, pulling my head firmly into the two small leather pads that lifted my head clear of the table. Those were the last two words ever spoken to me.

A cloud passed over the sun and the shadow darkened the room. It seemed like the right time to close my eyes and ready myself for this. Even with my eyes closed I could see myself, strapped to a table, the center of a collection of man and mechanisms. I did not, even now, feel connected to my body, the bonds were already loosening. Sharp pressure, but no pain came as the finely crafted knives spun crisp round penetrations in my skull. The sound was the worst. The pressure stopped and I knew, without wanting to know, that the next sound was a bit of my skull dropping into a small porcelain bowl that lay next to my head on the table. It was white with blue flowers. It's lower half covered in a dull layer of lead.

When the boilers were new, an old water man on the docks had been caught by an exploding boiler. A shard of curved metal had sliced through the side of the ship and sheared off the top of his head. I remembered looking at him when they brought the body to the dock. The pinkish gray that filled the skull contrasted sharply with the white bone and the blood matted hair. I was glad the woman shaved my head for this. At the time, the loss of my hair, as it fell in razor driven swaths bothered me more than did the current sound of my own skull dropping into the cold glass of the bowl. I think the opium juice, but for the taste, would be preferable to the sour ale down at the Floating Pig. I thought of the Floating Pig as I lay strapped to the table, being carved like one.

I had inspected the boring tools. The combination of pulleys, bracings, and tiny poured-lead bearings, with the lingering mark of graphite powders were such that I had tried to rise from my bed to inspect them closer. As with all of the devices I had observed in the infirmary, the precision was superior to anything I had ever seen. I felt no curiosity now. Simply resignation. After a sixth soft sound of the bowl being filled, the rattle of the pulleys and spin of the knives stopped.

The small brass spheres were next. They pushed into the cutouts until my head was held secure; it was as if the hand of god held my skull between his fingers.

There were no more words, no re-assuring voices. Just the

sound of a switch slammed shut and my vision shattered into a thousand streaks of light. Invisible forces pushed me through the gleaming brass spheres. For an instant I felt my spirit tear free. A bitter thought of what might be left in the remnant of my body to suffer death arced across my mind, but vanished. Left behind.

◇

Darkness came first, followed by silence and then memories, not all my own. They slipped through my mind like shadows in the moonlight. I am in the transfer casing. I push back against the unknown memories, pulling from my own to shape what I know is me.

They warned me about this. They told me about this when they gave me the choice. The choice to die or not die.

It was in the ward, earlier. They'd lain me next to a corpse waiting to be rotated out for a living body on one side of my bed and the sound of a rasping cough from a fluid filled lung on the other. The young doctor with the long, thin fingers and the small blue glasses seemed to be a fine option to fix my gaze upon. My lack of family, I sensed, was a factor, but the constant brain reddening waves of pain and a desire to avoid being the next corpse to be wrapped in a soiled sheet and placed on the trundle was a bigger one.

This was followed by hours in a room with only the doctors and engineers and finally the young woman with sad eyes who had shaved my skull.

And then I was in the tiled room looking up at the skylight. And now it was darkness. And now I was an automaton. They didn't use the derisive word "Tommy" then, that came later.

"Your body will die." The doctor with the blue glasses had said at my briefing. It was only my closeness to the engine room hatch when the explosion happened that kept my cooking from being more than skin deep. But that was enough. Enough to teach me more about pain than a man should know, enough to see a friendly smile on death's face.

It was done now. In the deeper recess of what was now my mind I felt other deaths. The past occupants of this device. I would be here until I transferred into my new casing. I wasn't the first occupant, nor would I be the last. I heard a scream as I fell and saw the carriage coming, the hooves splaying my hands. The wheels crushing my hips. The scaffolding cracking before the fall. The knife, cold in my chest. I pushed them all away, until I was alone again. So many ways to die and leave a mind intact. Or as I fought against other darker memories, I realized that some minds had never been intact. These were echoes they told me. They would pass. My own echoes would haunt the future occupant of this device. I strived to leave better memories. I forced memories of myself and Robert at the Floating Pig tavern. Darts, I remembered darts. My mind tried to smile.

I didn't notice the silence until I heard the sounds. They were not so different than those I imagined, but these were real. I could tell the difference. It was music. It came slowly and ebbed and flowed, the speed slowly growing even if it had no direction I was awash in it as if submerged.

I felt, an odd term to use, nothing but the music. It vibrated through me, each sound a thousand waves pouring over me. It was ecstasy beyond words.

How long this lasted, I didn't know. I let myself drift with it and after an eternity of the bliss, the music faded and again I was alone in my darkness. I heard the closing of the case as the violin was put away.

The voice, when it came, was female. I felt her approach as a widely spaced series of steps. Like the music, the spacing of the tread told me my perception of time was changed. But so was I.

"Hello," she said. The words drew themselves out but I could still recognize her as female. Memories of the scent of woman came from a corner of my mind. "Each of you has made the transfer successfully." There was silence; as if she was awaiting a response.

I was not alone? Had I been so entranced in my own pain

that I considered myself unique? The only one? I was not alone. I was legion.

"Your vision, assuming a fully successful transfer, will return."

She did not lie. Vision came, first a glimmer, then shadows. Within the hour or day or week it become vision, not as I had known, but thousands of tiny colors that formed patterns that I grew to recognize as jagged lines smoothed. Shades and colors I'd never seen before.

She was the sad eyed woman who had shaved my head. Beneath her clothes I could see the form of her body in waves of heat that outlined her breasts, fading in her hands. Later I was to learn that this was heat vision. The ability to see heat. I desired her, but as the thought came, I realized it was not desire, simply the memory. I wondered how many more such memories I would have.

<>

Robert's hat was a wadded ball in his huge hands. He shifted constantly on his feet. A habit learned on the choppy waters of the Thames. He and I had graduated Apprentice together. It had been he that I pushed ahead when the deafening roar of live steam had burned my flesh. Before the steam and iron boilers took over the waters, we dreamed of our own boat. Now he stood as if I were a banker and not his friend.

"Jared?"

I had grown accustomed to the fullness of sounds now that there was nothing between me and them. I have not yet had such a point where I was faced with sounds I knew as well as I knew Robert's voice. I could hear the strain.

I nodded in response and with as much grace as I could manage I pumped my bellows. The squeaks and workings of the rubber bellows pushed out a wheezing "Robert."

He winced at the sound. His head turned in a scan of the room. "This is a good house." I nodded. We were in a sitting room on the Doctor's estate. A room designed for sitting. A sitting room. The marvelous directness of the wealthy.

"You look," he hesitated, "well."

I wished for a moment I had the ability to laugh.

"Sit," I croaked and gestured to a chair. I hadn't yet managed much more than the basics of locomotion. And only with the assistance of a wicker-framed leaning box could I shuffle through the massive corridors of the estate. I did not rise.

"They're resetting the boilers," he said. "We're without pay while they do it. The bastards. They'd have us all tied to the machines like—" He stopped. His mumbled apology was clear in my ears. Again I longed for the ability to laugh. I too had resented the machines. I was raised by a Luddite father until my tenth year. He didn't come home from a march on the mills. The family dissolved. I'd found myself walking the docks until I earned an apprenticeship as a waterman. I'd—met Robert there, we'd become fast friends and drinking mates.

I nodded. He stared. Something I wasn't used to yet. He made further talk of the fixes on the Ferry and the goings on at the pub. Mostly focusing on the notion that I might no longer be the best dart player in the pub. I nodded where needed. I'd push out an answer to a simple question. The voice, if it could be called that, bothered him. The others here at the estate seemed to understand. Most even understood the finger signs we used. A language of hand movement not words. Like being reduced to the level of an infant for whom speech was not yet discovered, or in our case, speech made difficult. Finally he stood. "You'll be coming back to the ship then?"

I nodded.

"I'll be telling them then. They'll have to hold your spot." He turned to go and then he stopped.

"Is it really you, Jared?" He dropped to one knee and leaned forward. His face close enough to the glass plate that separated my tank from the blistering air for me to see the wetness in his eyes. "You're not just a machine now? Are you?"

I reached out and let my hand drop onto his shoulder. With the other I pumped my bellows. The brief vision of my body twisted in impossible ways on the table under a white domed ceiling flashed into my mind.

"I'm Jared."

<>

I slipped my arm through the bag's strap and lifted. The gyros in my chest shifted as the sum of what remained of my life settled on my back and I prepared to leave the estate. I could hear the soft footsteps in the hallway. I turned.

Elsie stood at the door, her eyes were still sad. She was the Doctor's sister. She had been the one to explain the intricacies of filling the feeder jar for my solution. Of draining the waste jar. How to check the leather gaskets. All of the things to keep me alive. Alive was a relative term. I was not so much alive as were the tiny water creatures in the solution that carried what was me. For all my years on the water I had never known the amount of life it contained. More than just the fishes and green slime.

She reached out and slipped a small blue flower in the button hole on the jacket I wore. The jacket was a pointless thing, I couldn't feel and had nothing that demanded modesty. Parliament had not agreed. Automatons were not exempt from the rules of modesty. I shifted focus to the flower until I had explored every tiny petal. Memories of how I should feel circulated. I felt the rustle of her skirts, the sound of her pursing lips as she kissed the brass panel that approximated my cheek. For a second I was more than chemistry. Like the flower, I lingered in life, but never to return to it.

"Good bye Jared," she said and slipped out of the room.

I shifted to the Doctor. The ever present blue glasses were, for once, riding high on his nose.

The Doctor moved his hands in a quick motion of hand speech, I responded in kind. "And goodbye to you as well, Doctor."

There were eight of us that were released that day. We each held a pouch with twenty pounds sterling and powders for mixing boiled and filtered spring water into new feeder solution to replace the dark foul smelling waste that drained out into a third chamber. If you fail to drain the waste jar, we died. Don't fill the feeder jar, we died. Break any of the jars, we died. We were not supermen.

Even so, the long walk to London that day was filled the promise of returning to life. We were not the first.

<>

The room that Robert and I shared seemed smaller after the Doctor's estate, yet the walls seemed taller. I had known I was shorter, few of us, and none made by the good doctor, were bigger than an Irishman. I could barely reach the peg by the drafty door that held our coats.

Robert had changed nothing. The room was clean, not clean as the estates were, but clean as two men living on the docks might measure it.

I settled into my shelf and lay in silence as I listened to the sound of Robert's snores. After a time I drifted into what passed for sleep among the automatons. Neither awake or asleep, simply alive.

Loud noises brought me out of it. The landlord's man was a fat Scotsman. He was drunk, as usual, and standing in our doorway.

"What's this?" He pointed at me. Robert stood in the corner, his razor scraping against his face. He didn't respond.

"What's it look like you fat bastard."

"You watch your tongue. I've got a family of fish eaters that'd pay double your rent."

Robert paused his shaving. "Will they kick your arse if you don't leave us the bloody hell alone?"

The fat Scotsman ignored him. "You'll be paying extra for it."

"I pay rent for two. This is Jared. He's back."

The Scotsman looked at me. "You're dead."

I shook my head.

"I'm Jared." I pumped the words out.

He opened his mouth as if to challenge.

I held out two crowns.

He pocketed the coins. "It'll be a crown a week extra for the Tommy. They ain't natural. They make people do things. I don't want anything to happen to this." He spread his arms and laughed.

◇

"Blooming Tommies." The words came from behind me. I ignored them and took another step toward the hall. The Ferry was nearing completion and both Robert and I received notice. We would be crossing the Thames again.

The rock bounced off of the brass bar that made what passed for my shoulders. It likely further damaged the coat I wore. I leaned forward, my semblance of a hunch. I heard the running footsteps coming up close behind me. It didn't frighten me, even though I knew in my core that I could readily become a heap of twisted metal underneath bludgeons of these sorts. We were metal men, automatons, now reduced to simply Tommies. The walking dead. Abominations they called us. We were not, as feared, maniacally strong, we did not need the blood of babies to replenish our fluids. But we were no longer men.

I focused ahead, still a hundred yards to the safety of the Guild Hall.

The footsteps drew closer. They were running. Something else I could not do.

"Hey Tommie," the voice called, "we're talking to you."

One on either side.

"Where you going?" the one to my left asked.

I focused on them for a moment. Dregs. Likely fresh from the poor house. Had I anything to steal, they would take it. These were the types that left sailors dead in alleys behind whorehouses.

I pumped my bellow. "No money."

I kept walking. 75 yards. I would make it or I wouldn't.

"You don't need money." The larger one said. His broken

teeth brought to mind a vision of rancid decay. They both carried knotted cudgels.

He shoved me. Hard. I stumbled, trying to keep my balance. I failed. My left arm broke my fall. I rolled and "faced" my attackers. They did not hesitate, they raised their cudgels and struck. The first of the blows fell on my legs. The sound of the blows directly to my frame blocked out all other sounds. I had no eyes to close.

"We don't need your kind," one of them hissed. "You should be dead—"

He literally flew through the air, landing against the wall I cowered against. Robert's frame seemed to block the sun. The second one, quicker, swung his cudgel in an arc toward Robert's gut. Robert stepped into the swing and pulled the man into a bear hug.

Years of rowing on the Thames gave him strength. He was known among the Watermen for it. Among the bruisers on the docks, he seldom lost.

"You know how you get to be a Tommie." His face was nose to nose with the squirming man. "You get hurt so bad you decide that you have to die or be a Tommie."

He squeezed so hard the thug's face contorted in breathless red.

I pumped my bellows with my working arm.

"No."

Robert looked at me. He'd barely heard.

"No." I pumped again.

With a roar he dropped the man into a groaning mass. He planted a foot on the man's chest. "I hear of you hurting a Tommy, I'll make one of you, and then I'll kill you." He pushed with his foot. "Now move."

The two ran until they paused at the corner. "Who the fuck is you?" they shouted at him from a safe distance. "It's just a Tommy."

Robert waved them off.

With cudgels still in hand, they backed away. The larger one gripping his bollocks and waving his cudgel, shouting obscene threats. Robert ignored him and knelt over me.

"You're broken." It wasn't a question. "I'll get you to the shop."

I tried to get up, but my legs wouldn't work. They seemed tangled.

The ship's engineer did not share his concern.

"He's a bloody Tommy."

"He's a waterman."

"He was." But with a look on Robert's face, he muttered a curse and reached for a tool. "He's bent up pretty bad."

They seemed to forget I was there as they discussed my injuries. Even Robert began to look at me more as a pieces of brass and iron as he held my arm. I could only endure the endless poundings on my frame. It was sweet relief when after a discussion they pounded out the pins before trying to straighten my damaged leg.

I don't know how long I was there. I simply watched. Time is something hard to measure. I know the work passed well into the evening. It was dark when my leg was re-attached. Coins slipped from my rapidly emptying pouch into his hands.

After that, Robert and I walked together.

One of the advantages of being an automaton is that we don't breathe. I fit back well into the engine room. Days spent shoveling coal into a boiler. Nights spent throwing darts in the Floating Pig. I was not Jared Thompson, as I remembered him, but I was something. With Robert at my side, I did not fear the roaming gangs of scrappers that would pound me into scrap metal. The shop took care of my needs. I was better than when I left the Estates. I was alive again.

<>

"No Tommies." The sign was new.

Robert looked at me and shrugged. "Wait." He said and disappeared into the dark opening of the Floating Pig. I could see his hand reach into the window and grip the sign. Inside I could hear him slap it on the planks that made up the bar. There was shouting. Not all of it from Robert. I heard the crash of wood against flesh. The shouts of "Tommy lover." The wall next to the door shook under an impact. Bits of dirt cascaded from the gaps in the wood.

"Screw you all," Robert shouted. "He's more of a man than any of you. You got no right to treat him this away. No right at all!"

He slammed the door as he came out. I stood and looked at him. In the window the sign leaned again against the glass. The broken halves next to each other. I walked past them every day for near two years before a new sign was made. Robert walked in the door and broke it in two. It stayed in the window in its broken condition and for all I know, it is still there.

◇

The posters had been up for weeks. The Automaton Registration Act. All unregistered Automatons would be subject to disassembly. It was a big word that meant death. The registration period was a week long, beginning on August 2. There were words and threats of violence. The Queen had been spirited away for her own good. For the time leading up to the registration she would be vacationing on the Isle of Wight.

Times were hard. The Irish famine was still killing by the thousands. The Irish flooded the shores. They were cheap workers. So were automatons. Neither of us was popular.

There were mobs at all of the registration centers. In London it was Kensington Commons. A large bright pavilion had been erected and dozens of tables and men with tools and benches beyond them. It was surrounded by a cordon of peelers, their police uniforms dark in contrast to the 300 brightly colored cavalry men who sat silently on their horses. The crowd screamed challenges and pelted us with whatever they could throw.

A rock struck my leg. It jarred me but I stayed on my feet with Robert's steadying hand on my arm.

More rocks flew through the air. "Abominations."

"Unholy." I could see the robes of a clergyman leading his congregation in a steady chant of "Unholy." Among the crowd I could see jugs of what I presumed to be spirits. The line of Peelers opened ranks and the horsemen trotted out. The bright red uniforms and the tall hats gave them the appearance of giants. The crowd jeered.

Hand speak erupted. The imminent danger vs. the risk. Compliance won out. We stayed. Almost a thousand of us were gathered. Ten times that many citizens were opposite us. Shouting and pelting us. The horsemen were pitifully few.

At first the crowd drew back from the horsemen. It was an empty bottle that changed that. I could see it arcing through the afternoon sun until it shattered against the forehead of a mounted trooper. He fell from his horse and lay limply on the green. An order was shouted and the trumpeter put a silver trumpet to his lips. At the call to arms the horsemen drew into ranks. Again the crowd fell back. It was the congregation with the robed clergy that didn't.

"We should be for getting out of here." Robert didn't bother to whisper. He knows me well enough now to know that I would hear him. I shook my head. Around us a flurry of hand motions. Many agreed with Robert. We had no safety in numbers. And straggling away in the face of this crowd would easily be worse.

To the left and right of the clergy and his sour flock, the crowd had fallen back until he and his followers formed the point of wedge aimed at the small line of horsemen. I looked at the crowd. A mixture of dock workers, bludgers, and Irish. They hated us. Among the crowd I saw banners like those borne by my father in the Luddite marches.

"Abominations," shouted the clergyman. His flock took up the shout and soon it became a wave of pouring hatred.

The clergy and his flock stood their ground. He faced down the cavalry officers with their tall hats. More bottles and rocks flew through the air. The trumpet sounded again. The horsemen turned in an easy arc and trotted away from the crowd. A shout arose. It faded when, after a hundred yards the men and horses stopped and spun again. The horn sounded once again. The horses started forward in a rapid trot.

Men in the crowd turned to run. All but the clergyman. The horn sounded one final time and the horses broke into a run. The thunder poured through my feet and my soul shook at the sound of it. I could see the faces of the men on horseback. Focused on the points of their sabers, held forward as they charged. I heard scattered pops as irons from the crowd were fired. A horse stumbled. In the final moment, even the clergy ran. People scrambled in all directions. A knot of then broke toward where we were massed. They carried short iron bars, bars made to bend our frames and break our chambers. For a moment I was alive again. We fell by the dozens, they fell to the man. Behind the cavalry, stretcher bearers carried off the fallen soldiers. A horse ate calmly from the lush grass growing in the late summer.

A group of men stepped out of the Pavilion and walked until they stopped in front of us.

"Let's get this moving then," he said, oblivious to the screams as the horsemen broke up what remained of the crowd. Screams rose from the fallen. I wondered how many of them would become automatons.

"Form three lines." He motioned to me. "You," he pointed to a spot of earth, "there." He pointed to two others and similar spots of earth and we stepped into place. Others stepped in behind us. Robert stood beside me.

"You are not a Tommy. You be best be moving on."

"He's my friend," Robert said.

"It don't matter," said the man. His suit was worn when seen up close.

"He's a Waterman. I'm his guild mate." The man paused and inspected us closer. There were still spatters of blood on my coat.

"So be it," and the man waved Robert's direction as if he were nothing. Robert accepted it and stood beside me.

"Bugger." Robert signed. For a moment I remembered a desire to laugh. So the afternoon passed, and each of us was made to lie upon a bench and have a numbered brass plate hammered onto our frame. I would forever be 159647, Automaton, General

Class.

The day would be known forever as the Tommy massacre. Nearly thirty men died on the grass that day. Horrific pictures of clawed metal men ripping women and boys asunder were on the newspaper and magazine covers. Within a year not a single automaton remained in England.

THE RUBY CURSE
S. A. BOLICH

There are days I wish I knew more swear words.

I took one look at the Drake house reduced to random bits of rubble and stinking like an abattoir and knew Malus had been here ahead of me. I dared not stop the buggy for a closer look; the bony nag between the shafts had caught the stink of magic curling thick out of the smoke and displayed the first spark of liveliness he had shown all day. The reins, slick from the damp fog, began to slide through my chilled fingers. Furious, I let the gelding exorcize his fears in a brisk trot up the narrow lane, no longer caring if he flipped mud up in my face in his haste.

My anger threatened to burst out into uncontrolled mayhem. Quietly, as befitted a lady, I said aloud the only three really vile epithets Jim Drake had ever taught me, careful to pronounce them correctly lest the magic choking the evening air twist them into curses to plague what was left of the neighborhood. A brooding sense of danger still crept from the ruins. I urged the gelding on faster, rounding a bend shrouded in tall pine trees that hid the remains from the road. A glance in the tiny mirror mounted to my spectacles showed me only frowsy brown hair escaping from its neatly coiled braid, a sliver of ear smudged with soot, and darkness swallowing the fog behind me. Reflexively I tucked up the hair to see better, but nothing followed me from the ruins save grief and an unholy miasma of dark magic.

Sweet Savior. Jim...and Malus. Tears stung my eyes for that kind, brave man, my mentor, my friend. He had been like an uncle to my son. Had affection crippled him at the end? Clearly it had not slowed Malus. *What will he do when he discovers who is hunting him now?*

But I knew. Fear shivered up my spine.

Two miles down the road the gelding had run out of steam and the night had drawn in thick. I let him amble on alongside a broad and lively river toward the glow of the bustling little frontier town over the next hill. Wearily I tried to shape a course of action. For three days, from the moment I learned that Malus had escaped his magically warded prison, my driving imperative had been to warn Jim Drake. Retired and happily puttering with his experiments in a country house far from Guild problems and politics, he had refused the modern magic of telephones, resenting a device that could intrude upon his privacy willy-nilly without so much as the courtesy of sending in a card first. He had, of course, surrendered the mirror of the Wizards' Guild upon his retirement. Poor honorable fool. But then, after six years, perhaps we had all believed Malus would actually stay where Jim and Sophia and I had put him.

The hired nag knew his way home. I wrapped the reins loosely around my wrist and left him to it while I unbuttoned one of the hidden pockets in the sturdy bloomers I wore even under ball gowns. I dared not use my own mirror; Malus might have obtained one by now, and I scarcely needed his spying eyes ascertaining my location. From the time he was small, however, I had been able to spy upon him without his knowing, a mother's prerogative, one might say—or necessity, given the circumstances of his birth.

Both the police and the Guild would be scandalized by half the things I carried in my bloomers. Certainly they would not appreciate the two-inch, handleless magnifying glass I drew out, bound in gold, its lens oddly cloudy, as if someone had spilt milk upon it and let it dry. A ring of tiny, evenly-spaced rubies around the rim gave it the appearance of a rich woman's toy. Only a discerning eye would see the fine marks around the top edge, and only one who handled it would discover that an outer ring of gold turned around the inner holding the glass itself.

I had not had the heart to line up the marks since the day my son went to prison for murdering half the ruling council of the Wizards' Guild. Today, I could die if I did not.

A shout from the road ahead sent my heart leaping straight into my throat. I dropped the glass back into its pocket and drew the knife strapped to my calf instead. With it on the seat beside me I put both hands to the reins, ready to hie the horse on if trouble spilled out in front of us. Only a hundred yards separated the gelding's homeward-questing nose from the first buildings at the edge of town, spilling light into the drizzly dusk from narrow, grimy windows. Dark figures ran and shouted, coalescing around two men engaged in a fistfight in the middle of the street. *Men!* I thought in exasperation, seeing no way around the thickening crowd. Quite apart from the exasperation of fending off unwanted attention from a mob of rude, female-starved men, I could not defend them all if Malus showed up.

The horse protested when I turned the buggy aside into a muddy lane that seemed to lead behind the noisy wooden saloon that had spawned the fight. The spindly wheels struggled in the ruts and the horse put his head down, snorting with the effort. Light and shadow spilled over us from the windows. I prayed that all eyes were on the excitement in the street and checked the little mirror on my spectacles obsessively.

We came to the dark but level yard behind the saloon and the horse picked up a trot, his ears pricked, eager for his warm stall in the livery beside my boarding house. Congratulating myself on avoiding the fight that seemed to be turning into a general riot in the street, I let him forge ahead into a narrow lane wending toward the more respectable brick establishments in the center of town.

I caught only the barest glimpse in the mirror of something bright, a flash of brilliant emerald, before the whole buggy rocked as something impacted the ground just behind. For a moment the entire alley—dripping roofs, blank walls, rubbish heaps, stray cats and all—glowed an eerie, unnatural green. A most unladylike word escaped my lips in fear and awful recognition of the thing powering that ill-aimed strike. The horse ripped the reins through my hands and bolted, uncertain what to be afraid of but taking no chances. Quite unmindful of a buggy wider than its skinny self in full flight behind it, the beast took a corner too short and hooked the off-side front wheel. Wood splintered and the buggy tilted up at an angle that promised disaster. I grabbed the upright holding up the leather hood and launched myself into the rainy night, nearly smashing myself to bits against the wooden building that had refused to yield to the buggy's passage. My shoulder connected with a solid thunk; I caromed off and landed on hands and knees in the mud. Being already down there, I bundled my skirts immodestly up around my waist and scuttled like a crab through the dripping dark into the deeper shadows under an unlighted window. I thought bad things about the horse, realizing that my knife had gone with the buggy, which, from the sound, the gelding, in full mindless panic now, seemed to be dragging down the lane on its side.

They'll make me pay for that, my mind informed me primly. Then the practical half of me snorted, because I very much doubted my life would stretch beyond the next few minutes. My skin still crawled from the knowledge that Malus was behind me with a dimensional screw in his hands. *How did he get his hands on* that *so fast?* my mind wanted to know, but my nerves were more interested in evading the next microsecond burst of energy drawn from the veil between dimensions. Cursing Charles Babbage and his clever machine that allowed even cleverer men like my son to dabble in things best left to God, I crept farther up the alley.

Voices shouted in alarm somewhere along the horse's path. Perhaps someone would come looking for the luckless driver. Ahead of me, light and noise and many strangers would all stand my friends, but I pinned no hope on rescue, for Malus occupied the darkness behind me. Halfway along the alley, a many-armed construction machine, banked down for the night, puffed quietly like a dragon in the dark, leaking small jets of steam and smoke. I slunk toward it, wondering if a little magic might goose the thing to useful life without stoking its engines. Those heavy arms could smash the whole half-built brick edifice beside it straight onto Malus's head could I but spot him.

Movement behind me, blacker than the shadows, froze me in place. I watched it in the mirror, not daring to turn my head.

"Mum-sy," a voice crooned teasingly.

I had never given much thought to the cliché of one's blood running cold, but mine seemed turned to ice. I could not even breathe for horror. *Oh, my child,* a tiny voice mourned, deep inside. How could the loving, eager little boy of my memories own that chill, timbreless voice, so belying any human origin?

The technology-loving folk who labeled me a witch would have been gratified, for a cat saved my life. Malus, a broad-shouldered shadow silhouetted against the dim gray wall of the building behind the one sheltering me, took a step too near some feral stray's hiding place. It shot out with a mad howl, driven, no doubt, by the crackling aura of the dimensional screw. Malus cried out in surprise. I leaped up and ran, snatching at a lever jutting from the quiescent machine as I passed. To my astonishment the thing snorted and plucked one of its thick arms up from its resting position on the ground. I ducked as it jerked aloft, its four-fingered placement hand swinging ponderously in a half-circle a few feet over my head. I breathed a Word that drove the business end down the alley, metal fingers spreading to grab, as I scampered by.

Malus's startled yelp echoed through the darkness but no green fire smashed the machine to impertinent bits. The screw had not had time to recharge. I seized the opportunity and fled into the street, screaming, "Help! Oh, help, murder!"

A curse snapped down the alley. I leaped up onto the boardwalk out of the way but felt the air turn foul and thick behind me. Malus did not need the screw to commit murder. Shaking, I ran past darkened windows, my shoes booming on the boards. I went on screaming, willing to play the helpless female if it got me quick, staunch action.

My screeching penetrated the excited roar of the mob settling their drunken differences outside the saloon. Startled faces turned my way, then a few onlookers broke and ran toward me. I bolted straight into the midst of them, little fearing the attentions even of drunkards when my choices were between them and my son. Voices shouted questions; I babbled of an attack on my buggy. Men began to stream down the street, happy to move on to new excitement, outraged by an attack on a lady. Feigning tremulous flutters, I allowed a large man with a magnificent walrus mustache to guide me toward the light and safety of the saloon. He was so kind I almost regretted twisting my dainty Guild signet ring in his face.

I held my breath against the puff of fine powder. He broke off mid-word, his hand slipping from my elbow. He blinked, his mind hazed past coherent thought for a precious few seconds. I slipped away, avoiding the telltale light spilling through the windows. No one saw me go; everyone was too busy with the hunt for the supposed murderer. With the wreckage of the buggy and the frightened horse for evidence, I had no doubt they would look all night. No stranger would pass unquestioned.

Odd tremors kept passing up and down my body as I made my way through shadowed alleys toward the boarding house. I needed a quiet place to think, to plan, to plot a way to lure Malus out of this vulnerable little town and onto ground of my choosing. With Jim dead I had no idea if my power alone could manage what three of us had barely accomplished before. Binding a demon is a chancy business, not for the faint-hearted. And not for middle-aged ladies with a weak spot for the intended victim.

I needed help, and right now.

I slipped in the back door of the boarding house, all over mud and not eager to explain to the fussy woman who owned it, who had become rather stiffly polite when her eye fell upon my signet ring. For all that the Guild had clawed its way to respect over slow centuries of service to the public good, those of us born to wield magic still bore the stigma of ancient fears. Malus's very public assassinations and sensational trial had certainly done nothing to alleviate them, despite that he had used technological marvels men would happily fight over.

Safely behind the locked door of my room, I shed the filthy

dress and bloomers and fished the little magnifying lens from its pocket. My room overlooked the street, its lacy curtains of precious little use in blocking prying eyes. Tucked up in a dressing gown drawn from the battered valise I never unpacked save to launder its contents, I pulled the rocking chair into the corner and sat down facing the door with the lens in my hand.

Grief and memories nearly overwhelmed me as I gently traced its clouded surface with my forefinger, remembering a giggling infant in his crib, an adventurous toddler, a small boy certain he was braving the wilds of the lower garden all alone, unaware of his mother watching for danger in his path. Even then he had been fearless. Only later—much later—had it slowly dawned on me, on Jim, on the entire Guild, that he *could* not feel fear. My child, born of rape by a father unseen, unknown, had after all inherited a dark heritage no loving upbringing could overcome.

I drew a slow breath and let it out in a soft sigh, blowing life's breath across the surface of the glass. It began to glow, glass and gold and rubies warming to life and color. Small red pinpoints danced on the walls as I slowly rotated the outer ring, concentrating on aligning the proper engraved marks. I imagined a faint click as they lined up, but I did not imagine the sudden flare of golden light or the instant clearing of the milky glass. A room dominated by an angry face leaped into view in the lens, lit by a single lamp that drew sharp lines of light and shadow onto cheek and brow and jaw. Tawny hair spilled over ears and collar and framed a mouth set in a thin, hard line. The square jaw was hidden by an unkempt beard, the vivid blue eyes lost in shadow. But I knew him, however the new, gaunt intensity of his face appalled me. Such had prison done to my free-roaming son, who had ever fought the restrictions of the nursery and his bedroom and the four walls of any classroom.

Would that he had shunned the inner sanctums of the Guild as thoroughly, but no. Power was an irresistible lure to any demon—as it was the surest trap. Thus had he engineered his own downfall, with a little help from the Guild. And me.

I watched him pacing his room, realizing with a stark

thrill that he could not be a quarter mile from where I sat. By morning he would have a very good idea where I was if he dared the streets filled with men still calling to each other, hunting whoever had attacked the lady who had disappeared at the saloon. My unwitting allies made an admirable barrier between me and Malus, but the solution was temporary at best. Shaking, I moved my hand slightly to left and right, swinging the view around the room, studying the window. By dint of careful angling, I managed to bring it close enough to peer through it at the building opposite. Tall, brick, with a decorative marble frieze shining pale three feet below the eaves. The bank. Faintly I could see the rear corner of the building, which told me Malus had taken a room in the back of the hotel—or seized it from its rightful renter, with what consequences to the renter, I could guess.

I watched the emotions raging in his face, and my skin crept with the knowledge that whatever fragile bonds of respect or love had held him in check had dissolved over the past six years. Whatever demon thing had warred with his better nature all his life had won that war. Was he merely mad, tormented by the unfathomable mystery of his father, his mind flawed from birth, as my kind friend Dr. Hagen maintained? Or was there true demon blood in him, untamable, doomed from birth to master his human half and live up to the strictures of the name he had chosen for himself, adhering to all that was malicious and evil?

Looking at the rage driving him in tight circles around the neat hotel room, I saw that it did not matter. The results were the same, and dear Lord, the Guild had reinforced his inborn power with the tools to kill us all.

Without conscious volition my fingers spun the outer ring, snuffing the view of my son. The glass clouded again. I put it away in the stout and practical underwear so de rigueur for female wizards and dug in the valise again. My landlady would doubtless have approved the miniature gadget I set in the fire snapping on the hearth. Carter's All-Purpose Cleaner might have worked wonders on the stain in the rag rug by the bed, but I confined my labors to my mud-spattered bloomers. With the cleaner breathing steam and industrious little brushes into every stiff seam I scrubbed and scoured and let fright ooze away until at last I felt calm again. I laid them out to dry on the hearth and dozed for a precious time, using Guild techniques to wring every benefit from such nervous rest. I badly needed to renew the ebb tide of magic at my core.

The clear tinkle of the landlady's mantle clock striking eleven woke me. I lay a moment listening to the stillness in the house. Sensible folk would be going to bed.

I did not expect Malus to be sensible.

The bloomers were still damp. I put them on anyway and laced a stiff bodice like a suit of armor over a brown and green dress with rather remarkable properties. Then I drew out a device that would have driven Mr. Bell to despair had he known how the Guild had improved upon his grand invention. Unlike Guild mirrors, this had but one mate, impervious to eavesdropping.

I hesitated, weighing merits and dangers. I had fled the moment my friend Elaine rang up to inform me that Malus had vanished from prison. Out the door I had gone on the instant, with only a nebulous plan for amending that unhappy situation: find Jim, collect Sophia, and see if once more our combined talents could stop a monster. Jim was gone, but unless Malus had found some means to fly, he could not have reached Sophia yet. Provided she had not entirely lost her nerve, we might yet bring him down.

I held the small brass box in my left hand, its weight warm against my palm. Sophia had many faults, including laziness, but her inventiveness in reducing the inconveniences of daily life knew no bounds. Without the cumbersome speaking tube and listening cones, the tiny telephone in my hand solved her anxious need to stay in touch with her own kind even as she cowered in her remote Canadian mansion atop its fortified hill.

I trickled a thread of magic into the box with my forefinger and dialed. One-seven-two-three, a carefully random series of digits. Gears clicked and whirred, achieving whatever mechanical magic they required to send my voice into the ether. More mundane magic spun a wire between my device and

Sophia's, invisible, ephemeral, untraceable.

The box began to glow gently. "Diana?" Sophia's voice came from nowhere, tinny and distant and almost drowned in a strange whooshing like a strong wind. "Did you find Jim?"

"Jim's dead," I said, blurting it out with brutal lack of grace. Sophia lived on hope a good deal of the time. She needed a jolt to ground her in the reality that Malus had *not* been either reformed or neutered by his time in prison.

"Oh, no." I thought Sophia would surely faint, judging by the feeble sound of her voice.

"Don't you melt on me, Sophia Grierson. I need your key."

"Diana!" Oh, how I wished the box could show me her face at the other end. I found it instructive that she cried neither *Yes* nor *No* in response to a demand no wizard makes of another, but rather my name.

"I know my name," I said, with dawning suspicion. "Do you know yours?"

An uncomfortable silence stretched over the miles between us. Sophia pondered that non-rhetorical question for much longer than she should, and finally said, a bit dubiously, "Yes."

"Say it," I said softly, with the hair creeping on my arms.

Another heart-stopping second or two of silence. "Sophia M-Mor—" I heard her struggle to say it, but *Morgana* would not come. Sorrow seized my heart.

"What have you done?" I whispered.

"Forgive me," she said, and the glow faded from the box with the speed of a heart stopping.

I stared at it with tears blurring my vision for the second time today. Dear, gentle, maddening Sophia, who could be counted on to do exactly the wrong thing in every situation save those requiring the courage of conviction. Time was, she would stand like a lioness in the face even of Malus and his kith ... but times change. Was it really fear of what he would do to her if he breached her walls that led her to strip herself of her own gifts? Or had she simply drained the cup of courage to the dregs?

Be safe, dearheart, I wished her, but could not help one moment's indulgence in white-hot anger. I was alone now,

needing a key Sophia had rendered useless. That it made her—
and it—of no use to Malus might or might not save her. The
Guild was not supposed to deal in superstition; the geas that kept
wizards of every level from attacking each other for the power
triggered by their personal keys was powerful and binding on all
sane practitioners. Malus was not sane, and Sophia's childlike
wishing away of her power might only make him angrier.

Once again I longed for a broader vocabulary, muttering
imprecations as I put the telephone away. Jim was dead. Sophia
had caged her talent in the probably vain hope that it would profit
Malus nothing to kill her. Yet my son had killed Jim with magic
powerful enough and black enough to level the whole house. I
could not doubt he had Jim's key.

Mine tingled in its hiding place in my hair, a most wondrous
tattoo at the base of my skull, done when I was so young I barely
remembered my uncle placing it there. My hair had grown back,
yet all I had to do was touch the hidden circle to unleash its
power. I longed to do so now, to take reassurance from its ruby
flare, but I did not. Malus might sense it, and home instantly on
this dingy boardinghouse.

After six years spent brooding on his downfall, he had to
have arrived at truth, however incredible. Jim and Sophia and I
had done what no one else had ever attempted—combined our
keys to contain the raging monster that was Malus. Back then
he had been armed mostly with the inventive toys of his own
making, the dimensional screw and others I had thought long
destroyed by the Guild after his fall. Had he made some hidden
cache before we caught him? What else might be waiting
for me in that hotel room, Malus's answer to the unwelcome
limitations of his magical heritage? My skin crept at the thought
of him harnessing Jim's key and mine to his own. What unlucky
coincidence of power might it produce? I could not tell, and
knew that Malus would not care. So long as it brought down his
betrayers, he would be content. If it also leveled the whole busy,
bustling, lively little town of Spokane Falls, likely he would
only laugh.

Something hard and implacable inside me raised its head. A

thing I never saw had once raped my body; I refused to let Malus rape my soul. If I must do this thing, then I must steel myself to do it right, forgoing useless wishing for Guild assistance to take the hard decisions from my hands. Malus was my problem. I had given him birth. Perhaps I should have taken wizardly advice to ensure he never took his first breath, but the time was past for wallowing in failure and guilt. I saw clearly now that some things cannot be righted without pain.

I left the lamp burning in my room. Let the landlady note the light under the door and inform any searchers that all of her guests were safely at home. The frumpy lady in No. 4 had not set foot outside all day so far as she knew, let alone hired a rig she had been careless enough to wreck.

The damp night closed around me as the stout door of the rooming house closed at my back. I lingered in the rain-spattered yard to let my eyes adjust and then set out to hunt, slipping through noisome alleys empty even of dogs shivering in the spring darkness. I regretted the warm cloak on its peg in my room, but the brown dress resisted the rain and the walk kept me warm enough without its hampering folds. I did miss my knife, pondering the irony of Jim's long insistence that I carry a needler instead. He had, liking the cold lethality of programmable spread patterns and gear-driven precision. I noted that it had done him no good.

In the pouring darkness the trek seemed much longer, but eventually the facade of the hotel loomed across the street from the alley where I stopped to survey it. Five full stories, a bold statement to a young town, and well tenanted, judging by the number of lighted windows and the heads showing in the dining room. I needed no questions from some stuffy proprietor with pretensions; I abandoned the front door and made my way down two more buildings to where a telegraph office showed a lighted window.

I stopped in the shadows at the edge of the yellow square it threw onto the mud and worked the rings on my precious lens again. Malus had calmed, lying on his bed staring hard-eyed at the ceiling. Taking a deep breath, I put it away and slipped across the nearly-deserted street, down behind the hotel to where I could judge the floor opposite the frieze on the bank. Top floor, which put Malus's room—there.

You are a fool, Diana Niniane Applegate, I told myself sternly. But love or grief or anger drove me now. I scarcely knew which, so tangled were the feelings I carried about Jim Drake, about Malus, about my duty to the Guild. *I* had persuaded them to let Malus study our lore, hoping inclusion in so elite a body would ease his fevered restlessness. Mine the mistake. Mine the remedy.

Only an empty hall and the open door into a bustling kitchen confronted me when I cautiously opened the rear door of the hotel. The back stairs came down just inside on the left, convenient access to the upper floors—or the lower, if one thought like Malus with an eye ever cocked toward a quick exit. I made my way up, shedding droplets of rain and testing each step for creaks. Sound scarcely mattered save that somewhere deep inside I felt that Malus would know my tread.

I arrived slightly out of breath on the top floor, pushed the stairwell door open a cautious finger's width, and waited a full five minutes on the top step, peering through the crack at the door opposite. No light showed now under No. 512, but I dared not assume Malus asleep. Even as a child he seldom slept, and then fitfully, sometimes with his eyes wide open, staring at vistas known only to himself. *What* had accosted me that night in London? What had it spawned to haunt a town trying to raise itself from wilderness in Washington Territory, the very edge of America, six thousand miles away?

Mum-sy... The memory of his cold, teasing voice made me shudder. Before I could lose my nerve I opened the stairwell door and crept soundlessly across the carpeted hall, exposed to the softly merciless illumination of the gas lamps beside every door. The barest trickle of magic touched to the door of 512 told me the key stood unturned in the lock on the other side. I had only to twist the cut-glass knob.

Gulping down great breaths of air to steady my jumping heart, I reached up under the damp straggle of hair escaping its braid and touched the key at the base of my skull.

Instantly power flamed from the crown of my head to the soles of my feet. Armored in magic, I kicked open the door and leaped inside, dodging immediately to the left. Green light flared. Inspired by terror, I plucked out a hairpin and drove it with all the force of any needler straight into the heart of it. Fortune really does favor fools. It jammed the mechanism of the dimensional screw a split second before it could drill through the veil between worlds and siphon off a deadly dollop of energy.

"Very good, Mumsy," that cold voice whispered on a glacial trickle of a laugh.

"You never believed me that gears and valves were less reliable than magic."

"But, alas, that's all the priggish Guild chose to leave me." A man-shaped shadow beside the bed made a mocking parody of a salute.

"I'm sorry your magical talent was never as great as you wished it to be, but did it never occur to you that draining the barrier of energy between incompatible worlds might eventually collapse it? To no good end?"

"Well, yes, that was the general idea. How else was I to meet my father?"

Horror nearly killed me. A familiar blue light flamed in the corner. I recognized Jim's entwined initials glowing mid-air an instant before a malevolent yellow glow encircled them, driving chains of light through the beautifully flowing curves, suborning their might to the brute force of Malus's key. The air in the room raged with the release of energy that all but seared me where I stood. I flung up both arms, letting the flowing sleeves of the dress shelter my face. Its specially woven folds drank in that raging force and fed it into the hundred thin dry cells sandwiched into the bodice, a battery sucking down the raw power of lightning until it reached its limit and threatened to burst into flame. I backed against the wall, bracing myself with shoulder blades pressed flat to the flowery wallpaper, drenched in sweat and straining to redirect all that power into my own key.

"Father sends his regards," Malus said, his voice reaching

effortlessly over the roar of invisible flames. "He taught me how to escape a warded prison. Most kind of him. Did you know he used to whisper to me in my sleep? I saw him capering in the landscape of my dreams, a horned devil with cloven hooves, beckoning, always beckoning. Why didn't you stop him, Mumsy?"

The accusation tore straight to my heart. "Why didn't you tell me about him?" I whispered.

Somehow, he heard me. "I didn't think you cared."

Such calumny should have melted me. Instead it stiffened my knees. I felt caged in lightning, my dress so stiff with crackling energy I wondered it did not burn straight through the wall. Malus lifted his hands, snatching at the ruby power of my key flaring over and around what he had flung at me. A frightful vision of the entire town going up in a fireball of magic and multi-colored flame shocked me out of my daze.

Gasping for breath, I took a ridiculous chance and tried to suborn all that ravening power under the aegis of my own key. Leaning against the kindly wall, I raised both hands and... *pulled.*

Malus shrieked in rage as control started to slip from him. The walls and floor and window looked to be melting, rippling and flowing as unnatural forces fought to align themselves into a new order. Only one shape came clear in my mind, a double ring shot with rubies, caging a secret world within. As footsteps began to pound up the stairs in response to Malus's shout, I began to unravel the sickly yellow chains of his power from Jim's key and bend them into a closed circle of *my* fashioning.

"Mother, don't!"

My control shattered, shocked to shreds by the sound of a voice whose every whisper and intonation I carried in my heart. Fear, plain and simple, laded my son's voice. I gaped through the ripples of raw magic flowing and twisting between us, and saw wide, bewildered blue eyes staring at me as though he had never imagined such a sight.

My lips shaped his name; I had no breath to say it aloud. His head cocked as though trying to remember something long forgotten. The half-formed circle hung in the air between us, inches from trapping his power within mine. He glanced at it, his tawny brows twitching into a frown, and then again, the dazed look draining from his face. His features melted like hot wax into a mask of unmitigated hatred.

His mouth opened. With the inspiration of pure terror I seized on a Word learned from James Drake in a moment of frustration—his—and sly delight—mine. With all the fear and power and grief boiling up from the depths of my frightened soul I spat it at my son and heard the very air groan as I bound the curse around his true name.

"Malignafacis, Arthur Merlin Applegate!"

Oh, sometimes magic is simple after all.

He snapped to his full height with a shriek that shattered the glass in the window and blew out the lamps in the hall. Only the circle of power in the air shed light into the room. It snapped closed, a double ring that flamed to purest ruby as it sucked in the magic of three wizards and made a new sigil bound to none of us. I staggered, feeling something snap inside, but Malus burst, roaring, from his trance. Quick as the cat he had stepped on earlier he slammed the hallway door closed and lunged straight through that ruby circle at me.

I clenched my fist. The circle cinched itself around his shoulders, hampering the wild movement of his arms. He was between me and the door; I ran for the window overlooking the alley, where a vague memory of a drainpipe plunging down from the roof fed me a faint hope. I scrabbled my skirts together, listening to him galloping after me, his boots heavy on the rose-patterned carpet. Five stories and a quick broken neck, or a slow throttling by my enraged son before the rescue pounding down the hall could pry him off? All in all, I preferred the drop. I clasped both sides of the window and prepared to launch myself through, ignoring the remaining shards of glass grinding themselves into my palms.

His hand snatched at my skirt even as a voice outside the window screamed, "Diana! Jump!"

Something whirred and whooshed outside, a sound familiar and yet so incongruous I could not grasp its presence outside a hotel room window. Sophia shouted something unkind and jerked her hand up. A jolt of pinkish light snapped past my startled eyes, accompanied by a high and wicked whine. Malus howled and dropped like a stone.

"Jump, you silly sylph!" Sophia cried, her slippered feet planted securely on the deck of her tiny airship with its busy propeller whooshing out a gale in my face.

I jumped. My skirts fell in a cloud around me, greatly reducing the grace of my landing. Sophia laughed a wild, hysterical laugh and yanked the cord controlling the steam. The airship shot straight up into the rain-washed sky, above the hotel and the broken window and the head that popped out to hunt for the female escaping from the lunatic in 512. He did not look up, fortunately. Sophia poured on steam until we had cleared the lights of the town and flew unnoticed over the rolling, wooded hills north of its wild river. We outran the rain pattering harmlessly onto the glass shielding the pilot's platform and whirred on through torn clouds shot through with shy moonlight, two wizards in Sophia's much scoffed-at answer to the inconveniences of horse-drawn conveyances and sooty trains.

I looked up at her from my huddle on the quivering wooden floor as she stepped down from the sheltered platform to give me a hand up. She looked like an overdressed Valkyrie standing there with the wind raking her blond hair back from her delicate face and whipping the entirely inappropriate morning dress around her ankles.

"You lied to me!" I shouted over the wind of our going.

"How was I to know he wasn't using you to trap us both? You always were a fool about him. And he never knew my true name!"

A wizard's most prized secret next to his key. In sorrow I guessed what Jim's last words had been.

Shaking my head in mingled disbelief and rue that after all these years she could still surprise me, I let her pull me up. "We have to go back," I said, thinking of a raging Malus, newly stripped of his power and unrestrained in his bullish fury.

"Malus—"

Sophia turned her head. A stray shaft of moonlight caught her face, illuminating the sad, strange mix of regret and satisfaction pulling at the corners of her mouth. I sat down abruptly on the wicker railing, heedless of the five hundred-foot drop to the spiky tops of the pine trees. Pink light seared my memory.

"He's dead," I said flatly.

Sophia made a small, helpless gesture that drew sparkles from the silver-plated needler still in her hand. "He would have killed you, *cher*," she said simply.

I looked down at my hands, that had painted power in the air and irrevocably altered the magic inside me. Slowly it occurred to me that perhaps that had been the purpose all along, some long-term scheme on the part of Hell to suborn a wizard's power. My son had been born with a wizard's magic, but he had never mastered the final tests. They required trust and a surrender of will that I saw at last he was not capable of. But...had I been fool enough in my maternal indulgence of his faults to help him past that obstacle—

Oh, clever trap. Clever demon.

Had Merlin's namesake ever been innocent? Ever uncorrupted? Or had his father visited him in the cradle and twisted his unformed mind before ever I had a chance to guide him down a different path?

Anger and grief closed my throat on the knowledge that the devil had won a different victory. The soaring magic born in my blood was gone, wrapped in that ruby sigil with Malus's.

But a devil is dead, came a fey, shivering thought inside my head. Perhaps it was worth the price. Had he really seen a horned demon in his open-eyed dreams?

Slowly I reached under my battered skirt and drew out the ruby-ringed glass. Sophia gave me a curious glance as I tilted it toward the uncaring moon and rotated the ring. Expecting nothing, I blew on it. And nothing happened.

Sophia clucked and snatched it out of my hand. "Silly sylph. Have you forgotten everything I ever taught you?"

I gaped at her as she rotated the ring *backward*. The milky cloud bloomed to ruby light pouring out over the gold rings, engulfing her hands. She thrust the lens back at me so suddenly that I nearly dropped it as live magic swarmed up my arms.

"What good is a spyglass that doesn't look backward as well as forward?" she asked scornfully, and took herself back to her pilot's platform.

Quivering under the magic writhing its way home, I slid to the vibrating floor, torn between joy and horrid guilt that the thing I loved most had come back to me. *Ah, my son, was it my fault after all?* I put my head down and wept for the boy who had laughed in my lens, for the taste of Jim's bound magic on my lips, for the taint of Malus's rage entwined forever in my own. I wept for a good man and a bad one, a gentle elder and an eager boy, the gilded past and the unrealized future. Is every mother inevitably linked to her child's legacy? Should I consider it a curse or a gift to have borne a son?

The clean night air, laden with the scent of rain and pine and spring, blew the tears over my hands and through the wicker sides of the airship. We flew on through the moon-washed sky, raining shining tears of sapphire and ruby and gold.

THE THIRD DRAGON
GEORGE S. WALKER

The Imperial Inventor wasn't entirely sane. A twitchiness of her eyes was one clue. And her silk gowns had many, many pockets—another clue. Servants whispered that the madness was due to an elixir of quicksilver she drank to keep herself youthful. For though she *appeared* young, she walked like a crone.

Nevertheless, the smiths had turned Madame Chong's diagrams into a traveling apparatus of elegant beauty, filled with polished brass gears that ticked through their orbits. A bamboo ladder affixed to the side of the mechanism led up to a curtain-shrouded cabin. An embroidery of dragons climbed the curtains.

From atop the ladder, the Emperor's daughter, Princess Mei, peered between the curtains. She saw a bench with two red silk cushions. In front of the left one was a wooden ship's wheel.

Careful not to catch the hem of her yellow gown in the gears, she descended the ladder. "Who is the second cushion for?"

"I shall be operating the controls. I need an assistant. Someone who can shoot a crossbow."

"*I* can shoot a crossbow. The Master at Arms taught me," the Emperor's daughter said.

A smile twitched on Madame Chong's face, then she bent forward, leaning on her cane. Mei could see the lacquered combs that bound her black hair. "Too young," the Inventor muttered.

"This should be a task for your brother."

Mei knew that her brother Ling had no interest in travel. Like her father and most of the court, he spent his days playing *weiqi*, pondering each move of the stones. If Madame Chong invited him, he would simply put off the decision. Meanwhile, someone else might be chosen.

"You can't risk Prince Ling," said Mei, "for he's heir to the throne. I am the least likely Emperor."

"Empress," Madame Chong corrected her. "But your counsel is wise. Have you a crossbow?"

"Of course." She had begged her father, and the Imperial Armorer had made it especially for her, with a crank to draw the bowstring.

"Perhaps you should get it, then."

Mei ran to the Armory to fetch it.

When she returned, Madame Chong was placing two skyrockets into a woven basket below the cabin on the other side.

"Where are we going?" she asked.

"Not where, Princess. When."

"Today, I hope."

"You misunderstand. Have you ever seen a dragon?"

"Many paintings. And the ceramics at the palace." She pointed up. "And your curtains."

"But a real one?"

Mei shook her head.

"You will, Princess. This invention is a reverse clockwork that will transport us back to the time of our ancestors, who painted the dragons they saw."

"And the crossbow? To shoot a dragon from the sky?"

"How foolish! No. From whence do young dragons come?"

Mei thought for a moment. "Eggs?"

"Just so. But if we take an egg from the Mother Dragon, she might take offense."

Mei looked at her crossbow. "I have three bolts. Is that enough?"

"Three is a fortunate number, Princess."

The midday sun shone brightly. A breeze shook blossoms from cherry trees in the Imperial Inventor's courtyard. Servants had taken down cloth banners from the day before, announcing a *weiqi* tournament in the Imperial Library.

Madame Chong mounted a third skyrocket, smaller than the two in the basket, to the outer rim of a great brass wheel at the front of the travelling apparatus. Then she instructed Mei to climb the bamboo ladder. The Inventor followed her into the cabin, clutching her cane.

Below the ship's wheel were two small levers on the floor and two long levers that reached up beside the wheel on each side. Madame Chong lifted the hem of her green gown to place her feet on the small levers, then handed flint and steel from one of her pockets to Mei. "Light the rocket."

To reach the skyrocket, she had to climb out of the cabin on the right side, balancing on a narrow platform as she waited for the turning wheel to bring the rocket to her. When the fuse was before her, Mei struck flint and steel together. A spark lit the gunpowder fuse, and it began to spit sparks of its own.

"Quickly, Princess! Get inside!"

She climbed back inside the cabin, landing on the cushion beside Madame Chong's, and straightened her yellow gown. The Inventor pushed one of the long levers just as the rocket ignited with a whoosh of flame. The great wheel stopped, then began turning backward, faster and faster.

Choking gunpowder smoke engulfed the cabin. Mei heard the gearwork screaming, and the cabin shook. Madame Chong gripped the wheel before her like a sailor in a typhoon.

In the courtyard, day changed to night, then day again, flickering faster and faster to become a blur. Leaves on the trees shrank to nothing. Then leaves flew up from the ground to join the branches and turned green.

Soon the Inventor's workshop vanished, then to Mei's astonishment, the palace itself. All the while, the rocket spun the clockwork faster and faster. The city itself receded, and a forest sprang up around them.

The rocket began to sputter, then went out with a final puff of smoke. The gearwork whirred for a little longer, then slowed to a halt.

Madame Chong pulled on a lever, and the clockwork began to tick forward again.

A winter forest surrounded them. On the ground lay a thin dusting of snow, and a cold wind blew through the curtains. Mei shivered, wishing she'd brought a coat.

Madame Chong pulled a compass from a pocket of her green gown. As she studied it, Mei wondered if all inventors carried compasses.

"That way," said Madame Chong, pointing to her left. "Bring the crossbow."

Mei followed her down the ladder. "Where are we?"

"This is an elder dynasty. In the time of dragons, cities were smaller. We must find the oldest part."

Mei walked beside her, carrying the crossbow. They struggled through underbrush, Madame Chong batting at it with her cane to shake off the snow. Their silk gowns snagged on bushes and brambles. Twigs stuck in Mei's hair. Her feet grew cold.

"Has your father spoken to you of last evening's wager?" asked the Inventor.

"What wager?"

"Hmm," was all Madame Chong said.

They came to a part of the forest where the trees were frosted stumps. A faint cry reached her ears. She peered through gaps in the trees to see a man trapped beneath the branches of a fallen tree. An animal crouched before him. At first, Mei thought it was his faithful dog. Then she realized it was a wolf.

"We may need your crossbow," said Madame Chong. Her eyes twitched.

Mei began winding it as they advanced. She heard the snarl of the wolf and saw the trapped woodcutter struggling to fend it off with his ax.

Once the bowstring was taut, Mei notched a bolt in it.

Madame Chong shouted at the wolf and waved her cane, but instead of fleeing, it leapt toward them. Mei raised her crossbow and pulled the trigger. The bolt struck the animal in the chest, killing it.

"Now I have only two bolts," she said.

"Just so, Princess. And yet kindness may be its own reward."

Lifting one branch at a time, they helped free the woodcutter. He stared at their rich gowns and Mei's crossbow before bowing in gratitude. His own clothing was leather and coarse fabric, his shoes woven straw.

"We seek audience with the Emperor," said Madame Chong. "Kindly lead us to the palace."

The man looked up, confused. He opened his mouth, closed it. After a long pause, he said, "Emperor?"

His accent was so strange, Mei barely recognized the word.

"Yes," said Madame Chong. She made a grand sweeping gesture with her cane. "Take us to the palace."

He bowed his head again, trembling. "Palace?"

Mei spoke up. "Where are the dragons?"

At that, the man seemed relieved. "Dragon, yes." He bowed repeatedly. He beckoned for them to follow. "Dragon."

He led them along a path they would not have found on their own. Madame Chong tugged on the sides of her gown, holding the hem above the snow. Mei hurried after them, unable to hide her excitement.

They emerged from the forest into a field. Ahead of them stood the buildings of a town. Dragons flew in the sky above.

"Look!" said Mei.

"Just bamboo and silk," said Madame Chong. "Kites."

"Oh."

Reaching the outskirts of town, they entered on an unpaved road. In the cold air, wisps of smoke rose from the chimneys of houses that were little more than huts. The town bore no resemblance to the Imperial City of Mei's time. A wooden palisade lay ahead, and a peasant herded goats through its open gates.

"The Zhou Dynasty, I think," said Madame Chong.

It occurred to Mei, a princess, that an emperor who lived in a palace made of sticks wasn't much of an emperor.

The woodcutter led them across the fort's grounds toward a stone building. Men were busy at various tasks, and colorful banners flew from poles. One with the yellow silhouette of a dragon struggled in the wind.

The woodcutter took them into a room where a soldier sat. He looked up as they entered, and the woodcutter bowed. The two men spoke rapidly, and Mei caught only a few words, but understood the two men were brothers. The soldier seemed fascinated by Mei's crossbow. He pointed to it, raising an eyebrow questioningly.

"Crossbow," said Madame Chong.

The soldier repeated the strange word carefully.

Mei shivered in the cold. Yellow light flickered from a lantern, but the room held no fireplace. She looked at a strip of painted fabric hanging from the wall. She could read the characters: Bravery, honor, respect. And a character similar to the character for the Imperial City, but missing two strokes. One final character for sky dragon, but again, slightly different. Other than the fabric, the room was quite plain. There was not even a *weiqi* board.

Madame Chong rapped her cane on the floor. "We would see your dragon."

The soldier bowed and led them from the room. The woodcutter followed.

In the center of the building, the soldier fumbled with keys. Mei stood back from the heavy wooden door, listening for the dragon's breathing. She heard nothing. She gripped her crossbow, wondering if now was the time to crank it, preparing for battle.

The soldier unlocked the door. The interior was dark as a dungeon, and the soldier held up his lantern. They entered the chamber.

Mei saw a shadowy outline on a platform. Two eyes stared, yellow in the darkness, and her heart beat faster. The creature didn't advance. The eyes didn't blink.

The soldier used the flame from his lantern to light a second, then a third lantern. As the flames brightened, Mei saw the full length of the beast crouched on the table. There was no breathing, no slithering of scales. The creature's head was completely motionless, like an oracle awaiting a question. Sharp teeth glistened around long jaws.

"A real dragon," whispered Mei.

"Hmm," said Madame Chong. She strode forward and rapped her cane sharply on its scaled snout. Mei gasped, tightening her grip on the crossbow.

"Stuffed," the Inventor announced.

Mei exhaled, letting herself breathe.

"Dragon," said the soldier, frowning at Madame Chong.

Madame Chong pursed her lips.

"Should we ask about eggs?" whispered Mei.

"This was no dragon," said Madame Chong, "but a saltwater crocodile from South China, purchased from some charlatan."

Mei hid her disappointment. She looked at the two men, who appeared puzzled. She doubted they understood Madame Chong's words.

"Thank you," said the Inventor. She bowed, turned with a swish of her gown and a rap of her cane, and marched out of the room.

Mei hurried after her. She was glad she'd rescued the soldier's brother, for it occurred to her that Madame Chong might not be following proper military etiquette.

The two men followed. "Dragon," said the soldier, with a note of pride.

"Hmm," said Madame Chong. She marched down the hall and out the building.

As she strode across the grounds of the fort, the two men came up beside her.

"Go?" asked the soldier.

"Yes," said Madame Chong. "We go."

The soldier regarded Mei's crossbow with curiosity, and she could tell he wanted to try it. They kept pace beside Madame Chong as she led the way out of the fort.

They retraced their path out of town, across the field, and finally, into the forest again. From there, the woodcutter helped guide them.

"Your father's wager involved you," said Madame Chong.

"Me?" said Mei.

But Madame Chong said nothing more.

Eventually, they came to the Inventor's clockwork machine, now coated with a dusting of snow.

Seeing it, the soldier's eyes widened even more than they had at the sight of Mei's crossbow.

Madame Chong pulled the medium sized skyrocket from the woven basket. She mounted it to the great brass wheel.

"What is?" asked the soldier.

"A rocket-propelled reverse clockwork mechanism to transport members of the Imperial Court backward through time in search of dragons."

"Wha– what?" said the soldier.

"We shall demonstrate," said Madame Chong. She gestured for Mei to climb up into the cabin, then followed up the ladder.

"Light the rocket," she said.

Mei took the flint and steel and climbed forward. As the two men watched from the ground, she waited for the wheel to tick around its orbit, then sparked the fuse.

She hurried back into the cabin, straightening her gown.

"What is?" shouted the soldier from below.

Then the rocket ignited with a blast of flame, and the two men leapt backwards.

As the wheel reversed, they leapt forward, then began walking backwards beside two shadows in gowns. The four moved faster and faster. Madame Chong gripped the wheel tightly as gunpowder smoke swirled around them. The gears screamed louder. Leaves jumped onto the trees and turned green.

The terrain around them rippled. Trees grew and shrank. A wall of ice approached from the north, then receded as vegetation swirled in a blur of green. All the while, the sun raced around them in a fiery blur. This rocket lasted much longer than the first, but finally sputtered out. The great wheel gradually slowed, and with it, the racing of the sun.

Madame Chong pulled her lever, and the wheel began

ticking forward.

Mei looked around. To her relief, it was a hot summer day. The trees around them looked like giant ferns. Insects buzzed, but they were like no insects Mei had ever seen. A dragonfly bigger than her head flew near, and she ducked. The ground was swampy, with scattered puddles of water. She felt thuds up through the travelling mechanism, making the puddles shake. There was no sign of the Imperial City.

"Bring the crossbow," said Madame Chong.

She descended the bamboo ladder, and Mei followed.

Consulting her compass, Madame Chong said, "That way."

Far in the distance, Mei saw large flying creatures, but kites had fooled her before, so she said nothing.

"Your father lost the wager," said Madame Chong.

"What prize did he lose?"

"You. You are betrothed to the winner."

The princess stared at her, unbelieving, but the Inventor said no more.

They made their way through grass and ferns taller than her head. Mud seeped into Mei's fine shoes, thawing her chilled feet. Madame Chong briefly carried the bottom of her gown above the mud, but gave it up as hopeless. Her cane sank in the earth. Both their gowns grew wet and dirty. Insects buzzed all around them, and Mei heard animals in the distance. There was no sign woodcutters had ever visited this part of the forest.

"This, too, is an elder dynasty?" she asked. "Still China?"

Madame Chong turned to speak as she walked. "Just so, Princess. But I have traveled and seen much, so it is curious I have not seen paintings of this landscape."

Her eyes were on Mei, not the way ahead, when she slipped and fell in the mud.

Mei heard words that had never crossed the lips of a lady of the court. Madame Chong sat in a puddle shaped like a huge dragon's foot. Mei set down her crossbow and helped Madame Chong to her feet. The Inventor's gown was ruined, the green silk in back covered with mud. Even her hair and combs were spattered brown.

With a sniff, Madame Chong gripped her muddy cane and marched on. Mei picked up the crossbow and followed. Within the forest, Mei couldn't see the sky where she'd seen the dragon kites earlier, but thought they were still headed in that direction.

Soon they heard loud hissing and sounds of something large moving in the forest. Mei stopped.

Through the foliage, she caught a glimpse of a large animal ahead, then realized there were two.

"Dragons?" she whispered. Quietly she moved forward.

The hissing became fiercer. A fern-like tree ahead shook off rain as something collided with it. It occurred to Mei that a creature that could shake a tree with such force might be dangerous. She wound her crossbow as she listened to the thrashing ahead.

"Wait, Princess."

She turned to see Madame Chong hanging back.

"I'll gather their eggs while they're distracted," Mei whispered.

"Too dangerous." Madame Chong's eyes twitched.

Getting closer, Mei caught glimpses of two battling creatures that looked like huge lizards. The larger one had a long neck and small head. But even the smaller one's head was bigger than the saltwater crocodile she'd seen in the other dynasty. With longer teeth. She finished winding the crossbow and notched a bolt— just in case—then began searching the ground for eggs.

"Princess, come back." Madame Chong's voice became urgent.

As Mei shushed her, the smaller of the lizards turned. She saw its head clearly, one eye looking sideways at her. Its jaws opened hungrily as it stepped toward her. When it parted the vegetation, she saw that it walked on two powerful hind legs. The forelegs were tiny, unlike dragons in paintings.

She raised her crossbow, sighted and pulled the trigger. The bolt struck it in the belly.

It responded with a hiss like a scream, tilting its head to look at the bolt buried in its flesh. Its short forearms strained to reach the bolt.

She hadn't killed it.

Its eye fixed on her.

At that moment, the tail of the larger lizard lashed out, knocking this one off its feet. It fell heavily against a tree.

"Run, Princess!"

But Mei was already running. She reached Madame Chong, who began hobbling back the way they'd come. The Inventor's cane sank in the ground. Mei grabbed the cane from her, put her arm around her waist, and helped her forward. The Inventor leaned on Mei's shoulder for support.

"I saw no eggs," Mei panted, "and I don't think they were dragons."

"Just so," said Madame Chong.

Mei struggled to hurry Madame Chong forward, her feet sinking from the added weight. She lost both her shoes in the mud. Glancing back, she saw movement. The long-necked lizard was retreating in the opposite direction. But there was motion under the tree as well.

"Your betrothed will be dismayed if you are eaten," said Madame Chong.

"Who is my bethrothed?"

"Master Hui."

"Master Hui! But he is nine times nine years old!" exclaimed Mei.

"Just so," said Madame Chong, "but a formidable *weiqi* player."

Mei spotted the clockwork ahead, beneath giant fern trees. Thrashing came from behind her and she turned to look. In the distance, the lizard on two legs limped after them. It must have used its jaws to pull the crossbow bolt from its belly. Blood spurted from the wound, but the other lizard had probably hurt it more than she had.

At the clockwork, she hopped anxiously on bare feet as Madame Chong removed the last skyrocket from the woven basket and fastened it to the great wheel.

Then Mei hurriedly climbed the ladder, followed by the Imperial Inventor.

Mei set down the crossbow and cane, snatched the flint and steel from Madame Chong and climbed out of the cabin. She waited impatiently as the brass wheel turned, so slowly, bringing the rocket closer with each tick. From up here, she could clearly see the lizard limping nearer. She'd left her crossbow in the cabin.

When the rocket was nearly within reach, she leaned forward precariously and sparked the fuse. The beast saw her atop the machine and opened its jaws, hissing loudly.

She scrambled back to the cabin and picked up her crossbow as the lizard lunged toward them.

The rocket ignited.

The wheel stopped.

Madame Chong pushed the lever, and the wheel reversed.

The beast stopped in mid-lunge, then reversed, followed by two shadows in gowns. The sun raced through the sky.

This rocket was the largest of the three, and a choking cloud of smoke engulfed the cabin. Mei saw Madame Chong clutching the wheel, then she disappeared in the haze. Mei closed her eyes against the stinging smoke. She coughed, covering her face with her muddy yellow sleeve. The cabin shook and gears screamed.

The rocket seemed to burn forever, and she couldn't get enough air. Just as it seemed she would faint, the roar of the rocket dropped to a whistle. Then that faded, leaving only the whir of slowing gears. The smoke gradually dissipated and she opened her eyes to glimpse the racing sun overhead.

As the gears spun to a stop, Madame Chong pulled the lever. The normal ticking resumed.

They were in the middle of an ocean. The world was void except for the small island that the mechanism stood on, and water to the horizon in all directions. Thin pieces of algae-covered shale littered the island. With relief, it occurred to Mei that she had traveled as far from her betrothed as possible.

She looked at Madame Chong, whose eyes twitched.

Mei picked up her crossbow, and they descended the ladder. A cool breeze blew gently from the ocean. Small waves lapped at the shore, but she saw no birds or any sign of fish in the clear water.

"How lucky to find an island just here," said Mei.

"Hmm," said Madame Chong. She pried at the overlapping black shale with her cane, trying to break off a piece.

Abruptly, the island heaved, and a row of spines unfolded, rising from the rock. The row extended out into the water in both directions. A new strip of land rose from the ocean beneath the spines. At the end of the strip, hundreds of feet away, steam bubbled from the water. Then the head of a great dragon emerged from the sea. It curved toward them at the end of a long neck. Mei's heart pounded in her chest.

Madame Chong bowed. Mei did the same, but her eyes watched the dragon's black head that swung into the air before them. She held her breath. The dragon's head was bigger than Mei's entire body. She could tell this was a true dragon. Its dark eyes looked big enough to swallow her up. She let her crossbow slip from her fingers.

Water dripped from its jaws as it spoke in a deep voice. "Welcome."

Madame Chong leaned on her cane, looking up. "We came to—"

"I know why you have come."

Madame Chong's eyes twitched.

"I foresaw your coming," said the dragon, "and waited here for seven times seven days."

"Why did you wait so long?"

It's great eyes looked at them, through them. "You sank."

"We did not," insisted Madame Chong.

"Before the when that is the now, I saw your bones at the bottom of the sea."

"Hmm," said Madame Chong.

Mei pulled herself to her full height. "I am the Emperor's daughter, and Madame Chong is his Imperial Inventor."

In the reflection of the dragon's eyes, Mei saw the mud on Madame Chong's gown and her own, and their disheveled hair. She wondered if the dragon had foreseen someone more regal-looking.

"Someone awaits your return," said the dragon.

"Just so," said Madame Chong, bowing.

Mei shuddered, remembering Master Hui.

At that, the dragon's head swung back over the sea and sank into the water, which bubbled and hissed.

Mei and Madame Chong looked at each other. The island shuddered beneath them, rattling the clockwork mechanism. The Inventor gripped her cane tightly.

It occurred to Mei that there were no more rockets. No way home. No fish. No birds. Only water and a dragon who'd lost interest in them.

But then the island heaved again, and the neck rose from the water. The dragon's head emerged and arced back toward them.

"Princess," it said. "Hold out your hands."

A bright red tongue slithered from its mouth, and as the tip of it uncurled, she saw a single blue porcelain egg. It was nearly the size of her head. She felt the heat of the dragon's nearness.

She reached out and took the egg. The shell was warm and hard against her palms.

"It will awaken at a time of your choosing," said the dragon.

Mei bowed.

"We are most grateful," said Madame Chong. "May we come again?"

"Only if you wish your bones at the bottom of the sea." And with that, the dragon's head plunged into the sea with a hiss. The spines on its back lay down. The island began to sink.

"Hurry, Princess!"

"But there are no more rockets!"

"Just climb!"

She ascended the bamboo ladder, cradling the blue egg to her chest with one arm. Madame Chong followed. Mei turned to see a wave sweep her crossbow into the sea.

As water lapped at the base of the travelling apparatus, Madame Chong pulled on both levers and stood on the pedals with all her weight.

Mei heard the twang of a coiled spring, and the great wheel began to accelerate forward, faster and faster. The dragon's head whipped upward from the sea, then back down. The sun flew faster and faster through the sky. The sea drained away. The land grew green, then white with ice, then green again. All the while, the gears screamed, driven by the spring uncoiling within the clockwork. Mei realized she was travelling forward this time, to the time of her father and brother. To the time of Master Hui.

The return took a long time, but there was no gunpowder smoke, so Mei could breathe. And think. She cradled the egg protectively, feeling its heat through her gown.

Forests of different types grew up around her, then receded, replaced by a quick growth of buildings. The wheel began to slow. She saw cherry trees in the Imperial Inventor's courtyard, changing with the seasons. As they blossomed one last time, she saw the banners announcing the *weiqi* tournament.

She leaned forward and pushed on the lever.

The Inventor looked at her in surprise as the wheel came to a stop.

"Today is yesterday," said Mei.

The Inventor stared at Mei for a long moment. "Just so." She climbed down from the cabin.

Mei descended the ladder after her, carefully cradling the egg. "I shall return to the palace."

"Shall I accompany you?"

"No," said the princess.

Madame Chong bowed.

Mei walked through the palace grounds, into the palace, and toward the Imperial Library, where the tournament was held.

The guards at the entrance bowed and opened the doors for her. Within, the players sat before their boards, all attention focused on the games. She saw the low *weiqi* table where her father sat across from old Master Hui. A half-dozen members of the court observed the emperor's game in silence. She took a deep breath, then marched across the floor, carrying the egg.

Master Hui looked up at her, grinning toothlessly. Her father, frowning, was too engrossed in his game to notice. Mei saw he was sweating, and that Hui's white stones controlled most of the board. One of the spectators whispered into the emperor's ear, and he looked up, startled.

"What is this, Princess?"

Master Hui reprimanded her, "You must never disturb a game of *weiqi*, bride-daughter."

Mei's eyes narrowed. She brought the egg down sharply upon the solid wooden table, scattering stones. The shell shattered like porcelain into a thousand fragments. From the shards, a serpentine red dragon uncurled. The onlookers gasped.

The dragon arched its neck, looking around. It hissed, sucking in air. After so long confined within the eggshell, it grew larger, stretching legs and coils across the table. The motion caused stones to slide from the table onto the floor. The dragon had the attention of everyone in the Imperial Library.

"You've ruined the game!" exclaimed Master Hui. He struggled to his feet and raised his cane to strike the dragon. It drew its head back and opened its mouth wide. A ribbon of fire jetted forth and the cane burst into flames. Master Hui dropped the cane and staggered backward, his robe smoldering. With a cry, he turned and hobbled from the table as quickly as his old legs could take him.

The dragon closed its mouth and turned to Mei. She stroked its neck, feeling the warm scales. It climbed down from the table to curl affectionately around her bare feet.

She saw that everyone in the room was staring at her, open-mouthed.

Ignoring the stares, she said, "That will be quite enough *weiqi* for today."

BIJOU LAVOIX AND
THE COAL DUST FAERY
MALON EDWARDS

If anyone could descry the gold fae, it was Oliver Cobbler. His eyes were keen, his ears were sharp, and his heart was greedy. His friends Robert Shepherd, Tobias Baker, and Bijou LaVoix all knew that.

Intimate associates of Ollie's for the better half of a decade, Bobby, Toby, and Bijou were very much aware of their nominal leader's selfishness and greed. Were Ollie to somehow (emphasis on the word somehow, since pennies usually eluded the thirteen-year-old boy) obtain a sweaty, grubby handful of Ms. Violet's penny candy, he would, with great haste, cram the ill-gotten pieces into his mouth before his companions could beg him for some, let alone do anything about it.

And were Bobby, Toby, or Bijou to whine at Ollie's stinginess or complain about his rudeness, they would be right away shushed by his vibrant but hard North African green eyes and bunched, knotted fists. While Ollie was stingy, he also punched like a piston, which was no hyperbole since the lad's left arm was made of metal and powered by a steam piston.

So come one early Tuesday morning, before first bell in the New City Elementary School play lot, when Ollie uttered the word "share" in the midst of divulging his plot for the foursome to kidnap a gold faery and steal her most prized element, Bobby, Toby, and Bijou were struck dumb by his word choice. However, they soon regained their voices as they realized Ollie's scheme was not playful jest.

"Your scheme will not work," said Bijou, bluntly.

Ollie raised his clenched left fist and pressed iron knuckles against the pleats and ruffles of Bijou's black high-collared, short-sleeved blouse, just above the dark brown leather chest harness bodice that cupped nothing, right over where her heart used to be.

"Keep sayin' stuff like that and you won't work. Ever again."

Grasping Ollie's metal forearm with courteous, careful honey-hued hands, Bobby shook his head, sending the loose dark brown curls framing his face flying.

"Don't."

Ollie smirked. "Don't what? Touch your flat-chested girlfriend? Or what? You gonna beat me up?"

Bobby pulled the bigger boy's iron fist away from Bijou, utilizing the majority of his strength to do so, even though the piston in Ollie's arm wasn't offering much resistance. As a result, steam vented from Ollie's armpit. The foursome guffawed, allowing the tension to slink away for the moment.

"What I think Bee meant," Bobby said, turning his almond-shaped eyes upon Bijou in a brief but adoring gaze before casting a nervous but neutral one on Ollie, "is how we gonna catch a gold faery?"

"Yuh." Toby pulled his Harris Tweed sporting cap lower. Tightly-woven, back-length dreadlocks bound with a thin leather strip obscured his dark brown eyes. "Those fings are majickal, fer flip's sake."

"But not when inside this."

Ollie removed a small, wrinkled grayish pouch from the front right pocket of his high-waisted, rust-colored, navy-striped trousers. Bobby reached for it.

"Is that what I think it is?" he asked.

Ollie smacked Bobby's hand. "Don't touch."

Toby pushed his sporting cap further back on his head to allow for closer scrutiny of the pouch. He glanced sideways at Bobby.

"An' jus' what the flip do you fink it is?"

"A goat scrotum."

Bijou arched an eyebrow at Bobby then looked to Ollie for confirmation, her hazel eyes sparkling with amusement. Ollie nodded, an errant thatch of his straight, raven-black hair bobbing with the motion.

Just then, first bell sounded and hundreds of children frolicking on the play lot plodded toward their respective primary, intermediate, and senior grade entrances, reluctance apparent in their heavy tread. With his good arm, Ollie yanked Bobby, Toby and Bijou away from the school and against the tide of children, toward the black wrought iron fence bordering the play lot. There, a shabby, threadbare rucksack sat on the ground.

"For the gold," Ollie said by way of explanation. He continued to lay out his machinations. "We kidnap the faery, put her in the goat scrotum, and tell her she ain't never getting out until she makes us enough gold nuggets to fill the rucksack." He picked up the empty rucksack, stuffed it into his school bag, and then shrugged the equally threadbare knapsack onto his shoulders. "Got it? Good. Let's go."

Toby and Bobby grabbed the bars of the wrought iron fence and made to climb it, eyes fixated upon the spear point finials topping the barrier. Bijou glanced back at New City Elementary. Schoolmarms with folded arms and stern gazes watched the hordes of children climb the cobblestone steps and make their way through the entrances, ever vigilant for mischief.

"Tarry awhile, if you would," she said.

Ollie gave a mock flourish with his metal arm as he bowed deep to Bijou. Toby snickered.

"What is it that you wish of me, O Queen of New City, And All That Is Flat and Smelly?" Ollie asked her in a grand voice.

Two years ago, the affected manner of speaking Ollie frequently adopted to mock Bijou's elocution, diction, and enunciation would have troubled the Creole girl so much that she would not have uttered a word amongst her companions for a week or more. These days, however, Bijou more often than not neutralized the teasing by blowing a kiss at Ollie with her naughtiest of fingers—which she did now—refusing to be aggrieved.

And why should she have hurt feelings? Now that Bijou no longer spoke Louisiana Creole outside of her home (at the behest of her New Orleans-born mother), her school marks had showed drastic improvement and her mother was a much happier woman. For Bijou, that was all that mattered.

"You did not tell us where we are traveling, nor did you disclose by what means."

Ollie looked at Bijou, his eyes flat with annoyance at her perpetual reluctance to follow his lead without hesitation. He took a deep breath and expelled it through flared nostrils.

"Norfolk Southern locomotive at Forty-seventh Street Station in Canaryville to Lake View and the Red Line; Red Line locomotive to the Gold Coast mines and the gold fae." Ollie bowed again, however, this time with his naughty iron finger raised to Bijou. "Art thou now pleased, milady? Excellent. Then make haste."

◇

Fifty minutes later, the foursome was standing before the decline portal of the Palmer Gold Mine, located at the far eastern edge of New City, within a bedrock valley, flat remnant of millennia-ago glacial activity, not far from the ribbon-shaped Lake Michigan.

Ollie crouched on the ground, slipped the rucksack from his back, and unbuckled its leather straps. His mates huddled close, peering with curious intensity over his shoulder. Relishing the attention, Ollie made a show of searching the rucksack; his movements slow and deliberate; his iron hand soft and gentle. Finally, he removed what seemed to be an over-sized Chinese finger trap woven of bamboo and Lady Fern.

Toby scowled. "Oi! Ollie, we ain't got time fer games, fer flip's sake."

"No games here."

Ollie put the green cylinder under Toby's nose.

"It's a faery trap. Yeah, I know; it looks like a Chinese finger trap. But it ain't. It's a faery trap. The old lady assured me of that."

Bijou creased her brow in skepticism. "What old lady do you speak of?"

"Well, milady, I speak of an old Chinese lady with a small, quaint shop just a stone's throw from the Cermak Road Station. She has nothing but two teeth in her head and looks like she could be Bobby's grandmother on his mother's side."

Ollie resumed his normal manner of speaking.

"The old Chinese lady said it works the same as a Chinese finger trap, but instead of catching fingers, it'll catch any gold faery within a twenty mile radius."

Bobby tried to keep the dubiety off his face. "How?"

"Inside are dew drops, nectar, sunlight slices, moonbeam bliss, and all that other good stuff gold fae like."

Ollie placed the faery trap on the ground near the box cut entrance of the mine.

"There. Now scram for an hour. Go stoke your boilers; explore the area or something. Just stay away from the trap. Fae won't come to eat if big galoots like us are nosing 'round."

The foursome moved off in different directions toward the vivid green wooded slopes, slowly picking their way through the small boulders of the Gold Coast Valley flats, searching for a secluded copse or discreet brushwood. Stoking one's boiler was just as private a ritual as urinating or defecation, but even more so given the naked vulnerability of the act. Ten minutes later, Bijou had discovered a thicket of trees and was feeding the tiny fire in the boiler in her stomach a scoop of coal dust from her rucksack so that the steam clock serving as her heart would continue to tick.

Bobby, Ollie and Toby were at that very moment engaged in similar behavior, though the measure of their coal varied:

Bobby stoked the boiler in his midsection with one lump of coal to energize the tiny pistons in his metal knee; Ollie stoked his somewhat larger boiler with two lumps of coal to power the steam piston in his metal arm; and Toby stoked his boiler—the largest of the foursome—with half a dozen lumps of coal to fuel the numerous steam pistons that ambulated his entire lower body.

Bijou still remembered the beating of her flesh heart. She missed feeling it pound in her chest when she got scared or excited or after racing the boys to the Forty-seventh Street locomotive when school let out. But that heart was replaced with a steam clock heart seven years ago when she and more than sixty percent of the adult population, and eighty percent of children under the age of seventeen were infected during a polio epidemic that ravaged New City.

Thousands died, but thousands more were left with various body parts and organs withered by the disease. Instead of living a life of pain and hardship, the polio survivors turned to metallurgists and steam surgeons to improve their health and quality of life through iron, copper, coal, and steam.

As a result, life expectancy for polio sufferers was extended by decades. But for most of them, whether they were healers, cobblers, bakers or shepherds, the sacrifice was great and entire life savings were wiped out.

Bijou knew she would not be alive if it weren't for her steam clock heart. But as she and the boys gathered back at the mouth of the box cut mine mouth an hour later, she longed for the organic pounding of her flesh heart to the dull knock she felt now.

The foursome regarded the faery trap with apprehension and distance: it buzzed and jittered angrily. Ollie nodded at it. "Bijou, go get it."

"Me? Why me? It's your stupid trap."

"You have the smallest hands."

Bijou scowled, but said nothing, unable to think of an appropriate retort. She didn't move toward the faery trap, either, though. Instead, she fussed with the simple cloth hair band holding the exquisitely coiffed henna-tinted cornrows that exploded into a dark, wonderfully massive supernova fro at the back of her head.

"Aren't you tired of being poor?" Ollie hissed.

"Aren't you?" Bijou hissed back.

Ollie shoved her toward the faery trap and Bijou stumbled on the dusty, uneven ground, nearly losing her footing. She gave him a dirty look over her shoulder, but did not hold it for long; the faery trap had quieted with abrupt silence.

"Well, go on," Bobby whispered.

Bijou crept toward the faery trap, stepping with soft care upon the sand-colored dirt and gravel so that the stones didn't crunch. When the faery trap was at her feet, she bent over it, cocking an ear toward it to listen for more anger within.

"Oi! Watch out!"

Toby startled Bijou so badly that her steam clock heart stopped a tick or two and she nearly jumped out of her thick-soled, knee-high brown leather boots.

"It's gonna bite yer thrupenny bits!"

Toby grinned and slapped his chest with the flat of his palm.

"Oh wait. You ain't got any!" He and Ollie brayed with laughter.

"Wretched boy."

Bijou picked up the faery trap, surprised at the dense weight of it. She closed her right eye and peeped inside the narrow opening of one end. The bright day could not penetrate its innards.

"Just reach in there and yank it out."

Ollie circled his index fingers and rolled his wrists in a vigorous, impatient hurry-up motion.

"No."

Bijou squared her shoulders and pressed her plump, burnished bronze lips together.

"No?"

Ollie was taken aback. None of them had ever said no to him before.

"No."

Bijou lifted her chin in defiance.

"Give it."

Ollie snatched the faery trap from Bijou, his voice more snarl than pubescent teen.

"Stupid girl."

He thrust two fingers and a thumb into the cylinder, splitting it down the middle with a violent rent. His fingers probed and dug for a few moments before he withdrew them from the wrecked mass of bamboo and woven grass.

"What the hell is this?"

Held tight and fast in Ollie's hand was an ebon-skinned faery with a pewter mohawk. She was clad in a high-collared intricately laced sleeveless and backless pewter blouse and a deep purple ankle-length wrap skirt. Two sets of lavender-tinted translucent wings—a larger pair sprouting from her shoulder blades and a smaller pair from her lower back—were trapped by Ollie's index and middle fingers.

"Release me! "Her voice was high-pitched and ethereal, but loud and clear as it bounced around the slopes of the valley.

Ollie peered closely at her. "What are you?"

The ebon-skinned faery looked down her pert but African-wide nose at him.

"I am Asha, the Coal Dust Faery."

"Faery?" Toby snorted. "More like bug."

"And an ugly one at that," Ollie added, frowning. He tossed Asha aside. "Flippin' hell. That Chinese lady tricked me. I'm gettin' my money back." He snapped his iron fingers at Toby, Bobby and Bijou. "Let's go. We're goin' to Chinatown."

Ollie turned and went a mere three steps before he yelped and slapped at his right earlobe. He looked at his hand and saw a dazed Asha crumpled in his palm.

"Stupid bug. I'll teach you to bite me."

And with the glee of a wicked child who takes pleasure in inflicting pain upon the defenseless and weak, Ollie plucked both sets of Asha's wings like the petals of a forget-me-not, ripping them out of her back. The coal dust faery issued an unearthly scream from her distended mouth.

For Bijou, time, at that moment, seemed to accelerate. Ollie flicked Asha and her rent wings away. Bijou rushed to Asha's discarded body. Toby and Bobby gaped. Bijou pleaded for strips of cloth to stem Asha's bleeding. Ollie ordered Bijou to drop the faery. Bijou refused. Ollie excommunicated Bijou from the group. Bijou begged Bobby to help her. Ollie commanded Bobby to stay where he stood. Bobby vacillated between Bijou and Ollie. Bijou searched her rucksack. Bobby fell in behind Ollie. Ollie shoved Toby and Bobby toward the trail to Gold Coast Station. Bijou withdrew a deerskin pouch from her rucksack. She selected vial of powdered goatweed from within. She sprinkled the goatweed onto Asha's ragged wounds. Asha moaned. Bijou spit upon the powder, forming a paste. She tore a ruffle from her blouse and wrapped Asha's lacerations. Asha shrieked again and fainted despite Bijou's gentle fingers. Bijou removed a small crocheted drawstring purse from her rucksack. She placed Asha inside. She slipped the purse around her neck. She searched on hands and knees for Asha's torn wings. She found them half-buried beneath the gravel. She tucked them into the front pocket of her leather trousers. She sighed, pressing her full lips together. And then, with swift urgency, she set off for the best healer in all of New City—her mother.

<><

"I am so very sorry." Bijou's eyes brimmed with tears.

"For what, child?" Asha's voice was husky and tired, but absent of pain.

"For that."

Bijou pointed at Asha, indicating her current state: naked to the waist and face down on a shabby throw pillow, weak, her mohawk flattened on one side, and, what threatened to wrench a sob from Bijou's throat and embarrass a girl who thought she was too tough to cry, the ugly, red scabrous wounds on the faery's back.

"Child, it was you who saved my life, correct?"

"My mother mostly."

"Then I am forever indebted to you and your mother. For as long as you both shall live, I will be your servant and attend your needs."

"My mates and I just wanted to catch a gold faery so we would be poor no longer." A tear trickled down the left side of her nose.

"And no longer will you be." Asha pushed herself up on her knees, gritting her teeth at the pain. Sweat stood out on her brow.

"What do you mean?" Bijou's face was scrunched in confusion.

"Child, I am a coal dust faery."

Asha made a fist, blew into it, and opened her palm. Upon her tiny hand sat a small mound of the black powder.

"Never again will your mother have to take bread-coin or rent-coin and haggle with the collier so you can stoke your boiler. At your heart's desire, you shall have pure, high quality coal dust, the kind coveted by every child with a small boiler."

"But I don't deserve it."

"Child, the sins of that hateful boy are not your sins. Be grateful for your reward."

"But Ollie—"

Asha snapped her fingers—a sharp, cracking report from appendages so diminutive—startling Bijou.

"*He* was the one who did this to me?" The coal dust faery reached behind her and ran light fingertips along the rough wounds where her wings once were.

Bijou nodded.

Asha touched a finger to the girl's chest. "The one whose flesh and blood heart is no measure at all to yours of steam and gears?" Bijou nodded again. "Leave him to me."

Asha rubbed her hands together with such vigor that they warmed from the friction. When she opened them, a perfectly round and smooth black pebble sat within.

"Do you see this pebble, child?"

Bijou nodded again.

"Take it to the entrance of the Palmer Gold Mine at dusk

this day, just before the sun dips below the horizon. Wait there with your hand outstretched toward the entrance of the mine until my friend the Tikoloshe comes."

"The Tikoloshe?" Bijou shivered as the word rolled off her tongue.

"Do as you're told, child."

◇

Bijou arrived at the Palmer Gold Mine exactly at dusk, her nervous breath visible as white puffs in the chill valley air. She did not have to wait long for the Tikoloshe. Just as the red-orange sun slipped behind the valley slopes, Bijou heard heavy shuffling and stertorous, bestial bellows from deep within the bowels of the mine growing louder, coming closer. Her knees weakened and twitched to flee down the trail back to Gold Coast Station, but Bijou stood her ground, her wavering hand outstretched. It was the least she could do for the coal dust faery.

And then she saw it.

The Tikoloshe was a hulking monstrosity, resembling a shaggy man-sized teddy bear, but with a sharp, bony ridge atop its head. Drool slavered from its terrible, fanged jaws; a tangible, animal musk hit her like a slap across the face, bringing tears to her eyes and causing her to gag. The Tikoloshe bent forward to regard her, its large black eyes unblinking. Bijou shrank from it.

"Please," she whimpered. "I beg of you. Do not hurt me."

"It delights me to no end that a human—a child no less—visits my mine but does not seek my gold." The Tikoloshe snorted and Bijou could feel its exhalation upon her face.

"Please."

Chuckling, the Tikoloshe reached out a furry claw and snatched the pebble from Bijou, scoring her hand with angry red weals.

"You may go now, child," it growled, and swallowed the pebble. And just like that, the Tikoloshe was no longer there.

Bijou searched the growing darkness with frantic terror, whirling and turning, attempting to look everywhere at once for the horrid faery. It was not until she heard its chuckle again—close and intimate—that she screamed and fled to the station.

<>

That night, as Ollie turned down the covers of his bed and blew out the flame of his thermolampe in preparation for slumber, the most wretched stench permeated his bedroom. Thinking it to be a dead rat, he checked the traps behind his wardrobe and chest of drawers, but found them empty. Determined to root out the smell that was beginning to turn his stomach, Ollie searched every corner of his modest and sparse room, taking quick, shallow breaths through his nose to keep as much of the stench as he could out of his mouth and lungs.

His search did not take long. Perplexed, Ollie was stumped as to where the foul odor could be emanating from—that is until he walked past his slightly ajar first-floor window.

Levering the crank within the windowsill, Ollie swung the window wide and the stink assaulted his nostrils. Curious as to the source of the out-of-doors foulness, Ollie pinched his nose and leaned his upper body through the window, turning his head left, then right, as he sought the source of the malodor.

Ollie could make out little in the darkness. Shrugging, he made to withdraw into his bedroom, but froze when he heard a low, slow chuckle that caused the dense hair on his desert brown flesh arm to stand on end. The last thing Ollie ever saw was wickedly curved fangs and a solid mass of shaggy fur before he was swiftly snatched out into the night.

All Ollie's parents found of him the next morning was his metal arm on the ground beneath his still open window, glinting dully in the wan sunshine.

DAMNED IF YOU DO, DAMNED IF YOU DON'T

JOYCE REYNOLDS-WARD

"Someone to see you, sir," the maid announced, her tone carrying just the slightest hint of disapproval as she tucked a strand of chestnut-colored hair behind her ear.

"Who is it, Hilda?" Peter McLoughlin asked. He took the interruption as an excuse to stretch to his full six-foot-four height. His long back ached as he pushed the newfangled steam-powered typing machine on its rolling metal stand away from his desk. The hoses almost toppled the pile of messy papers next to the machine, field reports from the past winter's unicorn hunting brigades. Peter growled and switched off the steam, letting the hoses collapse. The speed of the typing machine didn't make up for its inconvenience. "Send them away unless it's something important. I need to have this report done by the time Grandfather's back from Victoria."

A grimace twisted Hilda's lips. "Some stin—" She checked herself and the lips were firmly disciplined into a neutral line. "Some Injun, sir. And he's *dirty*."

Peter scowled at her. An Indian, straight from the bush. That meant something important had happened. Why hadn't she sent the Indian in? He thought he'd made it clear to all the staff that any Indian, at any time, in any condition, was welcome in his office. Even with deadlines pending. You didn't make valuable allies and friends wait, not in this business, not in this Oregon Country. This girl was a new immigrant from the States, and while she was good at bookkeeping as well as housework, her attitude toward nonwhites meant he couldn't afford to risk having her work in the office.

"You're not in the States anymore," he snapped. "You're in the Oregon Country. Indians are fellow citizens here."

The stony look on her face stopped any further scolding. Not the first time he'd had problems with this maid with regard to Indians, but it'd be the last. He scribbled a quick note to the housekeeper, asking her to send Hilda back to the agency for retraining. He took the precaution of sealing the note before handing it to her.

"Take this to Maria. Now, where's this Indian gentleman?"

"He's in the front parlor, *sir*."

Peter nodded thanks and quickly rushed down the stairs to the front parlor. As he entered the room, he could see what Hilda meant. The Indian stood with his back to the parlor door, still wearing ragged and dirty traveling clothes. The peculiarly sweet scent of unicorn blood tinged with a sharp bite of something vaguely rotten struck Peter's nostrils. *Something urgent.* Most of the Indians working for him took the time to change into their best town finery before riding into Oregon City. That this one hadn't spoken, meant either dire urgency, or of ignorance.

The Indian turned to face Peter. Wahhisit, from the Nimiipuu. Urgency, not ignorance.

"Wahhisit, my friend," Peter extended his hand.

"My friend Peter," Wahhisit said, his hands closing around Peter's, his grip less than half of what it had been. He sagged forward and Peter caught him.

"What's wrong?" Peter asked as they sank to their knees, shocked at how light his friend was, aware of the growing scent of what he now identified as putrefaction.

Wahhisit blinked rapidly at Peter as he collapsed the rest of the way to the floor. "The dead are walking," he croaked. "And only the unicorn's blood has kept me safe to give you the news."

"Wahhisit—"

"Tuekakas knows. Holding the line. Sent me." He gasped, then fumbled in his pocket, coming out first with a sealed note that he shoved into Peter's hand. Then he brought out a triangular-shaped case and popped it open to reveal the point of a unicorn horn. Peter instinctively flinched back from the horn, still oozing venom. Wahhisit's hands shook as he aligned the point with his throat. Peter grabbed at the horn, but Wahhisit shook his head.

"Dead. In life. Danger to you, to Oregon City. Let me go!"

"My grandfather will be here within the hour. Let him doctor you."

Wahhisit shook his head. "The dead got me. Dead now." He glared at Peter. "Don't want to live like that!"

Peter froze. Wahhisit plunged the point of the horn into his throat. Blood spewed over Peter's hands, not the huge spurt of fresh blood but the clotted, slow pulse of someone dead in life. Skin parted smoothly as the horn slid into Wahhisit's throat and faded from sight, the magic-driven death stroke of a North American unicorn. Wahhisit's body sagged; sinking into itself until the skin barely covered the skeleton.

The dead are walking, Wahhisit had said. Shuddering, remembering the lore about those dead in life, Peter wiped his bloody hands on his coat and went to the weapons cabinet, returning with a machete he'd used for killing unicorns. Whispering apologies, he severed Wahhisit's head from his body with a single slice of the sharp blade. Wahhisit's eyes popped open as his head rolled away from his body. For a brief moment, Peter almost thought his friend smiled at him.

And then the eyes closed again. Rotten blood stink filled the room, foul enough to make Peter gag. He dropped to his knees beside Wahhisit's body, fighting back sour bile and failing. He vomited until he could retch no longer and his gut tightened in dry heaves.

The dead are walking, Wahhisit had said. Peter'd only heard whispers from the Company's West Indies counterparts about the phenomenon the African slaves called *zombie*. At that time, he'd thought they were stories meant to spook an unsophisticated traveler from the wilds of the Oregon Country.

But what he'd just seen fit those descriptions from the Indies.

The dead are walking. Peter carefully cleaned his machete and resheathed it, hanging back inside the cabinet. He placed Tuekakas's note in his pocket. Then he rang for servants to help him. Wahhisit might have been dead in life, but at the least, Peter could ensure that what remained of his old friend was handled with respect.

<>

"Aye, I heard tell of zombies at the Company meeting today." John McLoughlin sagged over his cane as he and Peter stood in McLoughlin's medical quarters, studying Wahhisit's body and head. "Never thought it would come so quickly."

"Tuekakas says he's having trouble holding the line at Snake River," Peter said. "He has reports of zombies riding unicorns."

McLoughlin nodded. "Other districts are getting similar reports from their brigades. The Americans are most likely involved, along with the British. There are rumors of secret meetings and secret alliances. Some say they've already divided the Oregon Country and the Canadian Republic between themselves."

"Why the Americans?"

"Unhappiness over being turned back at the border. Losing California to the Mexicans and Indians there. East of the Mississippi isn't enough for them, even though the French practically gave it away to Jefferson. The dregs of Europe push in on what land they have, and they've got hungry eyes for the lands of Lewis and Clark. Napoleon was smart not to sell them anything west of the Mississippi."

"But zombies?"

"If the Americans have their slaves making zombies for war, then those slaves don't have time for rebellion. Zombies can't use guns, counteracts the magic, or so I have been told.

That means those slaves must make many zombies. But that doesn't solve our current problem, boy. Read me that letter from Tuekakas again."

Peter pulled the letter out of his pocket.

"Tuekakas of the Wallowa to my dear friends in Oregon City," he read. "I send you Wahhisit by the fastest means possible, to bear news of a dread new danger arising at our borders. The dead walk amongst us. They ride the horned ones. Our kinsmen struggle against the dead riders, and word has come to me from the great grassy plains that our Lakota friends seek refuge with the Absaroka from the constant attacks. A Lakota reports seeing bluecoats riding with the dead, and directing their attacks. I have not seen this.

Dear friends, come quickly. Danger sits at our borders. Heinmottooyalakekt has seen it. Ollokot has faced it. Wahhisit has been infected, and will need the final grace, but assures me he can keep control until he has delivered this message. I have had others of my hunters infected. The sickness spreads quickly, I know not how."

"Bites," McLoughlin growled. "I know that much."

Peter continued to read. "Come quickly my friends. Bring help. Your friend Tuekakas sees danger ahead for our nation if you do not come. Tuekakas through Heinmottooyalakekt."

"It's bad if that tough old bird is calling for help," McLoughlin muttered. "Tuekakas and his relatives can hold off the US Army under normal conditions and *have* done that, to my everlasting thanks. But the Army with zombies?" He sighed. "Gather a brigade, Peter. See if you can talk Ogden and Smith into giving up married life for the moment, and make all speed to the Wallowa. The Parliament is meeting this evening. I'll make the request for troop support. You get the brigade going."

"I will do it," Peter said. If his grandfather—Father of the Oregon Nation—requested troops, he knew the Oregon Parliament would move quickly. John McLoughlin asked for little that was trivial. "We will ride tomorrow."

"Don't short yourself on provisions," McLoughlin advised. "If I know Ogden and Smith, they've got their gear packed and ready to go at a moment's notice."

Just like I do, he thought. Out loud, he continued his thought. "You might pull Joe Meek aside at Parliament tonight," he added. "Meek would be a welcome addition to the brigade, and he might be tiring of political life, be ready for a little adventure."

"He would, indeed," McLoughlin agreed. "I'll speak to him. Go! Time is short."

"I will," Peter said.

As he hurried through the house, calling for Maria, he spotted Hilda sliding out the side door, now attired in a plain gray calico dress that seemed oddly plain contrasted to the length and thickness of her bright chestnut-colored braid, carrying a big bag.

Wonder if all that is hers? He dismissed the thought. Maria would have checked carefully and watched Hilda pack. There were more important things for him to do than worry about one inconsequential maid.

<>

"You're sure going by dirigible is the best course?" Peter Skene Ogden scowled at the airship waiting for them.

"Tuekakas sent that he'd have horses ready for us at Fort Walla Walla. Speed is of the essence," Peter told Ogden. "Speed and skill."

"Waugh! Well, they'll be getting skill all right," Joe Meek snorted, eyes bright as he chomped on a chew of tobacco, then spat. "Can't say much for our speed."

"From what I've heard, skill is going to be the greater need," Peter said.

Meek nodded. "Us old unicorn hunters ought to be able to figure something out with these whatchamacallits? Zombies?"

"Zombies," Ogden growled. He shook his head. "Shades of the Indies. Never thought I'd see one. Still, Tuekakas asked. And we owe him. The entire Oregon country owes him."

"Aye." Jedidiah Smith, the silent one, chimed in. "Young

McLoughlin. Cap'n says he's ready to load up."

"Then let's get it done," Peter said.

Smith nodded. He and Ogden headed for the rest of the quickly assembled brigade, for the most part old-time unicorn hunters now retired to a comfortable life in Oregon City and the Tuality Plains, with smatterings of younger, newer hunters who'd been in Oregon City on a summer break from unicorn pursuit.

Meek stood near Peter. He spat a wad of tobacco skillfully into the nearby urn. "We're going to lose a lot of people, you know," he said quietly to Peter. "If Tuekakas can't hold against this invasion, what are we going to do?"

"Hold until the Parliament's troops get there," Peter said.

Meek snorted. "And they'll be better than Tuekakas's hunters? If it's an American plot, there'll be hell to pay. Might not be the American government itself. Ever since they impeached my cousin Polk just before the start of the War, there's been enough speculators out there willing to do the government's dirty work."

"We'll know more when we get there," Peter said. Telegraph had its limitations, especially when dealing with Indians who didn't trust the wires. And the interference of unicorns, who liked to rub against the poles and bring the wires down. He'd seen the big ones of the karkadann breed do just that.

Big and smart. Hard to kill. And now, coupled with the walking dead...

Someone has to be controlling them, he told himself. *It's a matter of finding out who and why.*

Maybe if he kept on telling himself that, he'd finally come to believe it.

<>

Tuekakas himself met them at the dirigible landing at Fort Walla Walla, along with a sizeable guard of well-armed, grim-faced Nimiipuu.

"Wahhisit?" he asked Peter right away.

"Grace has been administered."

"Thank you." Tuekakas inclined his head slightly. "Did he—"

"He used the horn, and I severed his head. As I learned during my training in the Indies."

Tuekakas visibly relaxed. "Good. I would not care to be named as the cause of the plague in our capital."

"None would dare blame the Holder of the Line."

Tuekakas snorted at that. He glanced over at Meek, Smith, and Ogden, waiting behind Peter. "Friends. It's been some time."

"Since the Battle of the Flag," Ogden acknowledged.

"And now we face another battle." Tuekakas gestured and his men moved to help the brigade unload. "As soon as your men are ready, we ride. Heinmottooyalakekt and Ollokot are holding the line at the gold mines."

Peter exchanged a worried glance with Meek. The gold fields between the towns of John Day and Baker City were, along with the horns and hides of unicorns, part of the Oregon Country's treasury.

"They're attacking the mines?" Meek asked.

"Yes. You shall see."

"I'll need to send a message before we go," Peter told Tuekakas. "Any details I can send the troops that follow will be helpful."

"As few details as you can," Tuekakas cautioned.

"It's not that bad—"

"They intercept communications by the wires. That's why I sent Wahhisit to you. We've found copies of dispatches sent in the pockets of the dead. We must hurry. We'll face fighting before we reach the mines."

"What are we waiting for, then?" Meek asked. "Let's ride." He picked up his possibles bag and headed for the Nimiipuu. Smith joined him.

Ogden paused. "The route through John Day might be the best," he advised.

"That way is clear. So far," Tuekakas said.

"I'll let my grandfather know where we're engaging," Peter said. "We've a code, so even if they're reading the wires, they won't know what's happening."

"Good," Tuekakas said. "Do not take too long." He turned and followed Ogden.

◇

They rode due south through the desert, curving around to approach John Day from the west. As they passed through the Umatilla lands, a sizeable band from that tribe joined the Nimiipuu, bringing in even more fleet horses and skilled riders.

This is like the Battle of the Flag, Peter thought suddenly, as they dropped down from the mountains into the John Day valley. He'd been a little boy during that decisive battle that had established the Oregon Territory as its own country, but he'd heard enough about it while growing up. Every Oregon Country child his age had heard the thrilling stories and seen the woodcuts from that battle. A combined force of Indians, unicorn hunters, fur trappers, scattered settlers from the United States who had no desire to participate in the country's doomed war against the South, and rebel factions of the Hudson's Bay Company had defeated a combined British-American army to earn independence.

But how much longer can we keep it? he wondered.

Miners and Indians from John Day rode out to meet them. Tuekakas exchanged words with the Nimiipuu leader, then came back to Peter and Ogden.

"Ollokot's fighters are engaged," he reported. "Many, many losses. The battle's there." He pointed to the southeast.

"Let's ride!" Ogden snapped.

Tuekakas called to his riders. Ogden surged forward and Peter followed his lead, urging his short-coupled chestnut gelding forward.

They galloped through town to the cheers of grim-faced townspeople. Men, women and children alike were armed with scythes, long knives, and pitchforks, all more effective tools against the dead than guns or arrows. Peter shivered as he caught a glimpse of a frightened child's face as he raced by. *We can't let this fight get into the town.*

He smelled the battle before he could hear or see it. The sick miasma of decay rolled toward them, almost visible in its thickness. Peter coughed and choked before he could pull his bandanna up over his face. His eyes teared even after his nose and mouth were covered. For a moment he felt his mount hesitate. Peter urged the gelding forward. If even the horses lost heart, then they were defeated before they'd begun.

Then the gelding spotted one of the unicorns. He surged toward the foe that breeding and training had conditioned him to fight. Peter dropped his single, continuous rein over the saddle horn and drew his machete, using seat and leg to guide his horse as he fought. The gelding squealed and pinned his ears as the unicorn lowered its horn to charge. As the unicorn charged, the gelding nimbly danced aside, giving Peter a chance to strike at the zombie.

Peter's first blow whacked the arm off of the zombie. No blood. The zombie swayed. The unicorn dropped his head low, ears pinned so hard against his head that it didn't seem like he had any at all. As the unicorn charged a second time, the horse ducked low and under the horn, positioning Peter for a clean stroke at the unicorn's throat.

Peter took it. Unicorn first, then rider. He used both hands on his machete, nearly severing the unicorn's head from its neck. The sweet scent of unicorn blood triggered a surge of powerful energy. Peter felt more awake, able to move faster, fight longer. *Unicorn fever.* The strength that allowed hunters to take on entire herds single-handedly. It led to great profit from the hides and horns, but it could just as easily lead the unwary into a painful death.

As the unicorn buckled to the ground, Peter pulled the machete free and struck at the zombie. His horse would have flinched away except for the obedience trained into him as Peter pressed him close. The zombie grabbed Peter's fighting arm with its remaining arm.

That deflected the blow. Peter wrenched his short knife from his belt and slashed at the zombie's head. He managed to free his machete hand without getting bitten through his gloves and, somehow juggling short knife and machete decapitated the zombie.

Harder to kill than unicorns, he thought, as the zombie collapsed in upon itself. He felt tired but oddly elated, the typical effect of smelling unicorn blood. His horse shook his head, and prepared to charge again.

Peter lost track of time as he fought. With the unicorns, the zombies seemed harder to vanquish. Dismounted, they could be killed. The cumulative effect of the blood scent of so many dead unicorns was hard to shake off, however, and added to the unreality of the battle scene. By the time he caught a glimpse of a familiar chestnut-colored braid, he was almost ready to consider it a unicorn blood-induced hallucination, especially since the rider was mounted on a saddled unicorn. Then the unicorn turned to meet his horse and Peter recognized the rider. Shock flitted over Hilda's face, followed by rage.

She's not a zombie, Peter thought. *But how did she get here? And what is she doing on a unicorn?*

His horse lunged at the unicorn and caught it off-balance, biting it in the shoulder. Hilda swung her sword at Peter's horse, and he blocked it with his machete. He noted she needed one hand on the reins to control the unicorn while he rode freehand. *Advantage to me.* He shifted his weight, and his horse danced away sideways from the unicorn, then turned and let hind legs fly on Peter's cue, catching the unicorn hard in the barrel with both hinds. Hilda screamed as one hoof smashed into her leg. Another weight shift, and Peter brought the gelding around parallel to the unicorn, while Hilda, both hands on her reins, the sword dropped, wrestled with the recalcitrant unicorn to try to pull away, her right leg dangling uselessly along the unicorn's side.

Kill the unicorn, capture the rider. Peter's horse slammed hard into the unicorn's side and Hilda screamed again as they smashed against her leg, her face going white. The unicorn staggered sideways and Peter's horse spun, putting Peter in place. He slashed hard and deep and grabbed for Hilda with his left hand, just as a living, blue-coated rider pulled her off from the other side. Hilda slid easily onto the other horse despite her injury, displaying a riding skill Peter hadn't known she possessed.

Peter chased Hilda and her rescuer. The braid of chestnut-colored hair guided him as Hilda and her rescuer dodged through the fighters. Hilda was a key to what was going on. How?

Not wires that the bluecoats are getting information from, but a spy, he thought, sick at heart. *A spy in my household!*

A horse crashed into Peter's. Peter cursed and straightened his mount out. The other rider grabbed Peter's reins.

"It's over! Let them go! They're fleeing the field!" Joe Meek yelled at Peter.

"I've got to catch that girl! She's no zombie!"

"Girl? Fiend, maybe! She killed Tuekakas, she and her unicorn! She's poison, man!"

Peter froze. "She killed Tuekakas?"

Meek nodded. "Caught him off guard, and her unicorn got him with its horn. Dead. True dead, not zombie dead."

"That unicorn won't kill again," Peter said. "But Meek—that girl—she was a maid in my household."

"No. Couldn't be. Didn't fight like a housemaid!"

"She wasn't a very good housemaid," Peter said. "But I think she was a much better spy. That's how information's been getting out, Joe. Not stealing off the wires—but through spies." He tried to pull his mount away from Meek. "I've got to catch her, Joe! Find out how bad it was. I've *got* to find out how much she stole from me!"

Meek shook his head, keeping his hand on Peter's reins. "Next time, Peter. Otherwise she'll trap you, just like she did Tuekakas."

"Meek—"

"What am I going to tell your grandfather if I let you get killed? Damn it, Peter, *she killed Tuekakas*. You think you're better than that old unicorn fighter?"

"I killed her unicorn," Peter countered.

"You did. But look at them now!" Meek gestured toward the fleeing pack of riders with his free hand. "Don't you think all of us want to catch her?"

"We could."

Meek shook his head again. "Not this time, Peter."

"If we let her get away—"

"She's gone. We've got a mess here. Shake the unicorn fever and look around, man!"

Peter took a deep breath. Slowly, the haze from unicorn fighting started to fade. Grim-faced warriors and unicorn hunters progressed amongst the dead, hacking heads off as they went. A smaller group worked at harvesting horns and hides from the fallen unicorns. An even smaller group, mostly Nimiipuu, clustered in the center of the battlefield.

"You can't chase after her right now," Meek continued, his voice softening. "We've too much of our own to deal with."

Peter nodded, finally accepting Meek's words. "Tuekakas?"

Meek nodded toward the group of Nimiipuu. "They're preparing to take him back to their camp."

"He should receive a hero's funeral."

"He will."

"And he'll get honors in Oregon City as well," Peter said firmly. Meek eyed him carefully, then let go. Peter turned his gelding toward the group of Nimiipuu.

But still, he took a moment to look after Hilda.

I'll catch up with you, he vowed. *And when I do—*

He wasn't sure just what he was going to do. But he'd have his revenge on this spy.

I'll get you, and find out how much you've betrayed me. How much you've betrayed Oregon.

He wondered how much worse it could get.

OF BLOOD AND BRASS
K.L. TOWNSEND

If she could understand shame, Kyoka would have felt it long ago.

The sweet sounds of her shamisen filled the backroom of the tea house. Each string popped with a distinct twang as Kyoka danced, poised and measured, like a blooming lotus. The flower song had always been the house favorite, and even now she performed with the same control expected of a lady. She bent her legs and swept open her arms, slow, dignified, mirroring the stately bonsai behind her.

One of the Chinese opium dealers glanced at the stage as she transitioned into the next step. The young man licked his lips and shifted in his seat, but never caught her eye.

She caught his. Pupils dilated. Cheeks flushed. He was new.

He wanted to touch her. Maybe she would let him. The other girls had always told her it was forbidden. Kyoka could never understand why. Wasn't touch good? Wasn't that part of living?

An older man, a face she recognized as a frequent guest, nudged him with his elbow and shook his head. The young man sighed, stealing one last glance, before he joined his companions in their business. Grinding sputtered in her chest. Was she disappointed?

The opium dealers paid her no mind. They frequented New Toyko every weekend, eager for the regulars who brought their airships to port. Opium dealers were always busy. The others had told her not to mind them; they were bad for business.

She couldn't understand why. Why did no one ever tell her anything?

The dealers attracted the pilots, and the pilots were always looking for something new. Kyoka had always liked the pilots who came to the tea house. They were generous.

She glanced at the trinkets on her table: a gold locket, a silk scarf, and a lapis lazuli pendent. She wanted to hold them again, if she could only finish her dance.

She turned, gliding across the bamboo floor, and slid out her well-worn fan. It fluttered with every careful hand wave, gentle and graceful. Many compared her to a butterfly searching for the perfect lotus petal. Every movement carried centuries of tradition and honor, and Kyoka was determined to capture the meaning, even if it still was beyond her understanding. The lone strings vibrated inside her, their rhythm carrying both fan and feet alike.

Kyoka was an artist. The men had told her so. The other maiko and geisha had agreed, even if their lying eyes told different tales. She had been made to know better. Kyoka could codify and process the hot jealousy in their eyes.

The tea cooled on the table beside the stage.

Once she had performed these dances for many clients. Cursed with the memory of each transaction, Kyoka could envision every man's smile and wide-eyed enthusiasm. When she danced, they would lean forward, lips parted, following her every step. They had many conversations, interesting and human, she supposed, though small talk was a required part of her job. The other geisha had told her no man enjoyed her words, only her everlasting youth. Kyoka knew they were wrong. The men came from all over the world in their steam-powered ships and clockwork rockets, bringing trinkets of gold and diamond and silk just for her. Whether American, British, or Moroccan, they came to see Kyoka, not the other girls and their imperfections.

Kyoka was the star, the light in the dark. That is what the banner had said, so it had to be right.

The world was different now. For some of the weary captains, Kyoka had been a novelty. To others, she had been a mere curiosity. In these times, she was nothing.

If only she knew shame.

She dipped low and opened her palms. The metal joints in her arms popped and grated together, threatening to seize. Kyoka had no choice but to ignore the strain and pushed her body into a low sweep. Many men had said her grace was like that of a goddess. Was she still graceful? If one of those kind men were to return, would they look at her the same?

Kyoka clung to the memories. The images were clear and sharp like watching moving pictures on a screen. If she could judge, those times had been good times, the days before she had been given to Takahachi.

She circled the floor with restrained steps, slipping into her snow dance performance, and called on those old memories to mask the peeling paint and the dripping water pooling in the corners of the building. The weathered walls melted away, and once again, the ochaya sprung to life, new and fresh in muted colors of red and yellow, serving the best in entertainment.

The opium dealers had left, leaving her a new audience. The chittering of rats as they scurried across the floor undermined the sweet music she played. Kyoka never liked the rats. They would chew on the wiring and get lost in the pipes. She wondered if they would chew on her. Takahachi had always been the one to chase them away.

She continued her dance and shielded the rats from her vision.

Takahachi had loved her. He had loved her dances best, her grace, and everything special included in her packaging. The business man had loved her so much that he had wanted Kyoka not to just see the world, but also feel the world. The world contained more than dance and song, he would say with an old smile that held the years Kyoka's face denied.

Takahachi had sowed the seeds to make her feel, for her to

begin to understand.

Sometimes she believed she missed him. Sometimes she wished she could dance for him again. Most days those feelings floated above her, strange and alien. If only Takahachi had not left her caught between two worlds, trapped between knowing and feeling.

Kyoka smiled her unending smile and bowed, finishing the final move in her performance. The gears inside her breast would reset, and she would begin her neverending rituals again: the tea, the talk, the dance.

All for the man who sat dead in his chair, unable to finish his final programming.

THE PIRATES OF BAJA
DAVID LEE SUMMERS

Ramon Morales stepped up to the door of a shack near the waterfront in San Pedro, California. The sign over the door read "Southern Pacific Railroad." The railroad had just finished its line into Los Angeles and was now pouring money into the port so it could compete with Central Pacific's rail and shipping interests in Northern California. Ramon was tired after spending the day talking to numerous foremen and supervisors. Three of them said they might have work for him next week and that he should check back. All of them suggested he should talk to Bryan Burke at the railroad office. Ramon rapped on the shack's door.

"Come in," came a voice from the other side.

Ramon entered the shack and was greeted by a tall, lanky, balding man with a sly but affable smile. "Mr. Burke?" asked Ramon.

"That's me." Burke indicated a seat in front of the desk. "What can I do for you?"

Ramon introduced himself, then turned and closed the door. "I'm new in Los Angeles and I'm looking for a job."

Burke nodded and sat down behind the desk. He steepled his fingers under his nose. "What kind of experience do you have, Mr. Morales?"

"Most recently I was a ranch hand in Mesilla, New Mexico." He sat down opposite Mr. Burke. "I've done a lot of repair work on corrals and barns. I'm good with a hammer and a saw."

Burke frowned. "What other experience do you have?"

Ramon chewed his lower lip, debating how much to tell the railroad man. He didn't want to lose a potential job because someone asked for references and found out he was a wanted man. Finally, he took a deep breath and let it out slowly. "I was a sheriff in New Mexico territory." He settled on the truth without too many specifics.

Burke's eyes widened. "Really? Are you a fast draw?"

Ramon pursed his lips and shrugged. "I'm pretty good."

"Can you show me?"

Ramon chuckled. "I'm afraid I don't have a gun. I didn't think I'd need it for construction work."

"No worries, my boy." Burke walked over to a cabinet in the corner of the room. He retrieved a gun belt and handed it to Ramon. "It's a Navy Colt. Sometimes people try to steal supplies. It can come in handy around here."

Ramon took the belt and strapped it around his waist. He had to admit it felt good to have a gun on his hip again. "Are you looking for a security guard?"

Burke's brow furrowed. "Something like that." He stepped back and held out his hand. "Let me see that draw."

"I'm a little out of practice. Give me a minute to get the feel of this rig."

"Take your time."

As Burke returned to the desk, Ramon drew the Colt and evaluated its weight. He slipped it into the holster and drew it a couple of times, getting the feel of the metal against leather. Finally he took a stance, narrowed his eyes, reached for the gun, and aimed.

"I'm impressed," admitted Burke. "Are you as accurate as you are fast?"

"Yeah, I'm pretty good."

"Let's see." Burke opened the shack's rear door. They walked out onto the wooden pier. At the end of the pier, a target was set up.

"Do you do a lot of target practice, Mr. Burke?"

"Let's just say I'm looking for some highly qualified men for a job I have in mind." He indicated the target. "Let's see how you do." He retrieved three rounds of ammunition from his coat pocket and handed them to Ramon.

Ramon placed the cartridges into the revolver and snapped it shut. Holstering the gun, he took a careful stance and evaluated the target. He drew quickly and fired all three rounds into the bull's eye.

Burke nodded. "I think you might do nicely, Mr. Morales. Come inside and let's discuss this job I have in mind."

<>

"You've been hired to do what?" Fatemeh Karimi stood with her hands on her hips.

"Apparently a group of pirates have been harassing ships leaving the Port of Los Angeles. Southern Pacific Railroad wants it stopped." Ramon shrugged. "They offered to pay me a year's wages for a few weeks' work."

"A lot of good that will do if you get killed." Fatemeh shook her head. She walked over to the window of the hotel room they shared and looked out at the whitewashed walls of the surrounding buildings.

"These pirates haven't killed anyone." Ramon stepped up behind her. "Apparently they disable the ships, subdue the crew and steal most of the cargo, then leave."

Fatemeh turned around, her brow furrowed. "How do these pirates disable the ships? Do they fire cannons?"

Ramon shook his head. "Mr. Burke was a little unclear about that. All he said was that the pirates somehow break the rudder. Didn't sound like cannon fire to me."

Fatemeh dropped into a chair with a deep frown. "I still don't like it. It seems like there are a lot of ways you could get hurt."

Ramon moved to the chair next to hers. "There were a lot

of ways I could get hurt when I was sheriff of Socorro." He sat down and met her eyes. "This isn't the job I was looking for, but I think it's a lucky break. We're out of money, but he's already paid me enough to buy a new gun, rent the room for another month, and I should even have enough left over for you to stock up on some new supplies."

Fatemeh sighed. "You know how I feel about taking lives— any lives. Even if these people are pirates, I would not be happy if I found out you killed one of them."

Ramon looked down at his hands, then back up into Fatemeh's eyes. "I know, corazón. But, if what Mr. Burke says is right, I don't think I'll have to fire a shot. These pirates aren't used to encountering resistance. Our ship is the *Stockton*. It's under the command of an experienced Navy captain named Mercer. Our goal is to round up these pirates and bring them to port for trial." He held out his hands. "For me, that sounds like pretty easy work for a year's wages."

Fatemeh closed her eyes and considered what Ramon had told her. She tried to think how pirates could disable a ship without firing a shot. "I presume they'll be careful to make sure the crew of this *Stockton* is trustworthy."

"I would think so. They would need to know they could rely on the crew."

"It seems like the easiest way to disable a ship without firing a shot is to have a spy aboard." Fatemeh inclined her head. "How do you know the pirates will even attack if everyone aboard the ship is loyal?"

"I guess that's a chance we'll have to take." Ramon shrugged.

"Will this Mr. Burke pay you if you don't capture the pirates?"

Ramon looked down at his hands again, but did not lift his eyes. "He says they've been spreading the word that the *Stockton* is carrying a valuable cargo. He's pretty certain the pirates will strike."

"Pretty certain, Ramon?"

She saw Ramon's Adam's apple move as he swallowed

hard. "I'll get to keep the money we've already been paid, even if we don't meet pirates."

Fatemeh nodded. "At least that's something." She stood and looked out the window again. "Be safe, Ramon. I'll say a prayer of protection for you." As she spoke, she considered there might be a more direct way to look out for the man she loved.

◇

Ramon stood by the rail of the *Stockton,* looking out at the vast expanse of ocean. Having grown up in New Mexico, he had never seen so much water in his life. He'd been afraid he might feel seasick, but the gentle rolling of the ship didn't bother him at all. The calm seas had been no worse than riding on a horse or in a train. However, the unbroken seascape all around did make him feel somewhat claustrophobic. He was all too aware that he stood on the deck of a small ship surrounded by many people.

Still, he felt somewhat relieved to have some time away from Fatemeh. He felt a prickle of guilt at that thought—he did love her, after all. However, he was still glad to have some time alone with his own thoughts, to think about the events of the past few months and evaluate their relationship. The voyage gave him some time to consider whether he was ready to settle down and spend the rest of his life with her.

He turned his attention to the afterdeck and saw Captain Mercer watching the horizon. The stout man wore a blue Navy coat and black captain's cap. His cheeks were covered by gray, bristly sideburns. Standing behind the captain was the lanky form of Bryan Burke. Ramon's own concerns about the voyage had been put at ease when he saw that the railroad man would accompany them. Ramon doubted Burke would put himself into more danger than necessary to protect the railroad's interests.

Black smoke poured from a single stack amidships. A steam engine below decks turned the two paddle wheels—one on each side of the ship. The ship also sported three masts. Ramon didn't know much about ships, but assumed that sails could be deployed from the spars if the engine broke down. Lookouts stood in crow's nests at the top of each of the masts.

The boatswain appeared on the *Stockton's* afterdeck and blew his shrill whistle. The first watch of the day was over. A man pushed past Ramon and began climbing up the lines next to him. Ramon looked up, glad that he was spared that duty. He noticed that the man climbing down from the crow's nest didn't seem as dexterous as the man going up. The one coming down took his time and his foot reached around and searched for the ropes below more than other sailors. Finally, the sailor reached the deck. He started to pass Ramon just as the ship lurched and the two bumped into each other.

"Sorry," apologized the sailor in a surprisingly familiar high-pitched voice.

Ramon looked up and blinked at the quickly retreating, olive-skinned sailor. He noticed long black hair tied back and tucked under the shirt collar. Ramon rushed forward and blocked the sailor's path. His mouth dropped open when he realized he was looking into familiar green eyes. "Fatemeh?"

Her cheeks flushed red and she grinned sheepishly. "Hi, Ramon."

"What are you doing here?" Ramon looked up and saw that several sailors were beginning to take notice. He took her by the arm and led her back to where he'd been standing by the ship's rail.

"I wanted to come along and make sure you stayed safe." She shrugged. "Also, it allows us to make a little extra money from this voyage."

"How in the world did you get hired as a sailor?"

"When I came to America from Persia, some of the men showed me how to handle sails and climb the rigging into the crow's nests." She inclined her head. "I'm not as good as all the men on the ship, but I'm good enough that I was able to get a rating as an able seaman."

Ramon opened his mouth to say more, but was interrupted when one of the lookouts shouted from above. "Ship off the larboard bow!"

Looking up, Ramon saw the captain open a telescope and begin scanning the horizon. He turned around and thought he could make out a black cloud in the distance. He realized he saw smoke from another ship.

"Is there something between us and the other ship?" Fatemeh pointed toward the smoke on the horizon.

Ramon tried to see where she was pointing. After a moment, he caught sight of white, roiling water, like a ship's wake moving rapidly toward them. However, he couldn't see any signs of a ship or a boat. "What's going on? Is it an invisible ship or something?"

"I don't think so. Look closer."

Ramon held up his hand to shield his eyes from the sun. There was something dark, very low to the water—maybe just below the surface of the water—generating the wake. "Maybe it's a whale or a dolphin."

"If it's a whale, it's the fastest one I've ever seen."

Ramon nodded. "I'd better go tell the captain." He ran back to ship's stern and climbed the ladder to the afterdeck where Mr. Burke towered over Captain Mercer.

"The ship is definitely coming toward us," said the captain, peering through the telescope.

"Do you think it's the pirates?" asked Burke.

The captain grunted. "We'll soon see."

"Captain," called Ramon as he stepped up to the two men, "there's something between us and that ship, down in the water and approaching fast." He pointed.

The captain turned his telescope toward the place where Ramon pointed. "What the blazes?"

Burke inclined his head. "There's steam coming from the water's surface."

Ramon looked around again. The dark shape in the water was closer and he could see white clouds of vapor billowing just over the water.

The captain gritted his teeth and slammed his telescope shut. "If I didn't know better, I'd say that's a submersible, like the *Hunley* during the war." He turned toward his first officer.

"Beat to quarters, action stations."

The mate nodded and stepped forward calling out, "Action stations!"

A boy—Ramon guessed he must be about thirteen years old—rushed to a locker near the ship's stern. He opened it and retrieved a drum and two sticks. He began beating out a martial rhythm. Armed crewmen rushed out from below decks and lined the rails. Ramon caught sight of Fatemeh near one of the masts. He climbed down from the afterdeck and went to her. "You better get below decks."

Before she could respond, there was a loud crash and the ship listed. Looking up, Ramon noticed that the starboard paddle wheel no longer turned. There was a cry of "All stop!" from the afterdeck. With both wheels stopped, the ship settled upright in the water. Ramon rushed to the rail and saw the dark shape in the water pulling back. It turned and made a wide arc toward the ship's stern. Ramon drew his revolver and fired two shots. Both made a loud clang and a whistle as they hit the metal hull and ricocheted.

Ramon rushed back to the ship's stern and ascended the ladder. Just as he reached the top, there was another crash. He nearly toppled, but held on. The man at the wheel cursed. "They've broken the rudder. We've lost helm control!"

Ramon stepped up next to the captain and saw that the other ship was nearly upon them. He could just make out the ship's name, *Tiburón*—Spanish for shark.

"With no helm and no engines, we're sitting ducks," said the captain. He turned to the first mate. "Prepare to repel boarders."

The first mate bellowed out the order. Ramon felt the level of tension on the ship increase. He drew his revolver, snapped open the cylinder, and replaced the two cartridges he'd already fired.

As the *Tiburón* came alongside, men on the other ship hurled grappling hooks on ropes and grabbed onto the *Stockton's* rails. Ramon took careful aim and picked off one of the men on the other ship. The rest of the pirates ducked below the rail with curses and a few exclamations of surprise. Ramon's brow creased as he began to wonder just how experienced these pirates actually were.

Orders were shouted and three of the pirates leapt to their feet, wielding six-guns. The captain, Burke and Ramon all hit the deck as a hail of bullets flew over their heads. When they looked up, pirates were swinging across from the *Tiburón* to the *Stockton.* Some of the *Stockton's* men fired at the pirates. Two of the buccaneers were hit and fell from the lines, but others landed on the decks. In the close quarters of the ship's decks, the pirates drew knives and flailed them at the men. Others simply waded in with their fists. Ramon went to the afterdeck rail and tried to get a clear shot. He saw one lone pirate and fired, cutting him down, but others turned their attention toward him.

"Uh oh," said Ramon. He ducked as one of the pirates pulled a revolver and fired up at him. By the time he lifted his head, he saw pirates swarming over the afterdeck. Two pirates rushed forward and grabbed the captain's arms. Ramon tried to raise his pistol, but another pirate knocked it from his grip. He put up his hands.

Below, two pirates lowered a rope ladder over the side. Ramon saw the black shape of the strange submarine craft come to the surface. A hatch popped open on the top and a man emerged. As the man climbed the ladder, Ramon noticed that he seemed strangely out of place. He wore a white shirt and a bright blue silk vest, the attire of a gentleman. Around his neck was a black cravat. The only anachronisms were the denim pants common to sailors and a black hat similar to the one Captain Mercer wore.

"Well, it would seem this ship wasn't all we were led to believe," said the man who had appeared from the submersible. He turned and ascended the ladder to the afterdeck. "Who's in charge here?"

"I am Captain John Mercer of the USS *Stockton.*" The captain struggled in the grip of the pirates who held him. "I demand you release my ship."

"You are not in a position to demand anything." The dapper pirate waved his hand. "I'm guessing this ship is not carrying the silver and gold heading for China I expected to find. However, I see quite a fine cargo of ammunition. That would do nicely in exchange for your life, Captain."

With a nod of his head, the pirate captain sent members of his crew below decks to see what they could find. A moment after they left, a pirate led one of the *Stockton's* crew up the ladder. Ramon's breath caught and a knot formed in his stomach when he saw Fatemeh. Her shirt had been ripped and he could discern the soft swell of her breast.

"Ah, it would seem the *Stockton* transports other things of value besides ammunition," said the pirate captain with undisguised delight.

"No!" shouted Ramon. The back of his head exploded with pain and everything went black.

◇

Fatemeh was taken aboard the *Tiburón* and locked in a small, but nicely appointed cabin. There was a bed—more comfortable than the hammock she had aboard the *Stockton*. There were some books on the shelf. She took one and leafed through the pages. It was written in Spanish. On the cabin's small desk was a locked box. She picked it up and found it was rather heavy and rattled. Looking around, she saw a trunk. Opening it, she found shirts and pants. She replaced her shirt, torn in the scuffle with the pirate crew.

Opening the cabin's window, she saw she was on the opposite side of the pirate ship from the *Stockton*. She lay down on the bed and listened to the sounds of the pirates scuffling on the deck above and outside her door. She tried to discern exactly what they were doing. Loud bumps and thumps came from different parts of the ship and she could imagine cargo being secured. She wondered if the submersible was stowed aboard the ship or traveled alongside.

The engines soon fired up and she thought she could discern motion. Kneeling on the bed, she craned her head as far out of the window as she could and saw the *Stockton* receding in the distance. She hoped Ramon was okay—he had taken a nasty blow to the back of the head. She lay back on the bed, chewed her lower lip, and wondered what was going to happen next.

The sky was darkening when someone rapped at the door. A key rattled in the lock and a sailor in a torn and bloodstained shirt looked in. He said something in Spanish and gestured with his hand. She gathered she was supposed to follow and it appeared that he was being polite rather than demanding.

Fatemeh followed the sailor to a cabin at the ship's stern. He opened the door. Inside, a table was laid out with a sumptuous meal. There was meat in a rich, brown sauce, a cauldron of soup, a bowl with beans, and a basket that appeared filled with tortillas. The ship's captain sat at the head of the table. He stood and held out a chair. "I am Captain Onofre Cisneros. Welcome to the *Tiburón.*"

"Thank you." Fatemeh entered the cabin and the sailor closed the door behind her.

"Do you like your cabin?"

"I do, thank you." Fatemeh sat in the chair held by the captain. "I hope I'm not putting its owner to any discomfort."

The captain returned to his seat at the head of the table. "I'm afraid he won't be needing it again. The cabin belonged to my first mate and he was killed today." He looked down at his lap and sniffed. He took a deep breath and blew it out, then looked up again.

"I'm sorry for your loss."

The captain shrugged, then reached out for a flask of wine. "I suppose it's expected when you engage in piracy." He poured a glass of wine for Fatemeh and then one for himself.

"You suppose?" Fatemeh's gaze narrowed. "From what I was told, you've been menacing ships for quite some time."

Captain Cisneros laughed outright. "Is that what you were told?"

Fatemeh sat back and thought about what she had seen. The pirates were not well armed. They only had a few knives and pistols. "You weren't expecting the kind of resistance you met on the *Stockton,* were you?"

"I should have known better." Captain Cisneros lifted the glass and took a drink. "After taking two ships easily, I should have expected heavier resistance with the third."

"You've only taken two ships?" When the captain didn't answer, Fatemeh lifted her own glass and took a drink. She nodded appreciatively. "I don't normally drink alcohol, but this wine is quite good."

"It is made from grapes that grow near my home in Ensenada." Cisneros reached out and spooned some of the meat in brown sauce onto his plate. "Try the chicken molé. My cook outdoes himself."

Fatemeh took the dish and served herself.

Cisneros leaned forward. "What else have you been told about me and my pirates?"

"Only that you somehow disable ships without firing a shot."

"Nothing about the submersible?"

"No."

The captain's eyebrows came together. He looked down at his plate and shook his head. Fatemeh sensed that Cisneros was frustrated.

"These raids... they're not really about piracy, or even gold, are they?" Cisneros remained silent, so Fatemeh ventured another guess. "You're trying to get attention for your submarine craft, aren't you?"

Cisneros retrieved a tortilla, then took a sip of the wine. "Ten years ago—when Emperor Maximillian was on the throne—I owned a gold mine in Sonora. I had a number of wealthy French investors and I did quite well for myself." He took a bite of the chicken in molé sauce and took another sip of wine. "However, Mexican resistance to the French proved too costly and they finally withdrew. I was afraid my mine would be seized by President Juárez's soldiers, so I took what money I could and fled to Ensenada." He took a bite of his tortilla. "I always loved the sea."

Fatemeh took a tentative taste of the chicken molé. Her first impression was chocolate. Then hot spices danced on her tongue. She washed it down with a sip of wine. "So you turned to piracy to make a living?"

The captain pursed his lips and shook his head. "Not really. You see, when I still had the mine, I came across plans for a submarine vessel from Spain called the *Ictíneo*. It was built by an inventor named Narcís Monturiol i Estarrol. Even before I was a mine owner, I was an engineer. Estarrol's plans fascinated me and I wondered if I could improve on his design. I hoped I could sell it to the Mexican Navy. However, by the time I finished the craft, President Tejada wasn't interested."

Fatemeh nodded. "From what I've heard about submarine boats, they're rather dangerous aren't they? The *Hunley* was lost with all hands during the American Civil War." Her stomach rumbled and she took a portion of beans.

"The *Hunley* was a poor design. The men only had the air aboard that was there when they closed the hatches." The captain shook his head. "Estarrol solved that problem by inventing a chemical reaction steam engine. My *Legado* uses the same type of engine. Fuel rods create a chemical reaction that heats the water. Oxygen is released as the fuel rods are used up. You can stay under water as long as you have fuel."

"Legado?" asked Fatemeh around a forkful of beans.

"That's the name of my submarine vessel. The English word is legacy." The captain took another sip of wine. "Anyway, when the Mexican government refused to buy the *Legado,* I was left with no money. I had to find a way to recoup my investment."

"But why piracy?" Fatemeh narrowed her gaze.

"To get attention," said Cisneros. "I had hoped that word of my boat would make it to the owners of the ships I attacked, or even President Grant himself. That's why I ordered my men not to kill the crews of the ships. I hoped someone would seek out the creator of the submarine to learn more about it."

"You didn't think they would hunt you down?"

Cisneros snorted. "Again, that's why I left the crews alive. I thought people would be more curious than angry."

The captain and Fatemeh ate in silence for a time. Finally, Fatemeh paused and pointed her fork at the captain. "Would you be able to use your submersible to repair ships?"

Cisneros sat back and wiped his lips with a napkin. "I suppose so, Estarrol imagined that he could use the *Ictíneo* to rescue divers."

"Scientists might also pay to use such a craft to explore the ocean." Fatemeh leaned forward. "Is Ensenada a good port?"

"It could be, with some development."

"You've raided two gold ships at this point. Have you made back your investment in the *Legado?*"

The captain nodded. "Very close."

"I think you see that piracy isn't going to get you the attention you want. Maybe you should find a better way to make people aware of your submersible. Perhaps Ensenada could be developed into a port to rival Los Angeles or even San Francisco. The *Legado* could be used to make repairs more efficiently than they could be made at other ports."

The captain placed his napkin on the table and stood. He walked to the windows at the back of the cabin and looked out toward the night sky. "The only problem is that I'm now a wanted man. I suspect the captain of the *Stockton* would like nothing more than to see me swinging from the yardarm of his ship."

Fatemeh sighed. She didn't approve of Captain Cisneros's decision to pursue piracy, but he had avoided killing. He was a good engineer. "Perhaps we could speak to Captain Mercer and Mr. Burke aboard the *Stockton*. If they would drop the charges against you, would you give up piracy?"

"Do you think they would listen?" The captain's eyes remained locked on the darkened ocean outside his window.

Fatemeh chewed her lower lip. "To be honest, I'm not sure."

"Why would you suggest this?" The captain turned his head. "Even though I've only attacked three ships, I'm still a pirate and I have taken you hostage. Even if we succeed, how do you know I would not simply return to piracy?"

Fatemeh nodded. "Your actions speak louder than words, sir. You could have chosen to lock me in your brig, rape me, or even kill me. You could have used the *Legado* to sink the

Stockton. Instead you merely disabled her and you've left the crews you've come across alive. You would rather get rich selling the plans for the *Legado* than stealing gold."

Cisneros looked at his feet but did not say a word. Turning, he went to the door and summoned one of the sailors. The sailor escorted Fatemeh back to the first mate's cabin. She heard him turn the key in the lock. Sitting on the bunk, she wondered what the captain would decide.

<>

"Ship approaching!"

Ramon was lying in his hammock aboard the *Stockton* when he heard the call from on deck. The *Stockton* had been adrift for two days and he wondered how long it would be before they were rescued. He rolled out of the hammock and as soon as his feet hit the deck, his head began to throb anew. He closed his eyes until the pain subsided just a bit, then made his way outside.

In the distance, Ramon saw the smoke from a ship's steam engine. He climbed the ladder to the afterdeck and stood next to Captain Mercer and Mr. Burke. The captain scanned the approaching ship with his telescope. After a moment, he snapped it shut. "I'll be damned if it's not the *Tiburón*."

"Why would she come back?" asked Burke. "They already took everything we have of value."

"There are a few things that fancy-pants pirate could still take and I'll be damned if I let him have them." The captain stormed off the afterdeck, leaving Ramon alone with Burke.

As the *Tiburón* approached, Ramon noticed that she flew a white flag from the stern. He hadn't noticed if there had been a flag there before.

Burke watched the ship through his own telescope. "They're launching a boat."

Ramon picked up the captain's abandoned telescope and looked toward the *Tiburón*. His heart skipped a beat when he realized one of the people in the boat was Fatemeh. The others were the dandy captain and two of his sailors. Before long, they came abreast of the *Stockton's* side.

Captain Mercer appeared on deck wielding a Navy Colt revolver. Ramon realized he must have had it hidden in his cabin and the pirates missed it when they were cleaning out the ship's store of weapons and ammunition. The captain took aim and fired at the boat. The shot went wide and there was a splash of water next to the boat. Seeing the danger to Fatemeh, Ramon launched himself down the ladder and tackled the captain.

"This is mutiny," growled Mercer.

"They're under a white flag and Fatemeh is aboard that boat," countered Ramon.

The captain pushed Ramon off and made a grab for the revolver. Ramon kicked it further out of reach. "She was aboard under false pretenses," said Mercer. "As far as I'm concerned she can hang with the damned pirates."

As he spoke, Bryan Burke descended the ladder and picked up the captain's revolver. "Just so, I would like to hear what they have to say. As Mr. Morales points out, they're under a white flag."

The captain sneered. "Very well."

He motioned for two of the crew to lower a rope ladder over the side. Once the boat from the *Tiburón* came alongside, the pirate captain and Fatemeh climbed aboard. The pirate bowed to Captain Mercer. "I have come to offer assistance to you and your vessel. Furthermore, if you agree not to pursue me, I will cease my raids on American vessels."

"The only thing I'm interested in is your unconditional surrender!" shouted Captain Mercer.

Burke's eyes narrowed. "Are you really willing to give up your raids on our ships? Why the change of heart?"

Fatemeh swallowed. "Captain Cisneros realizes that piracy isn't as profitable as he once thought."

Mercer turned toward Burke. "Don't trust them. They're pirates. She came aboard under false pretenses. She's probably a spy for him."

"She is no spy," interjected Ramon. "I would trust her with my life."

"All I want is to see these pirates hang!" Mercer's face was beet red.

"You forget your place, Captain Mercer." Burke's voice was calm. "This is not a Navy ship. This ship is under contract to the Southern Pacific Railroad and I decide what is in the best interests of the mission."

"I am captain of this ship," growled the captain through gritted teeth.

"Not anymore." Burke motioned for the first officer. "Mr. Reed. You're in command. Please escort Captain Mercer below and then join us on deck."

Reed saluted. "Yes, sir." He called for two of the sailors to help him.

"I will not stand for this," Mercer shouted as the men led him below decks. "I will be calling a maritime board of inquiry!"

Burke looked to Captain Cisneros once the door closed on the captain's shouting. "What can you do to help us?"

The pirate captain smiled. "I would like to offer the services of my submersible, the *Legado*. I believe we can use it to repair the damage to the *Stockton.*"

Burke nodded approvingly. "I would like to see that. If it works out, would you be interested in licensing your patent to Southern Pacific Railroad?"

"We could certainly discuss that." Cisneros smiled and looked to Fatemeh.

She winked at the pirate. "See, this is a far better way to get attention for your craft and a far better application than naval warfare."

Burke and Cisneros shook hands. As Mr. Reed came out on deck again, Burke's expression turned hard. "Although I am interested in your submersible, I must warn you, if I agree to this and then find you've returned to your ways of piracy, I will not stop the next captain I send to hunt you down." He cast a meaningful glance at Reed.

Cisneros nodded. "I understand."

With that, Burke followed Reed up the ladder to the afterdeck.

Cisneros looked at Fatemeh. "You've given me new hope. What can I ever do to repay you?"

Fatemeh looked from Cisneros to Ramon, then she looked back to the *Tiburón*. "I do have something in mind."

<>

Ramon sat in a small seat looking out through windows in the *Legado's* side. He had never imagined there were so many varieties and colors of fish. The submersible dove deeper and they moved along the floor of the Pacific. The former sheriff of Socorro, New Mexico marveled at the sight of the corals and forests of undersea plants that swayed in the currents. He looked to the seat opposite him and smiled at Fatemeh, who was similarly enraptured by the sights visible through the windows. Captain Cisneros stood at the helm. His head disappeared into a small pillbox-shaped protrusion that rose above the submarine's hull with a window facing forward.

Ramon turned and peered out at the ocean again. Although the submarine was smaller than the *Stockton,* Ramon no longer felt claustrophobic. Instead he felt like he was seeing the future, and he could see no limits to the possibilities.

TIME OF AUTUMN
AIDAN FRITZ

The sweet smell of boiling azuki beans swirled through the flat. Weighed down with helium canisters, one under each arm and a third strapped to her back, Hana avoided her father's glance. He wore his head-mounted monocular loupe and as long as she didn't drop the canisters, she should escape to the Jade's team meeting. Her hand touched the door.

"Hana!" He placed the clockwork ancestor on the table, the heart gear still turning, thwapping a rubber band against the body cavity. "What day is this?"

She stared at the bamboo floor. "Chuseok." The Time of Autumn was the harvest festival, a day to remember her ancestors and the day of the ceremonial match, her Jade Buddhas against the Ice Tigers. "The team needs me."

"Your ancestors need you."

"Old brother bears my responsibilities."

"Shin isn't here."

Older brother had followed her father, learning the art of clockwork ancestor construction. He had spent the night at the shop to finish last-minute flairs requested by clients. Normally, her father would have been at the shop as well. Normally, her grandfather would've still been alive. She missed him. If she kept herself busy with her team's last-minute preparations, she could keep the emptiness away.

Her father's knees creaked as he stood. His callused hands—crisscrossed by tiny scars where gears and needle-sharp crankshafts had cut his fingertips—daubed at the tear threatening to fall. "You meant the world to him. He would have wanted—"

"I can't." Her father wanted too much. She had to help the team. Scouts from the engineer's guild would attend the preparation beforehand and the game itself. She'd learned how to work with compressed helium from her grandfather, and she could best honor his name by helping her team win. Grandfather would be proud if the scouts saw her and selected her as an apprentice.

"You must. Your mother and I need you."

"I'll miss the game."

"Forget the game." He stepped away to withdraw into himself. He'd always said anger had no seat in arguments. "Sorry. You won't miss the game. Your mother needs help with the songpyeon." Hana always liked the songpyeon, traditional sweets for the ancestors.

Her mother's voice called from the kitchen. "I can mold and stuff the rice dumplings, but we're out of pine needles. Hana."

Hana bit her lower lip. She'd planned to go into the hills last night, but instead she'd spent the evening at the clubhouse working on the finishing touches of the woven mat of their team's wooden ship. It'd taken longer than she had expected. "Do you really need the pine needles? The songpyeon is only for our ancestors."

"Hana!" Fire flashed in Father's eyes. Hana knew some of her friends were hit by their fathers, but hers had never done that. Yet.

She would disappoint the Jade's captain, Bai, if she arrived late. It had been her idea to use balloons to lift the ceremonial wooden ship so the team pushing the ship could focus on maneuvering instead of lifting. Many of the team lived in the farm districts beyond the reach of the pressure-driven helium network of pipes that brought the lighter than air gas to their flat. She'd promised to bring the canisters.

"You shame your mother and me. Is this how you will treat

us when we die?"

"I promised them I'd help with the preparations."

Her father scowled. "Plenty of time to gather needles before attending the game."

"I can't."

"You will or this house will be closed to you."

Breath whistled through Hana's lips. Even if the scouts selected her as a candidate, the guild wouldn't accept a houseless apprentice. She had no choice. When her father was worked up enough that he clenched his fists, she knew she couldn't change his mind. She crossed her fingers hoping the last-minute preparation would distract Bai and he wouldn't notice her late arrival. She wouldn't count on that luck because lately he'd become cross with her and she didn't understand why. She wanted the same thing he did, a Jade Buddha victory.

She slammed the two canisters she carried against the bamboo floor. She'd collect them when she returned with the pine needles. She stormed out the doorway of their flat to their balcony where she unslung the canister from her pack, selected a rubber balloon and pulled it tight over the canister's nozzle. The air inflated the balloon and she hooked the woven steel-line mesh over the balloon and to her harness.

Her safety anchor held her to the balcony and with the balloon full, it tugged toward the crisscrossing lines above her. She released the lock on the anchor and kicked toward the lines. She drifted near a wire and waited until one of the transports passed, a helium balloon pulling the gondola upwards faster than she could walk to the edge of town where the forests began.

Catching a rung on the bottom of the gondola, she tugged on the lever that opened a flap on the top of the balloon to release helium. She hooked the carabiner onto the hold and swung rhythmically over the city, flinching a little at the screeching of the wires, which was louder outside the gondola than inside where the walls deadened the noise.

<>

Hana held the ceremonial spear as she stood on the spare wooden ship the Jades used in scrimmages. Bai swiped his spear at Hana's legs, catching her behind the knee and spilling her to the woven rice leaves of her platform. Her breath caught. The platform shook as the boatpushers carrying her boat retreated so she could regain her feet. Bai waited.

He had been upset when she'd finally arrived with the helium canisters. The scrimmage was his idea even though they should be conserving strength for the competition this evening. He proposed the scrimmage so the boatpushers would grow accustomed to the decrease in weight afforded by the balloons. She couldn't argue against that plan or his proposal she captain the scrimmage boat. He'd known she would look like a coward if she declined. But, it was clear he was upset. Bai didn't try to spill her ship, knock it to the ground to force the end of the battle. No. Bai's boatpushers engaged so Bai could pummel her with his padded spear.

Clambering to her feet, Hana gripped the spear. Her boatpushers heaved against their wooden holds. The wind curled against Hana's face. Bai might think this was a lesson for her. She didn't understand his motives. She decided if he was going to punish her, she'd find a way to make the challenge end. The boatpushers needed their energy for the bout this evening.

Bai swung at her, but this time she got her spear in the way, deflected his thrust so he spun and the spear tangled itself in one of the ropes of the balloons holding his boat. She swung upwards, seeing the balloons, and pierced one of them. The hiss jerked the wooden boat as the balloon swayed while it deflated. Bai fell to his platform.

"Unfair."

"Rules say nothing about balloons."

Bai swung, catching her shoulder twisting her around, but her stumbling foot found the edge of the boat and kept her upright. Her ship rammed the side of Bai's and the grip of his men slipped and their boat crashed to the ground.

Jae-kwan, the leader of Hana's boatpushers, shouted, "Hana wins!" His cheer was echoed by the others. "The balloons were her idea. She's defeated Bai. I vote she captains the ship tonight."

"No," screamed Bai. "It was practice."

Hana leaned against a balloon's rope, catching her breath, startled at Jae-kwan's support. She looked at the faces of the others, and saw them looking to her for guidance. It surprised her. Even the boatpushers who had carried Bai's boat, moved away from him. Hana knew the balloons would impress the scouts for the guild. They would ask questions, and someone would tell them she had proposed the change. But, captaining the ship. Everyone would see her then. If they won, the engineering guild must accept her.

"Everyone for Hana as Captain, shout aye." A thunderous roar answered Jae-kwan. "Those against."

Bai's shout was tortured. He sulked toward the back of the crowd as the team crowded close to congratulate Hana. She lost sight of him, but he was the least of her concerns. She hadn't worked with the rest of the boatpushers on the strategies and signals they would use against the Tigers.

Jae-kwan would act as second to the leader of Bai's boatpushers. The three discussed the calls she'd use to direct them and prepared herself for the competition. She found it hard to concentrate on the strategies and the vocal calls. She was going to be captain.

An explosion rained bits of plaster onto the square where they had scrimmaged and where Hana still worked through the strategies for tonight. She looked up the hill as a silence lingered in the wake of the explosion. It was in the direction where her family lived, but explosions happened all the time. Usually in the steam pumps housed in the ceiling of the buildings. It happened frequently enough that she and the other boatpushers returned to strategizing.

"Hana." Her older brother's cheeks were stained with ash.

The boatpushers retreated to leave Hana with Shin. "Why aren't you at the shop?"

"Father. You must come." He turned and jogged back the way he'd come. Hana's throat constricted, and she ran after him, catching him. People crowded the streets around them and she thought she saw Bai as she neared their flat. He didn't live near this part of town and when she looked to see if she'd seen true, she couldn't find him in the crowd. She had a sick feeling when she saw the flat, a hole gaped from where their balcony usually stood, exposing her father's workroom.

<>

Shin left her father's room with the doctor. Their faces were unreadable as they walked toward the balcony with its makeshift door and the rubber that Hana had stretched over the hole blasted in the wall.

"Where are you going?" Hana asked.

Shin stopped on the threshold. Ash still stained his cheeks. "The shop. The dead do not wait." The door slammed behind him.

Her father waved when she peeked through the door to his room. Straps lifted his leg to the side with bandages thick around it, red blood staining the knee. Hana entered the room and knelt at the edge of his bed while her mother fidgeted in the kitchen. The whole place stank of steamed pine needles. Her father opened his hand. In the palm, the clockwork ancestor figure of her grandfather rolled, wooden pins for his arms swinging with the motion and his head bobbling on the thin neck.

She looked at the clockwork ancestor, the eyes blinking up at her, the wrinkles around them caught and carved for eternity around her grandfather's eyes in the same crinkled pattern he'd had. Her gut twisted. Her father wasn't in the shop because he needed to finish the clockwork ancestor. Once completed, he would have taken the clockwork figure to their ancestor's cave on the side of Mt. Deokamsom along with the customary songpyeon. She placed her hand over his palm and the wooden limbs pulsed against hers with their clockwork life.

"I can't take your grandfather to the cave. I know you wanted to watch the competition, but Shin must work the shop. I need—"

"I know." The journey by balloon up the sides of Mt. Deokamsom was slow, but not that slow. A plan formed in her mind. The helium pulled the gondola sleds and would pull a lower-weight rider much faster. She'd have enough time to get to their ancestor's cave and back if she hurried. "I will take grandfather."

<>

With a tank of helium on her back, Hana marched to the center of Bugok village where the sleds launched up to Mt. Deokamsom's heights. The square also contained a public nozzle for drawing helium, but she wouldn't need that.

The crisscrossed wires ran in parallel groups of three. The sleds moved along the wires and a driver could pull a lever to loosen the sled from the outside wire and flip it to the other side. This allowed one to pass a slower moving sled. Hana would need that maneuver in her ascent. She grabbed a single-person sled from the stack.

The sledrunner began to fill a small balloon for her, cinching it onto her harness. She grabbed his hand to stop him. "No, I need one of the gondola balloons."

"Not for you."

"I can handle the speed." Hana hoped she could. She'd never actually done this before, but it would be the only way to reach the ancestral cave and return before the competition began.

"Not safe."

"Are you a fan of the Jade Buddhas or the Ice Tigers?"

"The Jades of course. Has nothing to do with this."

Hana scrunched the sleeve over her right shoulder to expose the Buddha tattoo. "I'm the captain."

"No. I know the lad who drives for them."

"Bai no longer captains." She made the sign of the Jades. "I do. I need speed."

He released the latch on the top of the balloon and it sagged. "Don't crash. You risk more than your life." If she crashed into a gondola, knocking it free from the wires, there would be an investigation and a scapegoat needed. He grabbed the larger balloons used for the gondolas, and latched it to her harness. A bit of tension left her. Getting the sledrunner to give her a gondola balloon had been the biggest risk to her plan.

When he released the anchors, the force of the balloon slingshot her into the air, her harness swinging; the clockwork ancestor of her grandfather pushed by the force of the wind against the packet strung around her neck to press against her breastbone.

"Almost there, grandfather." At her words, the clockworks vibrated.

She flicked the lever holding the sled in its path and jumped into the oncoming traffic as she raced past a floating gondola. Faster than the swans, she rose into the sky. The flats disappeared as she moved further from the city. The ground greened with well-watered rice leaves as she left the city and flew over farmer's fields.

She approached another gondola and placed a finger on the lever. The open wire vibrated; a tell-tale note of a solo traveler descending downhill. They'd cross the gondola about the same time she arrived at that position. Gritting her teeth, she pulled the lever for the brake as she approached the gondola.

The brake squealed and sparks flew. A puff of smoke popped where the brake had ridden to the side of the wire. Light glinted from the sled's brake housing as it fell. She hadn't slowed at all. She would ram into the gondola, or the person sliding. Neither acceptable.

Hana climbed her sled's rigging while grabbing the helium canister from over her back. She pushed it against the wire above her head. Sparks flew into her face, scorching her skin, but none of them flew upwards. Lucky. She hadn't planned that part, but she slowed, just enough to feel the rush of air as the solo traveler passed her. She swung into the side path and passed the gondola. Once her heart had calmed, she returned the canister to her pack.

The rice fields became discontinuous as they moved into

the forests on the side of the mountain. Something manmade glinted with reflected sunlight. The direction of the light made it impossible to be a pool of water. Moments later, a knife flew through the air, blade spinning end over end to cut into her balloon. Air hissed. She slowed and fell backward, sliding toward town.

Hana placed a hand over her grandfather. She would get him to their ancestral cave. She didn't have to continue. She could ride the sled into town, could forget her duty, but that was not a choice she could make and face her father. She'd accepted the responsibility and would see it through. She pulled the lever to release both ends of the sled and fell. The rags of the balloon held just enough helium, combined with the drag of the rigging, to slow her fall. She rolled when she hit the ground.

The descent had brought her close to the place where she'd seen the glint of the knife before it caught her balloon. In the brush under a tree, the leaves shuddered. She leaped the final distance and knocked the person on the other side to the ground. Bai stared at her.

She hadn't expected to see him. "Why?"

"I am captain." Bai punched her. Hana's grip loosened and he rolled away.

"They won't let you."

Bai pulled another knife from his belt. "When you don't return, no choice."

"You don't need to threaten me. I'm returning my grandfather to the hall."

"You stole my position as captain. I can't trust you."

Hana fell backward, her ankle colliding with a root. Her back hurt when she landed on the helium canister. Bai charged her. She parried the blade with a stick. He gripped the knife with two hands, kneeling over her, preparing to stab down. She flinched to the side, just far enough. His strike, aimed at her neck, hit the strap of the pack holding the canister. Her shoulder ached. She rolled away, getting distance between them before she collapsed against a tree. Her pack hung from one shoulder. She pulled the canister in front of her as Bai neared. She sprayed helium into his face, knocking him to the ground. She pulled another balloon from the pack and held it over the nozzle. Unanchored, she rose into the air.

Bai threw another knife. The handle hit the side of her shin to deflect into the forest. He chased after her, but even though the balloon didn't move that quickly, she didn't have to evade the trees and other obstacles as she climbed the mountain's flanks. She 'just managed to avoid crossing the wire paths. The wind might turn at any point to blow her away from the mountain. When the leaves stopped flapping from Bai's struggle through them, she opened the flap to release some of the helium and descended.

<>

By the time Hana had climbed to the ledge where the entrance yawned to the cave of her ancestral hall, her stomach growled. The hike had taken longer than the balloons would have and left her starving. She smelled the pine scent of the songpyeon and the thought of their sweet azuki bean filling made her mouth water. The clockwork ancestors had no need of a food offering, but she did. She dangled her feet from a rock ledge and ate while the sky started to turn the color of cherry blossoms.

Her stomach full, she turned to the cave where the sun, low in the sky, splayed into the cave to illuminate the platform where dozens of clockwork ancestors stood. She placed her grandfather amongst them. The other clockwork figures didn't move to accommodate the addition of her grandfather. The new clockwork ancestor twisted, moving with a shaking step as he approached the right side of the platform. A nozzle extended from the cave's wall. Geothermal heat created steam that was captured in these pipes and used to power the clockwork figures.

Near the nozzle was a stack of bark plates with dark songpyeon stains. With a twinge, she placed the plate she'd brought on the others. The living were more deserving than those who'd died. Her grandfather pushed against the nozzle. She expected a puff of steam to escape before her grandfather's gasket closed. Instead he backed away from the nozzle and approached it several times before turning toward her, clockwork arms held so the palms flapped on the edge of the wooden pins.

The pipe had no condensation on it and she shifted her fingers toward it, careful in case it would burn, but the metal was cold. Feeling backward along the pipe, her hands moved over the boiler that collected the geothermal steam with a one-way permeable seal. It had a compartment for fuel, but that wasn't used, just the chamber to collect the steam. The pipe on the other side was also cold and she explored until she found a bend in the pipe where rust had eaten through the metal. Upset, wishing she wasn't here, wishing she was on a wooden ship at the moment, preparing for the competition that would start after sunset, she knew she couldn't leave her grandfather here without fuel. Or the other clockwork figures.

She searched through the cave. She'd overheard her father talking with her brother. One need not carry tools from the city but could use the set in the maintenance toolchest. The door was stuck and when she yanked, it came loose, spilling across the floor. Pieces of pipe rolled to the sides of the room, but none of the pieces could replace the rusted bend. She grabbed an endcap. Using a wrench she removed the bad pipe, and replaced it with the end. In twilight, she collected sticks and lit a fire in the boiler compartment.

The roar of a cannon rolled over the hillsides below her. It signified the beginning of the competition. Hana wondered who captained the ship in her place. Without her, the scouts wouldn't even know that it was her idea for the balloons. She'd failed her team and she'd failed her grandfather.

"What is wrong my daughter?"

"You...you talk."

"Of course. What would be the point of clockwork figures if we were nothing more than the wood from which we were constructed? If we could not communicate with our children?"

"But, why haven't the figures talked to me before?"

The clockwork head bobbled. "Did you know my father?" The hand jerked to point at his chest cavity. "Must be a tie, a reason for speaking. A twining of knowledge and service."

The figure moved towards the nozzle and Hana's eyes fell upon the bark plates. She should have known the dumplings had a purpose. "The songpyeon. But I didn't—"

"Sometimes, one provides more necessary service." Steam hissed before the gasket formed a seal. He returned to her side, placing a hand on her knuckle. "You did not answer my question."

Hana closed her eyes and saw a brief imagining of herself guiding the Jade's boat to a win, but the dream faded out. It wasn't so much that dream she wanted, but the dream of entering the guild. A future that moved out of reach. She felt the loss but worried her grandfather would think it inconsequential compared to his loss of body. "It is nothing."

"Never lie to your ancestors. I still remember the heat of my body, but as time passes it will grow harder to understand more than a surface of your words. Remember, the heart is never nothing. You mourn captaining."

She'd never been able to hide anything from grandfather. "How do you know?"

"I heard that boy."

"It's not the captaining. It's entering the engineer's guild. I let you down."

"No, daughter. Don't treat life like balancing on a log over whitewater rapids where one misstep leaves you battered on the rocks. Rather make your life like the yellow-throated marten climbing a tree. You can't take all forks, but remember multiple paths lead to the tree's crown."

"But Bai will say the balloons were his idea."

The clockwork figure climbed up on the platform to look Hana in the eyes and tapped his wooden hand against her forehead. "Ideas come from here. There will be more. And besides," he motioned at the other clockwork figures around him, "we talk. The truth will be known. Most important, you keep your word and others will see this and respect you for it."

Hana hadn't lost her grandfather. The empty spot she'd felt since his death vanished. She knew it wasn't the same, especially for grandfather, but she needed him. She needed this. "You'll always be here for me."

"Well, yes." His voice clicked in his throat with what must be laughter. "Collect some twigs so I can feed the boiler while you're gone and come back often."

"I will."

THE FESTIVAL OF FLAME
CHRIS WONG SICK HONG

Symbols could only contain the infinite for so long. That was the great flaw in Western magic. They treated the occult like science, another force to be mastered like galvanism or alchemy. Fa Xui's own symbols, traced lightly in chalk on the wooden floor around him, were instead echoes of the immutable laws of the universe. As soon as they were no longer needed they would dissolve, leaving no record of their brief existence. Nothing in Heaven-and-Earth was permanent and it was arrogant to believe otherwise.

Ever since the guizi had arrived in their ships filled low with opium and demonic mechanisms, they'd chased nothing less than the destruction of the Middle Kingdom. The drought in Shangdong, followed by vicious floods uprooting hundreds of thousands, was only the most obvious sign of Heavenly displeasure.

Even this house, which was once and should still have been a bright and intricate flower, one among hundreds in the garden of Beijing, was a sign. The cracking plaster walls, hastily thrown up to please the Europeans, bore soot from squatters' opium pipes like tattoos of shame.

Finishing the bagua circle, Fa Xui arranged his offerings: sweetmeats, bajiao incense, a small bowl of sticky rice, and a handwritten scroll bearing a phrase from the Tao Te Ching. "Heaven-and-Earth are not sentimental. Everything is as straw dogs." Fa Xui knelt in the center of the circle and chanted the words to commune with the spiritual world.

The crumbling, decrepit house faded away, replaced by a cultivated garden. Small bushes and shrubs defined the space around him, themselves respectful and unobtrusive. Its furrows perfectly aligned, a raked dirt path approached a red footbridge. The footbridge spanned a small stream. A shrine to the ancestors nestled in the green on the other side, and the path continued to a pair of ornately carved and painted double doors. A chime sounded, subtle yet clear, and Fa Xui prostrated himself.

From bitter experience, he knew the Western guizi would consider this a degrading affront to their dignity. Such was their arrogance. There were forces in Heaven-and-Earth far beyond any mortal striving, and the virtue of the superior man lay in obedience.

A voice spoke. "The Jade Emperor recognizes you." It was deep, cultured and dignified.

"I am honored to serve," Fa Xui replied, neither moving nor lifting his eyes.

This wasn't the Jade Emperor himself, of course, only a functionary sent in his place. Nevertheless, it was an overwhelming honor.

The functionary entered the circle and inspected his offerings. Here was another vital difference between China and the West. Their magic circles were used to trap, separate and confine. Taoist circles excluded nothing, instead fostering harmony and interconnection.

"Your obeisance is pleasing," the functionary said. "The manifold blessing of the Jade Emperor upon you."

A red envelope was placed in front of Fa Xui, a handbreadth from his bowed head. The smell of morning springtime faded. Waiting the respectful fifty heartbeats before rising, he gave thanks to his ancestors and silently vowed to defend China with his life once again. It was only when the trigrams of the bagua circle had completely faded that he opened the envelope and read the name of his target.

◇

Stepping into the evening, Fa Xui adjusted the frog clasps and stiff collar of his formal silk shirt. His long black hair was slicked back and impeccably braided, several stiletto-thin knives concealed therein. His task would be difficult, but after tonight the West would know that the Middle Kingdom would never be bowed again.

The paper lanterns of the Yuan Xiao festival were everywhere—dangling from roofs, perched atop poles, carried by revelers—and cast muted color throughout the cobblestone streets. Young men and women, most properly chaperoned, searched for love, the matchmakers clucking to themselves about this break from tradition. Merchants in flimsy stalls sold the rice balls said to ensure a long and prosperous life.

"If it isn't the ghost tiger. In the flesh." This voice spoke passable Chinese, but the lack of tonality and inflection marked it as irrevocably foreign.

A gentleman stepped out from under the eaves of a 'restaurant.' He was dressed in a two-piece suit, with a matching waistcoat over a linen shirt. A brightly colored cravat cradled his neck. His top hat was worn and scuffed, and the gold-rimmed monocle dangling from his breast pocket caught glimmers of light. It looked as though a fire were being kindled within.

His thick but carefully waxed moustache outlined the broad grin below.

"Dr. Ambrose S. Tyrrell," Fa Xui replied in English.

The good doctor corrected his pronunciation. "It's Tyrrell, actually, though I don't suppose I should hold that against you." As usual, Dr. Tyrrell reeked of laudanum, though he never partook himself. Doubtless he was on his weekly rounds.

"To what do I owe this honor?" Fa Xui replied, bowing slightly.

"Yes, I do suppose it is. Shall we walk?"

The way Dr. Tyrrell's overcoat bunched in the back suggested

~ 225 ~

something concealed, but that wouldn't be unusual. The doctor was known as Victoria's Mongrel on the streets, and whenever the British needed something distasteful done, he was always happy to oblige. In his spare time, he applied his alchemical knowledge to developing ever more potent tinctures of opium.

They walked side by side in silence through the crowds, turning onto a main thoroughfare. All around them, commoners carried lanterns. The hiss and pop of small fireworks punctuated the murmur of excited conversation. The good doctor and the assassin stopped at a stall selling meat on a stick. Dr. Tyrrell offered to buy Fa Xui dinner. Fa Xui declined.

They conversed briefly, with the good doctor espousing the merits of Victorian ideals and how lucky the Chinese people were to have the civilizing example of the British. Fa Xui responded with skeptical silence.

After a time, Dr. Tyrrell leaned in. "I can't let you do this. Nothing personal, you know."

That, at least, Fa Xui could agree with. Fate never was.

<>

Ensconced in the Legation Quarter, the Rt. Hon. P. Neil Perry looked up from the sermon he was penning by lamplight. Not one of the flimsy constructions of the natives, but a proper kerosene lamp. A particularly loud firecracker had disrupted his thoughts. He'd spent years in this country spreading the word of God and witnessing all manner of depravity, but their heathen ceremonies still disturbed him deeply. At least the wall surrounding the quarter would keep them out.

Still, there was hope. Just fifty years ago the Chinese had refused even to trade, considering the British inferior vassals. What gall, especially since they'd traded with the Russians on equal terms. It was as if they were intentionally trying to bankrupt the West by selling silk and other baubles, taking nothing but silver in return. The love of money was the root of all evil and the Rt. Hon. Perry's calling was to scour out evil wherever it lay, saving sinners from themselves.

Not that many would listen. Despite his exemption from local laws and nearly untouchable status—the better to preach the gospel—the locals treated him and Holy Writ with derision, preferring the blasphemy of Kong Qui and Laozi. The White Man's Burden of civilizing the lesser races was indeed onerous, but the Lord had been crucified for his efforts. The least the Rt. Hon. Perry could do was bear the contempt of backward locals.

And then there was the matter of the assassin, Fa Xui. He was connected with the Boxers—the Society of Righteous and Harmonious Fists as they arrogantly called themselves. With the Empress Dowager's recent show of support, they were breeding like vermin.

Setting aside his self-propelling fountain pen, the Rt. Hon. Perry rose from his desk and paced the confines of his study. The pen was a marvel of Western ingenuity. More a cage for one's hand than a pen, miniaturized pressure plates and springs translated simple hand gestures into letters, syllables and words, even preset sentences. A skilled operator could give the machine orders then withdraw his hand, and the contraption would wheel itself across the page, scribing as it went.

Normally, the Rt. Hon. Perry could write as quickly as he thought, images of salvation springing forth fully formed, but tonight the pen lay motionless, his sermon lost to more worldly concerns. He didn't know for sure what Fa Xui was planning, but rumor was the Boxers considered it an important blow against the West. Ambrose, that rude lout with the pretension to call himself a doctor, should be able to handle it.

<>

The fight was not going well. Monstrous mechanical arms, clicking and hissing like a demon spider, had sprouted from Dr. Tyrrell's back, tearing his overcoat to shreds. Each of the multiple sections clacked and whirred, while the three-fingered claws spun and spasmed in the night. The lack of chi running through them was as obvious as it was chilling, made them difficult to anticipate. They struck like scorpions as the good doctor advanced, grinning, and Fa Xui was hard pressed to dodge and parry.

At first the passersby thought it yet another street performance, but had since scattered, dropping brightly colored lanterns in their wake. Hungry flames within devoured thin paper coverings and delicate wooden frames. The few exposed fires flickered in the night.

Laughing, Dr. Tyrrell attacked again. A wide, reckless sweep nearly knocked Fa Xui's head from his shoulders and destroyed a noodle stall. Undaunted, the doctor grabbed the wreckage and heaved it at the assassin. Within the confusion of splintered wood and soy-scented ceramic shards, Fa Xui spied an opening and struck for the pressure points directly above the doctor's heart.

He nearly broke his fingers on concealed metal armor.

"Serves you right for trying that death touch hocus pocus," the doctor gloated. "Ingenuity and science will always triumph over ancient superstition."

All four mechanical arms closed in, impossibly fast, grabbing Fa Xui by the arms and ankles. They brought him close enough for the doctor to grab by the shirtfront and headbutt, breaking his nose, before tossing him through the air like a child's doll. Fa Xui crashed through three merchant stalls before landing, but righted himself just enough to roll immediately to his feet.

The river at Fa Xui's right, calm and broad, was blocked off by only a flimsy guardrail. An unconcerned cat inspected an abandoned bowl of soup in the stall to his left. Dr. Tyrrell charged. The bottoms of the doctor's pants split, revealing mechanical boots. The pistons and valves therein churned and hissed, leaving a trail of steam behind.

Wordlessly, Fa Xui traced the character for wind in the air. A concussive blast rocketed at the doctor, who shielded himself with a mechanical arm. Magic shattered against lifeless metal, no more effective than a bamboo sword against the Great Wall. The two thrown knives, however, were considerably more so.

One cut a bone-deep gash across the doctor's right cheek. The other embedded itself in his thick-lensed protective goggles.

Bellowing in pain and rage, Dr. Tyrrell ripped a small phial from his cravat and ate it, glass and all. The bleeding stopped and he charged Fa Xui inhumanly fast, swatting aside spells like disrespectful flies.

Knowing a direct confrontation was futile, Fa Xui traced the symbol for wind again but angled the blast downward. The remains of lanterns on the cobblestone street scattered as he launched himself away. Dr. Tyrrell followed suit, his mechanical arms vaulting him into the air.

There Fa Xui's superior agility proved deadly. He watched calmly as the doctor approached, and when an arm lashed out to swat him to the ground, he grabbed the cold metal and levered himself onto his opponent's back.

"I knew I should have built them to bend backwards," Dr. Tyrrell bellowed.

Fa Xui traced wind after wind, angling each blast upward to send them plummeting faster. The waiting lanterns below, pinpricks of light in a darkened city, twinkled like fireflies.

<>

Dr. Tyrrell's body went limp on impact, skidded several feet through the dirt. Fa Xui was flung into the courtyard wall. After several motionless moments, the noise of their landing lost among the cannonades which had joined the festival fireworks, Fa Xui rose first. Covered in masonry dust and staggering toward Dr. Tyrrell's unmoving form, he intended to snap the doctor's neck. Instead, the mechanical arms erupted into violence.

"Got you, you bastard." Dr. Tyrrell chuckled weakly, face down on the ground. "As soon as I reach my vitality serum, you're as good as dead." The doctor tried to move his real arms, failed and relented. "Maybe I'll let my arms finish you off."

Fa Xui smiled a grim smile. Here was another potent difference between China and the West. Their alchemy was limited to symbols and potions, which did nothing when one was incapacitated. He however was trained in Neidan, and even though he was immobilized as the mechanical arms slowly crushed the life from him, all he needed was his mind and his breath and the gates of power were his to fling open.

Ignoring his ribs as they cracked, Fa Xui mentally traced the symbol for fire on his lower tan t'ien. His chi grew from a steady flame to a roaring inferno. As he channeled the power into the meridians along his arms, his muscles spasmed with sudden, supernatural strength. This would take a year from his life, but one unwilling to sacrifice was unworthy to serve Heaven-and-Earth.

Roaring like a bull, Fa Xui bent the metal arms backward enough to free himself, ripping one apart at the joints. Gears and springs dislodged by dismemberment vaulted through the air and the arm itself bled a viscous, bubbling oil.

His breathing laced with fire, Fa Xui shook his head to clear the double vision and turned back to Dr. Tyrrell. If he'd had any doubt about the guizi's demonic nature before, this had quelled them. Fa Xui placed one hand on the back of an impossibly meaty neck, its muscles and veins grotesque and bulging. The other grabbed across the doctor's head, fingertips hooking underneath eyebrows. Fa Xui pinned the neck to the ground, pulled and twisted with his other hand. Muscles slowly gave way and vertebrae started to separate.

"It's nothing personal," he whispered, almost to himself.

"Eat ether, you yellow demon," the doctor grunted through gritted teeth. Spurred by the immediacy of death, Dr. Tyrrell wrested a large vial from an inside pocket and smashed it on the ground in front of him. Anesthetic vapor filled the air.

<>

The Rt. Hon. P. Neil Perry returned to his desk. The sermon wasn't going to write itself. He'd already listed, in detail, how the ridiculous native beliefs were nothing but a perversion of Christianity. Their superstition held that, untold years ago, the God of Fire had decreed Beijing was to be burned down on this very evening. In order to save the city, an advisor to the emperor ordered that red lanterns be hung around the city, bonfires built in the streets, and firecrackers and cannons set off constantly. Thus, when the heavenly armies were sent to raze the city to the ground, they would be deceived into thinking Beijing already ablaze and return to the heavens, reporting the deed accomplished.

The fires, the lanterns, the explosions, even the color red itself, was clearly mimicry of Hell, a way for the Great Deceiver to trick these deluded souls into chasing away the heavenly host of saints. One day, when the light of truth illuminated this Godforsaken land, this festival and all like it would be abolished. It was the Rt. Hon. Perry's sworn and ordained duty to oppose these demonic machinations until such time as these false prophets brought upon themselves swift destruction.

He knew that God's time was not man's, but every day the Rt. Hon. Perry fervently prayed for such destruction to appear.

Calming his passions, he looked at the intricate horometer mounted on his desk. It showed 11 of the clock. Unsettling. Ambrose should have returned by now. Sighing, the Rt. Hon. Perry set his self-propelling pen down once again. There was always so much left to do, but he needed to prepare for the worst. God's work was never done.

◇

Fa Xui, bruised and bleeding, stood at the south end of the Legation Quarter. While this side was protected by a moat, that also meant that the Water Gate was the least guarded. He'd need Taoist magic to get through, but had no fear of upsetting the natural balance. The Jade Emperor himself had given him this task and he was not going to shame himself before the entire Heavenly Kingdom.

The Legation Quarter's protective walls thrummed with the sound of hidden machinery. Between Fa Xui and the moat was a stripped-bare killing ground strewn with rubble. Limelight flood lamps atop the walls, harsh and bright, swept the killing ground, sure to catch anyone foolish enough to sneak across. Bitter, burning chemicals filled the air.

But as yin was the core of yang, darkness was the core of light. Taking a deep breath to steady himself, Fa Xui traced the symbol for spiral, intending to turn one of the lamps around, night-blinding the barely visible sentries.

Once again, magic failed to affect dead metal.

Grimacing, Fa Xui appealed to Heaven-and-Earth for guidance. Metal and magic were not enemies, as evidenced by magic swords, and Chinese artificers worked in harmony with universal laws. While a Western clock could not be enchanted, Chinese clocks often were, the oldest being over 1,000 years old. Only Western technology defied magic.

Fa Xui looked to the looming walls of the Imperial City, which rose above even the old city walls. They dwarfed the walls of the Legation Quarter by comparison. TiananMen Square lay just beyond, the Imperial Palace further still. The heart and soul of China.

"Aid me," he prayed. "I do this in defense of China, the holy Middle Kingdom, against the foreign barbarians who have conquered this ancient nation and shamed it to its knees. If it be the Heavens' will to see me succeed, show me my path. If not, allow me honor in my death."

A long silence. The spirits of the stones rose, then subsided. A shadowy figure emerged from the moat.

"I am Ch'eng-Huang of the city walls," it wheezed.

"Please," Fa Xui asked, "ferry me into the foreigners' dwelling. I have a task entrusted by the Jade Emperor himself."

"I cannot," Ch'eng-Huang replied. "Their artifice has made me weak. Like all of us, I am about to die."

"Surely you have the strength for one last miracle!"

Ch'eng Huang laughed, a soft, gurgling sound. "I cannot aid you, but I will take your plea to those who can."

"A thousand thanks, great Ch'eng-Huang."

"Not so great anymore." The spirit coughed, then vanished.

Moments later, Fa Xui felt himself enveloped by a mystic wind. His inner vision flew across the world to the backward, barbaric countries of Europe. Guizi swarmed the streets of strange cities. They usurped the countryside, mining metals and coal, stripping down forests. These were turned into boards and steel, guns and ships. But rather than giving thanks and working in harmony with universal laws, the guizi flouted their mastery of nature. Injured and offended, the spirits fled the constructions, leaving them more inert than corpses.

At once, Fa Xui realized his mistake. He had been trying to work with the spirits of the lights, to coax them to his aid, but there were no spirits within.

He traced the symbol for revenge. *Come*, he whispered to the spirits of Europe. *Come. You have been shamed and driven from your rightful homes. Help me, help yourselves, help your brothers and sisters in China to exact revenge, and you shall always have a place of honor among us.*

It exhausted what remained of his inner strength, but the flood lamps turned. Creaking and protesting, the three closest to him spun inward. Giving thanks, Fa Xui sprinted across the killing ground while concerned sentries shouted above him. Placing a fu, a protective paper talisman, across his mouth, he dove into the moat.

The fu allowed him to breathe water. Even the Water Gate itself evidenced soulless gears and levers, but they caused no trouble as he swam through. Once in the Legation Quarter's interior canal, he passed the U.S., Russian and Spanish compounds, under the South Bridge, and emerged next to the British Legation. Shuddering with effort, he pulled himself onto the bank.

◇

The Rt. Hon. P. Neil Perry stood at his pulpit, staring out into the pews. Word had come that Ambrose had failed to stop the Chinaman. Fa Xui would be here soon. Even if by some means Ambrose had survived, he obviously wasn't as good as he self-advertised. Lower pay was clearly in order.

To steel himself for the confrontation, the Rt. Hon. Perry mouthed Psalm 23. "Yea, though I walk through the valley of the shadow of death, I will fear no evil..."

The door to the church opened. Fa Xui, dripping wet, stepped inside, a soggy strip of paper draped on his shoulder.

"I see Ambrose failed to stop you," the Rt. Hon. Perry said.

Fa Xui raised his gaze. Hatred and rage lit the assassin's eyes like those of a rabid beast. The votive flames behind the priest flickered.

"He died a warrior's death," Fa Xui replied in broken English. "As will you."

The assassin traced a demonic sign in the air. Nothing happened. "Don't bother with your heathen magic. It won't work in a house of the Lord." The Rt. Hon. Perry laughed to himself. And to think he had been afraid.

Rather than argue, Fa Xui drew a pistol in the form of a dragon and fired. The dragon belched flame and the bullet exploded on impact. Collapsing, the Rt. Hon. Perry muttered, "Technology? Impossible..."

Fingering the sides of his sucking chest wound, the Rt. Hon. Perry reached for his pulpit, but didn't have the strength to grasp it, let alone lever himself to his feet.

"So," he rasped as Fa Xui stood over him, watching him die, "you killed me after all. I suppose I should congratulate you."

Fa Xui shook his head. "I didn't come for you."

<>

"I came for him."

Ignoring an outraged gurgle from the false priest, Fa Xui looked up at the crucifix mounted high on the rear wall. Jesus Christ, spirit emperor of the barbaric Western countries, hung from his cross, his pain a reflection of the agony he had commanded the British and the Dutch and the French and the Spanish and the United States to inflict upon the Chinese people. Jesus Christ looked down at Fa Xui with a baleful gaze, a crown of thorns upon his head. Once his power was broken, the Western armies, bereft of spiritual sustenance, would collapse like the paper-thin ghosts they truly were. China would at last be free.

Fa Xui bowed deeply. Though they were enemies, Jesus

Christ was still a god and an emperor and deserved respect. Despite the corrupting influence of the West, the Chinese were still civilized.

Because this was not the only demonic sanctuary he'd have to burn this night, Fa Xui withdrew a small knife from his shirt. It was squat and silver, weighted to be thrown, and had a fu of its own attached. This fu contained the words which would allow it to kill any demon, no matter how powerful. The knife struck home in Jesus Christ's throat, and Fa Xui was gratified to the see the image of the demon emperor bleed from his crown of thorns and side. The magic was working.

Fa Xui piled Bibles and hymnals in the main aisle, started a fire with the votive candles. Thin paper crisped and burned. Delicate gold leaf peeled away. Infernal words turned to soot and crumbled. When the fire engulfed the wooden pews, now too large to be stopped, he considered his next target. The French had an ostentatious temple. It should burn nicely.

He opened the outer doors and came face to face with Dr. Ambrose S. Tyrrell.

"Thought you could leave me in the river to die, did you, you Goddamned chink? Well, think again. I'm going to send you straight to Hell!"

Fa Xui felt no surprise. The doctor had suffered enough wounds to kill an ox several times over, but demons were known for supernatural strength and fortitude. The lenses of the doctor's protective goggles were cloudy and cracked, water still pooling inside. Most of his waistcoat had been torn away, revealing the pack from which the metallic arms had sprung. Only stubs remained, vomiting oil. The protective metal armor, dented and rent, caught the dancing light of the church fire.

Fa Xui warily backed away, gaining himself space to fight. Digging past his exhaustion and burning his irreplaceable life energy for fuel, Fa Xui traced one last symbol: death. The spell rippled through the air, striking Dr. Tyrrell in the forehead.

The good doctor's eyes rolled back and fell dim. A thick dart launched itself from the stub of a mechanical arm, burying itself in Fa Xui's chest.

◇

As he died, Fa Xui watched the growing flames, felt their heat. The walls of the church faded away and then he was in the air, looking down.

The church was on fire. With all the red lanterns, Beijing was on fire. The lights on the ships in the harbor, European and Asian alike, were also flames. The whole world was burning and it would burn for centuries, feasting on the bodies of the slain.

Above, the stars were clearer and brighter than he ever remembered as they slowly faded away.

UNDERBELLY
EDWARD MARTIN III

Another man had been torn asunder and strung up high in the support wires of the Floating City of Nessez.

The Police had been tracking the fiend for three months, but so far, their searches revealed not one single usable clue. Ever higher, the reward offers climbed, as each victim's family added their share to reflect not only their grief, but also their solidarity.

A grim social paralysis gripped the city, and no one went out after dark, but still, somehow, every week, a new body was found, torn to pieces.

No one except, of course, for the most foolhardy.

Neville Moore and Constance Crane stepped into a pool of light, in a dark street near the less respectable warehouse sections of Nessez. Long loops of mist billowed about them, industrial remnants from the many shops working full thirty-two hour shifts.

Each wore long leather cloaks against the night chill, hats to keep the wind's bite at bay, and strapsacks filled with gear.

Mr. Moore adjusted his glasses and surveyed the area.

"The Police," he declared, "are fools of the highest order. They are trying to find a common thug, when our quarry is neither."

Miss Crane raised an eyebrow. "Such an extraordinary claim," she said, "requires extraordinary evidence."

Mr. Moore buttoned the top two buttons of his cloak. He reached into a large pocket and withdrew a weapon—a deadly weaving of brass, copper, and glass. He handed it to her. "I shall collect such evidence with this," he said.

Miss Crane examined it carefully. "Although we are in the pursuit of a most heinous murderer," she said, "I think our Police, even at their least competent, would be keen to confiscate this. The catalyst load is twice the legal limit—which makes it more likely this would simply explode in your hands—and I believe the projectiles are explosive. Also highly illegal."

She handed it back and he slipped it away.

"I see your training was not completely substandard," he said. "You are proving an adequate apprentice." He shrugged off her glare thinking she should be most appreciative of his compliment. "We are hunting something considerably stronger than the average human being, so while this... tool... is illegal, it's the only logical solution as far as weaponry goes."

As they moved through the patches of light and shadow, no one challenged them.

"Curfew is effective," observed Miss Crane.

"Self preservation is one of those few traits even stronger than the desire to cause mischief. It is also perfectly logical, as well as being convenient for our work."

In a few moments, they arrived at one of the elevator banks of the city's Central Hub. Mr. Moore pressed a button.

"Why down?" asked Miss Crane. "All the murders occurred in the city, in the support wires."

"Correction, Miss Crane—the murders did occur, but did not occur in the wires. The bodies were deposited in the wires, but the murders occurred somewhere else."

The doors opened and they stepped inside. Mr. Moore pressed a button for the lowest level.

"It's true there was no actual murder location determined," murmured Miss Crane. "That much blood would have been most significant."

Mr. Moore nodded as the elevator descended. "Exactly. You have just concluded what I concluded several days ago, while preparing for this adventure."

"But the bottom level?" asked Miss Crane.

Mr. Moore offered her a look that, under other circumstances, might have been considered withering, and said "The farthest point from waste disposal, of course. It's perfectly logical."

"Ah," she said, and nodded.

After fifteen minutes, the elevator stopped and the doors hissed open. A wave of cold washed in over them both, carried by a stronger wind than topside.

"I've never been down here before," said Miss Crane, wrapping her arms around herself.

"Most women haven't," said Mr. Moore. "There's no reason for such—the underdecks are more exposed to the weather, and a place of difficult, dangerous work. Mistakes are invariably fatal. It's simply not safe for women."

She replied with only a sniff, which he dismissed as an effective of the chilly air.

They stepped out. The deck beneath their feet was solid, but it was obvious that there were no protective shrouds or walls on this level, nor the typical heating vents that kept topside so temperate.

Miss Crane stepped near the edge of the walkway and looked down. Another half-dozen levels seemed evident, but much less substantial than this one. This was the bottommost level that still boasted a solid floor. The rest were expanded metal, or metal mesh stretched between supports.

Wind whistled through the structure, low and moaning, but with gusts. Far, far below, she saw the tops of clouds, hypnotic tan swirls of vapor.

"Don't fall," advised Mr. Moore.

She glanced, irritated, at him, but he was already sweeping his way down the platform. She caught up quickly, at a most indecorous gait.

"You think," she asked "that the killer is down here?"

"I'm quite certain of it," he said. "It's only logical." He waved his arm around. "The underdecks are largely automated, and the few workers down here are strictly protective of their privacy."

"How could they have privacy down here?" Miss Crane looked around. Other than pipes and other solid tubes and conduits, the structure was basically open. "There are no walls, no shrouds, no nothing."

"That's what feeds it," he answered. "The very fact that they don't have privacy reinforces their need to maintain it, even if it's artificial. So, they don't talk to each other except when necessary and they don't interact socially. Not like civilized people, of course," he nodded upward.

They descended via a metal staircase. This new level had a flooring of expanded metal, and Miss Crane was fascinated by the surreal sense of hovering midair that the mesh afforded. She inhaled softly and looked around, as if seeing everything anew.

The underdecks seemed practically magical to her. She felt as if she were moving through a delicate crisscross of spun steel, of cable and rigging, of hoses, pipes, and girders.

She looked up, and imagined the entire city of Nessez above her, held aloft by the impossibly high Lifters, and kept in place by powerful engines deep in the heart of the structure that throbbed softly and eternally, and provided a constant rhythmic of life in the background; a heartbeat for every citizen.

She could, briefly, picture the entire city in her head, imagine it, from the highest point to the lowest point, and feel the flux of material to and from. She could sense the cycling and recycling of fluids through it like blood, the passage of people through it like cells, and the myriad of parts hanging onto the hovering skeleton like muscles from some great and wonderful creature. She could sense the trapships circling through clouds, collecting water and other vapors, and bringing them back to the collectors. She could sense the flash and pulse of steam, powering most of the city's machinery, each engine's heat catalyst a pinprick of energy.

It was an amazing city, and she marveled at the combination of intricacy and—

"Miss Crane!"

She looked back. Mr. Moore was staring at her with a

combination of curiosity and mild contempt.

"Are you well?" he asked. "Are you experiencing any sort of dizziness? Vertigo is a common problem for people new to these levels."

She shook her head slowly. "No, no dizziness," she said. "Just woolgathering."

"Well, stop it," he snapped. "I already have doubts about my logic in bringing a woman out on such a harrowing adventure— the very last thing I want is to find myself regretting it even more by bringing out someone for whom woolgathering is an occupational hazard."

He shook his head. "I swear, the next time I decide to—"

Something crashed to the deck in front of them, dropped from high. Something heavy, that bounced oddly.

They both stared.

It was a man.

His clothing was shredded on his body, and his skin and hands streaked with blood and deep slashes. His left leg was twisted and broken.

Despite his injuries, he rattled in a breath and tried to roll over.

"Are you... can we help you?" asked Miss Crane.

His eyes flew open. One was deeply bloodshot—practically black. He waved her away.

"Run!" he croaked. "Run before it sees you! Hide!" He coughed up bright blood.

Above them, she heard something moving. Something big, heavy. Something impossible. She backpedaled quickly, but there was nowhere to hide.

Mr. Moore pushed her around and the two of them ran a few steps away before the man's screams stopped them.

Although they spun reflexively, it was Miss Crane's instinct to pull Mr. Moore down, into a crouch, exposed, but small.

A *thing* dropped down to the platform above the man, who continued screaming. A thing like a crab, with eight legs and heavy armor plates covering its body. A thing with razor sharp claws that reached out to the man, who writhed and screamed on the deck. The claws grasped him and held him steady. His screams continued.

In horror, Constance watched blood and effluvia filter down through the deck, some pattering on the grill below, and the rest falling away, falling forever into the deep clouds.

The thing bent its head down toward the man. Slowly, the head peeled open, the armor unrolled and an inner head showed itself—a pink, soft, toothed and fearsome head. The broad mouth opened and engulfed the man in one bite.

As he was stuffed into its throat, his screams muffled, and then stopped entirely.

Then, the head raised back up, and the armor plates slid back across.

"I'm not sure even an overloaded projectile could penetrate that carapace," Mr. Moore whispered. "We may have missed this chance, but perhaps, er, what are you—"

Miss Crane had extracted from his coat pocket the weapon. By the time he realized what she was doing, her foot was already raised, leg coiled behind it. She kicked hard, and because he was already unbalanced, Mr. Moore tumbled a good ten feet before coming to a halt near the base of the creature.

Instantly the claws whipped out and pinned him.

"Miss Crane!" he cried out. "What have you done? Miss Crane!"

He writhed, but as with his predecessor, there was no hope.

Again, the head slid out, unpeeled itself, and the cavernous mouth opened.

Mr. Moore screamed.

Almost unheard next to his scream was a hissing pop.

The thing's head punched backwards a few inches, and its emerald eyes rolled in confusion.

There was a deep and powerful sound, a kind of whump, and instantly, from the neck of the beast, a slurry of red erupted. The head fell forward, pushed from behind. The claws fell from the still-screaming Mr. Moore, who was then instantly covered in the filth and debris from inside the monster.

It fell to the cold metal deck, completely dead, and practically empty.

Constance looked down at her hand. As expected, the overcharged weapon had blown itself to pieces, most of which had fallen to the deck around her. Although she had all her fingers, they were black and she could not feel the lower two.

She tore a strip of cloth from her petticoat and bound her hand, which was starting to throb slightly. She stepped over to the corpse.

Coiled up with it, the figure of Mr. Moore stirred, moaned, and struggled up.

"We… we could have come back," he muttered thickly.

"I doubt it," she said. "I think it would have seen us anyway, and surely killed one or both of us, and you might have fired your single shot uselessly against its shell."

Slowly, he nodded. "I probably would have," he said.

"I needed another opportunity to penetrate," she said, "And I am a much better shot than you, plus a less enticing target, being small and female. Apparently, it is accustomed to feeding on males."

He glared at her for a long minute, still recovering his breath. Then, he brushed enough gore from himself to be able to move somewhat freely. He was doused.

He straightened himself and reappraised her more carefully.

"You don't need to say it," he growled. "I recognize it as quite the logical choice."

RUMIKO
ALEKSANDAR ZILJAK

Chapter I

In which we meet our heroes.

A whistle pierced the sooty autumn evening. Gaslights were turning on. Although Ilica Street was one of the main Zagreb streets, chill kept most people home. Marin let a blue steam omnibus pass before crossing the street. He stopped in front of a shop. The sign above the entrance read "WATCHMAKER—est. 1873—S. Sigsfeld, prop." Marin removed a lock of dark hair from his forehead, turned the doorknob and entered the shop.

The doorbell announced him merrily. The young man at the workbench raised his eyes from a pocket watch he was working on.

"You arrived at last," he said, removing a magnifying glass from his eye. Unruly curly hair gave him an artistic look, but his eyes were curious and calculating at the same time. On occasions, Marin found the look in those eyes cold.

"I was a bit delayed, sorry," Marin apologized and took a bundle of papers out of his worn-out bag. "Here, these are today's lectures. But, really, Jakob, I don't see how you're going to manage—"

"You know I cannot close the shop," Jakob replied, leafing through the notes. Marin noticed he was worried. "Somebody must run it while father is ill. Anyway, this doesn't look much. Digital mechanics, data structures, numerical calculus... When do you need the lectures back?"

"In two or three days. But what are you going to do with exercises?"

"All right," Jakob shrugged. "I'll attend the exercises. Fortunately, they're not being held every day. Thank you for these."

"Oh, it's—"

At that moment, the doorbell rung again and an unusual pair entered. The gentleman could have been more than sixty, of undoubtedly oriental origins, piercing steel-gray eyes, white hair, and neatly trimmed moustache and beard. He was dressed in a dark suit: the work of a first-rate tailor was immediately obvious. He held a bowler hat in his right hand and a simple but elegant wooden cane in his left.

And then his escort followed him into the shop. A lightning bolt pierced Marin's chest upon seeing her. Never in his life did he meet such a beautiful girl, her rich black hair arranged into a chignon. Her lovely complexion was pale, reminding Marin of snow. She wore an expensive dress. Their gazes met for an instant. Smiling, the girl looked another way, but not before Marin spotted a mischievous glimmer in her almond eyes.

"*Gutten abend, Herr Watanabe*," Jakob greeted in German, putting down Marin's notes. "Your watch is finished. But let me introduce you! This is Marin Stipanchich. A fellow student," Jakob added. "Mister Watanabe and his daughter."

"Watanabe Ishiro," the old man bowed. "And this is Rumiko. We are honored." His German sounded fluent, although with an accent. Marin bowed in return. He found it difficult to divert his eyes from Rumiko. He hoped he would not look impolite.

"Mister Watanabe was kind enough to entrust me with his watch," Jakob explained as he took a golden pocket watch out of a drawer. Watanabe took it, raised the lid, brought it to his ear and smiled, satisfied.

"Are you in Zagreb for a long time?" Marin dared to ask.

"Three months now. Expert delegation," Watanabe replied

after pausing a second or two. As if he was assessing Marin, weighing how much he could tell him. "You see, our Empire must modernize. So our delegations visit developed countries worldwide. We gather experiences we can apply in our homeland."

"Oh," Marin nodded. "And what precisely are you interested in, if I'm not being indiscreet?"

"Railroads. As you must have read in newspapers, the Austrian State Railways are hastily laying mountain tracks through Bosnia. And as you also probably know, mountains predominate in Nippon, and so..."

"Isn't this a Babbage engine?" Rumiko asked suddenly. Marin looked at her. She stood before a showcase in the corner. Among various broken watches, serving merely as decoration, there was a rather small brass box on a wooden pedestal. Its winding key was inserted on the side.

"Precisely, Miss Watanabe," Jakob replied and opened the case. "The original IBM portable Babbage engine, weighing a mere 14 pounds. A bit old, though." Jakob released the locks and raised the engine lid. Rumiko leaned above the frame supporting a complex tangle of axles, cog-wheels and levers comprising a Babbage computer. Her eyes shone in excitement. "Beautiful, isn't it? Of course, their monopoly expired long ago, but still, nobody makes them as good as Intelligent Babbage Machines Co. It's powered by this spiral spring here, see? It's wound up by the key. Of course, this is a small model. Compared to steam analytical engines..."

"Does it work?" asked Rumiko.

"Unfortunately no, Miss."

Rumiko turned, visibly dejected. Marin understood her: a running Babbage engine, even when running idle, was a fascinating sight. "The tape reader is broken, and the writer is missing altogether. And some bearings are gone, one axle is broken: this is one of the earliest models, after all. Subsequently, they improved upon the hardness of the parts. Anyway, I'm afraid I couldn't afford myself a functional engine."

"Such a shame..."

"Maybe, once you finish your studies, you will find means to repair it," Watanabe noticed. "And now, it is time to go. Rumiko-chan..."

Once they we're alone, Jakob closed the engine. "Watch your step, my fellow," he nudged Marin, winking mischievously.

"I don't know what you're talking about, my friend."

"Come, come, as if I didn't see the way you ogled her. He's got a cute daughter, doesn't he?" Marin said nothing. He couldn't take Rumiko out his mind: that desire for knowledge as she leaned above the engine, unruly lock falling on her forehead, eyes admiring the perfect precision of the Babbagean mechanics—in Marin's opinion, the greatest achievement of the modern era of progress. Whenever he tried to describe that harmony—required to carry out complex numerical and logical operations, supervised by algorithmic structures—to some young lady, her stare would wander, her face assuming a dull look of complete disinterest for any matter technical.

"...but one must be careful."

"I beg your pardon?" Marin started.

"They are foreign people, their clothes regardless. We don't know their customs and traditions."

Foreign or not, Marin mused, *we shall all be finally united by steam, Babbage engine and telegraph.* They'll weave us all into a new world, into a bright future for young people such as Jakob and Marin. And Rumiko, too. Somehow, Marin felt the pale girl fully belonged, in some beautiful and unusual way, to that new world.

<>

Chapter II
In which Rumiko and Marin meet again.

Marin and Jakob got off the steam omnibus that stopped, whistling, before the entrance to the barracks, festively adorned with flags. Carried by cheerful Sunday crowd, they passed the guards and went to the former drilling-ground. Four moored airships rested on its edge.

The traditional air meeting at the Borongaj field was at full course. Crowds circulated everywhere. Prominent Zagreb gentry mixed with common folks, students courted ladies, mothers held their children firmly for their hands, lest they lose them. The military brass band, playing merry marches from a specially erected stage, contributed to the mood. Several balloons were rising above Borongaj, each carrying two or three passengers in a basket.

Marin and Jakob gave wide berth to the stand of the Ladies' Lilienthal Club "The Falcon". They both agreed there are easier ways to break one's neck than throwing oneself, hanging under a flimsy biplane flyer, from the top of some cliff, hoping to reach its base in one piece. They also skipped bingo and stalls with hot sausages, sweets and children balloons. They rushed to the edge of the airfield, where the constabulary had a hard time preventing the crowd from spilling in merry disorder across the grassy field.

One airship, painted grey, belonged to the Imperial and Royal Navy. She flew all the way from Kotor Naval Base to magnify the event. Two ships proudly carried the sign of the Imperial and Royal Air Postal Service on their sides: a pigeon, its wings widespread, carrying a sealed letter in its bill. There were no Army ships. The relations with Kingdom of Serbia regarding Bosnia had grown tense again, and most of them were stationed in Petrovaradin and Sarajevo, from where they took off to patrol borders. Instead, the Kaiser—newspapers claimed, as a sign of support and a warning to the Karageorgevichs—sent one of his dark scouting ships from Berlin.

While Marin and Jakob were making their way through the crowd, a handling party gathered beneath one of the postal airships. A mustached *Oberleutnant* was issuing orders under a vigil eye of an aeronaut who was to fly her. The soldiers grabbed the ropes holding the ship and started pulling her in unison toward the centre of the field. An experienced crew it was, and they handled quite a large ship as if she was a toy. Soon she was away from the others and the time came to prepare the steam engine driving her. The aeronaut and the engineer climbed into the car: sometimes, it took half an hour to prepare the engine.

In all that elbowing through the crowd, Marin earned a kick between his ribs.

"I'm sorry! Oh, I'm so sorry!" he heard a lady's voice and turned. And his heart fluttered. He was facing Rumiko! "I'm sorry... Err..." Apparently, it took her a moment to remember. "Marin! Marin Stipanchich!"

"Look who's here, Jakob!" Marin happily held Rumiko under her arm and pulled her from the crowd. She nodded in gratitude.

"Well, Miss Watanabe! Such a small world!" Jakob bowed, and then he looked left and right. "I presume your esteemed father is here somewhere, too?"

"My father had to leave on businesses. So I was free..." She looked aside mischievously. "You won't tell my father? He'd disapprove were he to know I was here unaccompanied."

"Let's say you're not unaccompanied anymore, Miss Watanabe," Marin said, smiling. Rumiko replied with even more mischief: Mr. Watanabe would approve the student company, in which Rumiko found herself, even less.

At that moment, the music stopped. The Mayor of Zagreb climbed to the stage, followed by the postmaster and the airfield commander. Somebody passed him a megaphone and he, his nose ruddy after some wine, cleared his throat and announced above the murmur and shouts from the crowd:

"Ladies and gentlemen! Dear visitors! It is time to draw the awards of our bingo! I call our Lady Luck!"

A young leading lady of the Croatian National Theatre climbed pertly to the stage, followed by applause and an occasional merry whistle, and bowed, with lots of laughter. Excited, Rumiko took her number from her purse. Marin sincerely wished her luck while the actress on the stage, followed by the Mayor's witty comments, drew the winners.

Seemingly, everyone who paid for the bingo got something: there were so many lucky ones. But, Rumiko's number didn't come up. However, she didn't seem bothered at all. *Didn't it matter to her*, Marin was puzzled, *didn't she care for prizes*? At least half an hour must have passed before the Mayor announced the drawing of the three main awards: a panoramic flight for two in the postal ship that was just being prepared at the field. At that moment, Rumiko grew attentively tense. So, that's what she was hoping for!

The first number drawn wasn't hers. An elderly gentleman climbed to the stage, leading an eager grandson. Rumiko had no luck in the second drawing, either: the winner was a fatty man of clerkish look and his drab little wife, not really happy about it, as if she put no faith in all those novelties. Rumiko slowly prepared herself for disappointment. The actress reached for a number for the last time. She picked one, handed it to the Mayor, who read it aloud: "Thirty two!"

Cheering happily, Rumiko jumped and raised her number high up! And then she remembered it was a prize for two and, not even thinking about it, drew Marin forward by his arm. He looked first at her, then at Jakob, confused.

"C'mon, lucky man, what are you waiting for!" his friend laughed and pushed him. Marin took Rumiko under his arm, as if they were a couple, and together they pushed through the crowd surprised to see a foreigner from some far away country.

Some twenty minutes later, after the Mayor, the postmaster and the airfield commander congratulated them, and the aeronaut—reassuring them they had nothing to be afraid of, since the ship was perfectly safe—gave them firm instructions on how to behave during flight, lucky winners, followed by fanfares and a march, climbed into the car. Rumiko and Marin settled into wicker chairs right behind the aeronaut. The old man and his grandson sat behind them, while the clerk and his still-not-too-happy wife sat at the very end, next to the engineer.

"All set?" the aeronaut turned and checked once again if everybody settled. Then he gave a sign to the officer on the ground. He gave an order and the soldiers released the ropes. The ship began climbing silently. Marin grew stiff in his seat. He felt uneasy, watching the field and the cheering crowd become smaller and smaller. Rumiko watched carefully over the aeronaut's shoulder, without the slightest fear or discomfort. Part of her courage crossed to Marin, and he looked at the others. The boy pressed his nose against the window pane, enraptured. His grandfather appeared calm: it was possible he flew an airship before or simply always appeared unruffled. The clerk's wife was squeezing her husband's arm. "You'll see more if you open your eyes, dear," he reproached her quietly.

Marin smiled. Unconsciously, his hand reached for Rumiko. Equally unconsciously, she took it and held it. Marin was filled by indescribable sweetness. He didn't let go of her hand when the aeronaut, taking a steam pressure reading, started the propellers. He didn't let go when he set course for the northeast. He didn't let go throughout the entire flight, as Zagreb spread below them in full splendor.

Their silvery ship glided quietly above the Maksimir park, painted in autumn. They startled swans on the lakes, and perplexed rowers and their ladies in boats. Racing an omnibus from Maksimir, they run west for the center of the city. They alarmed maids at the stalls surrounding the statue of Viceroy Jelachich, resembling a toy soldier from so high above. The newly-built towers of the Cathedral seemed within reach. They greeted buzzards above wooded hills north of Ilica Street and spoiled the lining up of soldiers in the Prince Rudolph's Barracks. They flew across the railroad, and coughed at the smoke from Treshnjevka heating plant chimneys. They followed the Sava river, and then the aeronaut turned back north, venting the gas at the same time. The Borongaj barracks grew closer, marking the end of the flight.

When they finally landed, the handling party grabbed the ropes and moored the ship. The impressed passengers got off, all a bit sad that the flight had to end. (Only the clerk's wife was sincerely glad to tread the firm soil again.) Rumiko threw herself into surprised Marin's arms and planted a kiss on his cheek. Only then did she recall it was inappropriate for a well-mannered young lady. But Marin didn't object one bit as he was leading her back to the crowd, where Jakob awaited them. Not one bit.

<>

Chapter III
In which great love blossoms.

During the next days, Rumiko and Marin seemed inseparable. For the first time in two years, Marin neglected lectures he otherwise attended regularly and scrupulously. Instead, he guided Rumiko through Zagreb, showing her the sights. From uptown walls, churches and towers, narrow streets and leaning shacks, across the new wide parks and pavilions downtown, all the way to peaceful Maksimir lakes, where Rumiko fed pieces of bread to showy swans.

Marin was amazed at how well Rumiko was getting along. She adopted all the customs—so different from those in her distant homeland—with an ease of someone born in Zagreb, the capital of all Croats. She spoke German as if it was her native tongue.

"For several years now, we travel across Europe," Rumiko explained when Marin asked her. "From construction site to construction site. I almost forgot the ways of home." Rumiko tossed a piece of bread. The swan stretched its neck and got it right before the bill of another. She tossed a piece to that one, too, and there was enough left for several mallards joining them. Finally, when there was no more bread left in the bag, the swans paddled away, wiggling their tails in goodbye.

Later, in the Zoo, Rumiko paused before the wolf cage. She contemplated the wolf and his mate as they circled the cage, every so often pausing to sniff the air.

"It's sad," she muttered, "when your entire world is a cage like this. They are almost no more in my homeland," she whispered sadly. Marin said nothing. But he, too, felt compassion for the imprisoned beasts. And then Rumiko walked on and he followed her to the tropical house, where chattering parrots and gaudy finches were sheltered during those chilly days.

They took a steam omnibus back to town. The bell-tower clock chimed nine when Marin finally escorted Rumiko home, a house on Tushkanac hill rented by her father. The overgrown garden, arched by cherry trees, maples and spruces, was entered through a wrought iron gate in a stony wall, covered in ivy and creeper. A hushed blackbird call greeted them from dense shrubs when they stopped before the gate.

Rumiko turned to bid goodnight to Marin. Then she paused.

"Come, let me show you our home!" she decided finally.

"I'm not sure it's appropriate," Marin objected. Indeed, should anybody see them, it could have most embarrassing consequences for Rumiko.

"Oh, come on, there's no-one!" She took his arm and led him through the gate and up the stony stairs. She unlocked the entry door and let Marin in. He paused until she turned the lobby gaslights on, and then he followed her into a large reception-room.

The house was obviously rented with all the furniture. Marin saw nothing reminding him in any way of Nippon. (And he had studied several books in the last few days, even Racinet, and believed he had a pretty good idea of an average Nipponese home and dressing customs.) Apparently, when in Rome, Mr. Watanabe and his daughter wisely did what Romans do.

Rumiko left Marin in the reception-room and disappeared. He waited politely, and then she entered, changed into a traditional *kimono*. Marin lost his breath. A dress so simple and convenient, and yet elegant—embellished with camellias in fool bloom and tied with a broad *obi*, the sash—accentuated her sweetness even more. She carried a small tray.

"Won't you sit?" Rumiko asked as she put the tray on the table. Marin sat on a divan. Rumiko settled in an armchair opposite him and offered biscuits and tea. The biscuits were delicious, some rum was found to put in the tea, and so time flew in pleasant chatter. At one moment, Marin became aware that a large clock in the lobby was striking eleven and realized he remained for indecently long. He rose to leave, but then, to his greatest surprise, Rumiko stood before him and took his hands.

"Sometimes, I'm very lonely here," she whispered. Marin felt his mouth drying. He melted in her almond eyes, longed for those sweet lips. And then, as if reading Marin's mind, Rumiko—so much shorter than he, tall and wide-shouldered—rose to the tips of her toes, embraced him and kissed him on the mouth. Marin was afraid a single word would break that magic, scatter that intoxicating fragrance enveloping him, destroy that beauty before him, lost in the desert of solitude.

Then Rumiko led him upstairs. Without a word, because words were no longer necessary. *What am I doing?*, Marin asked himself, but gathered no strength to resist Rumiko. And why should he, what wrong were they doing? Rumiko opened the door to her bedroom and led Marin in. The room was decorated simply, with taste. The bed invited with fragrance of freshly starched sheets and pillow-slips.

Rumiko kissed Marin once again. He embraced her, casting away any doubt, and pressed her against him. He caressed her fragile body, surrendering to the whirl into which her eyes lured him, greedily drinking nectar from her lips. Rumiko moaned through clenched teeth, undid her sash and opened her *kimono*. Marin went with his palm beneath the soft cloth, slipped across her pale flesh, lost his breath upon touching her firm breast. Rumiko unbuttoned his shirt and took it off. He laid her on the bed. It squeaked under their weight. She was opening to him, surrendering, desiring someone to drive away her solitude, a stranger in a strange land. They looked into each other's eyes, and then she whispered: "Please, don't think bad of me."

"Never, my love! Never," Marin whispered back before finally sinking his entire being into sweetness named Rumiko.

<>

Chapter IV
In which bad news arrives!

Marin was awakened by a phone ringing. It came from a study adjacent to Rumiko's bedroom. He opened his eyes and sat up in the bed. It was well after dawn. The phone wouldn't stop, persistent, loud, like an intruder turning sour the sweet taste of the last night. Then he heard quiet footsteps and Rumiko lifting the receiver.

He reached for the shirt thrown to the floor. Trousers, where did he loose his trousers? *"Moshi-moshi? Hai?"* he suddenly heard Nipponese. Perhaps it was her father calling, it would be awkward... *"Nanda?"* Rumiko screamed in fear and Marin realized something happened. He put on his trousers, listening at her agitated voice. She asked a question. Tense silence as she listened to an answer, and then another question and silence and quick reply and finally putting down of the receiver. Silence. Steps. Rumiko bursting into the room, her eyes full of dread.

"What was it? What happened?" Marin jumped out of bed and took Rumiko by her shoulders. She started, as if she completely forgot she wasn't alone in the house.

"An accident on the track. There are dead among workers."

"Father?" Marin shivered.

"They don't know." Rumiko shook her head. "He's gone!"

"What do you mean, he's gone?"

"I don't know. They phoned from the consulate. I should report as soon as possible."

Rumiko stared in all directions, scared, not really knowing what to do. Marin held her to himself. He felt her against him, the fragrance of her hair, the freshness of her skin and last night returned to him, passionate and sweet.

"Don't worry," he whispered into her hair, calming her. "Everything will be all right. I'll come with you!"

Rumiko looked at him, shaking her head. "You don't understand! Father—"

"Don't be afraid! You'll see, everything—"

Rumiko tore herself from Marin's arms. "Father had enemies in Nippon, perfidious enemies that will stop at nothing! This is their doing, I'm certain of it!"

Rumiko was kept in the Nipponese consulate a whole day. Marin waited for her on a bench under young plane-trees. Dusk was drawing upon the Zrinski Square when she left the consulate. Marin rose from the bench and went to meet her. She kissed him, and they went through the park to the Jelachich Square.

"What did they tell you?" The first gas lanterns were turning on. Several couples strolled the paths, their steps rustling in the fallen leaves. An elderly lady with a small dog was passing Rumiko and Marin. The white dog stopped suddenly, looked at Rumiko and started barking.

"Quiet! What's the matter with you?" his mistress reproached him immediately. But the dog wouldn't stop. The woman lifted him off the ground and slapped him gently across his muzzle. "Quiet! You're naughty! You are! Forgive him," the woman asked, "he's a bit nervous today."

"It's all right," Marin smiled and they left the woman and her little dog behind.

"Nothing new," Rumiko answered Marin's question. "There was an explosion followed by a landslide, and the entire train overturned. An engine pulling three wagons and two coaches. Seven people dead, God only knows how many injured. Father's body wasn't found. He's not among the injured, either. Officials said they'll let me know as soon as they learn something new."

"Did you mention your suspicions?"

"It's better I keep what I know to myself. I'm not sure who's loyal to whom in the consulate."

"I don't understand." Marin didn't miss the concern in her voice. Several times, she looked behind her, as if afraid somebody was following them. *What's going on?*, he wondered.

"It's not easy to explain to someone who's not completely familiar, but when Black Ships arrived to our ports in the middle of the century... And when commotions and rebellions began soon after... My father, although a *daimyo*—a landlord—contributed greatly to bring down the *bakuhan* and to force the *shogun* to capitulate. Many never forgave him that. And with time, some of them regained influence and power."

<>

Chapter V
In which dark forces attack!

It was already night, foggy and dank, when Marin saw Rumiko home. He did his best to cheer her up. He took her—by a funicular she otherwise enjoyed—to an uptown cellar for supper. In a quiet booth, he tried to convince her everything would be all right. But Rumiko seemed absent-minded: unspeakable horrors swarmed in her head. Finally, Marin took her hands into his.

"You're not alone, Rumiko", he said. "Whatever happens, you're not alone."

Rumiko smiled and—relief in her eyes, as if his words were the first ray of comfort in uncertain darkness surrounding her— merely whispered: "*Arigato*. Thank you."

And so, after taking a stroll, they found themselves before the house, and as Marin held the gate to let Rumiko pass, he wondered if it would be appropriate to follow her. Last night, so sweet, came back to his mind and shame filled him immediately! No, it was not fair to take advantage of her worry and weakness and...

"Come with me," Rumiko invited him quietly.

"I thought..."

"I know exactly what you thought," she smiled, driving the fog surrounding them away. "And that's nice of you. But you promised I shan't be alone."

Rumiko climbed the stairs, Marin following her, and the two of them sank into the darkness of the garden. She unlocked the entry door. She was about to step inside, when suddenly she turned stiff, tense, as if feeling some danger! *What is it?* Marin wanted to ask, but she pressed his mouth with her palm.

"We're not alone," she whispered into his ear. Marin froze. Without a sound, knowing precisely her whereabouts in the darkness, Rumiko reached for a stand in the lobby and drew a cane out of it, quite similar to the one carried by Mr. Watanabe. She held the cane firmly in her left hand. Marin wanted to go ahead, but she pushed him behind her.

"Let me!" she ordered quietly, but in an uncompromising tone. She gripped the end of the cane with her right hand and pulled lightly, enough for Marin to see her tender hand drawing a blade. *A sword!* he realized with horror. What he took to be a cane was actually a sword!

Suddenly, something whizzed next to Marin's ear and thrust into a wall behind him! It resembled a sharp-pointed steel star. Resonant clash of steel against steel echoed across the lobby and another deadly star was deflected by the Rumiko's sword. Before Marin blinked, much less realized she had just saved his life, a dark shape charged at them. A masked burglar, dressed in black, drew his sword and struck, but Rumiko skillfully repulsed his blow, crying like a beast.

Marin watched in consternation as his fragile girlfriend turned into a dangerous warrior, excellently trained in the deadly skills of far-away Nippon. Swords clashed and it was obvious Rumiko would quickly overpower the mysterious fiend. And then, her foe reached deftly under his black jacket. Some dust spilled out of his hand across the lobby. Marin screamed as it irritated his eyes. He panicked, thinking he'd lost his sight! Someone rushed past him into the night, pushing him aside. The burglar escaped!

Marin dropped to his knees, rubbing his tear-filled eyes. It stung, bit, burned! And then, Rumiko knelt next to him and pleasant cool water spilled from a jar over his eyes,washing the devilish powder away. Marin blinked. Rumiko poured more water on his face. "Do you feel better now?"

Marin nodded. He saw again. "What was that, for God's sake?"

"*Metsubushi*. A blinding powder. Ashes, ground pepper, stinging nettle hairs and sand, all mixed together."

"Who was that?"

"A *ninja*. A spy and assassin. Stay here!" With these words, gripping the sword, Rumiko disappeared. She returned after several minutes—they seemed like eternity to Marin. "Good, he didn't steal anything. And he was alone. Let's go, he's the only lead to my father!"

"But who knows where is he by now!"

"Don't worry," Rumiko led Marin back into the garden. "I'm certain he's up there!" He looked where she pointed. And indeed, a dark shape of an airship was discernible, like a giant fish, in the fog. Did it just seem to him, or was there a rope hanging from a car, somebody holding tight at its end?

"Now we shall never catch them! We should inform the constabulary!"

"No time! An airship is not fast, we can catch up with them."

"But how?"

Instead of an answer, Rumiko rushed down the stairs to the street. Puzzled, Marin followed. At that very moment, luck smiled at them: two eyes glowing in the fog, a pair of lanterns. A new and shiny topless Stanley Steamer was coming down the street. A driver sat in it: a gentleman of pointed moustaches, obviously of newly-acquired riches, and his fair lady, both dressed warmly against the damp cold piercing to the bone.

Rumiko jumped before the steam car and the driver braked suddenly and honked angrily, startled. "Are you insane, Miss? To jump out—"

Rumiko drew her sword and grabbed the man for his fur collar. She pulled him out of a leather seat. His cap flew off his head as he landed on the pavement where, upon seeing a shiny steel blade, he remained, purple with helpless rage. His lady, screaming, got off by herself, hiding her face before the insane foreigner. Rumiko climbed behind the steering wheel and looked at Marin. "Coming?"

Still disbelieving his eyes, Marin jumped next to her. Rumiko knowingly turned the lever under the steering wheel and the car jerked and rushed down the street at full steam. She held the wheel firmly, cornering, as the owner yelled furiously behind her, completely forgetting himself: "It's not gonna end with this, you'll see! You'll end in the slammer! In the slammer, I tell you—"

"Was this necessary?" Marin asked, looking across his shoulder.

"Either that, or running to the Head Post Office!"

<>

Chapter VI
In which exciting and terrible things happen!

"Rumiko, I forbid!" Immediately next to the Head Post Office building, on a spacious field cleared of cots and fenced for that purpose alone, a small airship was moored. Her steam engine was ready, the ship was to take off soon.

"Those *shurikens* were meant to kill you, Marin! Those people know no mercy! And father is in their hands."

"I mean, stealing an airship," Marin whispered angrily after her. The aeronauts and the entire ground crew were in the Post, warming themselves with hot tea and rum before departure, recklessly leaving the ship without supervision. Rumiko and Marin were cloaked by the fog as they stalked the wrought iron rail fence with spikes on its top.

"What else? They went south, they're somewhere above the Sava river by now..."

"But, you can't steer!" Rumiko didn't hear him. She sprang, grabbed the rail and jumped across it, and landed on the other side, deftly and quietly like a cat. Marin was amazed. *What else does this girl know?* He grabbed the rail, too, and climbed, slipping clumsily, but brought himself over. His coat was caught by a spike, he heard cloth tearing. Damn, he cursed through his teeth, and jumped to the other side. He landed and fell and bruised his palms on the hard soil. A piece of his coat remained hanging on the spike, as a trophy of sort. Stooping, he rushed after Rumiko.

"Cut the ropes loose!" she whispered an order and sat behind the steering wheel. Marin obeyed, wondering if he was committing a major stupidity. The airship, free of her tethers, went up slowly. Marin run, jumped and caught a door-frame at the last moment, pulling himself into a cramped car. At that moment, a clerk exited the Post building, carrying a tied bag. He saw the ship climbing and called in surprise. At his shout, the crew rushed out, cursing and screaming and running after the ropes hanging from the ship. Marin spotted the three mail bags. He threw the first one out, followed by the remaining two.

"What are you doing now?" Rumiko demanded.

"Stealing an airship is one thing. Stealing Imperial and Royal mail something else entirely, believe me! And we also lose ballast that way!" As if hearing him, the ship rushed up even more briskly and none of their hands reaching for the ropes caught one. Several tense moments later, they were some hundred feet above the building spires.

"What now?" Marin closed the door and settled behind Rumiko.

"Did you forget the air meeting? I watched how to run this thing!"

"You watched how to run this thing? Oh, God!" Of course he remembered the aerial sightseeing of Zagreb. That ship was of a different mark, considerably bigger and of a more spacious car. But, her levers and dials didn't differ much from these: it all seemed very complex to Marin. And Rumiko's entire aeronautical training consisted of watching how it worked! *What was I thinking?*, Marin stewed, angry at himself for not restraining this crazy child from rushing mindless into peril!

At Marin's surprise, Rumiko pulled the lever knowingly, releasing steam into cylinders. The engine came to life and propellers behind the car turned, pushing the ship. Watching the compass, she turned the steering wheel and gave more steam. Almost without a sound, the ship rushed above the city toward south, leaving whitish trail behind. The fog below them was like a grey sea, out of which roofs and spires broke here and there, pointing to the sky. Then they flew over the railroad. In the distance, Marin saw the roof-top of his faculty building. From then on, only fog and tree-tops. Then, after some ten minutes, two lines of poplars and willows. It was the Sava river: the trees outlined its course.

"I can't see them," Marin muttered. "What if they're following the river to Sisak and on, into Bosnia?"

Rumiko said nothing. She merely released some ballast. The ship bolted up, rising and rising until she stabilized again at about half a mile altitude.

"Is there a flare gun here?" Marin looked around and

indeed, he found a pistol and flares right behind his seat. "Fire three flares downwards. In different directions!"

He obeyed, puzzled. He opened the pistol, inserted a flare and closed it again. Then he pushed the barrel through a round opening in a window—seemingly meant just for that purpose—and fired and understood. A screeching rocket flew toward the ground, merrily burning above the landscape veiled by fog. Marin fired the second flare through an opening on the other side, and then the third one. The bright flare illuminated the fog, resembling an opaque white glass pane. But, against such a reflected light, Marin spotted a black airship silhouette, some two hundred feet above the Sava course and some two miles away.

"Down there!" he pointed. Rumiko nodded, turned after the second airship and accelerated.

"What if they saw us, too?"

"Maybe they haven't yet," Rumiko replied. "Although, now they know somebody's chasing them." The flares fizzled and they lost their prey again. But they knew she couldn't get far. After several minutes, Rumiko ordered: "Fire another!"

Now they spotted the chased ship above groves growing on a fertile flooded soil south of Sava. She didn't gain altitude, but she looked closer. They flew above a village, leaving behind the bell-tower and Lombardy poplars sticking from the fog. And then there was forest below them, seemingly spreading into infinity. "You think your father is onboard that ship?"

"I wouldn't know," Rumiko shook her head uncertainly. She pulled a lever and valved some gas. The ship descended. "Another flare!"

"But—"

"Unless they're blind, they know we're at their heels! Another flare!" Marin obeyed and the flare shone upon the forest shrouded in fog. "Oh, bloody hell!"

The enemy ship was straight before them, presenting her side, several hundred feet away, like an ambushing pirate. Only then did Marin realize she was painted black. That is why they didn't see her climbing in the night. And now she obstructed their path! "What...?"

A flame followed by loud staccato burst from the black ship's car. A Gatling gun! "Down!" Rumiko screamed, throwing herself from the chair, grabbing Marin and covering him on the car floor. Not an eye-blink later, the car windows burst, shattered by the hail of bullets. Slugs ripped the wooden boarding, tore the wicker seats, broke levers and severed control chains. Another burst tore the rudder off and again the slugs rained on the car. Glass shards cut Marin, he felt blood flowing down his forehead. Steam hissed behind Rumiko and Marin. Fortunately, a bullet pierced the pipe outside and steam whistled into night, otherwise the heat would scald them like pigs.

A new burst hit the ship. Bullets pierced the envelope and the gas, hissing, rushed through countless holes.

"Burners out!" Rumiko yelled and Marin cut the fuel to the fire-box burners at the last moment. The ship was relentlessly losing altitude as the envelope lost gas. The fog-shrouded ground grew closer and closer. "Hold tight!"

Marin squeezed Rumiko in a tight embrace, trying to protect her. And then a jolt, breaking, cracking of branches, tearing and ripping of the envelope, hissing of gas. They fell through a tree-top and hit the moist soil with full force. Impact shook their bones. Marin thought his spine would break.

"Out!" Rumiko pushed him away, grabbed her sword and kicked the door open with her foot. They both shot out of the smashed car and splashed into mud. Marin rose to his feet and stumbled through the quagmire, following Rumiko. Behind them, a detonation and hot blaze burst up, devouring whatever was left of their airship.

Veiled by fog, surrounded by centuries-old oaks, Marin and Rumiko paused. Somewhere behind, in the forest, the fire was slowly dying out.

"Did we lose them?" Marin whispered. His face was bloodied, his clothes completely muddy. Rumiko was no cleaner, but from her bearing, he deduced with relief she wasn't injured. He couldn't believe what they passed through! Even the most experienced officer, even the toughest soldier, would be shaken after a night like this, and here a fragile girl stood next to him, brave and unflinching in her quest to rescue her kidnapped father. *What would the spoilt Zagreb young ladies say to that?*, Marin wondered. He wanted to praise Rumiko for her courage

She put the finger to her mouth and he turned mum. She listened to the night tensely. Distant hooting of an owl. Rustle somewhere behind them. Marin turned, uneasy. Beasts foraged here, and it would be no good should they stumble upon a wild boar. Rumiko pulled his hand and he run after her. Where? He didn't know. They would not be able to find their way before morning, when the fog cleared. Suddenly, Marin thought he heard the quiet running of a steam engine and transmission and propellers! He strained to hear. Yes, he was right! He cursed. The black ship was quite close! He looked up, but the fog hid her.

"They're at our heels!" he whispered into Rumiko's ear. She merely nodded. She gripped her sword, ready to draw it. *Are we already surrounded?*, Marin despaired. *Is it possible they are so quiet, like apparitions?* He looked around and saw a branch lying on the ground. He grabbed it with both hands, it felt like a good club. Rumiko looked at him, expression of pity on her face.

Suddenly, behind an oak, some twenty feet away, a human shape stepped out and stood facing them. They were on a small clearing. Marin turned when he felt—by the instinct of a beast pursued—that somebody was behind them. Two men cut off their retreat, and one each approached them from left and right. Apart from the first man, they were all wearing black, with black hoods and masks on their heads, and swords in their sashes. *Ninja*, Marin recalled. And the one before them, dressed in an expensive-looking *kimono*, must have been their leader. He wore no mask. He appeared almost as old as Watanabe, but stronger, with black moustache and arrogant bearing. He was wearing a long and a short sword in his sash.

"Watanabe Rumiko?" he growled.

Rumiko replied in Nipponese, then asked a question. The man replied contemptuously in several sentences. At that,

Rumiko shuddered and staggered. Marin realized the worst had happened. But then she clenched her teeth, drew her sword and gripped it with both hands above her head, challenging all five of them to try their skills. Their leader lifted his hand and spoke in a not-quite-fluent German: "I think the esteemed gentleman, since he was foolish enough to find himself here, deserves an explanation why he will die."

"Indeed, I do. Only, it is custom here for gentlemen to introduce themselves first."

"You are right, I apologize! I am Seki Kaneda" the man replied and bowed.

"Marin Stipanchich." Marin tried to keep a tremor out of his voice. He had no more doubt blood would be spilled here. He only hoped it wouldn't be Rumiko's and his. But, hope alone would not be sufficient to save them.

"You met Watanabe-san, I believe. And I noticed you realize he's dead. We caused the accident and kidnapped him in the subsequent commotion."

"So, you are the followers of the deposed *shogun*," Marin interrupted. Seki laughed.

"I see Rumiko-san hinted at our recent history. True, Watanabe-san and I were on opposite sides. But my side grew interested in his subsequent work, work that became his obsession. We approached him discreetly, not revealing who we really were, and we offered him significant funds. He—let me put it this way—used them against our agreement."

"So that's why you killed the man?" Marin squeezed through clenched teeth.

"After several years, Watanabe-san realized whom he made partnership with and to what cause," Seki ignored Marin's interruption. "After that, his work became completely inaccessible to us. It took a long time for a good opportunity. We had to find out how far he got with his research. We failed. He bit his tongue off instead of telling us." Marin shivered. Seki admitted in cold blood they tortured the old man to death, as if it was something normal! "It is an act demanding great strength of will."

"And then you sent a *ninja* to break into our house," Rumiko cut him.

"And you came home at an ill time. But at the same time, you revealed yourself," Seki smiled. "As soon as my man told me what happened, I realized Watanabe-san indeed made great steps in his work. I realized he succeeded beyond all our expectations, he—"

"Enough!" Rumiko yelled and charged at Seki. He shouted something in Nipponese and the four ninja rushed at her. Weighted chains and a rope with a hook at its end flew at her from four sides. But, she evaded the attacks supposed to restrain her with incredible agility. Marin realized they wanted her alive! He charged at the nearest ninja, hoping to jump him from behind. But the man in black sensed his intention with some uncanny instinct—because, he couldn't have seen him!—and the weight on the chain hit Marin's temple. His vision blurred, he staggered, fell, rose quickly, still clenching the branch, but feeble on his legs.

The rope with the hook coiled around Rumiko's waist. The ninja pulled her strongly to him. But Rumiko skillfully switched her sword and stabbed the ninja between his ribs. He whined silently as she drew her blade out of his body. She cut the rope with the next strike and it fell from her. Seeing blood spurting from the ninja's deep wound made Marin realize how lethal the Nipponese swords were.

"Your father taught you well, Rumiko-san!" Seki murmured. The other ninja now approached with much more respect.

"Did you think *kaginawa* and *kusari-fundo* will restrain me, you swine? Better grip your *katanas*, lest I cut you all bare-handed!"

"So be it" Seki nodded. "If that is what you wish." The remaining three warriors drew their swords. "After all, if your father worked well, we can afford to cause you damage." Marin was afraid Rumiko's threat might have been a bit premature. The three men surrounded her. They completely forgot Marin, as if he wasn't an opponent worthy of any attention, merely a stranger to get rid of after finishing the serious business. His pride hurt a bit, Marin gripped his club and set to charge at the nearest ninja.

"Stay out of this!" Rumiko commanded him. "You stand no chance against them." Screaming like a beast, Rumiko attacked the first ninja. Steel rang against steel, blade screeched against blade. Next moment, without Marin even seeing what happened, a man fell down. With a victorious cry, Rumiko threw herself at the remaining two. The swords whizzed through the air, one ninja repelled the attack while the other charged. Rumiko struck back, the three of them exchanging savage blows. It was a fight with no mercy, to death! Seki merely watched from aside, his right hand resting on his sword, pleased with what he saw. And then, a scream, and one ninja stumbling back a few feet, blood splattering from his neck. A moment later, and the last ninja collapsed into the mud. With horror, Marin realized his belly was cut open. Finally, Rumiko was alone, surrounded by four corpses.

"This is all you planned to send against me?" she faced Seki with contempt. "I know a good *shinobi* is hard to find these days, but these..."

"I assure you they were among the best," Seki smiled. "Your father did a great work, Rumiko-san. And he taught you better than I could have imagined. After all, his skills were legendary. Even at his age, I doubt we'd overpower him if we didn't stun him with explosives first. Nevertheless, I don't believe you're better than me!" Seki drew his sword. The time had come for the two of them to face off.

Marin looked at them helplessly. Seki raised his sword in a slow, threatening movement. Rumiko didn't even flinch. They measured each other for several moments, and then charged at each other. They struck, yelling, and passed each other before stopping dead, frozen in the mud. *What happened?*, Marin was surprised, expecting a protracted fight. And then he noticed a bloody blotch spreading across Seki's *kimono*. When? How did Rumiko's sword find its way? What was that deadly skill that can cut a man in an eye-blink, in a movement seeming to stem from a pagan dance? Marin didn't understand. He'd witnessed some swordsmanship exhibitions, but this—This was an entirely new world, entirely different skills! And his Rumiko possessed them!

Seki opened his mouth to say something. Blood rushed out. The sword fell from his hand. He dropped into the mud. He was dead.

"It's over! You cut them down, Rumiko!" Marin rushed to her. Suddenly, without a word, Rumiko collapsed to her knees. Marin's heart froze. He grabbed her, she hung with all her weight against his arms, almost pulling him down. *No*, he muttered, *God, no!* He saw how deadly were those swords and he instantly realized that, in the same invisible manner Rumiko cut Seki down, he had mowed her, too. Her gaze was empty. Marin felt her dress getting soaked under his palm. Suddenly, something felt out of place. He looked at his palm and gaped in surprise. He smelled it. With all the mud and blood, his palm was soiled in—

Machine oil!

<>

Chapter VII
In which Jakob has a lot of work to do!

The impatient doorbell broke the night silence in Samuel Sigsfeld's shop. *Is it some drunken fool?*, Jakob asked himself. Or perhaps constabulary? But why? "All right, all right", he muttered. He opened the door a crack, only meaning to take a peek, but as soon as he unlocked it, an untidy, staggering apparition burst into the shop, surrounded by stinking fog that blanketed the city, carrying something wrapped in his arms, something—

"For God's sake!" Jakob exclaimed. Marin stood before him, his face dirty, his coat filthy and torn, his hair encrusted in blood, his stare half-mad.

"Where can I put her?"

"Put who, man?"

"Where can I put her? And lock the door!"

Jakob obeyed and indicated the workbench. Marin placed atop the work surface whatever he was carrying with care and stepped back. He wiped blood and mud from his forehead. He wiped his hands on his trousers and then unpacked— Jakob barely suppressed a scream when he recognized Rumiko bundled in coarse cloth.

"Is she dead?"

"No. I need—"

"Why did you bring her to me, man?" Jakob screamed. "You're wasting time here with me, instead of taking her to a doctor!"

"I can't, you'll see—"

"What happened? Speak!"

"Actually, I don't understand myself. Old Watanabe is dead. So Rumiko cut them all down with a sword... I know it sounds crazy, you should have been there and seen for yourself! And then she fell, too!" Marin shook, trying to tell what really happened.

"But why not the doctor...?"

"Because of this!" Marin hissed and uncovered Rumiko fully. Jakob saw her stained dress. He touched the stain, smelled his fingers. His eyes opened wide. Words failed him. Then he took a deep breath. *Not impossible*, he decided after thinking it over, *not impossible*... His brain started running like a clockwork.

"This is what we're going to do now," he looked at Marin with a firm stare. His voice turned calm. "Whatever damage's done, it's done. It's not an urgent case and we have time. Go upstairs to my room, tidy yourself as much as you can. Try not to wake up my father. And wash your hands well. I need your help, and if this is what I think it is, then we need clean hands."

It was in the small hours of the night when the two of them, after a slim supper and several cups of strong coffee, returned to the shop. Rumiko was laying there, her eyes staring dully into the ceiling. First, they took off her clothes. They both paused before her perfect figure, almost snow-white complexion without a slightest blemish, seducing bush hiding—

"Did you know her?" Jakob asked.

"In a Biblical sense, you mean?" Marin nodded after brief silence.

The cut, the only one, was deep, slanting across her belly. Jakob spread the cut skin, greasy with oil. Marin cast some light, steel spiral spring flashed inside. It was obvious something was wrong with it.

"Navel," Jakob murmured. "The winding key probably goes here. Do you have it?"

Marin shook his head. "Maybe at home. We left in a hurry."

"Never mind, it's easy to make a new one! Let's turn her over on her belly!"

Her skin was sewn in neat and firm stitches, from somewhere beneath her hair, down her nape and all the way down her back. "You didn't see this?" Jakob asked. If he didn't notice Marin's worried look, he might have winked.

"It was dark and she was wearing *kimono* and..."

Jakob dismissed it with his hand. He realized there was no time to waste, after all.

"Listen, you must go to their house! It will soon swarm with constabulary. Go right now, while it's still dark, and make sure that you're not seen!" Jakob also realized he'd have to think of some story. The investigators could easily visit his shop, too. He'd have to hide the body.

"What am I looking for?" Jakob's calculating coolness calmed Marin. He did a good thing, bringing Rumiko here. If anybody in this town could have fixed her, it was Jakob.

"Blueprints. I don't believe Watanabe took her around without any blueprints. Maybe they're on paper, maybe on transparencies..."

"All right, I understood," Marin nodded, grabbing his coat. He unlocked the door, peeked out as if checking for an ambush, and then disappeared in the fog. Jakob locked behind him, and took a thoughtful look at the body. Although he didn't yet check the damage, he already guessed what was the matter and was calculating the possible expenses.

◇

Chapter VIII
In which all ends well!

The doorbell rang merrily, in Christmas mood, as Marin entered the shop. He took off his cap, shook off the snow, unbuttoned his coat and removed his shawl. "It's cold outside," he rubbed his palms.

"Well, it's winter-time, isn't it?" Jakob replied and locked the door behind him. He looked at Marin. "It's finished!"

"Really?!" Marin rejoiced. He took his friend's shoulders. "I don't know how to thank—"

"It cost me quite a lot," Jakob said gravely.

"Look, I'll make it up to you one day..."

Jakob interrupted him: "There are interesting things in those blueprints. Things a patent or two could be made of."

Marin spent enough time with Jakob above the opened Rumiko to know how revolutionary she was. Instead of human bones, Rumiko had bamboo sticks. Lightweight, yet firm. Her vertebrae were made of jointed shorter pieces of bamboo. Only her skull was a two-piece steel case. And inside it...

The most perfect and complex Babbage engine Jakob and Marin had ever seen. Every part was a miniature masterpiece, and the complexity of the entire machine far surpassed even the large steam-driven IBM 11-30 college exercises were held on. And instead of punched tape, replacing the original looped Jacquard cards in modern Babbage engines, Rumiko's memory consisted of round plates, like disks lined on a single axle. Both students immediately realized the novelty introduced by old Watanabe. While data on tape could be accessed only sequentially, one after another, the memory installed in Rumiko could access data directly, the moment they were needed. They both realized the increase in speed of the Babbage engine inside her. And they both knew well-enough how much capital an interested party would invest into something like that.

The greatest expense was the spiral winding spring. Jakob

had to order it from Switzerland. The spring was driving the entire Rumiko, just like an alarm-clock. "I heard once that the Nipponese make mechanical dolls," Jakob said to Marin one night as he was leaning above Rumiko, studying camera obscuras she had for eyes. "I think they're called *karakuri ningyo*. Some use clockwork mechanisms, others sand or quicksilver. Some of them are even steam-powered. Not to mention de Vaucanson's and Jaquet-Droz's automatons. But something like this..."

They spent hours and hours studying blueprints. They passed nights and nights above the opened Rumiko until they understood all the fine points of that brilliant and deliciously beautiful machine. Jakob was right: Marin had found the blueprints quickly, neatly wrapped in wooden quivers. But he also discovered their copies, reduced on celluloid. He handed Jakob just the quivers. He also kept silent about some gold he found in a drawer of Watanabe's writing desk. He felt he was going to need it, once his friend finally repaired Rumiko. It was by no means fair not to cover his expenses, but the gleam in Jakob's eyes—as he was studying the blueprints—said he'd manage to make his effort profitable.

Marin kept another secret before Jakob: sketches and notes he found among the blueprints. Of course he couldn't read them, but the drawings were sufficient to finally understand all the allusions made by that cursed Seki. Watanabe was to build an invincible mechanical soldier! And where there was one, whole regiments would soon sprout. Then Seki's comrades could re-establish the overthrown regime. Marin could only guess what drove Watanabe to make Rumiko instead of a soldier: the old man took that secret into his grave.

A swine-herd discovered the destroyed airship and cut bodies the next day. Carrying Rumiko, Marin had used fog to make good his escape. The black airship disappeared, driven away by dawn: whoever was inside, gave up the chase. Of course, the investigators made enquiries on Watanabe. They interrogated Marin, too, but they didn't suspect for a moment he knew more than he told them. They didn't discover Watanabe had taken his watch to Jakob for repairs. Finally—no doubt, at the instigation from above—they concluded their investigation, explaining it all with some old political requitals.

Marin was well-aware that Rumiko was not safe in Zagreb. On the other hand, she'd be like fish in a school in Nippon. And there were quite a few foreigners in Nippon: their expertise was needed there. While waiting for the spring to be delivered, Marin decided...

"Coming?" Jakob started him from his musings. He held a lantern, the cellar stairs were steep. They stopped before a heavy locked door. Jakob took a key out of his pocket and unlocked. Marin followed him, holding his breath.

When Jakob turned the light on, Marin saw Rumiko. She was lying on the table, just like all the nights before, covered with a white sheet. All the tools around her were set aside. Marin approached the table and looked at Jakob. He nodded. Marin uncovered the lifeless body. The wound was stitched neatly and tightly. "The stitches will remain, I'm afraid."

Marin caressed Rumiko's cheek. "Key?"

"Here," Jakob passed him the tool. Marin took the large key. With his fingers, he carefully opened a hole at the spot where a navel would be in an ordinary girl, and inserted the key. He began turning it, and heard clicking from inside as the spring wound tighter. With every turn, the resistance grew stronger, and then, finally, the key would turn no more. Nevertheless, Rumiko didn't move.

Marin looked at Jakob.

"I don't know," Jakob replied with apology in his eyes. "I didn't try it, I don't know what happens when the machine is started after rest."

And maybe the machine shouldn't have stopped in the first place? Maybe Rumiko was dead the moment the cut spring ceased powering the mechanism? What if all the repairs were in vain and it would all be just a strange memory Marin should reveal to no-one, because who would ever believe he loved a machine, a doll? And that the doll responded with love, with more care and tenderness than any girl he caught sight of before?

Marin sighed with resignation, leaned above Rumiko and

placed a tender kiss on her lips.

There was complete silence in the cellar. Marin rose and wanted to turn away. He was about to leave that Hoffmanian fantasy behind, because it was all just a foolish dream, when all of a sudden—

Rumiko opened her eyes wide, leapt like a furious wildcat, and grabbed a screwdriver from the table next to a wall.

"Rumiko!" Marin yelled, facing a sharp tip. "Rumiko, it's over! It's over, you cut them! You cut them all down!"

It was only then she became aware of who stood before her. Her eyes darted from Marin to Jakob and back to Marin.

"You cut them all down, Rumiko! It's over, they're no more!"

Rumiko paused, keeping her eyes on Marin. As if it took time for the Babbage engine in her head to search all the memories, to remember after she'd been shut down for months. And then, with joyous cry, she dropped the screwdriver and flew into Marin's arms, nude as she was. Jakob wanted to object, her clothes were neatly stacked on a chair in a corner. But then, taken by some unusual peace and warmth in his heart—he came to the realization that a good deed was done—he silently sneaked out of the cellar, as befits a true gentleman, and left the enamored ones in tender and passionate embrace.

<>

Epilogue

Jakob Sigsfeld tapped his cigar. Ashes fell on stony slabs paving the terrace of his new villa. Before him spread the vista of the promenade and shoreline. Pines rose above and downy oaks arched. Beyond them, a dead calm sea. Several boats, a passenger steamer's smoke in the distance. On the rocks, gulls squabbled nosily above a morsel. Scaffolds on a new hotel: the construction was nearing its end. Warm hazy autumn morning in Opatija... Jakob reached for newspapers on a table next to him.

The IBM stocks rose again. Jakob smiled in satisfaction. They were not happy when he demanded partnership in the company instead of fixed fee for his patent of a random access memory. They were by no means happy, they could count just like he. But they had no choice, they couldn't let anyone overtake them. And Jakob invested dividends cleverly. Shares of a steam-shipping company. The hotel that was being built before his very eyes. Yes, and that fellow Schwartz... His patent of *Metallballon*—a rigid aluminum-clad airship—looked promising.

A servant stepped onto the terrace, carrying a smallish parcel. Jakob raised his eyes from newspapers. "Mail for you, sir."

"Thank you," Jakob took the parcel and dismissed the servant. He looked at the address, the package had gone first to his Zagreb apartment and was only then forwarded here. Then he saw the postage stamps, and read the sender's address: Nipponese. He frowned and his heart started beating faster at the same time. *Marin!*

Last he'd seen him was three years ago, that night he came to pick up Rumiko. He took her into the winter night and he hadn't called or written since. Until now...

Jakob tore the wrapping, taking care not to damage the chrysanthemum stamps. For a moment, his newly-discovered passion forced him to go for a magnifying glass and take a closer look at them, but then his eyes paused at what was in the package, carefully wrapped in fabric. A framed photograph. Marin and Rumiko, both in *kimonos*. And a boy, of Nipponese features, black hair, in a dark student's uniform. Jakob frowned, he didn't get it. Rumiko was perfect, but still... And then it dawned upon him. The blueprints! Watanabe must have had a copy. For a moment, Jakob grew upset, but then he thought it over. *Marin won't try to cash the blueprints*, he realized. It was his debt to Jakob.

Jakob looked at the photograph longingly. Who knows how many of them will soon walk this Earth, machines like Rumiko or the boy. Machines? *Or our successors on this Earth*, he concluded watching the happy family. The boy held a white puppy in his arms.

The puppy seemed alive, of flesh and bones.

THE WHITE SWAN
IRENE RADFORD

"Captain, black envelope, Ho!" Jimmy Seaforth reported, maximum telescopic lenses atop his goggles; five layers of glass piled on top of each other from smallest to largest. Reverse the order and he could see tiny objects close up as if they were as large as his fist.

"Distance?" I barked back, flipping four layers of lenses over my goggles. Even with correction in the goggles themselves I couldn't see as far or accurately as my young communications officer. But I loved the new technology, and took time to learn the intricacies of each new innovation so that I could work with it.

"One hundred miles, east by northeast, headed this way." Jimmy's Australian accent clipped and drawled in odd places, forcing me to listen more closely to him. My own French Swiss lilt had faded over the years since running away from the farm to go a-pirating. A profession I was much better suited to than being wife and mother to farmers. The only thing I'd kept from my old life was my name, Trudé Vollans. That and a sporadic line of communication to my sister, a spymistress in London who billed herself as the bastard daughter of a Gypsy King with the *sight*.

No such pretense for me. I was who I was, a pirate captain with a need for rebellion against authority. My tools enhanced my ability to keep any one company or government from controlling everything. Controlling me.

I picked out a dust mote in the sky beyond the envelope of my own dirigible, the *White Swan*.

"We got here ahead of them," I sighed with relief, then grabbed the speaking tube to the engine room and whistled a warning into it. "Take her up to seven thousand feet, Mr. Arbuthnot."

Dead silence filled the bridge until Mr. Forbes the navigator coughed delicately. Embarrassed heat drove further thoughts from my head. "Gods, I miss you Buthy," I whispered, not really caring who heard me.

We'd lost the grumpy old man who kept our boilers and engines working at peak efficiency and near silently in a clash with a Hudson's Bay Cargo battalion a month ago. First Officer Reginald Singe had gone in the same action. I hadn't the heart to officially replace either.

"Whoever is running things down there, you heard me, take her up to seven thousand feet. I want that slaver to see our white belly and not know they are looking at anything but sky!" I snapped at the entire crew. I knew they all listened even if they had other duties. The next tool I bought would do something to make communications less public aboard my ship. If I wanted to speak to the boiler room, I wanted to speak to the boiler room, not the weapons bay or the mess hall.

"Increase speed to thirty knots. We want to meet them over open water, not close to land." Close in, the men who bought slaves from the bastards ahead of us, and sold those slaves to Chinese warlords could launch their own ships in defense of their human cargo.

"Priming steam cannons, Captain," Forbes said briskly. Thinking ahead of me. Again. He had a few things to learn about protocol and obedience as well as prudence and diplomacy in his blatant attempt to step into Reggie's position.

In this case, having the cannons ready before we encountered the slave ship was wise.

"Hold off, Mr. Forbes. Arm them too soon and we lose steam while waiting." In my mind I traced the passage of hoses and gears, gauges and dials. I knew how long each cannon could hold enough pressure to discharge a silent salvo.

"Ninety miles, Captain," Jimmy spoke. I knew he was as anxious to take down that filthy ship as any of us aboard. His parents and two sisters were among the cargo. Prisoners. "Coming fast and trailing black smoke. She's burning everything she has to reach port in Shanghai ahead of the authorities." His voice wavered a tiny bit.

"They may outrun the Hudson's Bay Corvettes. They won't outrun us. Bring us in over top of them, Mr. Forbes. We'll take a bit out of their ballonets with the Gonne and force them down."

He looked up at me with hope in his eyes. "Yes, you'll get your chance to fly a dragon." A grin split his face. "I'll take the lead aeroplane. Mr. Seaforth you can take the other flank."

"If you don't mind, Captain, I'd rather stay aboard and fire the cannon that sinks those stinking slavers. Not an honest pirate among them."

Pirates and thieves we might be. But we also held to a loose code of honor: no murder of hostages, no rape of women or boys—though I'd been known to take a semi-reluctant man to my cabin upon occasion—always leave the crew a life raft and supplies. Independent traders had nothing to fear from us. Too much trouble for too poor a cargo. The HBC though dreaded spotting the *White Swan* in the skies above them. Especially if they carried otter pelts. I'd made five fortunes selling those to Chinese warlords. The bales of luxury furs in my cargo hold now was a reserve in case we had to ransom the slaves in the hold of that black monster, now only eighty miles away.

I didn't intend to let that ship get close enough to any port to sell those slaves.

"Seventy-five miles, Captain," Jimmy said. A grim determination firmed his chin and made him look taller than his skinny five feet seven inches. I topped him by half a head and a good fifty pounds.

No one, not even the husband I'd kicked of the ship last year, considered me a weak female who needed protecting or to be told what to do.

"Prep the dragons!" I looked around the bridge as men scrambled to do my bidding. "Lieutenant Margaret," I didn't know her last name, didn't care. She was a damn good pilot. I'd make her first officer in a heartbeat but she'd turned me down. This job was only temporary for her. When she'd earned the price of a farm in the Oregon Country, she planned to leave our crew and my ship.

"Yes, Captain," Margaret snapped a salute. Tall and whipcord lean she had a scar from right temple to center mouth that pulled her face into a perpetual grimace. The missing tip of her nose completed the off-center gruesome mask. We never knew what she was thinking, or where she got those scars. From her fierceness approaching this battle, I guessed she'd escaped a similar slave ship.

"You take the dragon on my left flank. Forbes you will be on my right."

"The Gonne, Captain?" Jimmy reminded me.

"You, Mr. Seaforth will have the honor of taking that ship down." I yanked a purple crystal from its lanyard around my neck. It glinted prettily in the bright light of the South Seas. A lovely bauble from India that belied its more deadly qualities.

Forbes gasped a little. He'd heard of the wondrous powers of pure Yuenite, but he'd never seen it. Mostly I used the less powerful blue Kenjite crystal in the Kinetic Galvatron—affectionately known simply as The Gonne.

"Well, stop staring and unrack her, Mr. Seaforth," I commanded. His jaw closed with an audible snap.

Mutely he strode to the brass-framed glass case to port of the forward view ports. He paused before the magnificent weapon mounted on a series of clips that held it in place through bad weather and battle. Pristine polished brass and blued steel proclaimed its value in both price and the care we took of this rare weapon.

"It won't bite you as long as you point it at the enemy and

not yourself."

"Of course, Captain." He swallowed deeply and opened the glass. The Gonne practically jumped into his hands the moment he released the clips.

I don't believe tools and machine have souls or intelligence, but sometimes...sometimes I have to wonder if the care we put into crafting, maintaining, and understanding them gives them something more. Call it a personality. Every machine has its quirks and preferences. The Gonne more than the crankiest boiler.

Jimmy went through the powering up routine carefully, following each step precisely to hook it to a steam hose, check all the dials, vials, and gauges, and shoot a small stream of hot compressed air out the muzzle, then a second stream to clear air pockets out of the system. My entire bridge crew and a few select others knew the procedure and drilled often. I let them practice with the Kejite crystals, learning some the Gonne's quirks, how she pulled to right, how she burped with the second dose of steam. But only I controlled the Yuenite crystal.

I slapped the purple gem as big as a quail's egg into his palm. Gingerly he fixed it into the brackets atop the barrel and pulled the switch that converted steam to light that would pass through the crystal. Almost reverently he propped it onto a tripod by the forward porthole. Margaret cranked open the glass window for him.

Then I left with my two fellow pilots.

"Say your prayers, slaver," I muttered. "This is the last sunset you'll see."

In the weapons bay, I checked and double checked my dragon. The little aeroplane only held enough steam for short range and brief flights. What we lacked in time and power we made up for in maneuverability. Buthy had been working on a method of self-propulsion for these valuable weapons (two of those five fortunes in otter pelts had purchased them). No one else aboard understood his notes and half-complete models. For now we had to make the best of their limitations.

I counted on the slaver not having any dragons of his own.

Slavers could make a lot of money in their disgusting trade. Still, few of them invested in perpetuating their "careers." First Officer Reginald Singe had direct communications with the factory in Madras. Until his death severed that connection, I had not heard of any other captain in the region commissioning dragons. They all went to my greatest enemy, the Hudson's Bay Company.

But that was six months ago, before this black-sailed, black-hulled slaver started raiding farms in Australia to feed the ever hungry market for human laborers and front-line soldiers.

Slave owners wore out their property. Cheaper to replace a slave than invest time, money, and understanding in tools and machines that could perform most of the same jobs cheaper and longer.

Forbes gave me a thumbs up in the bay to my right. The elegant and curving nose of his aero edged closer to the exit hatch. He understood the need to fly inherent in the machine and gave it just enough steam to keep it from leaping out too soon. Margaret on my left also gave me the signal, keeping a firm control of her dragon.

We were ready. I waved my hand at the Seabees. Three men jumped to lean heavily on the lever that propped open the wooden portal a quarter the length of my ship.

I had a clear view of the black envelope five hundred feet below and half a mile west of us. Forbes held his hand over the thruster, as eager and anxious to move forward as I. We had to wait.

"Now, Mr. Seaforth," I whispered, willing him to fire.

Twenty heart beats later a streak of deadly purple light traced a line across the top of the black fabric, just to the starboard of center, avoiding the solid strut along the ridgeline. A breathless moment later the envelope sagged from loss of invisible air contained in a full row ballonets.

She had enough air left to stay aloft, but not as high. The dirigible dropped a thousand feet. I imagined I could hear the screams of the human cargo at the sudden loss of elevation.

"Now!" I screamed as I signaled the launch of the dragons.

My stomach clenched as my little aero dropped free of the *White Swan*. I counted to ten and opened the retractable wings. Another drop until they caught air and stabilized.

We swooped and spun, maneuvering to the far side of the ship and the most vulnerable part of the hull nearest the boilers. We had to take out the engines and force the ship down.

The slaver had painted a red dragon's head on the bow. The eyes gleamed white. Gun ports. A flash and roar. Cannonballs powered by gunpowder sped toward us, faster than sight. The flash had betrayed them. All three of us pushed our aeros out of the way.

As I swept past the bow toward mid-ship the name of the vessel painted in red lettering that seemed to drip blood registered in my mind. *Black Hawke*.

I faltered in dread.

A cannon ball whizzed past my tail.

Margaret took out the cannon from the port eye with her steam musket. A missile shot straight up the barrel exploded on contact with the powder pan.

Ten square yards of hull disappeared.

I recovered and signaled with hands and flashing lights to change targets.

The captain of the *Black Hawke* would put his human cargo between the hull and the boilers. We dared not shoot the boat itself. We had to target the upper decks and the envelope.

If I were one of those captives I'd prefer death to slavery—especially if a Chinese Mandarin or warlord owned me. What remained of the short life of a slave was dreadful and painful. The reason the markets were always hungry for new slaves was that none of them lived more than five years. None of them. Even the children. Young boys as well as girls were sent to brothels. Anyone between the ages of five—*FIVE!*—and fifteen were highly prized by their new owners.

I shifted my target to the bridge on the bow above the cannons.

One, two, three shots from our steam cannons. Forbes and Margaret knew the *Black Hawke's* captain almost as well as I.

Forbes and I each had one shot left before we needed to refuel. I used mine on the strut connecting the boat to the envelope. Clean, through and through. My little dragon responded to my touch like a teammate. I don't know many who could make that shot. I trusted my eyes, my hatred of the captain, and my experience to shoot straight and accurate. The strut cracked and splintered. The weight of the hull weakened it further.

The bow separated from the envelope leaving five more struts in place; all straining to stay intact with the increased load.

Dirigibles are tricky things. They depend upon finely tuned balance as well as steam and hot air to stay aloft.

With the sagging bow below and the loosened envelope above, it drifted downward in an uncontrolled spiral.

Then miracle of miracles, Forbes took out both aft cannons with a single shot and Jimmy had recharged the Gonne for a second sweep along the side of the envelope.

I nudge my dragon back into the *White Swan* on the last gasp of steam. Inside the weapons bay, Markos, a swarthy Greek from the engineering crew with an engaging grin and a leering eye, passed conventional weapons to every crewman aboard.

Jimmy still cradled the Gonne. He relinquished her to me with an almost sigh. "She's too much for me to handle more than once." He shook his head and patted the butt. "Got a full head of steam, Captain. Use her well."

I nodded, understanding his desire to give back to me the responsibility of such a weapon. And authority over the ship and crew. A fine communication's officer and look out, not first officer or captain material.

"Captain," Markos called me with that blinding grin creasing his face. "Heard tell that the *Hawke* bought one of those new *IDjinn* valve regulators out of Persia. If you can salvage it, our Gertie would be forever grateful."

"Gertie?"

"Boiler number two. Number one is Mabel," Forbes whispered into my ear.

"We'll look," I called across the bay. Then sotto voce I said to Forbes with my body half-turned away from the others.

"When we get back, remind me to promote Markos to chief engineer."

"Why not do it now?"

"If I don't make it back, your new captain may have other ideas."

Forbes looked at me strangely.

"This is the *Hawke* we're dealing with."

"You kicked his butt off the *White Swan* once, all by yourself. This time you have the whole crew at your back."

"He has his entire crew as well."

"The *Black Hawke* is listing. The envelope is barely holding enough lift to keep it from sinking. We can't delay." I clipped a boarding rope to my belt.

Forbes cocked an eyebrow at me and gathered the crew, dividing them into two squads. Margaret headed up a team of twelve to liberate the prisoners and get them back aboard the *White Swan* safely. Forbes and I led fifteen a piece to secure the decks before accosting the *Hawke*.

<>

I knew no other name for the devilishly handsome man I'd married in a haze of lust. Thirteen months later, I fully believed the black-hearted devil must have drugged my wine. Aphrodisiacs were common and cheap in Dakar. How else could I have been so stupid as to stand before a tribal shaman and declare my everlasting love, devotion, and *obedience* to him?

One month later I found myself bound, gagged, and on my way to a brothel in New Dehli while he took command of *my* ship. I escaped, of course. I feigned insensibility all the while working at the hemp ropes around my wrists with the skinny blade tucked inside my sleeve. Other blades, a single-shot gun, and a barbed garrote removed all further obstacles to my escape. I desperately hoped he knew about all my weapons and expected me to escape. He needed me out of the way only long enough to steal my ship and truly intended me no lasting harm.

Margaret awaited me on the dock with a hot air balloon. We

followed the *White Swan* for three days, fortunate that the wind held.

By the time I lashed the basket to the upper decks and held a knife to Hawke's throat the entire crew welcomed me aboard, disgusted and appalled at his total lack of morality and concern for no one but himself. Many sported bloody lash scars on their backs and missing digits from their hands. They'd refused to convert their lucrative pirating to running slaves just because *he* said they could make more money.

I was too generous in giving him the hot air balloon—even if it did leak.

This time I had no intention of being generous. Or respectful. Or considerate.

<>

As boardings went, this one was boring. Not a single shot fired and every damn crewmember threw down their weapons.

I secured them to the remaining struts with rough hemp ropes (making sure I confiscated all their blades) not sure if I'd release them when I blew the hull or not.

Carefully I led the way to the bridge, confident that my crew would do their job in liberating the prisoners. I didn't trust anyone to take down the Hawke but me.

"Ah, Trudé, my love, my only love. I knew that fate would bring us together again," he proclaimed with arms open wide, ready to embrace me. Or drive a knife into my back. "You look magnificent, my dear." He surveyed me with lustful hope in his eye.

I blinked in the watery dimness as waves slapped the portholes, unsure of what I saw. One eye. An ocular-monoculux, in the place where his right eye should be, clicked and whirred as he shifted focus from my bust line to the men behind me, all of us heavily armed.

"Is that any way to greet your long lost husband?" His right arm jerked as it folded down to his side and gripped the sawed-off shotgun on his hip.

The gibbering fear he had induced in me at one time roiled in my gut turning into hate and disgust. "You aren't man enough for me," I said. At the same time I noticed his mechanical arm, I realized he wore a heavy canister strapped to his back. Long hoses draped away from the contraption to plug into a steam outlet in the interior bulkhead.

His articulated fingers closed around the gun grip, the trigger finger already curling into place.

No time to speculate, or distract him.

I stomped on the steamhose with my boot heel, releasing another of my hidden blades from my heel. A hot hiss followed the knife severing the hose.

Hawke turned to face me, each movement a calculated jerk. What he lacked in smoothness he made up for in speed. He already held the shotgun level with my heart. My crew backed away, spreading out, less likely to get caught in the scatter shot.

"Is that any way to treat your long lost husband?" Hawke snarled.

"How much steam do you have left?" I retorted, pointing to the hot mist shooting from the hose rather than into his body. I prayed that his artificial joints would lock up fast.

"More than enough, my dear." He threw his head back and laughed.

I heard a scurry of movement below decks moving upward. The prisoners, I hoped.

I stomped on the second hose and a new leak burst out.

"Safeguards. I have safeguards," Hawke said. His left hand reached behind him and yanked the hose out of the base of the canister. "Reserves." He held the shotgun steady. His finger jerked once, closer to contact with the trigger.

But the canisters continued to hiss. He hadn't unscrewed the hose ends, only yanked them free. The valves hadn't fully closed.

"You're alone, Hawke. Your crew surrendered without a fight. How much steam do you have? Enough to kill every last one of us?" My gaze flitted right and left seeking a weakness.

Weakness? Not bloody likely.

"You never did have much in the way of moral restraint," I said taking a more casual stance. My hands opened at my sides in a gesture of vulnerability. "But you would never stoop to running slaves while you worked with me." I let my contempt drip with each word.

"Times change, Trudé. Circumstances change. Now I want you and your crew to get out of my way. You've left my vessel somewhat less than airworthy. So now that you've transferred my cargo to the *Swan*, which should have been my ship as part of the marriage settlement, I'll relieve you of command. You may take the *Hawke* to port. If you can get it that far." He gestured with his shotgun for us to back away from the hatch.

"You've become a slave, Hawke. A slave to the machines that keep you moving and alive."

"And are you not a slave to your machines? Your ship, your guns, your dragons?" His mouth quirked up on one side in half a smile, the left side, not the side with the artificial eye and arm.

"My machines are tools. I work with them, I understand them, and I can fix most of them if they break. Technology should be a partnership to enhance our lives, not dominate it."

"You have your definitions. I have mine," Hawke sneered.

"What happened?" I asked, stalling rather than concerned for his welfare. I had cared for him at one time. Emphasis on the past tense. "Run into a jealous husband who's meaner than you?" I stood firm.

"Shark actually. The hot air balloon you gave me sprang a leak. Great white off the shore of Australia circled. I killed one by shoving my knife down his throat. The bugger tore my arm to shreds in the process."

"And the eye?"

"Infection I picked up in some rat infested flop house in Shanghai." He shrugged as if he'd lost nothing. "Actually, I didn't really lose anything, except some money paid to the Chinese gadget makers and magicians." That uncanny eye whirred and stretched out telescopically. He looked a little pale, sweating copiously across his brow and under his arms.

The signs of pain. Or opium withdrawal. Another form of

slavery.

"What are you looking for, Hawke? Can that thing see through my clothes to locate all my weapons?"

"Only one I want. The Yuenite crystal."

"Won't do you any good without the Gonne." It slipped from my hand with a clatter, bouncing and skidding across the deck.

Forbes lifted his foot over it. "I get my boots made by the same cobbler she does," he said. "Now let's see there is one spot, right here at the base of the barrel were the steam is converted to light..."

"Go ahead. I don't really need the Gonne. I just need the crystal." Hawke's eye made another slow and painful adjustment, bringing his focus back to me.

"Ah, you have truly become a slave to your machines; you need to constantly make them better, channeling all of you cunning, ruthlessness, and money into them. Running slaves, murdering innocent farmers, condemning children to brothels means nothing to you, because you see no difference between their condition and yours. Only your master is a machine instead of a warlord."

"And you aren't?" he barked back at me. His trigger finger seemed frozen in place. I hoped his steam reserves waned.

"You think fixing a Yuenite crystal to the eye will make it as good as a real eye?"

Forbes had inched around until he stood outside Hawke's peripheral vision. We had Hawke trapped. But he still held a lethal weapon aimed at my heart at nearly point blank range.

"The crystal won't help you, Hawke. It will only demand more power. All your steam will go to feeding it, and not moving your arm, or any other part of you that you've sacrificed to your master, the machine. Tell me, can you separate from the canisters at all? Can you walk about and lead a normal life without them? No. You are chained to your machine more so than any slave in a Warlord's army is chained to his bunk each night. You sold yourself to a machine.

"Give me the crystal, Trudé. I need the crystal." Each

word came out in an individual expulsion, as if he used all his remaining energy to speak.

I lifted my eyebrows to Forbes in a silent signal. He slid a machete out of the sheath on his back, soundlessly. In one swift arcing movement he severed the straps that held the canisters to Hawke's back.

Hawke whirled to confront Forbes, pressing the shotgun into my crewman's chest.

Forbes froze in place, holding the machete out to his side.

"You, you, y...can't...do..." Hawke stammered, his voice winding down with each breath.

"I just did," Forbes said blandly. Using the flat of his blade he flicked the shotgun out of Hawke's hand, the mechanical fingers convulsed, trying to press a trigger that was no longer there. His jaw flapped but no words came out.

He'd surrendered more than his eye and arm to the machine. His very lifeforce had been replaced. He should have died months ago.

Maybe he had. All that was left of the handsome adventurer was the machine.

The sounds of retreating feet had stopped.

"It's time to reunite Mr. Seaforth with his parents and sisters. We're done here. Liberate the crew and scuttle this damn boat. She won't run slaves again. Never again."

"What about...?" Forbes gestured with the machete.

"A captain goes down with his ship."

"Will you?"

"If I have to. But don't force the issue even if I do make you first officer. The *White Swan* is a demanding partner. If you don't keep a firm hand on her, she'll try to take over your life, become your owner."

We both spent a long silent moment of regret staring at what was left of Hawke, opening and closing his mouth without speaking, fingers still trying to pull a trigger that was not there.

I felt no regret. My Hawke was already dead. But not my *Swan*.

BIOGRAPHIES

S. A. Bolich is a fulltime freelance writer of science fiction and fantasy who lives in Washington State with a dog, four cats, and two horses. Her short fiction has appeared in such venues as Beneath Ceaseless Skies, On Spec, Damnation Books, and No Man's Land: Defending the Future IV, among many others. Her first novel, Firedancer, was released in September 2011, with its sequel, Windrider, due out in Spring 2012.

James Brogden was born in Manchester in 1969, grew up in Australia, and now lives with his wife and two daughters in Bromsgrove, Worcestershire, where he teaches English and Media Studies. His stories have appeared in the Big Issue and the British Fantasy Society's *Dark Horizons,* and his first novel, The Narrows, has just been published by Snowbooks. When he's not writing or trying to teach children how to, he gets out into the mountains whenever he can, exploring the remains of Britain's prehistoric past and hunting for standing stones. Fortunately they don't run very fast.

Bob Brown is a Health Physicist and one of eleven children deposited on the earth in the wilds of Central Texas during the Eisenhower administration. Ever since his early days he has excelled in the application of the shovel and the hoe, both of which are necessary to garden, something he does well, as did his grandparents who kept victory gardens at same time that Eisenhower was defeating the European Hun.

Bob has been writing ever since the Nixon administration, which was the same year he planted his first garden. He grew radishes. As he and his writing both matured he entered into a relationship with Northwest Public Radio where he served as a commentator for seven years. During this period he documented the Clinton era and the childhood of his daughter, Cheyenne in detail for the amusement of Northwest Public Radio patrons. He still resides in the Pacific Northwest, where he continues to work as a Health Physicist.

Brenda W. Clough is a meek mild-mannered reporter at a major metropolitan publication. She has published seven novels, many short stories, nonfiction, and innumerable book reviews that revolve around death, misery and grief. She has traveled around the world under the aegis of the US government, and now lives in a cottage at the edge of a forest, surrounded by animals.

Her latest novel, Revise the World, is available at Book View Café (www.bookviewcafe.com). A version of it was a finalist for both the Hugo and Nebula awards.

Malon Edwards was born and raised on the South Side of Chicago, but now lives in the Greater Toronto Area. Much of his speculative fiction is set in a near-future Chicago and features people of color. He serves as a Grants Administrator for the Speculative Literature Foundation's Older Writers and Gulliver Travel Research grants, which provides $750 and $800, respectively, for writers of speculative literature.

Christopher Eger is a military scholar and writer who has published more than 300 non-fiction articles on modern warfare in such magazines as *Warship International*, *Military Historian* and *Sea Classics*. His nonfiction book-length work includes contributing to the *Mississippi Encyclopedia* by the University of Mississippi Press. *Last Stand on Zombie Island*, Christopher's first fiction novel, is set for release in the Spring of 2012.

Mark J. Ferrari was a professional fantasy illustrator from 1987 until his attention was redirected to a long-suppressed passion for writing early in the millennium. His first fantasy novel, *The Book of Joby,* was published by TOR in August 2007, nominated for an Endeavor Award, and made Booklist's Top Ten Sci-Fi / Fantasy List the following year. It was rereleased as a mass market paperback in January 2012. Mark currently resides in Seattle, Washington, where he is hard at work finishing the next in a whole flock of novels, which have been circling the airport in his head for years. More info on these and other projects can be found at www.markferrari.com.

Livia Finucci likes to read ancient history and mythology. She has always been attracted to the fascinating world of once-upon-a-time stories, so she collects fairy and folk tales from various countries. She has been published in the anthologies *Greek Myths Revisited, Here There Be Dragons* and the magazine *Scifaikuest.* In her free time she practices sumie painting and studies Chinese. One day she intends to have a greenhouse where she will grow exotic orchids.

Aidan Fritz lives on an island in the San Francisco Bay Area and works part of the time in Sweden, which has opened his eyes to the varied perspectives through which different cultures view the world. He grew up in Michigan where his parents ran a campground in the summer and lacking a television, he read books from the library on rainy days, particularly captivated by the worlds found in science fiction and fantasy novels. He blends these two passions together in his fiction. When not writing, he can be found baking artisan breads, practicing his Swedish, playing the hammered dulcimer, or occasionally on stage as a Scottish Highland dancer. Aidan's home on the Internet is: http:// blog.aidanfritz.com.

Not yet award-winning author *Chris Wong Sick Hong* has now

established a beachhead on the shores of steampunk. Aided by his two armored cats, one dog and half an MFA in creative writing (the good half), his plans for literary world domination proceed apace. More of his work can be found at www.chriswsh. com and, if nothing critical kerplodes into a pile of broken gears and steaming oil, his near future urban fantasy, *Dick Richards, Private Eye*, will be published by Dragon Moon Press in 2012, just in time for everyone to read it before the world ends.

David D. Levine's story "Tk'Tk'Tk" won the 2006 Hugo Award for Best Short Story, "Titanium Mike Saves the Day" was a nominee for the 2007 Nebula Award, and "The Tale of the Golden Eagle" was a Hugo nominee. I'm a John W. Campbell Award nominee (2004 and 2003), Writers of the Future Contest winner (2002), James White Award winner (2001), and Clarion West graduate (2000). I've sold to F&SF, Asimov's, Analog, Realms of Fantasy, and anthologies including Mike Resnick's New Voices in SF and four Year's Best volumes (two Fantasy, two SF).

Rhiannon Louve's steampunk influences include *Girl Genius, Pride and Prejudice and Zombies*, Abney Park's musical oeuvre, "The Next Doctor" (among other recent *Doctor Who* episodes), and the various legends of Baron Munchausen. She has previously published scholarly essays on contemporary Pagan thea/ology, as well as numerous role-playing game supplements, particularly in Sword and Sorcery Studios' d20 *Scarred Lands* setting. She hopes to soon sell her first novel. Rhiannon provides vocals and keyboards for a geeky metal band, has taught World Religions at the college level, speaks French, co-runs a volunteer organization, and has personal experience with inter-planar airship combat.

Edward Martin III is a writer, an essayist, and an award-winning filmmaker from Portland, OR. He adapted and directed an animated adaptation of H. P. Lovecraft's "The Dream-Quest of Unknown Kadath", produced "The Cosmic Horror Fun-Pak", wrote and directed a 10-minute comprehensive period adaptation of "Lord of the Rings", and is wrapping up "Flesh of my Flesh," a ground-breaking independent zombie action movie. He recently published an anthology of peculiar horror entitled "Close Your Eyes—Tales from the Blinkspace," and is preparing two more manuscripts. He's the oozing beating heart of Hellbender Media (HellbenderMedia.com), as well as the gristle, the muscle, and a lot of the other moist stringy bits. Bones, too. Delicious bones.

Shannon Page was born on Halloween night and spent her early years on a commune in northern California's backwoods. A childhood without television gave her a great love of books and the worlds she found in them. She wrote her first book, an illustrated adventure starring her cat, at the age of seven. Sadly, that story is currently out of print, but her work has appeared in *Clarkesworld, Interzone, Fantasy, Black Static*, Tor.com, and a mighty number of anthologies, including *Love and Rockets* from DAW, Subterranean's *Tales of Dark Fantasy 2*, Flying Pen Press's *Space Tramps: Full Throttle Space Tales 5*, and the Australian Shadows Award-winning *Grants Pass*. Shannon is a longtime yoga practitioner and newbie swimmer, has no tattoos, and lives in Portland, Oregon, with lots of orchids and even more books. Visit her at www.shannonpage.net.

Irene Radford has been writing stories ever since she figured out what a pencil was for. A member of an endangered species, a native Oregonian who lives in Oregon, she and her husband make their home in Welches, Oregon where deer, bears, coyotes, hawks, owls, and woodpeckers feed regularly on their back deck. A museum trained historian, Irene has spent many hours prowling pioneer cemeteries deepening her connections to the past. Raised in a military family she grew up all over the US and learned early on that books are friends that don't get left behind with a move. Her interests and reading range from ancient history, to spiritual meditations, to space stations, and a whole lot in between.

In other lifetimes she writes urban fantasy as P.R. Frost and space opera as C.F. Bentley

In June of 2011 Irene returns to fantasy with a new series, *The Pixie Chronicles*. The first being *Thistle Down*." Look for "Chicory Up" in May 2012. The re-release of her masterwork series "Merlin's Descendants" begins in January at the Book View Café http://www.bookviewcafe.com

David Lee Summers is the author of seven novels and over one hundred short stories and poems. His writing spans a wide range of the imaginative from science fiction to fantasy to horror. David's novels include *The Solar Sea*, which was selected as a Flamingnet Young Adult Top Choice, and the wild west Steampunk adventure *Owl Dance*. His short stories and poems have appeared in such magazines and anthologies as *Realms of Fantasy, Human Tales, Six-Guns Straight From Hell,* and *The Santa Clara Review.* In 2010, he was nominated for the Rhysling Award. In addition to writing, David edits the quarterly science fiction and fantasy magazine *Tales of the Talisman* and has edited two science fiction anthologies, *Space Pirates* and *Space Horrors*. When not working with the written word, David operates telescopes at Kitt Peak National Observatory. His website is: www.davidleesummers.com.

Bruce Taylor, aka. "Mr. Magic Realism", writes magic realism. He has nine books published. A collection ("Alembical") with his novella, "Thirteen Miles to Paradise", received a starred review in Publishers Weekly. "Kafka's Uncle and other Strange Tales" was nominated for the &NOW Award for Innovative Writing (SUNY, NY). Other titles are, "Edward: Dancing on the Edge of Infinity", "Magic of Wild Places" and (with Brian Herbert) "Stormworld". With Elton Elliott, he co-edited "Like Water for Quarks", an anthology about the blending of magic realism and science fiction. Living in Seattle, he has a smashing view of Mt. Rainier. His website is: www.brucebtaylor.com.

K.L. Townsend has always been interested in finding the fantastic within the mundane. She has a background in history and anthropology, and uses her studies to help fuel her imagination. Her works tend to be influenced by her interest in other cultures. She has a short historical novel called "Song of the Swallow" due out the winter season of 2011-2012 with Hadley Rille Books and has sold the short story "Kiss of the Jade Fox" to Absolute Write's anthology. Prior works include "Convergence", a short story published in the Ruins Metropolis anthology and a scifaiku with The Shantytown Anomaly. When not writing, K.L. Townsend enjoys spending time with her dogs.

George Walker is an engineer working in Portland, Oregon. He has written numerous science fiction and fantasy stories, appearing in Steampunk Tales, Digital Science Fiction, Ideomancer, Mirror Shards, Comets and Criminals, Science Fiction Age and elsewhere. Links to a number of his stories are available at http://sites.google.com/site/georgeswalker/
He describes his story as: "A Chinese steampunk fairy tale, just like the ones Confucius used to tell."
Of course, Confucius would be rolling over in his grave at how the princess in my story behaves :-)

Joyce Reynolds-Ward is a middle school learning specialist, horsewoman and skier living in Portland, Oregon. Besides earning a SemiFinalist placement in Writers of the Future, she's had short stories and essays published in places like *Random Realities*, *M-Brane SF*, *The Fifth Di...*, *Nightbird Singing in the Dead of Night*, *Zombiefied*, *River, Trust and Treachery*, and *Gobshite Quarterly*. When not teaching, she's often thundering about on her intrepid reining mare Mocha, living la vida ski bum, and writing. Follow her adventures through her blog, *Peak Amygdala, at* www.joycereynoldsward.com.

Aleksandar Žiljak was born and lives in Zagreb, Croatia. He graduated on the Electrotechnical Faculty in Zagreb, and received a master of computer sciences degree there. Since late 1990s, he has worked as a freelance illustrator, writer and editor. Beside Croatia, he publishes stories in several European countries, as well as the USA. He has two story collections-"Slijepe ptice" (Blind Birds, 2003) and "Božja vučica" (The Divine She-Wolf, 2010)-as well as a book on cryptozoology in print. He has also won 6 SFera awards for SF art, stories and editorial work. The SF magazine "UBIQ", which he co-edits, was voted the best European SF magazine in 2011.

Books Published by Sky Warrior Books

Purchase them through online resellers and better independent bookstores everywhere. Visit us at www.skywarriorbooks.com for news and upcoming books and promotions.

Alma Alexander

2012: Midnight at Spanish Gardens (E-book, Trade Paperback)

Embers of Heaven (E-book, Trade Paperback)

S. A. Bolich

Firedancer (Book 1 Masters of the Elements) (E-book, Trade Paperback)

Windrider (Book 2 Masters of the Elements) (E-book)

M. H. Bonham

Prophecy of Swords (E-book)

Runestone of Teiwas (E-book)

Serpent Singer and Other Stories (E-book)

John Dalmas

The Second Coming (E-book)

Carol Hightshoe (Editor)

Zombiefied: An Anthology of All Things Zombie (E-book)

Gary Jonas

Modern Sorcery (E-book, Trade Paperback)

One-Way Ticket to Midnight (E-book)

Quick Shots (E-book)

Michael J. Parry

The Spiral Tattoo (E-book)

Phyllis Irene Radford (Editor)

Gears and Levers 1: A Steampunk Anthology (E-book, Print)

Healing Waves: A Charity Anthology for Japan (E-book)

Deborah J. Ross (Editor)

The Feathered Edge (E-book, Trade Paperback)

Laura J. Underwood

Ard Magister (Book One of Ard Magister) (E-book)

Dragon's Tongue (Book One of the Demon-Bound) (E-book)

The Hounds of Ardagh (E-book)

www.ingramcontent.com/pod-product-compliance
Lightning Source LLC
Chambersburg PA
CBHW020230260626
47156CB00002B/617